not being on a boat

ESMÉ CLAIRE KEITH

not being on a boat

A NOVEL

freehand books

Freehand Books gratefully acknowledges the support of the Canada Council for the Arts for its publishing program. ¶ Freehand Books, an imprint of Broadview Press Inc., gratefully acknowledges the financial support for its publishing program provided by the Government of Canada through the Canada Book Fund.

 Canada Council   Conseil des Arts
for the Arts   du Canada

Freehand Books
515 – 815 1st Street SW Calgary, Alberta T2P 1N3
www.freehand-books.com

Book orders: Litdistco
100 Armstrong Avenue Georgetown, Ontario L7G 5S4
Telephone: 1-800-591-6250 Fax: 1-800-591-6251
orders@litdistco.ca
www.litdistco.ca

LIBRARY AND ARCHIVES CANADA CATALOGUING IN PUBLICATION

Keith, Esmé Claire, 1964–
Not being on a boat / Esmé Claire Keith.

ISBN 978-1-55481-060-4

        I. Title.

PS8621.E39N68 2011   C813'.6   C2011-902059-9

Edited by Robyn Read
Book design and cover illustration by Natalie Olsen, Kisscut Design
Author photo by Paula Henry

Printed on FSC recycled paper and bound in Canada

for my mom
never adrift

Guildenstern: You can't not be on a boat.

Rosencrantz: I've frequently not been on boats.

Guildenstern: No, no. What you've been is not on boats.

— TOM STOPPARD

departure

CHAPTER ONE

We were slow getting out of port, and I was afraid something had gone wrong, and maybe we wouldn't make it after all. There was the press and the crowd and the celebration, like there should be when a major event is underway, and the launch of a big new ship is an event. But it went on and on, with speeches and jugglers and cracking a bottle of champagne on the bow. And I was tense and jumpy, and I knew I wouldn't relax until we were in international waters.

I watched while on the quay the Company laid on a show of shows. There were streamers and confetti and balloons and white doves. A marching band was playing. The sun hit the brass and blinded me. Further down the pier, teams from the regional cheerleading competition showcased their routines. The girls shot into the air with the doves and balloons, and then dropped back down again. There was a big crowd: investors, gawkers, guests of the passengers. Everyone oohed and aahed.

On board, the intercom kept it up: "Embarkation in forty-five minutes. All visitors proceed to land links on deck levels one and two for exit purposes. Land links will retract in fifteen minutes. Passengers are invited to the Hold, level minus one, the Tropicana Room or the Sunset Room, level five, the Voodoo Lounge, level six, the Crow's Nest, level eighteen midship, for cocktails and orientation. *Mariola* Health and Security Services present 'Cruiser Safeness and Personal Protection' hourly on the aft sports deck. Guests are reminded that feminine hygiene products must not be flushed. Please use the receptacles provided. Cabin crews to position fourteen beta. Bridge crew protocol sigma. Code viridian. All visitors to the land links. Embarkation in forty minutes." It went on and on.

I stood on deck, quayside, to watch the world slide back and away, holding my position at the rail against competition from my fellow passengers. The land links were open bridges running to the *Mariola* from the Company offices on the pier, and I watched the guests and Company VIPs filing off the ship, friends of the cruisers and Company men who came out for the party and to wish us well and be impressed by the luxury and the technical achievement, and then had to go back to ordinary life on dry land.

The links emptied out, and I thought, "Here we go." But there was another holdup. Nothing happened for a long minute. Then three or four security types wrestled a guy across one of the links. They had him under tight restraint, and he was resisting and shouting, but I couldn't hear what he said. We waited a few more minutes until security quick marched back on board, and then we were good to go. The links retracted into the offices. There was a pause and a hum, and the engines powered up. Slowly the pier fell back and away. The streamers stretched and broke.

On the pier people shouted "Bon voyage." They waved and threw flowers. The band played. Teams of two, three, or four girls launched themselves like fireworks. I watched it all through my binoculars. Last thing as we cleared the quay I heard explosions, a big gun salute to the maiden voyage of the *Mariola*, or another raid, maybe. I couldn't tell which.

on board

I stayed by the rail until I couldn't see land any more, and then I went to my stateroom. It took a minute. All the passengers were milling around, it felt like hundreds of them, and personnel was involved also, carrying things and pushing carts and giving directions. I shouldered my way through the crowd on the deck, in the hallways, waiting by the elevator banks.

Once I was inside my stateroom, finally, I took a moment to rest and reflect. I'd been working at speed for a few weeks, thinking on my feet and making hard choices and keeping an eye on the rear-view. Under these pressures and working against distractions, I booked into the *Mariola*, and I paid the pop for the deluxe package, the floating condo investment, the Lifetime-Lifestyles option. So I was fully committed. And now I was getting my first chance to sit back and review, take inventory, and see what I was getting for my money. After a long stretch of dodging and weaving, the last few days especially, full of deadlines and arrangements, there was nothing left to do. I did everything already. I had the rest of my life now to kick back and relax, to enjoy all the good things I'd earned. It was exactly what I wanted. But I didn't know how to start. So I had a look around my suite as an opener, to see how reality compared with the brochure.

I was on deck six, an exterior suite with a balcony, even though it jacked up the price. The royal yacht, it wasn't. Everything was nailed down, and the proportions were all junior, a size and a half smaller than life ashore. But the amenities were good. There was an ice machine twenty feet down the hall, clean sheets daily, laundry on demand. I walked around the living room and out through big sliding doors to the balcony and back through the other glass doors into the bedroom and I put my head in the bathroom and closet.

They had taken my bags at the check-in on shore, and I had been a little concerned about that. But I saw that all my luggage had safely made it to my suite while I was on deck and that someone had unpacked for me. All my pants and shorts were hung up, as well as my shirts, jackets, and ties. Socks, underwear, athletic gear, golf shirts, and sweaters were folded and stacked in drawers, with tissue between items. Everything was organized by colour, moving from light to dark, which I thought was a nice touch. I looked to make sure nothing was missing. I noticed a claim tag for my suitcases on the dresser, which they stowed somewhere for me, I guess.

It was a hot day, and I'd been through the check-in and beside the rail. I was getting ripe. So I took off my pants and shirt and put them in the laundry bag. Then I washed my face and armpits, talced, and put on khakis and a golf shirt. I sat down on the bed to put on clean socks, and I noticed a bell to call the steward. It was an easy arm's reach from the bed, which I thought showed good sense. And I was checking the amenities. So I looked at my watch and pushed the call bell.

It took about thirty seconds until there was a knock at the door of my suite. I was impressed, but I didn't want to show it. If you give your workforce too much praise too early in the game they can go soft, and I wanted service to stay sharp. So I finished putting on my socks and then my shoes and there was another knock before I went out to the living room and opened the door.

The steward wasn't what I expected, not really measuring up to the luxury standards of the *Mariola*. He was tall and lean, a boy still, not filled out to a man's bulk. So I was happy he was wearing long pants and not the shorts that some of the crew went for. But he had an old man's grey face; his skin looked dingy against his crisp white uniform. Still his manners showed respect. He folded his hands together like he was praying and he leaned in toward me.

"Welcome, sir, welcome. You called for steward service. How can I help, sir? A problem? A question? What can I do?"

I nodded him into the room and settled back for some conversation. "What's your name, my friend?" I asked him.

He touched a name tag pinned to his uniform. I hadn't noticed it. "Raoul," he said, a bit slowly, like he was sounding it out for someone just learning to read.

I thought about being offended, but passed. "Raoul," I said. "I'm happy to meet you, Raoul. I'm checking out the territory, learning the ropes. I'm wondering, what have you got to say? What's the drill? What are you going to do for me today?"

He looked hard at me for a minute and then nodded and straightened up. He kept his hand on his name tag like he was taking the oath. "First off, sir, I want to welcome you on board the *Mariola* and let you know you are in for a superb retirement lifestyle experience. I am the guy on the front line to deliver. It all starts with the amenities in your suite. Have you had a chance to check it out, sir? Did you find everything you need?"

I looked around. "I think so," I said.

"Let me walk you through it so you know what's where," he said. He waved his hands around. "You've got your living area." He walked back to the door and pointed at the panel beside it. "The a/c control for the living room is by the suite entrance, with your basic settings: on, off, max, min." He punched some buttons and turned a dial. "You've got a separate panel in the bedroom, so you can spot control conditions in each room for optimal comfort and convenience. You already know, but the Company likes me to remind you: you want to keep the balcony doors shut when you've got the a/c on, or you can run up your power bill."

I had the doors open because I like a breeze, and I had turned the a/c on also, because it's my right. I thought he noticed probably, but he didn't say anything out loud, which showed respect. Instead he came back into the room and pointed around some more.

"Light switches at each point of entry, and the lights are all on dimmers so you can set the mood." He went to a switch by the balcony doors and turned the overheads on full I think. It was the middle of the day and I couldn't see a difference. "Anything from a reliable reading light to a romantic glow," he said, and he turned them down, I guess, although I couldn't really tell.

He pointed outside. "Full outdoor living enclosure with standard features and portside exposure."

"Is that a good thing?" I asked him.

"It's the best way to go," he said. "Although it depends on our latitude and bearing and the time of day and if you like direct sunlight and so on."

Then he went over to the desk and picked up a remote and brought up the wall screen. "The Balcony Stateroom package includes standard entertainment and information systems. On-board closed circuit streams informationals about cruise destinations and on-board activities. In emergency protocols, the in-house channel keeps guests up to date and fully informed. It's part of our passenger safety package. You also find in-house pay-per-view selections on this menu. Reasonable charge. Also you've got satellite access to major broadcasters, depending on latitude and satellite availability like you'd expect." He ran through a menu on the screen while he was talking, but I didn't come to sea to watch television so I didn't pay attention.

Raoul put the remote down, pushed buttons on the desk computer, and looked from the desktop to wall screen. Menus came up and he opened and closed icons. "You've got an x-two-seven integrated desktop panel. You can run visual on the unit or send to the big screen. Also you can stream video to the personal screen in the bedroom. Audio facilities include four in-room speakers in the living entertaining complex, two in the bedroom area, and one in the bath. State-of-the-art surround sound in all arenas."

He gave me a second to be impressed and I said, "It's got a lot of features." He told me more about them. "You're enabled with docks for compatibles: cell, berry, reader, interactives. Standard software is pre-loaded: text, mail, chat, video."

"It sounds very complete," I said.

"Aerial and backup hardwire interface your console with *Mariola* central systems. Access and download services match dryland resources depending on our location and available broadband. Everyone has their own virtual style, but I recommend the Company home page for your default site." He brought it up so I could see Company advertising and promotions on the big screen. "Also on the home page you find the CruiseCalendar updated regularly with a full menu of dates, destinations, and excursions. On-board activities are posted concurrent deck by deck and room by room. When you see what you like, you can book it on site through your CruiseAccount."

It sounded convenient. "I should set that up," I said.

He nodded. "People set up their CruiseAccount before they book a suite sometimes. It is a useful resource for your cruising needs. We can do it now if you like. Fill out the online form, make a password."

I was polite but I didn't lie to him. "I'm not interested in technology," I said.

He straightened up like he just saw the light. "The virtual world is overrated," he said. "I prefer a hands-on approach." He closed up the console and the big screen shut down.

He looked around. "You chose the Balcony Stateroom package."

"I thought it sounded comfortable," I told him.

He was very firm. "You made a good choice I think. Some people are all about the specialty range, the Deluxe Stateroom and the Principal Stateroom and the Admiralty Suite packages. They get some extras, some additional menu choices. They pay a higher pop. So we offer them a wider range of activities and amenities, like you expect. But to tell you the truth, and maybe I'm out of line saying it, but I think the Balcony Stateroom package is the best deal for your money. The add-ons at the higher fare schedules look nice but they lack substance. Sometimes you hear about buyer's remorse.

"Then again, you can always switch it up. We've got a Company-Interiors franchise with feng shui consultants, fully bonded contractors, and specialty trades all on-board and ready to discuss design and renovation options."

"It's another service I will keep in mind," I told him although I didn't plan to take out any walls.

"You signed up for the bar fridge option," Raoul said.

"It was extra but I thought it was worth it for the convenience and the hospitality opportunities," I said.

"It's one of the finest upgrades on the menu," he said. "You won't regret it."

He waved at the desk. "You found the call bell, so you know how to reach me." He walked into the bedroom and I followed him. "You've got another call bell by the bed."

That was the one I used, but I didn't interrupt. He was on a roll.

"Lights in the bedroom are also controlled by switches at all points of entry." He turned them on and off again and went to the balcony doors. "All balcony access points have titanium bolt locking systems." He snapped something on the doors and put his weight against them like he was trying to open them against the lock and couldn't even if he used all his strength. "The *Mariola* is a luxury facility and our clientele are salt of the earth. Also our staff is fully bonded. But security is an important consideration in any environment, and the Company accepts no responsibility for goods lost from suites."

I didn't like this. "You're running the show but you're not taking responsibility?" I asked.

"The Company offers good security options and we encourage passengers to make use of them, such as the titanium bolt systems on the balcony doors, and we offer secure storage in the ship's vaults. You can set it up through the Purser's Desk. The charge is very reasonable."

He came back past the bed. "Queen-size, full support," he said and I nodded. There was also a night table and an alarm clock and a big mirror. I didn't see the point of the alarm clock, but it was a homey touch and there was no rule saying I had to use it. So I didn't mind.

He turned the lights on in the bathroom. It was done up in marble and glass with towels and a thick, white robe hanging on the back of the door. Raoul had more instructions. "The outlet in here is for shavers only, like you expect. You want music in the bathroom, you have a speaker in here, too. High-quality sound although you get reverb with the marble and the tile and the smaller space." He opened up the shower and pointed at the head. "Your shower comes with a variety of spray options: pulse, massage, mist. Take your choice."

He closed the shower door and took me back into the bedroom and waved at the closet. "Your standard feature walk-in," he said. He turned on the light and stepped in. "I unpacked for you already. You find everything all right?"

"You did a very good job with that," I told him, because he was busting his butt for me and I thought I could give him some encouragement.

"It's a pleasure, sir," he said.

He pointed at the safe in the back of the closet. "You've also got your security box." It was a good size vault. He stepped up and opened the door and showed me a card, which he waved at me and put back. "You follow the instructions to set up a combination, and you can keep valuables in there also. But you want to keep a record, because there's no override key. It's a good option, but like I said, the Company only takes responsibility for goods secured in the ship's vaults."

"I like to have my things close," I said.

"Convenience is also a consideration," he said.

We went out of the closet and Raoul turned out the light and closed the door, and took me back into the living room. "What else can I show you?" he asked me. "What else do you need to know?"

"You have very fine facilities here," I said.

"They're A-one," Raoul said.

"I'd like to hear about service, too," I said. "Are you my one and only, Raoul? Are you the guy who's looking after me this cruise? Are you part of a team? Paint me a picture."

Raoul snapped to it right away. "This deck is serviced by a first-class team of stewards, cleaning technicians, hospitality professionals, maintenance- and cruise-specialists," he said. "This cabin, and the thirty cabins on deck six, forward, are the personal responsibility of myself, Juan, Jimmy G, and Horst, with Ricky, Regina, and Leticia pitching in on Sundays."

"On Sundays?"

"They're your Sunday team."

"They work with you on Sundays?"

"Sunday is our day of rest."

"So they're instead of you, not as well as?"

"They look after your Sunday service."

I took a moment to think this over. He was glib and snappy, and I don't like to be rushed.

"Ricky, Regina, and Leticia on Sundays."

"Correct."

"And weekdays my team is you and those guys?"

"Juan, Jimmy G, and Horst."

"You, Juan, Jimmy G, and Horst."

"The musketeers."

"But there's only three scheduled for Sunday?" I was starting to smell a rat.

"They're very gung-ho."

"Three stewards and how many cabins? Is this a good arrangement?"

"With a professional team of three, we can maintain A-one steward service. If anything, we're overstaffed through the week. But the Company schedules a quartet six days a week to guarantee luxury standards."

This sounded like horseshit to me. Either the Company was skimping me on Sundays, or it was throwing money down the toilet six days a week, which could impact the financial security of my investment. As a stakeholder I felt that it might be an issue. Still it wasn't the kind of thing the guy who scrubbed the toilet could put right. So I held my peace and did more fact-finding.

"This Ricky is Richard, Ricardo?" I asked.

He held back again and I knew it was bad news. "Rochelle," he said finally. I didn't like the sound of this either.

"So it's men working Monday to Saturday and girls kicking in on Sunday?"

He thought for a minute, and I was glad he took the question seriously. Finally he said, "It works out that way, but it's not Company policy."

"I'm glad it's not Company policy," I said. "But I think it could be an issue."

"In what way, sir?"

"There are things I might need assistance with that might not be in the domain of a woman. Things that are male and somewhat private for example."

He took my point. "I didn't think about that," he said. "It's an issue. If you like, I could raise it with housekeeping."

"Could you raise it with housekeeping?"

"I could bring it to their attention. It's an issue. And for the ladies,

on board

~ 21 ~

too, because they might want service from a girl on a Monday or a Thursday or something, although I'd be happy to help if it came to it."

"That is another point."

"I will definitely mention the topic to housekeeping."

"You're a good kid."

"Somebody, maybe, I don't know, might be able to switch a shift."

"Just a couple of adjustments."

"It makes sense. Although." He looked troubled. "I don't want to get your hopes up. I have seniority, so they won't ask me. But Horst, Juan, Jimmy G. They don't want to work on Sundays."

"Is it better to have Sunday off?"

"Better for some. But Leticia, for example. She's Buddhist. Sundays don't mean anything to her."

"And you?"

He looked solemn. "The ship's chaplain does an interfaith service on Sunday, after brunch. Or at a port of call we can go ashore."

When people talk about themselves it pays to sound interested even though you're not. I said, "Raoul, I'm happy to hear that you're a man of faith. It shows character. But frankly my focus is on service. Do you think Horst might want to switch with Leticia? Then Leticia would be available for the ladies, if there were some kind of female issue during the week. And Horst would be around on Sunday, if I had some sort of masculine problem that it would be best to take to another guy."

"I will certainly suggest it to housekeeping. It sounds like a good thing to do." He looked worried. "But I should warn you. The schedules are set. Not everyone knows how to be flexible. And there's the union."

This surprised me. "There's a union?" I said.

He shrugged. "What can you do? But this switch. It might be possible. But you need to remember, female stewards aren't really a problem, because your team isn't just the stewards, although we're your first line. You've also got your cleaners, trainers, maintenance, tech support. So Ricky and Regina and Leticia are never your only options. There will always be someone around who can give you a hand when you need something."

He was making a good case, but always respectful. I liked his style.

"What about Ricky and Regina," I said. "Don't they ever get a day of rest?"

"They're on the c14 timetable. They get Mondays, I think."

"What do they do the other days?"

"Ricky, Regina, Leticia, a whole bunch of people are relief stewards all around the ship."

"That's what c14s do?"

"That's the c14 profile."

"Is it a good job?"

Raoul put his hands up like he hoped he didn't have to fight about it. "Socially it's a fine position," he said. "You get to meet everyone, and everyone has something to say to you. Myself, I like a fixed station. I know my post, where things are, like cotton balls and Visine that people sometimes need in a hurry. And I get to know my clients, so I can give them my best."

He was starting to sound boastful, which I don't take to. Plus he was drifting off topic, and I wanted him to focus. "Raoul," I told him, "You seem like a nice kid, and I'm encouraged by your suggestions. I'm glad you're going to talk to housekeeping about female stewards. I feel good that you're dedicated to my concerns. But I'm going to tell you, and it's nothing personal, that I'm going to take my concerns to the concierge as well, as I feel that may make more impact. This isn't totally a criticism of you. It's just the way I find that you get service in this world."

Raoul looked sad and sorry. "Of course, sir," he said. "But, let's slow down a second, because I think you're getting upset and you shouldn't. It'll wreck the first day of your cruise, and that would be a shame. Here. Have a seat. Let me help you."

There was only one soft chair in the room, and about half the size of my ass. But I let Raoul lead me over and lower me into it. He kept hold of my hand and knelt in front of me looking in my eyes and twisting his neck and back to stay small. He looked up at me and pressed my hand.

"Housekeeping will be happy to hear from you personally, Mr. Rutledge. If you like, I can set up the appointment, or send Bobby down to see you. He's in charge."

Raoul was full of surprises.

"You know my name?" I said.

"I studied up on the passenger list. I can tell you, my clients are my number one concern. Sunday service, don't worry. If there's a problem, I address it. It's my professional creed. Your job: eat, drink, and be merry. Tomorrow is in my hands. Trust me to do my job, Mr. Rutledge. Just give me the chance."

I heard him out, and I thought about it for a minute so he didn't think I was easy. Then I stood up and, after a second, he got up also, cringing in front of me in a way that I liked. He stood a little close. He had personal space issues that I needed to work on. But I liked that he kept his head down and his shoulders hunched. He stood eye to eye with me if he straightened his back, and that just felt wrong. About his creed, I told him I would take it under advisement, mostly because I liked him begging for it.

I reached for my billfold and found a crisp c-note.

"Raoul," I said, "This is going to be a long journey."

He bowed his head, and I folded the bill and pressed it into his hand. He closed on it without looking and tucked it away.

"Thank you, Mr. Rutledge," he said. "Let us look forward to a prosperous cruise."

the captain's mess

In any new environment the social landscape is a first priority. A responsible person checks out his options and test drives people and groups. A good policy is to seek out like-minded people for company and pleasure, although other options are worth considering, like finding people with scarce and valuable goods and services, or better social connections and status. For all these reasons, and because I paid for it already in my all-inclusive, I went out right away to the Voodoo Lounge for cocktails and orientation.

My fellow passengers were a mixed bag. For starters, there were too many of us in too small a space, and that always makes things difficult. I thought about going to the Tropicana Room or the Sunset Room. But I wasn't sure where they were, and the Voodoo Lounge was just down from my suite, which was convenient. So I stayed there.

The hostess at the door gave me the itinerary for the first week, and she tried to give me a name tag. But they're really for the service. So I passed. I had to struggle through the crowd to get to the bar, but I had better luck there. The bartender was sharp and professional. He poured me a large

G and T in an understated, stylish way. Then a guy with a Yankees cap cleared out of his bar stool, and I nabbed it. It was a decent vantage point.

The music was cranked. People were laughing a lot. Out on the floor people were dancing, couples, and older women, and girls, dancing alone or with each other or with the cruise gigolos.

The guy beside me put out his hand. "Bud Matthews," he shouted.

"Rutledge," I said, and shook.

"You in for the long haul?" he shouted.

"The whole enchilada."

"We're a privileged group," he said.

It seemed right to express interest. So I asked him, "What turned you on to it?"

"My wife talked me into it," he said. "She's out there." He nodded in the direction of the dance floor. "I don't dance. My hip is bad. But she likes it. She'll dance all night. I like to watch her, so it's okay. The *Mariola* was her idea. I don't know. It's a lot. It's a marathon. But Bailey is keen. This is what her dreams are made of."

The floor was full of girls who liked to dance. I wasn't sure which one was Bailey. Most of them looked like whores. High-class, successful whores, of course, and no offense intended.

"So far so good?" Bud was asking a question.

I don't like to come off like a rube, so I held back. "I have some concerns," I said.

"The music's too loud."

"I'm thinking safety issues. Service. Big picture items."

"It's a hell of an undertaking."

"The devil's in the details."

A pretty girl came off the floor and put her arms around Bud. "Hey, Buddy, wanna dance a slow one?"

"They don't play slow ones. It's been disco for three hours now. This is Rutledge."

She put her hand on my knee and squeezed it, making me think she maybe specialized in hand jobs. "Rutledge," she said. "Any friend of Bud's, etcetera." I filed this for future reference. She looked around. "Where's my drink?"

"I'll order you one," said Bud.

"I asked you an hour ago."

"I ordered it an hour ago. The ice was melting."

"You drank it?"

"I don't like to waste."

I thought it was the right approach, because people sometimes don't appreciate and let good things slip away. But Bailey waved a finger at him. Then she leaned over him to talk to the bartender. She had a fine ass.

"My husband drank my daiquiri," she said.

"Ma'am?" The bartender was very respectful. "A daiquiri?"

"All the bells and whistles. I like that stuff."

He was at the blender right away.

"You gotta admit, that's service," said Bailey.

The bartender made a show of pouring the drink out and decorating it. He had full professional skills. We all watched.

Bailey was reaching for the drink when the song changed. She lit up. "Oh, I gotta dance to this," she said. She waved her finger at Bud. "Don't touch my drink."

Bud and I watched her dance for a while. She had a fine, dynamic style with confidence and good posture. I could see why Bud liked to watch. Seeing the two of them and their good arrangement, where she danced and he watched her, I thought I should have held out for a trophy wife myself instead of letting Laureen talk me into marrying her when we were both too young to know better. Because as I know now but did not know then, when you take pity on someone you only get a kick in the head. But then I figured what's past is past and there's no point brooding.

Instead, I had another gin, and then another. I went to the head, and when I came back someone had taken my stool and he and Bud were shouting at each other over the music. So I circulated for a bit. I met a guy in biotechnology, and a guy with a trust fund. I sat at a table with a guy with an oxygen tank, but I didn't get his story.

o o o

When I booked my ticket, I pre-signed for the late seating at dinner for the first month. It was at eight-thirty in the Captain's Mess, the big, formal dining room. Instead, or to keep the pangs away, you could grab sushi or tapas or a steak dinner at one of the bars or restaurants. But I liked the idea of the Captain's Mess. You had to dress for dinner, for one thing, which sounded elegant. I bought two tuxes especially. I'd never owned a tux before, and I'd only rented one a couple of times in my life, like for my high school prom.

For the prom, besides the tuxes, we'd had a limo, and a bottle of vodka that we mixed into slushees, and the girls wore shiny gowns and big hair. I'd felt mature and sophisticated. It was the beginning of real life, I'd thought. But it hadn't sat right. The rest of the world was out of step. In the mini mart where we bought the slush, people were shuffling around in sweats and Birkenstocks. Back in the limo, we drove past strip malls and vacant lots. In the school gym, the chaperones patted us down. At midnight, Laureen spewed. It hadn't been the real thing. I'd been ready and dressed but the world around me was only so-so. I'd been disappointed by it all. That was my first experience with a tux.

So I wanted everything to be right for the first night on the *Mariola*, and I checked myself carefully when I dressed for dinner. And then I thought Raoul could make himself useful. So I pushed the bell and right away he knocked at the door and I yelled at him to come in and he used his pass-key and came into my suite and stood at the bedroom door showing respect. He took in my tuxedo pants and my cummerbund and shirt.

"The late seating," he said. He was a sharp boy. "It's the right choice. Chef Lousine really gets it together after dark."

I checked myself over again in the mirror. "I don't know about this tux," I told him. "I'd like your opinion."

He stepped back and looked me over. "It's a good one, Mr. Rutledge. A flared leg never goes out of style."

"Is the cummerbund okay?"

"I should take a crack at it?"

He ducked his head to show he was asking, and I put my hands up and he came in close and started pulling at the cummerbund and my shirt. It looked okay when he was done. I couldn't really breathe was all.

I had another good look in the mirror. I still wasn't sure. "I feel kind of overdone. You don't think it's too gaudy?"

"It's stylish, not flashy. You can probably wear it all the way through the Canal."

This was a bombshell. "I thought I'd wear it a long time, a few years at least."

Raoul smiled like he was trying not to. "It's good tailoring," he said. "It will last. But on these cruises, our clientele go for novelty. We see whole new wardrobes every six weeks, two months."

"I thought this was the maiden voyage?"

"With luxury cruising in general."

I looked at my closet stocked with top of the line khakis and so on. I thought they'd last me all my days. I'd already spent enough on clothes, in my opinion.

Raoul was reading my mind. "Your wardrobe is quality. But it will get old. New clothes are a kick."

"There aren't a lot of malls on the ocean."

"The ports of call have good shopping. But also right here on the *Mariola* we have the CompanyFormal boutique, it's a CompanyCruise-Wear franchise, a Jimmy Fleet's and a Bingham&Sons, and selected designer portfolios and prêt-a-porter shows quarterly. Also, there's Mr. Gualtieri, the ship's tailor."

I knew it was another scam, but I also appreciated him letting me know the drill. "You're a good kid, Raoul," I said.

"Thank you, Mr. Rutledge," he said. He was standing close again, and kind of waiting patiently. I thought it was pushy except he had given me useful fashion advice. So I found my bankroll and pulled out a crisp c-note. The bill disappeared in his hand.

"You're very kind, Mr. Rutledge," he said.

Then he went after the top button of my shirt. He didn't say anything while he hauled it through the buttonhole. I'd been maybe optimistic about sizing when I'd had it made up. But I had extensive opportunities for exercise in the fitness facility on the ship. Raoul flipped up the collar and got to work on the tie. It took him a couple of tries before he was happy with it. He picked up the jacket and held it up to me like a bullfighter. I turned around and he pulled it up my arms.

"Okay, Mr. Rutledge," he said. "Now you want to assert yourself into the shoulders, and give a good tug at each cuff."

He stepped back and gave me the once-over, then shrugged and nodded, and turned me to look in the mirror. He did good work.

"You're ready. And I should probably tell you: they're very punctual in the Captain's Mess."

o o o

I was late, anyway. The Captain's Mess was just two floors up, on deck eight. But you had to take the midship elevators to get there, and they were packed. I didn't like to crowd the people already in them. I was feeling shy. And I don't like the stairs. So I waited for an empty elevator, and got one finally, and it took me right to the foyer.

The Captain's Mess was a stylish dining room, big but with raised levels and sunken pits and an upper gallery running around two sides. There were trees and flowers and aquariums breaking it up so each area felt snug, even though there was seating for a crowd. And it was all decorated in a tropical theme, with ferns and palm trees and little lights and real songbirds in the trees and butterflies in the air. It was magical and sophisticated and exciting like it should be for the price, and I was impressed right away when I stepped inside.

A hostess called Ashley took me to my table, and on the way I asked her where the captain's table was. I'd read up on cruises, and the captain's table is a big deal. I wanted to get a look at it and book my turn. I wanted to say hello to the commander and make sure he knew my name. I like to have a personal relationship with the people in charge since I always find that it keeps service sharp.

Ashley pointed it out, on the far side of the room. It was up a few steps, like on a stage, against one wall, with a low bank of flowers and a sort of waterfall arrangement around it. It had a good view of the whole room, and all the diners had a good view of it. Several officers were seated there, in crisp white uniforms. And the guests at the table were instantly recognizable, even though these people always look different in person. There was a legendary entrepreneur, getting old now; a reclusive movie star; an heiress who I thought was in recovery. This was the elegance I'd been looking for, the beautiful women and the power and the wealth.

Then I saw three or four crewmen stationed in the aisles, looking casual and controlling access. There was no actual cordon, but it was set up like a private club, and this did not impress me. I can understand people wanting privacy. I too want to be left alone to get on with my concerns. And on a cruise, even a big liner like the *Mariola*, you're in a small town, and the best thing is to live and let live, because gossip gets around and people's feelings get hurt. But the bouncers, I thought, were unnecessary, since we were all on the same luxury cruise together, and I didn't like that line being drawn between me and them, like they would hurt if I got too close.

I'd stopped to get a good look at the table, and Ashley wanted to move me along. "We're just over here, Mr. Rutledge," she said. She took my arm like she wanted to dance, but she put some pressure into it and she leaned in like she was telling secrets. "Isn't she lovely?" she whispered. "It's a privilege to be in the same room as her. But service is starting so I want to get you to your table." We went through the ferns and up a couple of stairs.

the captain's mess

"She's okay," I told her. The movie star was showing her age. "So tell me, when do I get to sit at the captain's table? What's the drill?"

"Captain Moncrieff will invite every passenger to his table some time during the cruise. But for tonight, I think you'll enjoy meeting the Martins and the Tremblays."

"I'll enjoy meeting the captain, also," I said. I know how things work in the world. So I pulled out my roll and found a c-note for her.

She smiled like a good kid, and took it. "I'll be sure to tell the maitre d'. But I should let you know, it could take a few days. Several cruisers have already asked about the captain's table. Plus Captain Moncrieff can't join us for dinner every night."

"He's here tonight."

"He came to both seatings tonight. On the first evening he wants to welcome his guests."

"That's the way. The captain and his ship."

"Yes. But on other nights, it might be the first officer who hosts the captain's table, or the purser or the chief engineer."

"The first officer might be okay," I told her. "But I want to meet the captain. I'm not interested in the guy who oils the turbines."

"I'll be sure to tell the maitre d'."

She brought me to a table for eight with a big family group. There was a white-haired couple, two middle-aged guys and two middle-aged women, I couldn't tell who was with who, and a young guy, a kid, who slouched in his tux like it was sweats. Ashley rolled me toward them and everyone but the kid looked at me and they all looked surprised. And then one of the girls said very loudly, "Who is he? He isn't with us. He can't sit here." Her voice had power in it and people looked.

But everyone else at the table said, "Lily!" Some of them said it like they were angry and some of them laughed.

Lily made a face like she was above them. "It's a family table," she said. She leaned into it like it was obvious and anyone could see.

But the other girl had better manners and she was prettier. She said to me, "You sit right here. We have an empty chair. You sit down."

And Ashley introduced me and I shook hands all around: Eric and Steve, Della, who was friendly and polite and had a pretty smile, the old man, called Eddie, and the old lady, Katherine. Then Lily and the kid: Jason, Jamie, Jordan? I didn't catch it. A waiter pulled back the chair between Eric and the kid, and I sat down and everyone looked at me like they were waiting for me to start, and I smiled at them because Lily put me off but I was willing to move on and have an elegant meal with sophisticated companions and amusing conversation anyway. And then Lily put her foot in it some more.

"I only meant we're a family group," she said. "I assumed they were going to give us our own table, so we could dine en famille. I didn't know they'd put an outsider with us. I thought it might not be comfortable for somebody who isn't one of us."

"Then let's make him comfortable," Eddie said.

He sat low in his seat and he wasn't spry, but he looked at me and winked and he didn't pay attention to Lily. I took to him right away. He had a spark I liked. And I was there for pleasure and to enjoy myself. So I made polite remarks.

"It's a treat to see a big family all together," I said. "I know families you never see all in the same room, not even for a big event like a holiday or a funeral. It's nice when everyone is together. If I may say, in this world today, it's an achievement."

The old man had manners. He kept the old lady's hand under his hand, but he leaned toward me and made the effort. "It is an achievement to have your family all together," he said. "I've seen families bicker and I've seen families fall apart. It's not for me. It's not for Mrs. Martin either." He looked at the old lady for a minute. "Mrs. Martin likes to keep her family close."

It was a fine thing to see, although I wasn't sure the old lady noticed. Her head bobbled on its stem, and her eyes went around and around. I wasn't sure she was totally all there. Also, the way Eddie held her hand

and watched over her reminded me for a minute that Laureen was gone and nobody was watching over me. But I put it out of mind because I wanted to enjoy myself. There was a team of waiters all around. So I ordered a drink and one of them jumped to it right away, Eddie turned around to check the old lady, and Lily read the menu with dedication. Eric had his back to me while he was involved with Steve and Della.

"Nothing Latin," he said. "It's too complex."

"That's why it's good. You use your whole body," Della said.

"I'll show you a quickstep. That will get you moving. You cover the floor at speed."

"I don't want to run sprints. I want to samba."

Lily had said it out loud and it wasn't polite, but it's true that it's difficult to join a family party. Because everyone knows everyone else already, and even if they bore the pants off each other or get on each other's nerves, even if they could use new blood to shake things up, they're still a team. And coming into it is like being the new kid at school.

On my other side, the boy was staring down at his lap and twitching and shaking. He didn't look like much, but no one else had anything for me. So I gave it a shot. "Who do you belong to?" I asked him. He didn't look up, and I thought for a minute he was maybe deaf or backward. Then I saw he had a unit with him and jacks in his ears. He was humming, and rocking back and forth. It was funny, and I kind of laughed and looked around and Della noticed.

"Is he bothering you?" she asked me.

"No. He isn't bothering anyone. I didn't see the headset," I said. "I was asking him whether he came with you or with Lily."

"He's my little kitten," Della said. She gave the boy a big, bright smile, and he didn't notice. He was working his system.

Across the table, the old lady nodded forward until her head settled on the bread plate. Lily and the old man turned to and tried to sit her up, but it didn't take. Lily wasn't fully committed, I thought, and the old man wasn't strong. A waiter jumped in and he hauled the old lady up again. She lifted her head and opened her eyes wide and they started to circle around again.

Lily said, "I told you this seating was too late for Mother," in her loud voice.

"What can you do?" Della said. "Eric said it was all that was left."

"That's because he left it too late." Lily's voice went up a notch and she looked over at the guys. "They told us to sign up right away, and he waited deliberately."

Eric looked stunned. "Not on purpose," he said.

Then the waiter stepped in to move us along. "Has everyone decided?" he asked the old man.

"We should start," Eddie said. He put his hand on Katherine's hand. "Do you know what you want?" he asked her.

She smiled and stared around.

"Katherine?"

"You order for me," she said. She pushed it out in a sandpaper voice. She didn't have a lot of steam. But she knew what was happening.

Eddie halfway turned to the waiter and started telling him. I looked at the menu. It was short but select, and when my turn came I ordered a lobster bisque and a fish course since we were at sea, and osso bucco for the main meal. The waiter punched it all into his handheld. Then I had a good look at the wine list. They put a bottle of house wine on the table, but I steered clear, obviously. Instead, when the sommelier turned up I ordered a half bottle of white for the soup and fish, and a claret for the main course.

I thought about making a big gesture, like ordering a couple of bottles for the table. But you start out with that kind of thing and pretty soon people think it's their right, or sometimes they're recovering alcoholics, or they're allergic, or it gives them migraine. Even a generous gesture sometimes leads to trouble. So it's a better policy just to look after yourself.

Then I turned in my menu and the lights went down, like a movie starting. People stopped talking, and I heard Eric say, "White tie and tails are a classic look. I'm not dressing up like a bullfighter," before he noticed no one else was talking and looked around like the rest of us to see what was happening. All around the room, the wait staff went very quiet and respectful. I didn't know what it was but I hoped it wasn't going to hold up the soup, because it was late and I was hungry.

A light came up on the captain's table and a man stood up in a white uniform. He had a red face and white hair and he was going soft and spilling over his buckles, but he was cheerful. He had a microphone in one hand and a glass of champagne in the other, and while people settled down he started to talk.

"I'm interrupting your dinner but for a good cause, because everyone should have a drink by now and I can make a toast and say hello. Some of you have met me already, and I've met some of you too. But for everyone else, I'm Captain Moncrieff. I'm the skipper." He pointed at his pips. "You can tell by the brass if you know about that kind of thing. I want to welcome everybody to the maiden voyage of the *Mariola*, pride of the fleet and an exciting new experience in luxury lifestyle. That's right." He nodded at us. "Give yourself a hand. Go ahead."

We all did. Della said, "He's an old sweetie pie."

The sommelier turned up with my half bottle. He showed it to me and cracked it and gave me the cork and the tasting glass very fast and discreetly. It was a good Chardonnay. I was happy with my selection. But I was worried about the captain talking and if it was going to be a long speech. I wondered if I should have ordered a full bottle of white to see me through, since it looked like the first side of dinner was going to take awhile. But the wait staff were very professional. Nobody talked and they tiptoed around, but they didn't let the speech hold back service. They turned to, and the soup came right away. My bisque was very fine.

In the spotlight, the captain got down to the details. "I have a couple of notices they asked me to tell you," he said. He held up a tablet and squinted at it. Then he put his champagne down and felt himself. He tried his head and his pants pockets and he felt his chest, and the microphone hummed when he hit it. Finally he found his glasses in a side pocket and put them on and looked at the tablet again.

"Our first stop will be San Lazar, not Itamar like it says on the itinerary. We're not taking Itamar off the agenda. We're putting San Lazar on because we have the chance. Schedule changes and add-ons will pop up on your dailies, and hospitality updates the CruiseCalendar regularly. But they asked me to tell you about San Lazar here tonight because it's right away and they don't want you to miss out. Also a family special poolside tomorrow at nine, if your family gets up before nine. Mine never did. It's an interactive sea animal event and it features dolphins, seals, penguins, and a sea lion. One show only. We were lucky to be able to book them. They're touring the liners on the Atlantic circuit and they have a tight schedule. Sign up online. First come, first served."

A couple of busboys arrived and lifted the soup plates away, and another relay brought in the second course, just like it said in the brochure. I had studied up and found my fish fork okay, not that anyone noticed. The J-kid broke his fish off in chunks and ate with his fingers.

Lily got distracted by the new plates. "What's this?" she said.

The waiter hated to talk while the captain was talking. He kept his voice very low. "You have plaice napped in a mint and mango-infused beurre."

"Yeah. Nice." Lily didn't sound enthusiastic which was a shame as it was a very fine dish. She looked over at the old lady's plate and helped Katherine find her fork. "What did we order for Mother?" she said. Every word carried.

"For the lady, we have mixed greens tossed with walnuts and dried cranberries in a raspberry vinaigrette."

People were drifting at other tables also, looking around and eating and starting to talk somewhat, although the wait staff was discreet and respectful. I listened to the captain with half an ear and concentrated on my food. Lily got some salad into the old lady before she fell asleep again. The busboy moved out my fish plate. The sommelier turned up and showed me my claret. It looked okay, and I liked watching him open it and pour the tasting glass for me. I swilled it around for a while to keep him on his toes, but it was fine. The osso bucco came with polenta and asparagus.

Then the captain stopped talking about agendas and looked at another guy at the captain's table. He was younger and smiling and looking sharp in his whites, and he didn't look at the captain but he said something and kind of laughed and then they said a few words back and forth off mic and then the captain looked around.

"Well apparently I've gone on too long as usual," he said. "But hospitality told me to read the notices. So I read the notices. Now they want me to wrap it up. So I'll wrap it up. In conclusion, I'd like to welcome everyone to the *Mariola* and wish you all a happy cruise." He raised his glass. "Stand up everyone, and let's salute the ship and the flag."

So we all stood up except the old lady. Della gave Eddie an arm and a team of waiters moved in to help Katherine. But she was sleeping and Eddie and Lily waved them off because there was no point really in waking her up and hauling her onto her pins and then putting her down again. But the rest of us held up our glasses and said, "The ship and the flag." And we drank and sat down again. The old man checked on the old lady, and she was peaceful. And he looked at me across the table and winked. He knew how to have a good time.

Then the captain said, "And now I'm going to pass the mic to Father McGrath. He's going to give us a blessing. We sailors are religious and superstitious, but the blessing is non-denominational. So you can all bow your heads regardless."

He held the microphone out to the officer at the end of his table who was the padre it turned out. He stood up and ignored the captain and the mic. He was old also, but fit and ropy where the captain was soft, and with a fierce look on his face, maybe because he had to wait until the middle of dinner to say grace. He was the kind of guy that when he stood up everyone else sat straight and stopped fidgeting.

"I am an old man now, and I have given my life to the sea," he said. He could project. I could hear him fine even though I was a long way from the VIP section. "Through study and through trial, I have learned her cruelty and her splendour. I can plot a course and map the stars, but I do not know and cannot say how any voyage will end. Over the shallows and the deeps, our lives run their course. We strive sometimes against the current or test our strength in the tempest."

I wasn't sure what he was getting at, but I liked his style. He was solemn and dignified. He looked like a man who knew a thing or two, and I liked that he brought experience to his work.

He bowed his head for a second and we all stayed quiet and respectful. Steve crossed himself and then Eric did too. The moment stretched out. I wasn't sure if we were maybe supposed to clap. The captain stayed on his feet and he was watching hard like he was looking for a sign. He raised his glass up and brought it down again like he was ready to toast the cruise or pray for it, whatever the padre wanted. Finally Father McGrath said, "There are days, too, of pleasant sailing, when wind and water take us to our heart's content. With compass, crew, and keel, we seek safe passage and a following wind. Bless this ship and all her company."

We all said amen. It felt right and solemn and serious, and I was happy with it. And then the padre sat down and the lights came back up and the waiters got back to business topping up the wine or clearing plates. But the passengers didn't bounce back right away. There was a kind of pause all over the room.

Lily said, "So what does he mean?"

"I didn't follow," Della said.

I thought we were going to have some conversation finally. So I spoke up. "It was an unusual blessing," I said. They all looked at me again, and I liked it that they were paying attention. "I don't say I'm an expert," I said. "But I've been reading up on ships and the sea because I was looking forward to the cruise and because it's my first. I've never been to sea before."

the captain's mess

I waited for a second because I thought someone might want to say that it was their first too, or that they took a lot of cruises, or ask me what I usually did for a holiday if I didn't cruise. But no one said anything.

"From what I read, it looks to me like the captain sets the tone for the ship," I said.

"Like the emcee at a wedding?" said Della.

"Something like that," I said, although it wasn't what I meant. "And Captain Moncrieff was very friendly and welcoming."

"But the father had a different approach," Steve said.

"It is another side of the coin," I said. "The cruise is a serious undertaking, a significant thing. We are starting the adventure of a lifetime. The father told us the stars will guide us and the captain will set the course."

"But does he know where he's going?" Lily said.

"Of course he does," Eric said. "We have an itinerary."

"The captain doesn't do much anyway," said Eddie. "The officers and the crew get down to the nitty-gritty. The captain glad-hands the passengers. He's like the CEO."

"That's a fine way to put it," I said. "He's the public face of the cruise, the official representative."

"Why was the father talking about bad weather?" said Della.

"I think he meant the power and the strength, the *Mariola* riding out the storm," I said.

"I guess that's good," said Della.

She didn't look convinced. It didn't worry me, though, because we'd had some pleasant conversation and I was working with the team.

All through the room, people were quiet, like they were trying to work out the padre's speech. But eventually everyone shrugged it off and we got to work on our entrees, even the J-kid. He ate with his fingers, and chewed with his mouth open, or he closed his mouth and hummed and banged his head.

Dessert was gâteau with cream. I had cognac.

ports of call

Our first port of call was San Lazar and I got up early to watch. Common sense tells you that the ports of call are a highlight of a cruise. So I was excited, and I stepped out on deck to see the port come into view. I thought we'd steam into the harbour in a high style. But the real thing was cranky and technical. The wind was up, and we anchored in the bay. It wouldn't have mattered if we had calm weather. Their facilities were outdated and undersized, and the *Mariola* was a majestic ship of the future. It needed more room to manoeuvre than was on offer by the docks. And although it is always the best thing to have the most advanced and up-to-date technologies, there are interface problems sometimes if you want to connect with older systems. And so in San Lazar, we parked in the middle of the bay, and eventually went over in tenders, which were the *Mariola*'s lifeboats.

Before all of this, we'd gathered in the Silver Screen cinema for orientation, and the cruise director told us about the cultural and recreational opportunities on the island, a beach excursion or a steel band concert or a Santeria service and blessing. The security chief demonstrated self-defense techniques with volunteers from the audience. I was thinking I should check out the movie listings since the theatre was very comfortable, with reclining seats and a wide variety of snack and bar options, although my cabin was equipped with a flat screen and extensive programming access, and that was really more convenient.

Finally they took people down in groups to deck level minus one and into a hold. The hatch in the side of the ship was open just above the water, with a raft pulled up beside it. People stepped out of the hatch onto a raft, and then from the raft they got into the tenders. We climbed in one by one. It was a choppy kind of day, and you needed timing and coordination for it. The ship's hospitality specialists helped people who were old or shaky. And then a family of very large people had trouble also, and the hospitality specialists intervened in teams of two. We sat around rocking and heaving until the tender was full, with twenty-five or thirty people. The whole process took a while, and I was thinking that this was another aspect of the cruise that could use some work.

Still, it was a sight to see as we came in to dock. The smiling natives lined the pier waving and calling and selling merchandise from stalls that lined the quay. They had baskets of ripe tropical fruit, and fresh seafood snacks, cooked while you watched. They had shells and shell jewellery. One guy was offering tours of the historic colonial city in an air-conditioned bus, and another guy had tours of the historic colonial city in a horse and carriage; to each his own. There were snorkeling and scuba excursions. Everyone was friendly and everything was safe because there were soldiers patrolling the waterfront and security check-points all around the perimeter.

The buses laid on by the Company were parked at the far end of the pier. I looked at what they had on offer and I talked to the other guests who were waiting around. I decided against the beach and diving packages. I was feeling shy about my trunks, and I wanted to see what the other guys were wearing before I committed. The fat family, who were the McHughs, were on their way to a cricket match, all wearing white. They were nice people and friendly and they invited me to go with them.

"No one appreciates the game," Grant McHugh said. He was the head of the family and he had strong opinions. "It takes strength and athletics and hand-eye coordination. You come with us. We'll make you a believer."

I was polite and careful not to call him McHuge by mistake. But I said no, obviously, because I didn't want to be seen with them. You have to be careful about that kind of thing, especially when you're just starting out with a new group of people. Because the choices you make at the start impact the rest of your interactions, and other people judge you by the company you keep. So when more people came along, I put some distance between us, but in a nice way.

Bud and Bailey turned up with Bailey's new friend, Teresa. She was older but friendly and well-maintained. So I went with them on the tour called "City, Country, Culture." We all got on the bus, which had seats arranged in groups of four around little tables, and we waited around for it to fill up. It was air-conditioned, and a waiter came around and took our drink orders. I got a large G and T.

We rolled out of the pier, through the checkpoint, and into the city. It was small and ramshackle. We crawled up narrow, crowded streets till we broke through to a wide avenue with fountains and statues. At the top of it, there was a big building, the seat of government, in sort of a Spanish style. The guide made us get off the bus to see it. He wouldn't let us bring our drinks.

A guide from the site took us around first. She had a hat and a bad uniform, but she knew her stuff and talked fast and a lot. We walked through the grounds in the hot sun while she told us about horticulture and landscaping. When she was done, we clapped and tipped her, and I thought we'd go back to the bus. But instead they took us through another checkpoint and into the government building. A new guide picked us up in the foyer.

His uniform was bad also, and he also knew detail. He walked us into the middle of the foyer so we were standing under the big central dome, and he told us how tall it was and who painted the frescoes on the inside and where the granite for the building came from and how many people died building it. Then we took the stairs, because the elevator wasn't working, and we sat in the gallery of the senate chamber since they weren't in session, and the guide filled us in on the current regime, and the historical ties between our nations, and so on. Then we went to a committee room, where they served lemonade and dainties. The minister of tourism came in. He had a good suit instead of a uniform, and he embraced each of us warmly and kissed us on both cheeks in the European style. He smelled a little funky, but the a/c was down, so probably we all did by then.

It was hot and dull standing around the committee room. I am a patriot and I welcome the friendship of our allies. But I'm not interested in them on a personal basis. So the official reception didn't do much for me. But other people were committed. Bailey held on to the minister's hand, and said she fully supported his government. She asked him about the tourism and liberation theology.

"We will never yield to terrorists," the minister said.

Then we all line up for a group photo, and the tour people said they'd email it back to the ship when their server powered back up.

On the bus again, I ordered another G and T and settled in for the ride. We took the coast road, and admired the white sand beaches. The guide told us about the history of the island and the indigenous peoples and the colonial period. We stopped at a restaurant for lunch, and they served fish caught in the bay. Drummers played complex rhythms and some girls came out and danced in a spirited, tropical way.

Our last stop was a tourist market, for shopping. They had shoddy local goods and a fine selection of knockoffs. I bought sunglasses and a bottle of gin and a bottle of rum, since I was in the Caribbean. Teresa looked at the jewellery and the scarves, and she held them up beside her face and studied herself carefully in the mirrors at the kiosks. Bailey bought earrings with shells. Then she got a woven basket and then she bought some other things and put them into her basket. She looked good, with her basket and her sarong and her tan and her earrings. Bud gave me his phone and asked me to take a picture of Bailey and him, so I did. Then I took a picture of them and Teresa. Then Bud took a picture of me and the girls. He took our details and sent us the files from his phone.

On the ride back to the harbour, the guide talked about geology and oceanography and the formation of the islands and the reefs. Teresa and Bailey looked over the things they bought. I sort of dozed. But I clapped when the guide wrapped it up, and tipped him fifty dollars when we were back on the pier. We found the tender and waited around until it filled up, which was another waste of time.

But we were back in time for cocktails. Bud and Bailey took us up to the Crow's Nest, and it was a fine venue, at the top of the ship, with windows all around. We watched the show on the pier. The locals released a flight of white doves, to salute the *Mariola* as she left port, and then they set off a big display of fireworks. We could see them shooting and shimmering behind us.

o o o

We saw Itamar the next day and I took the tender again, and again it was awkward and difficult, and I got on a bus and saw the sights and met people, Vance and Amanda and Tom, who took an interest and enjoyed themselves like people should. It was a good day, although it was a lot like the day before, with the tender and the tour and the sun and the good things to eat and drink. You could see how it could get old.

Then when I was back on the ship, Raoul rolled in with my shoes while I was dressing for dinner. He had polished them and I was impressed with his initiative. And he told me about Maromed, where we were docking the next day. It was an island that the Company had bought and developed as a private resort, and the amenities sounded very fine. We had two days scheduled there. So I decided I'd sleep ashore in the resort accommodation, and I told Raoul to book it for me.

The next day, he turned up early to pack. He brought several of my suitcases with him, my flight bag, my twenty-one inch roller, a shaving kit, one of my garment bags, and also the laundry I'd sent out the day before and a box of tissue paper.

"Jeez, Raoul," I said, "I'm going in for one night. How much do I need?"

"We should look at that, Mr. Rutledge. I brought a range of bags. What you don't need, I'll send back to stowage."

I had been lathering when he knocked, so I went back to the bathroom to shave. He followed me into the bedroom and put the bags down and took my clean laundry into the closet.

"I signed you up for the Colonial Mansion," he said.

It was what I'd asked for.

"They told us about colonial life in San Lazar, so I know all about it now," I told him.

"For the Mansion, you'll need a tux, because they dress for dinner there."

That was one reason I signed up for it. It sounded elegant.

"I've worn the one with the flared leg several nights now," I told him. "I'll take the other one."

"Okay, Mr. Rutledge," he said.

I couldn't really see him, just his reflection in the mirror as he went back and forth to the closet. But I thought he sounded like he wasn't sure, and I wondered about my tuxes again for a second. He started bringing clothes out and packing them or piling them on the bed. He put the tux into the garment bag. Then he brought out some briefs and socks and put them in a stack.

"For today, you want shorts. It's a hot one. You want a polo or a button-up?"

"Maybe a loose cotton shirt would be good."

"Cotton is comfortable. It breathes. I'll give you a white undershirt and this blue button-down. It'll look sharp with the grey shorts." It sounded flashy to me, but I didn't like to hurt his feelings, so I didn't say it. He kept going. "Okay, what else you need. At the Mansion, you're near the bike trails and the hiking and climbing facilities."

"I don't know if I'm interested in those things."

"Maybe I'll put in your runners and some bicycle shorts? You don't want to limit your options."

I told him sure.

"There's a fine pool facility, and it's warm. I'll pack your trunks." He brought out my speedo and added it to the pile. I still wasn't sure about it, but it still was all I had. "Then you need shirts and shorts for two days. I'll put in one khaki and one navy for shorts, and black ones also so you have options. I'll do the red weave button-down and the yellow, in case you want colour. And we'll say four golf shirts. It's hot. You might want to change in the afternoon."

He was thinking, taking all the factors into consideration. I was impressed. But then I got suspicious. "Don't they have a/c in the Colonial Mansion?" I asked him.

"They do. They shouldn't. It isn't period authentic. But they do anyways. So you'll be comfortable indoors. Outdoors you will feel the heat, though, because it's tropical. You might want to change your shirt after lunch. I'll do you one pair of pajamas. The Mansion will have a robe for you. You want the black belt with the grey shorts, and we'll do a tan belt too, for variety. You need your black shoes for the tux. I polished them yesterday." He held them up and looked at them. "They're still okay," he said. "And some loafers. You want sandals, maybe espadrilles?"

He was very serious about it.

"Are they period authentic?" I asked him.

Raoul made a face like he was above humour. "Strictly speaking, no, although the design is longstanding. But they're good pool wear and they don't take much space in your bag."

ports of call

He sounded touchy and I wasn't trying to make him mad. So I told him he could throw them in.

"Yes, Mr. Rutledge," he said. I could hear him opening and closing drawers inside the closet. "Mr. Rutledge, you got a hat?"

"I don't like a hat, except maybe a baseball cap when I'm casual. I feel foolish in a hat."

"Doctors recommend good coverage, especially for the face, where your skin is sensitive."

"No part of me is sensitive, Raoul," i said.

I finished shaving and wiped the lather off my ears and neck and I gave myself the once over to see if I missed anything.

"You want some pants for the evening."

"I'll be wearing my tux."

"Or the early morning."

I thought it was possible and I admired his contingency planning.

"Sometimes in the interior you get a breeze off the hills," said Raoul. "Next port of call, or maybe at the CompanyCruiseWear shop, you might want to look into a tropical suit, light fabric, light colour. They're very practical in the cruise environment, and they're stylish."

In the meantime, he chose my lightest khakis, since even in the early morning it would still be warm.

Then he came into the bathroom and started packing toiletries. It was crowded and I thought he could wait until I was done. But he was being efficient and I admired it.

"They'll have soap and shampoo and mouthwash at the Mansion," he said. "You want to take your shaving kit, the talc." He rinsed things off and patted them dry and packed them. "Cologne?"

I slapped some on, then corked the bottle and handed it over to him, and I cleared out of the bathroom so he had elbow room. I dropped my robe and put on the clothes he'd laid out for me. He had a good eye. I looked sharp.

I could hear Raoul talking to himself. "Toothbrush, toothpaste, floss, deodorant." He was opening and closing doors. "You want to get sunscreen, Mr. Rutledge, and bug spray. You can pick it up at the pharmacy in the ship's mall, or they'll have some probably in the guest boutique at the Mansion."

He came out of the bathroom with my shaving kit and such and packed it in the twenty-one inch roller. Then he started on the clothes he'd piled on the bed. He folded things neatly and wrapped each item in tissue. Then he put everything into the bag. It all fit. He zipped the tux into the garment bag.

"You were right," he said. "You don't need the flight bag. I'll send it back to stowage."

He looked at my robe lying on the floor, and picked it up and took it into the bathroom and put it in the laundry bag. Then he took out the laundry bag with the robe and the other laundry in it, and he got a new bag out from under the sink and set it up in the hamper. He brought the old laundry out with him and he went to the bed and picked up the garment bag and the twenty-one inch roller and the empty flight bag and the tissue paper. I watched him work. He was a good kid.

"I'll move all this out for you," he said. "We'll deliver your bags to your suite at the Mansion." He was moving into the living room and I followed him. "You can disembark any time on the land links. You can have breakfast here, or wait and get something over at the Mansion. Resort hospitality meets you across the link at Maromed reception."

He was picking up speed, and it was hard to follow. So I just nodded and smiled like I was listening.

"There's lots to do," he said. "They have activities all day. So you don't want to sit around here too long."

I felt that he was getting close to a line. I kept smiling but I folded my arms so he could see I was serious. "I move at my own pace, Raoul," I told him.

I tried to show him how I felt without being mean about it, but it

ports of call

hit him hard that he offended me and he came to a full stop and stood in the middle of the room looking sorry.

"You bet, Mr. Rutledge," he said. "And no offense. I just want to lay out your options so you can make good choices. You can go ashore or you can go down to the Big Banana. They run brunch until four o'clock."

But that wasn't what I had in mind either. "I'm not hanging around until four o'clock," I told him.

"Exactly," he said. "You have your own timetable. We just give you the choice."

I told him I might look into it. I appreciated the good advice although I didn't like him telling me what to do. But he looked humble and sad about rushing me, and I felt sorry for him. So I told him to wait and I turned around to be private and checked my bankroll and found a c-note to cheer him up and in recognition of his fine service. The whole job had taken him maybe twenty minutes, including the advice that I didn't really want. He had the garment bag and the laundry slung over his back, and the roller and the empty flight bag in his other hand, with the box of tissue paper under his arm. So it took effort. But I rolled the bill up and tucked it in his pocket so he knew I didn't hold a grudge.

"Thank you, Mr. Rutledge," he said.

"You're a good kid, Raoul," I told him, and I let him go.

o o o

So I had coffee at the Big Banana and checked out the spread, and it was very fine like Raoul said, with a station for eggs, and a station for hotcakes and waffles, and chafing dishes with sausage and ham and prawns and lobster, and a big table with bread and rolls and cereal, and a table of fruit with bowls of melon and berries, and individual servings of yogurt and granola parfait, and a table with danish and croissant. I had coffee and eggs and then I walked across the link to Reception.

It was an easy landing, much more convenient than the tender process, partly because it was late and I was the only one crossing the land link maybe. But also because all of Maromed was custom-built and the Company took the size and scope of its fleet into account in the design process. The Company offices were right on the pier and the pier reached way out in the bay. The *Mariola* pulled up by the pier and deployed the land links so they ran from the boat to the offices. And there were no tenders, and no loading and no waiting and no rough seas. I just walked straight across and I was in Maromed reception.

There was a long desk with several people ready to serve you, and no lineup. The reception girl found my name on the list right away and she gave me some papers to sign and called up a driver. He shook my hand and told me he was Chaz, and he took me down to the parking lot and we got into a Land Rover and rolled out of the pier station. We went through the little town built around the Company offices, with houses and condos for the island crew. There were shops and cafes on the pier, and the big dock stretching way out in the bay, and a smaller marina further down the shore. There were parks and flowers and gardens. It was an attractive modern development.

"You want speedy delivery?" Chaz asked. "Or the scenic route?"

I told him to show me the island. So we took the coast road and went west along the north shore where the Company had extensive beach resorts and was building more. There was already a terraced hotel in glass and steel, and then in a small bay a marina with anchorage for yachts, and a complex with restaurants and discos on the shore, and then, a few miles further, there was the cabana resort, with private guest bungalows. Between the finished amenities you could see cranes and work crews and trucks and construction sites where the Company was developing more facilities. Chaz said there was eight miles of white sand beaches and the resorts specialized in beach activities on this side of the island. You could lie in the sun or swim in the pools or in the sea, and the sounds of construction didn't disturb the clientele as much as you might think, and they also had sailing lessons and water-skiing and surfing and deep-sea fishing excursions.

ports of call

We came south around some tricky bends in the road, and then drove back east. The south coast was rockier, with caves and cliffs but also small, isolated stretches of beach that looked private and inviting. There were smaller islands off the shore where there was a reef and coral and a variety of marine life.

On my left, the interior was tropical with lots of trees, and hilly. The tallest peak was called Hechuel, which Chaz said was a Carib word, or maybe Arawak, but nobody knew what it meant. There was an archeological dig there. The Company sponsored it and got a write-off, and the archeologists came from a big university.

We turned off the coast road and headed up the hills and through the forest. It was dark and cool for a while. Then we came out of the woods into a cleared plain, and we were in the Colonial Mansion's plantation. Chaz pointed out the sugar cane crops and he wanted to tell me about period agricultural techniques. But I didn't encourage him since I wasn't interested.

We turned off the road and went up a long drive. There were fruit trees and flower trees all along it, and it was shady and comfortable after the open fields. It took us up to the Colonial Mansion itself, which was a fine building, white, with lots of windows and terraces and colonnades. Chaz let me out and a doorman stepped up and greeted me and brought me into the lobby. The girl at the desk gave me some papers to sign, and she gave me a key, and the doorman brought me up to my suite on the second floor, which they called the first floor. We walked up a grand staircase, which felt stylish even though an elevator would have been more convenient. My room was just down the hall.

My bags were already in my room, and a houseboy was unpacking when I walked in. He flashed a big smile and kind of bowed at me, and went back to work while the doorman showed me the amenities, which included a fruit basket and a bottle of rum with the Mansion's compliments, and also a straw hat with a note that said, "From Raoul with respect," which I thought was sweet, although it was also bossy.

And then the doorman waited around not saying anything and the houseboy did too, and I told them thank you and found a bill for them each and they smiled like they were surprised and left me alone finally.

o o o

I went down to the front desk and signed up to see the dig in the afternoon, because it sounded educational. And then the Mansion curator was hanging around, and he offered to show me the facilities and I thought it would kill time until lunch. So I got my hat and we walked around the grounds and out into the fields and in the gardens around the Mansion and he told me all about it.

He said that Maromed had changed hands seventeen times during the colonial period, from the Spanish to the French to the English to the Dutch to the buccaneers to the rebelling slaves and back again. At different times it had been called San Isidoro, Dauphine, Karlsrutt, and Jarbit. It was complicated and the details weren't interesting, as he said himself. But it meant that the Mansion could showcase a variety of cultures. They offered a flamenco show to salute the Spanish heritage, and a billiards room to recognize the British colonial period. The kitchen mixed French and island techniques. I don't know what they got from the Dutch.

In the fields they had sugar cane, which was a big crop in the eighteenth century, and the workers, some of them descendants of the original slaves, worked the field with authentic period implements. They drew a decent wage from the Company, my guide said. Again I had to steer him off agricultural topics because my upbringing was urban and I'm not interested in ploughshares.

But then he moved onto the nineteenth century, when the sugar market crashed, and plantations tried different business models to survive. "Tobacco and cocoa and coffee and spices and exotic fruit," my guide said. "They tried everything." And now the Mansion had fields of all of these crops, also cultivated with traditional nineteenth-century techniques, and stands of pod- or fruit-bearing trees, and coffee bushes further up the mountain. I keep an eye on the stock market and I know the heartbreak of diminishing returns. So that was kind of interesting.

And the curator told me how they processed everything they grew on the plantation, and he wanted to take me to the works where they treated things or dried them or milled them. But it was getting close to lunchtime, so I passed, and he said that was okay because I'd be sampling the Mansion produce at the table.

Truthfully it was all more than I wanted with the facts and the details and examples. I could see why no other guest signed up for a tour and he had to hang around the front desk drumming up business. Because I came to the Mansion to experience luxury living, not to study history. But I was polite of course and I shook the curator's hand when we got inside again and gave him a bill, and found my way out to lunch finally.

They served us on the terrace. We had fish and vegetables and then coffee and exotic fruits. The waiter made a speech about each course. I didn't listen.

There weren't many guests, maybe a dozen of us spread around four tables, since most people from the *Mariola* went to the beach resorts or stayed on board, and some of the people who were staying at the Mansion had gone for all-day excursions that started before I arrived. The waiter put me at a table with Lou and Denise, who I hadn't met before, and they were nice people. We compared notes on the Mansion and the activities. Denise was making plans. She had a guidebook with her, and when Lou and I got onto baseball (he was a Bandits fan and we talked about their chances), she opened her book and started marking pages and reading out bits about the island: "First discovered by Columbus on his second voyage in 1493, he named the landmass San Isidoro, although it is unclear whether he meant to honour San Isidoro of Seville or San Ysidro the Laborer."

"Denise thinks there's going to be a test," Lou said.

"It's a rich history," Denise said. Her books had titles like *The Company*

History of Maromed and *Daily Life on the Plantation*. And they weren't on eReaders, and already she had broken their spines and folded page corners for easy reference, so you could see she was that kind of person. They had been to the buildings where they processed the coffee, and in the afternoon they were going horseback riding on the plantation trails, and the next day they were taking a nature walk. Lou said she kept him busy, but he looked happy. He lit up every time she read to us although it was dull and his heart was with the Bandits. He said Denise made so many plans he was thinking of asking for a day off once a week. She said they were retired and every day was a day off. He said he was working harder than he ever did when he drew a salary. They kidded around with each other. It was nice.

After lunch I changed my shirt because it was very warm, and then I went back down to find my transport to the dig. There were half a dozen of us in the party, and Chaz drove us in a Hummer. We went further into the interior, part way up Hechuel, and then the road ended and there was a shed and a few tents for the dig crew, who stayed near the site mostly, and a gift shop that sold books and postcards and souvenir spades and brushes and tweezers and knock-offs of Arawak carvings and activity kits for children to pretend to dig up relics.

We all got out of the Hummer and Chaz got folding stools out of the shed and we walked into the forest about a half-mile till we came to the foot of a waterfall. It was a pretty place and there was activity all around. There was a cave in the rock beside the waterfall and it was lit up with bright lights powered by a generator. An area was taped off by the mouth of the cave, and there was a kid working inside the ropes, shovelling dirt into a wheelbarrow. He filled up the wheelbarrow and then he wheeled it over a few feet and dumped it in a big sieve and another kid put the dirt through the sieve and sorted through the leftovers. It wasn't glamorous, and it was a warm day.

Finally Dr. Hewitt, the man in charge, came out of the cave. He was weeny, like you'd expect for an egghead, wearing big boots and shorts.

And he liked to be in charge. He clapped his hands together and took us a few steps away from the generator and told Chaz how to unfold the stools. And we sat down in a circle and Dr. Hewitt stayed on his feet and towered over us and explained it all. He told us about the peaceful Arawaks, who farmed and traded and worshipped nature, and the Caribs, who attacked and enslaved them, and Columbus, who wiped everyone out with his soldiers and his germs. He said the Arawaks were the first people on the island. So the deeper you dig, the more likely you are to find Arawak remains. They were digging pretty deep, here, he said, because the cave was an Arawak burial site.

Truthfully, I didn't like the sound of that. But Dr. Hewitt said burial sites and garbage dumps were great resources, because you can learn a lot about people by the things they throw away and the way they bury their dead. For example, he said, the Arawaks buried their loved ones in places of natural beauty, and so the experts knew that they were nature worshippers. He had a point about that, because with the waterfall and the trees, it was a nice spot.

"Also," he said, "when you go into the cave, you'll see faces carved in the rock wall, and we've uncovered small representations of Arawak nature gods also interred on site. These are conventional Arawak burial practices. The Arawaks summon the gods to watch over the dead."

And I thought that was nice, too.

"Furthermore, when we sent the first remains to the lab, the technicians found pollen," he told us. He was very excited about this; he bounced in his big boots and waved his hands. "The survivors put flowers in the grave with the corpse. This is a familiar practice. We do it ourselves. It's an emotional gesture."

So you could see that the Arawak loved their dead, and an Arawak cemetery wasn't the worst thing in the world.

Then he asked if there were any questions before we went into the cave and one of the women asked him how they found the site. Dr. Hewitt laughed. "Happy accident," he said. "A couple of kids on an eco-tour got separated from the group. They were young — the thinking is that they ducked out for a little tenderness. They ended up in the cave, and whatever else they got up to, they found a femur, a leg bone. They brought it back to the guides, who sent it up to the experts."

I went cold when he said it. I figured the kids, when they found the waterfall and the cave, they must have thought they hit the jackpot. And then I thought about them going into the cave and lying down together on the dirt floor and kissing each other, and then one of them, probably the girl, feeling something poking her in the back, and reaching around to move it, and figuring out what it was.

I couldn't really see the two of them getting back at it after that. It's hard enough to love someone from day to day, with the boss leaning on you at one end and the bank working you at the other, law enforcement breathing down your neck even though you're an honest businessman trying to earn a decent draw, and your kids getting into the usual scrapes. But for those two kids, they might have thought for a few minutes that the world was a beautiful place. And then they found out they were sleeping with the dead. It was a sick joke to play on young people in love. The whole thing made me sad.

Dr. Hewitt took us inside the cave, where more kids were digging a section of the floor. They were on their knees inside more tape, working carefully, taking out a teaspoon of dirt at a time, or using a brush or tweezers.

"This is an exciting time for us," said Dr. Hewitt. "We've just found the remains of another body, our third. Two days ago, we uncovered what looked like a human hand, and we are in the process still of carefully removing the accumulated earth from around the whole figure." I looked into the pit again, and sure enough, you could see the outline of a body curled up on its side. There were black bones and black fabric that blended with the black dirt they were buried in. The corpse's hands covered its face and it looked small and pathetic. It made me sad to see.

"We have to work carefully at this stage of the exhumation," said

Dr. Hewitt, "to preserve the burial posture, and of course to avoid damaging the remains." People in the group nodded like they knew what he was talking about. "Notice also the faces carved into the rock walls around us."

I looked around and sure enough you could see them. They were rough and unattractive, and if they were meant to keep evil spirits away, I thought they would probably do the trick. But if they were supposed to be portraits of the dead, I thought they were insulting.

Then I'd seen enough and I wanted to get out. The site wasn't like Indiana Jones, which maybe I'd been hoping in the back of my mind. It was more technical and morbid. You can dress it up with big words, but when you get right down to it, they were scraping dirt off bones. I say, let the dead sleep.

Dr. Hewitt took more questions from the group, but I skipped it and wandered over to the waterfall. It was a light flow but steady, and it came over a steep rock face and made a pool beside the caves, and then it drained away in a stream. It was a hot day, and the water was cool. I stood by the pool and dipped a toe in. Then I stepped in and found my footing in the pool bed and waded over to the rock face where the water came down. It was refreshing, with the mist from the water and in the shade of the rock. I leaned into the waterfall, and let the water splash over my head and the back of my neck.

When the girls ran out of questions, Chaz rounded us up and took us home. I didn't tip Dr. Hewitt, because I figured he was a professional and above that kind of thing.

the lottery

I had lots of time to dress for dinner, and I managed okay even without Raoul's good advice. Then I went down to the bar for a cocktail and Bud was there. We shook hands, and I ordered a large G and T.

"You hit the beach?" he asked me.

"I went to the archeological site," I told him. "It was very educational." I left it at that. I asked him, "You?"

"Bailey went snorkelling. It's something she has always wanted to try."

We talked about going to the billiards room to shoot a frame, but then Bailey came in wearing a tight dress. So she ordered a mojito and we hung around the bar with her. Then the dinner gong sounded, and they ushered us into the dining room. I took my drink with me.

The dining room was big and elegant with one long table. Windows were open at both ends letting in the air, and the curtains moved a little in the breeze. There were candles on the table, and silver and crystal and big bowls of flowers. It was very fine to look at. The ladies gasped.

There were maybe twenty of us altogether, and you had to go

around the table to find your place where your name was written on a little card. I sat between Denise, who didn't bring a book this time, and a younger girl, Jen, not really good-looking, but noisy and entertaining for a few hours. She was blonde and energetic, and I thought she was about my daughter's age, and that made me sad for a minute but I shrugged it off.

Bud was further down on my left, and Bailey was across from me. I had a good view of her cleavage. She was sitting between Eddie and the J-kid from my table in the Captain's Mess. I was surprised and let down somewhat because I'd been looking forward to new faces after a couple of nights with them and not getting any further really in terms of conversation. Not that I was suffering, because Eddie was a good guy and attentive to his wife, but the hospitality specialists were supposed to shuffle the tables every couple of weeks and I was looking forward to meeting more people. In the meantime, at least, Lily wasn't at the Mansion, and I enjoyed Denise and Jen, and the food was very good, although the waiters kept trying to tell us about produce and food preparation. I ignored them.

Jen had been riding with Lou and Denise, so they went over that excursion. Denise said how well-groomed the horses were, and Jen told insulting stories about the other riders.

"That girl. Natalie? Had she ever been on a horse before? She's going to be sore tomorrow. So will the horse."

"Natalie and Ben won the lottery," said Denise.

"What lottery?" said Jen.

"That giveaway, the promotional package they offered."

The waiters rolled into action around us. We didn't get to look at a menu or make a choice. Instead they served us from a fixed bill of fare that showcased plantation produce and history: we started in with plates of tapas, olives, figs, and wedges of tortilla Espanola. The waiter made a speech about it all. I ignored it.

"I remember that," I said to Denise. "To tell the truth, it made me think twice about booking. I wasn't sure about the quality of the product if they were giving it away."

"Can I sign up for it?" Jen asked.

"It's closed now. They did the draw. But it was the whole show, a Lifetime-Lifestyles cruise package," said Denise.

"An interior suite," I told them. It was an important consideration.

"But still," said Denise.

"You mean their whole thing is free?" said Jen.

"That was the prize," said Denise.

"For a couple of months?" said Jen.

"The whole contract," I said.

It took Jen a few seconds to process it. Then she looked mad. "You mean they're getting it for nothing?"

"That was the prize," Denise said.

"But why do I have to pay if they don't?"

"Because they won," Denise said.

Denise looked like she was trying not to laugh. But Jen looked angry. She thought about it some more. Then she decided.

"I just don't think it's fair," she said.

Denise did laugh then. "It isn't fair. It's luck. It's like being born with a trust fund."

"No, it isn't," said Jen.

"It isn't?" said Denise.

She wasn't trying to insult Jen, but you could see that Jen was irritated. Plus, Jen looked like a girl who would enjoy a cat fight, and I didn't think Denise was. So I was the good guy and came in to keep the peace.

"There is a difference," I said.

"That's right," said Jen.

"I don't see it," said Denise. But she was ready to listen.

"It's simple but it's fundamental," I said. "Anyone can win a lottery. You buy a ticket; you've got a chance. But if your family has money, that's not luck. It's family values."

the lottery

"Yes," said Jen.

The waiters cleared out the first plate and brought in coquille St. Jacques. It was very good and it came with its own fork, so I didn't need to look for it. But it was a small portion served on a half shell. I ate it in two bites and kept explaining.

"You work hard. You make a living. You put something away for the kids. It's work and it's love. It's what life is about. Your kids end up with something in the kitty. It didn't happen by accident. You made it happen. You earned it for them."

Jen nodded every time I spoke. But Denise didn't take the point. She was spearing prawns with attention. But I had strong views about the giveaway, so I kept going.

"I think that generally the draw for the cruise was a bad idea," I said.

"I thought it was a good promotion," said Denise. "Good advertising."

"No. Hear me out," I said. "In the first place, like Jen says, it's an insult to the purchasing customer no matter how you slice it. Here we are, paying full fees and we all know it's not cheap."

"Well, my parents . . ." said Jen.

"One way or another, we're financing this project," I said. "And we have to share the dance floor with people who haven't paid a nickel? People resent freeloaders. It's only natural. So it's better when everyone does their bit. Next, and I guess it's a dirty word in the welfare state, but I also think this is about merit."

"Merit?" said Denise.

"Merit," I said. "For some of us, we worked hard for this thing, making sacrifices and taking chances. And for some of us," I nodded at Jen, "our parents did." She nodded back. "Either way. You put your life into it, and then Natalie and Ben waltz in and help themselves. It's an insult to your efforts. I hear about Natalie and Ben, and I think what a fool I was to put my shoulder to the wheel to earn this lifestyle. I should just have bought a lottery ticket and taken my chances. Natalie and Ben are getting a free ride, and that is an insult to all my working days."

"You mean, you had to work hard and they should too?" said Denise.

I thought she was a bright woman with her guidebooks and her notes. But she was having trouble with this. "It's only fair," I said.

Denise gave me a big smile like she understood. But then she said, "Another thing about working for a living is you have the satisfaction of the work itself."

So however much she read, she had no common sense.

"Did you spend much time in the working world, Denise?" I asked her.

"A few years. After the kids, I stayed at home. When they got older, Lou said, 'Why bother?' He didn't mind, and I had other commitments."

The waiters took away the shells and gave us salads with ripe avocado and slices of orange. It was pretty and tropical but I wondered if we would ever get a main meal.

"You won the lottery, too," I said. "You weren't out on the chain gang. You've got no idea what the working man goes through to earn his place in the sun."

"Oh, I do know what you mean," said Denise. She finally caught on to an idea, and it was nice because she lit up right away. It made her happy when she could keep up. "Lou worked like a trooper his whole life. The first three years we were married he worked days and took courses at night. I was working then, too, and I took all the contracts I could. We hardly saw each other. I think about all the late nights Lou put in and the long hours and all that travelling. It's a wonder we survived. Still, I don't mind about Ben and Natalie. I say, more power to them. We worked hard; they were lucky. We're all happy to be here."

She kept trying to let them off the hook. I felt that she was too nice for her own good. I kept going.

"I feel that the lottery draw gave an unfair advantage to poor people. They were statistically more likely to win."

Denise laughed. "A rich person had the same chances," she said.

"But you're going to have more poor people buying tickets just because there are more of them. So the odds say that one of them is more likely to win. And look what happened: Natalie and Ben. They don't even know how to ride."

"The tickets weren't cheap," Denise said. "I don't know if really poor people bought them."

"But rich people don't need to since they can pay the pop," I told her. "And then, when Natalie and Ben, working stiffs, win the ticket, they think they're on easy street. But it isn't that simple." I slapped the table to make my point. "It's the lifetime lease, but it's a basic package. An interior suite and three meals a day. Also there are hidden costs, and they have to find the money to cover them."

"The prize included the monthly fees," said Denise.

"They don't have to pay those either?" said Jen.

"But they still have to find tips, for example," I said. And Denise nodded like she hadn't thought of that. "I don't know if you've noticed," I said, "but service doesn't take no for an answer. And then the Company keeps pushing a line of very attractive extras, the excursions and the spa and so on."

"I can't resist the tours," Denise agreed. "We've had such fine experiences."

"It's all going to add up."

"But some activities are very reasonable."

"Name one."

She had to think for a minute. But finally she said, "There's the pool."

"The pool is free, but when you're lying in the sun on a hot day, you're going to want a drink. A G and T runs you thirty, forty dollars."

"Forty dollars?"

"For a double, and one for your friends, and one for the bartender, and then the tip."

"Ah."

"And are you really going to have just one drink all afternoon?"

"If it's a double."

"You have to keep yourself hydrated. You can't even eat where you want to. Most of the *Mariola's* restaurants are extra."

"You get a gourmet meal in the Captain's Mess. And it includes wine." Denise brought it out like a trump card.

"A bottle of plonk. How far is that going to go? Sooner or later, you're going to want to splurge, and if you're a bus driver from the suburbs, how do you feel when all these good things are going on all around you and you can't have any?"

"Did Ben drive a bus?" asked Denise.

"You think he was on welfare, maybe? I didn't know, and I guess that is another issue, but I don't think welfare cases should spend their money on lottery tickets. The welfare cheque is supposed to cover the essentials and help people in a crisis. It's not a completely bad idea. But for someone to be collecting a government cheque and blowing it on lottery tickets. I can think of better ways to spend my tax dollars. Why should I pay for Ben to gamble?"

"I just meant, I thought you were saying Ben was a bus driver..."

"And, another example, they're not staying at the Mansion. So they can't afford the complete colonial experience."

"They might prefer the ship?" said Denise. I think she knew it was a long shot.

"More likely they can't do the riding excursion and the resort accommodation both. And, really, isn't that worse?" I said. "Once a month, you go out on your big day and mingle with the real guests. And then you take the tender back to your crumby interior suite and drink plonk at the early service in the Captain's Mess."

"I'd shoot myself," said Jen.

Denise smiled. "You think it might get dull? All that leisure and nothing to do really?" It was like she wasn't even trying to understand.

"This leads me to the social aspect," I said.

Finally the waiters came in with a proper meal. They gave us plates with tasting portions of curried goat and jerk chicken and pulled pork, and generous sides of fried plantains and beans and rice. I got to work but kept explaining my views.

"Ben and Natalie don't have a luxury background," I said. "They don't know its ways. They may feel excited about their opportunity to mingle with a better class of people. But they won't fit in and they won't keep up. Already we know that Natalie can't ride. She probably also can't sail and doesn't know anything about art or fine jewellery. She'll have nothing to say to her fellow passengers, and they'll have nothing to say to her. Eventually Natalie and Ben are going to figure this out, and it will only make them sad. So it's not like they'll enjoy the cruise anyway."

Jen said I was exactly right and Denise kind of smiled. So we were all agreed. And the two of them never got into a cat fight, which had been my main goal.

Jen took a liking to me after this. She started by saying she was out of practice riding too, and then she pulled up her skirt to show us her saddle sores. Her thighs looked red and chafed in places and I told her she should put some salve or something on them. And she said she didn't have any, and Denise said she had lotion with aloe if Jen wanted, and Jen ignored her and asked me if I had some salve. I said no since she was my daughter's age and I didn't want to get involved. We were going to be on the cruise for a long time, and I don't like complications. Also, although she had a nice ass, I thought it was strange for her to pull up her skirt at the dinner table. It didn't fit with the sophisticated room and the crystal and the name cards. It was cheap and obvious, and that does not attract me.

After dinner, they ushered the ladies out, in the English style. Jen didn't like it, but the waiters insisted. And the J-kid didn't understand and just followed the girls. We all tried to call him back, but he had things in his ears like usual. The waiters cleared everything off the table and put out nutcrackers and bowls of nuts. They put out new glasses and decanters of port and madeira, and we all moved around to new chairs, to stretch our legs and then to be sociable. I ended up beside Eddie, and he was happy to see me.

"I always like the English protocol," he said. "It gives you a chance to talk about important things, or other things at least." The decanters came around. "Port or madeira?" he asked.

I looked around, but I couldn't see what I liked. "I was thinking cognac," I told him.

"Cognac," he said, like it was a whole new idea. "I will too." He waved one of the waiters over. "Two cognacs," he said. "We'll take two fine cigars."

"The Mansion's tobacco station makes an excellent cigar," said the waiter.

"We'll take two Cohibas, the real thing, not Dominican yellow bands. And don't tell me anything else about local produce," said Eddie.

He knew what mattered. The waiter brought our cognacs and an ashtray and a box of Cohibas which were Habanas. I looked them over and chose one, and Eddie did too, and the waiter brought cutters and we trimmed them, and then he lit us up with a wooden match and we smoked for a few minutes and sipped cognac. The other guys were laughing and joking beside us, and the women were waiting in the next room. It was a comfortable time of the evening.

"The boy doesn't like a cigar?" I asked him. I ate dinner with them for several days and I thought it was too late to ask what the J-kid's name was again. I thought someone might mention it sometime. But so far no one did, although they looked his way and smiled every now and then.

"He's a kid," Eddie said. "I think he sneaks a smoke sometimes. His mother doesn't like it."

"She's a sweet girl."

"She's a prize. Eric got lucky."

"Eric?" I said.

I thought Della was married to Steve although no one said so. It's how it is when you meet new people. No one bothers to tell you who

the lottery

~ 67 ~

is married to who. It's a mistake I think and it can lead to misunderstandings, although it didn't matter to me in this case.

"They all went dancing," Eddie said. He was thinking his own thoughts. "They went to a beach resort where they can learn the lindy hop."

"Dancing is very enjoyable," I said.

Eddie smiled and sipped his cognac. "Mrs. Martin could dance," he said. "We used to burn up the dance floor. Of course this was a long time ago, before rock and roll and mosh pits and crowd surfing. People do whatever they want on the dance floor, even dance alone. It looks bad. It has no discipline and no style."

"It's a free-for-all," I said. I didn't mind watching a pretty girl shake it up on the floor, but I felt that Eddie made a good case.

He said, "We danced when there were dances and steps you could learn and music to dance to."

"It was a golden age," I told him. For a second I remembered dancing with Laureen, although I never knew the steps really. It was an easier, happier time when you just held someone close and the music played.

"It's coming back now," Eddie said. "They want to learn salsa. Della's talking about tango. They're all keen to learn."

I was still trying to work out the family. "Where does Steve come in?" I asked him.

"He's Della's brother. He went to school with Eric. It's how Eric met Dell."

It was all coming clear finally. Lily and Eric were his kids. It took me a while to sort it out, but I should have seen it. The way he talked to Lily for example or told her to be quiet should have tipped me off.

"Lily and Eric are Mrs. Martin's pride and joy," Eddie said. I liked that he called Katherine "Mrs. Martin," like he had respect for her in front of everyone.

"And everyone is travelling together," I said.

Eddie nodded some more. "Our children are attentive to their mother. They were our joy in youth and they're our comfort in age."

"That's the way it should be," I said, and I meant it. But I didn't want to think about it more since it reminded me of Laureen and the kids who were a joy to me off and on in their youth and who I hadn't seen now for years and maybe never would again.

"I thought Mrs. Martin would enjoy the Mansion — and she would have liked it. But she isn't feeling up to par. So she said, 'Take the boy with you.' She thought it would be educational." He shrugged. "I'd rather be with her, but she insisted. It makes her happy. I do it."

"She's a lucky woman," I said.

He thought about it while he took a long a pull on his cigar. "I'm a lucky man," he said. "I've had many good things in my life."

I raised my glass and we drank to luck and good things. And then the waiters started snuffing the candles and we joined the women in the lounge. There was a dance floor at one end and a guy came out and played Spanish guitar, and a woman came out and sang flamenco like her heart was breaking, and then there were dancers. It was passionate and fierce.

After they did their show, they brought us onto the floor and tried to teach us the Sevillana. By then some of us weren't steady, and Jen tried to dance on a table, which the waiters didn't like. Bud sat out with his bad hip and he and Eddie hit it off. Then I was tired after a day in the heat and a big dinner and fresh air. So I called it a night.

the transaction

The next day I went river rafting in the interior. It was a rugged activity, with some hiking first and hard paddling at intervals. Then floating in the sun or in the shade, with a refreshing spray blowing up. We had a luau for lunch, although it was the wrong ocean, with a roasted pig and rice and squash and pineapple and chutney and beer. The pork was very salty and good, with crackling the way I like.

When the sun went down, we went back to the Mansion to get ready for the jump-up at the pub by the main docks. The houseboy came in, packed my things to send back to the *Mariola*, and I gave him another tip and went down to the lobby where the drivers were lined up to take us back to the dock. I rode in with Jen and Lou and Denise, and Jen kept showing us her ass where the saddle sores were worse because she spent the whole day riding again, even though she was already chafed and sore. I thought maybe there was something wrong with her since she was hurting herself for no reason, and also lifting her skirt for everyone to see. So I was glad I didn't take an interest in her the night before but it also made me sad. By the time we got to the pub, I was feeling morbid and depressed and not really in the mood for it. But I started in with a G and T, and then it seemed like a good idea to get drunk and forget my troubles.

I overdid it, because at the end heading back to the ship I wasn't feeling good. I was thinking back to the crackling and the chutney and feeling regret. We were all stumbling by then. Bud's hip was giving him trouble. On the land link the McHuges rolled up behind us on mobility scooters. We made room and they drove across in a convoy. Jen tried to walk on the handrail. A hospitality specialist from the *Mariola* came out and made her get down, and she argued and he picked her up and carried her over his shoulder onto the ship, with her ass waving in the air.

I didn't sleep well that night.

o o o

The next morning I woke up and we were motoring and I could feel the hum of the engine. It took me a while to figure it out, but I was sick. I lay around for a while trying to ignore it, and then wondering if I should just go into the bathroom and get it over with. Finally I didn't have a choice, and I had to run for it. Then I just sort of lay by the toilet and brought some more up every few minutes. Nausea is a terrible thing.

After a while, I don't know when, someone knocked at my door, but I was too weak and pathetic to answer. They knocked some more, and then the door opened.

"Mr. Rutledge?" It was Raoul. He came into the bedroom.

"You just come busting in?" I said. I wasn't thinking straight.

"I brought your bags from the Mansion," he said. "I should unpack, get your laundry, make up the bed." He looked at me lying on the floor in the bathroom. "Bad night, Mr. Rutledge?"

"I think it's a bug."

"Those jump-ups can get pretty wild," he said.

"I can hold my liquor," I told him. "I think it was the pig."

"It isn't the food," Raoul said. "The Company runs a tight ship for food preparation."

Talking about food did it to me again, and I brought it up some more, not that I had anything left to deliver. I just heaved and hawked. Raoul hung around. He had advice for me, the way people do when it's too late.

"You've got to be careful with the water on these islands," he said. "It's different from what your system is used to."

"They gave me bad water at the Mansion?" I said.

"Definitely not at the Mansion," he said. "They've got a filtration system and they mostly serve bottled water anyway. But were you swimming maybe or did you go on the rivers?"

I remembered the waterfall, and the spray falling on my face, and the cool spray on the river raft. "The Company should have warned me," I said. "I should sue the Company."

"The Company isn't liable," said Raoul. "It's in the contract, and you probably signed a separate no-sue agreement at the Mansion." I signed papers, it was true, although I didn't read them so I thought probably they weren't binding. "But it'll pass in a day or two," Raoul said, "especially since you're getting it out of your system. I'll call the doctor up. He'll make sure it's a bug."

He went to the phone and I could hear him talking and laughing and joking around. Then he came back and told me to sit tight and that the medic would be down soon. I held on to the toilet. The porcelain felt cool on my cheek and forehead.

Raoul went back to the bedroom and started unpacking my bags. I could hear him working with tissue paper in the walk-in closet. And then the medic stopped by and told me he was Doctor Dan and he shook my hand and took my pulse and my temperature and told me I was sick. He said I should drink water and I told him water was the reason I was sick and I didn't trust it. And he told me the *Mariola* had reliable water and I needed to rehydrate. Then he went away and Raoul brought in a blanket and a pillow. I fell asleep on the floor in the bathroom and woke up every couple of hours and brought it up some more for the rest of the day.

○ ○ ○

I wasn't really recovered until we got to Uberstaad, a few days later. Before this it wasn't so bad, except I was weak and pathetic. But Raoul took care of me. He stopped by several times on the Saturday, and he brought me soup and scrambled egg and dry toast, which I didn't eat, but it was a nice gesture. And on the Sunday, which was his day off, he came by on his own time after chapel to see how I was feeling. So I told him I just wanted to sleep and gave him a c-note. But later that day, like I knew would happen, Leticia showed up, and I was sick and I smelled bad, but she wanted to change the sheets, and it was difficult and inconvenient. It made me tired again because I knew when I was better I was going to have to take it up with Raoul or with Bobby who was in charge.

So when we pulled up at Uberstaad, and I was feeling stronger, I decided that I was going to make the most of it and enjoy myself, because I'd been out of the action for a while and I wanted to make up for lost time, and also because I knew I was going to have to deal with housekeeping and get steward service sorted out, and I figured I had a right to some pleasure between chores. So I made up my mind to have a good time, and I went ashore. I skipped the official tours. Not that they didn't do a good job in San Lazar and Itamar and Maromed. But I figured a little of that kind of educational tour goes a long way.

Again I took the tender over, and it was rocky and slow. I was becoming more and more opposed to this process. Because if we only stopped at ports that were built for the *Mariola* and other top-of-the-line ships, where we could pull up to the specially designed pier and take the elevator down to deck level two or one and walk over on the land link, then the whole process would have been more inviting in my opinion.

Again the natives lined the shore waving and smiling. A welcome committee rowed out to greet us with singers and drummers in small, rickety boats. I rolled a bill into a tight nugget and tossed it to the nearest crew. It fell short and a guy dove for it. I started to feel better.

On the pier, like before, businessmen were selling merchandise. I hung around for a while, listening to their pitches, flashing my billfold, and enjoying a fine sense of well-being. When the sun got too hot, I went through security, where they warned me about pickpockets and the undesirable element. I walked up the hill a few blocks until I was hot and tired. Then I stopped at a bar. It was nothing special, but it looked authentic and there were a couple of locals inside. There was no a/c, just a ceiling fan stirring the hot air. So I sat outside, under the awning, and ordered a large G and T. Pretty soon the neighbourhood entrepreneurs spotted me and they came around, looking slick and running their lines.

"Tour of the city, mister sir? I got a rickshaw and a guide. PhD in demographics and urban sociology. Twenty dollars. Best deal in town."

"No thank you," I said. I was tired of being schooled, plus I thought it was probably a scam.

Another guy stepped up to the plate. "Parasailing, my man? Air-conditioned transport there and back, white sand beach, two hours in harness, fifty bucks. Top value."

Obviously this was out since I didn't have trunks with me, and since I was unhappy with the going style. From the bus on San Lazar, when we drove past the beaches, I could see guys wearing long, loose trunks. And on the river raft, when I wore bicycle shorts, the other guys were wearing skater shorts it looked like. I have issues with those, as I feel there's a danger with so much fabric getting waterlogged and heavy. To my mind a smaller piece of fabric with more elastic is that much more secure, but on the whole, guys seemed to be disregarding the risk and going for big beachwear. And I like to fit in with the group, so I was pretty much deciding to pick up big trunks on my way back if I saw any at the booths on the pier.

The parasailer kept it up. He had good stamina. "Some people tell you parasailing is dangerous, chief. They never tried it. I've got a sport and fitness professional running the boat. He straps you into the chute and gives you a fifteen-minute training session, no extra charge. The bay is two miles wide and we give you three circuits. Soft landing guaranteed. Team of medics on standby if anything goes wrong."

Alluding to risk is a classic sales error. I felt sorry for him, because he tried so hard but couldn't pull it off. I waved him away.

The guys I was waiting for made their pitches in a quiet, confidential way. They came at me sideways and one at a time, while their competition and the guys I already turned down hung around on the road and watched.

"I'm your best source, man. Quality product only. Good price."

"Mister tourist, sir. I know some very friendly women. Clean and naughty."

"Travelling man want to come to a party?"

I let them do their shtick. I enjoyed the variety and inventiveness of their offers. These people were thinkers, putting their skills and resources to work to entertain the client and generate a nice profit. They were my kind. Also, I enjoyed being at the other end of the transaction for a change, the guy that everyone is busting his butt to please, instead of the cringing toady who'd sell his mother, and totally with her blessing, by the way, because she believes in the free market too, if he could squeeze a bit more juice out of the mark.

It felt good sitting there, in a cane chair with my G and T. and the hot sun, letting these up-and-comers do the work. There was an elegance in the way they were petitioning me, like peasants and the king, and also because I was turning them all down. The waiter poked his head out, and I ordered another G and T, and when he brought it, I let everyone get a look at my billfold. I had their attention.

One of the pimps had a fine delivery, smooth and polite. "Lots of nice girls in Uberstaad, boss," he said. "Happy to meet a man of standing. I could introduce you to my cousin, sure. She's a talented woman. Very reasonable."

I kept an open mind.

"What does she look like?" I said. "I'm only interested in quality."

"She's a peach. She's my youngest cousin, boss, just out of school."

"I am not a pervert," I told him. It's important to be clear about that kind of thing or there can be misunderstandings. "I am not interested in children."

"She's a woman, boss. Full grown and very friendly."

I opened the bidding at ten dollars.

He looked sad. "I'd do it for you, boss, but this is family. Fifty."

"For family values I can go to fifteen."

"She's got three kids, boss. Forty-five."

"Three kids and she's just out of school?"

"It was a co-educational facility."

"That is the road to ruin. I sent my daughter to the nuns."

"The sisters know from discipline."

"Three kids," I said. I wasn't just trying to knock down his price. I had reservations. "I don't like stretch marks," I told him.

"She kept her figure. But say forty and you can go bare back."

"In this day and age? I don't think it's a good idea," I said, although in some ways it was an attractive offer.

"Thirty. She's a good sport. And she has her own room."

That was a real savings. "Can you bring her over here? I'd like to get a look before I commit."

"Yeah, sure, boss. You stay right there. Shereen likes to come out for a drink. She's a party girl."

He went off with his cell. I sat in the sun and waited. He came back and sat down at the table with me like we were friends. I thought it was pushy, but he thought he had the right. The waiter came out again, and they both looked at me, so I asked him what he wanted and he ordered a beer.

"She said ten minutes. That means twenty. Twenty-five. She likes to fix herself up. She likes to make a good first impression."

"We shall see," I said. Because I wasn't going to commit until I had a look.

"You at the big hotel?" he asked me. "The new resort?"

I told him yes, because it wasn't his business, and I invented stories about the beach and the bar to pass the time. He took it all in. I ordered another G and T, and he had another beer. We got onto politics and world affairs. I predicted North Asia would go up in smoke next. He agreed with most of my views. Shereen showed up about an hour after he put in the call. She was okay, with good legs and bad teeth, but I figured she'd do. The teeth put me off, but she'd taken the time to fix herself up, with makeup and jewellery and clips in her hair, and I didn't want to hurt her feelings. She sat down with us and drank a beer, and then she took me back to her room.

It was hot and smelled bad. There was no sign of kids. I told her what I wanted, which I decided I would keep simple, since she sounded like a bad risk. But she had no technique plus I was just getting over a bug. She made an effort but I had to take over eventually, which made the whole thing pointless.

Afterwards, I said I'd give her twenty, since she'd put some energy into it, although she didn't really do it for me. She tried to sweet talk me, but once my pants were back on and I put a bill on the table, she got angry and called me ugly names. It didn't matter because sticks and stones. But then her manager came in. I thought he must have been waiting outside, which I didn't like. And I realized the whole thing was getting involved and unpleasant.

"Problem, Shereen?" he said.

"He only gave me twenty."

He turned to me. "We said thirty."

He stopped calling me "boss," and I thought it was a bad sign. Plus he was standing between me and the door.

"I figured thirty for a blow job, but her teeth are so bad I changed my plans."

the transaction

~ 77 ~

"Give her thirty and she can get her teeth done."

"For thirty dollars?"

"She can put the surplus in the kitty, start saving up."

He wasn't showing respect like he should, but it is a good idea to look for a peaceful resolution as a first approach. I told him, "You're a nice kid, and I'm impressed with your financial sense. But you have to learn that you can only charge what the market will bear."

He said, "You shook on thirty. You pay it."

He was wearing a thin shirt, jeans. I couldn't see a weapon and I didn't like his attitude. So I crossed to the door, and when he came at me, I clocked him in the face. You move fast and hit hard and you're usually okay. The mistake people make sometimes is they hesitate, and then your target sees it coming and fights back. Everything gets more involved. So I just made up my mind and followed through. His head hit the wall behind him, and he dropped. Shereen screamed and ran at me and started flailing. I hit her, too, and she dropped straight down to the floor and lay there beside her pimp. Her nose was bleeding. She called me more names, but not so loud.

"You need to show respect," I said. "Otherwise people will take their business elsewhere."

I walked back to the dock. All in all it was a disappointing day. A couple of businessmen saw me and tried to interest me in their products. But as a consumer I felt dissatisfied with Uberstaad in general. So I had to turn them down. They followed me for a bit, but they didn't have the right papers at the checkpoint, and they wandered off. The soldiers waved me through, which I thought was maybe a little lax with the criminal element and the global situation, but then I figured they remembered me from earlier. Plus also I'm white.

I checked around the booths. They had sunglasses and knockoffs, but no trunks. So I found the tender and headed back with a gang from the ship. The other cruisers were checking each other's purchases and telling stories. I felt let down and tired. It was the heat maybe.

○ ○ ○

Next stop, Prince Clarence, and again I was unimpressed. We stayed two days in port, and on the first day, I went over on the tender like we had to. It was a calm day, and not as difficult compared to the other stops, but I had to wait on the tender for it to fill. On shore I bought trunks and toured a rum distillery. It was educational, and they gave us samples in small, decorative bottles. I took one for me and one for Bud and one for Bailey and one for Eddie, and that was all right.

Then I went back to the Captain's Mess that night. It was the first time I'd been down since Maromed, because I still wasn't feeling totally up to par, and I'd just been calling the desk and getting a cheese sandwich or a plate of eggs sent to my stateroom. But I wanted to give Eddie the rum sample, which I thought he'd enjoy.

But he wasn't there and Katherine wasn't there, and I had a bad feeling about it. And when I asked, Lily said, "Mother's fading. We got her settled in Sick Bay. Father's taking dinner with her." I said I was sorry to hear it. And Lily said, "What can you do?"

Then the next day, I didn't feel like going to the beach, even though I had my new trunks. So when I got into town, there was nothing to do but drink G and Ts and outsmart the locals who were trying to scam me.

So finally, that day, when I came back on board, I bit the bullet and took all my issues to Raoul. I started with Sunday service, because it just wasn't a good arrangement and the weekend was coming around again.

"We've been at it for a while now," I said to him, "and I've had a chance to see how the whole schedule works."

"Yes, Mr. Rutledge," he said.

He had brought back my laundry and dry cleaning and was folding and hanging everything carefully, with crisp folds and lots of space between articles so nothing creased in the closet. It was these little touches that impressed me when I noticed them. And he still listened and thought about my problems even as he was hanging my pants just so.

the transaction

"Leticia is probably a nice person, although I don't know much about her," I said. "And it isn't a question of professional know-how because she wipes down the fixtures and all."

"She's first-class," said Raoul.

I didn't let him head me off. "But I was sick and lying in bed. I was weak. And for a man in that state to have a woman come busting into his room," I said. "It isn't right."

"You had some rough days, there, Mr. Rutledge," said Raoul. "I was worried about you. But you're back on your feet and that's not going to happen again, because you know the risks now. You just need to watch your intake and be careful at the ports of call, like we discussed."

"The ports of call are another issue. I want to discuss them also. But we need to look at the female stewards first. I've thought about it and I have ideas."

Raoul gave me a big smile. It looked terrible because he was so bony and green. But he said, "Let's hear it, Mr. Rutledge. The sooner we can sort this out the better."

I said, "I was thinking about a rotating day of rest."

Raoul looked stumped. "You mean I get Sunday one week and Monday the next? I don't see how it helps."

"No. Each steward on any given team takes a different day. Maybe you take Monday and Horst takes Tuesday."

Raoul shook his head. "But then you have four days when only three stewards are covering the floor," he said.

"But we work in the c14s," I told him. "You reassign them so each one is part of a steward team. Then you have a team of five for each station. And in every team, each person on the team takes one day off, but you all take different days. That way you give the customer continuity of service. And that means there can always be a guy on the team who is available to help the gentlemen. And when I get sick and need special attention, I don't have to worry about a girl I don't know seeing me in my dirty pajamas."

"Don't even think about it. Leticia barely mentioned your pajamas."

"Just as an example. What do you think?"

Raoul stood in the middle of the room and looked serious. "It's a good idea, Mr. Rutledge. It's probably the way to go. The problem I think might be changing schedules in the middle of this thing. People fear change." He worried about it for a minute and then moved on. "But I appreciate that you are trying to help us. And I feel personally ashamed that you spend your time trying to solve our problems when that's my job and I should be way ahead of you on it. So I am going to take this idea to Bobby with my highest recommendation. He listens to me. And I'm also going to take it around to the guys and try to get the staff excited about it, build support in the grassroots."

"You're a good man, Raoul," I said. I'd have been happy to settle the whole thing, but I thought that was all I was going to get right away, and I'd let him shop it around for a bit to see if he could sell it. So I went to my next concern. "I need to talk to you about the ports of call," I said.

"They don't give satisfaction, Mr. Rutledge?"

"They do not."

"Maybe tell me what you're looking for? I have shore contacts. I could arrange things."

"I enjoy peace and quiet and no one trying to rob me."

Raoul opened his eyes wide. "Someone tried to rob you, Mr. Rutledge? That's no good. We should report it. These places want our business. They'll look into things. Find the guys. Settle them."

"It wasn't robbery per se."

"Not per se?"

"I just want to enjoy the amenities in peace."

Raoul made clucking noises and went back to work. He went into the bathroom and took out the bag of dirty laundry and set a new bag in the hamper, and he came out into the bedroom with the old laundry bag, but he was thinking about the issue the whole time.

"They do their best at these places," he said. "They value our business and they try to satisfy. But they've got problems. There's the geopolitical thing ongoing. On some islands the problem is drugs. On some it's insurgents. There are rough characters. You have to be careful." He stripped my bed and threw the dirty sheets in with the laundry, and then he started making up the bed again, snapping a clean sheet out over the mattress and smoothing it down. "They even get problems with some tour groups. The nudist cruise a couple of seasons ago. It upset people all over. We have an open culture, a live-and-let-live culture. A lot of these islands, we need to remember, were settled by Spain. The Holy Church is the bedrock and foundation. They have a conservative culture, some of them, very old world."

"I respect the Church," I said. "But I'm not taking vows. The brochure talked about 'a lifetime of pleasure.' That's what I'm paying for."

Raoul pulled the sheet tight and made a complicated tuck. I was very happy with his work. My bed was always completely professional, wrapped tight, nearly impossible to get inside of. And he focused on my issue, which I liked also.

"We have to do the ports of call," he said. "We're committed and many people enjoy them. You want to be absolutely sure about safety, you sign up on a Company excursion."

"I do that. I go over. I get on a bus. But it's hit and miss. I never know what's on offer. The tours aren't always what I want. I need information."

Raoul gave me the squint eye. "Did you open your CruiseAccount like we discussed?" he said.

It was a low priority, I admitted. Raoul made noises like he agreed.

"I'm in your corner on this one," he said. "Computers are overrated. I'd rather concentrate on the human element, the interpersonal aspect. But your CruiseAccount keeps you informed. You want some help setting it up, stop by the computer services. The improved information and enrollment opportunities will enhance your cruise experience. You'll check the CruiseCalendar daily, get the updates and add-ons. You can take advantage of group rates. And security is part of the package. If you stick with the Company tour, you never have to worry about the locals getting out of hand."

"What about the tender and the tour guides and the information. It's work."

Raoul had an answer for that too.

"Another fine option is just stay on board. The ship is good when we're parked, with so many clients ashore. We've got the pool and the casino and the shops and the spa. Even the cinema's mostly empty once the tenders have cleared out. People who stay on board can enjoy all the amenities without the crowds."

"That's what I mean. No pressure and no crowds. That's what I'm looking for."

"Then maybe a spa day on the ship tomorrow, at Port Esteban?"

"We have another stop tomorrow? I thought we were going around the world. We're just circling the Caribbean as far as I can see."

"This is the first lap, the Caribbean and the Yucatan. People like it. Then we make the Canal. I can get you an itinerary?"

"I got one. I just don't see the point. A cruise means a sea voyage. We spend too much time on land."

Raoul spread out the duvet. "Some people like it. But nothing says you have to leave the ship. You can enjoy the on-board entertainment. And you'll like the Pacific. Lots of water, not many islands. Not too many ports of call." He looked sorry again. "But, you know, we have to stop sometimes, hook up with suppliers and so on."

"What do you mean?"

"Food, fuel. The passengers see the sights, and the staff offload recycling, refuel, load stores. Fresh water and fresh flowers. We have to import them. We stock up at the ports of call."

I felt foolish when I thought about it. "I didn't know that," I said.

"The Company knows it," Raoul said. "They make the plans."

"What's the plan for the Pacific?"

"You want the Pacific itinerary?"

the transaction

"I mean, where do we stock up if there aren't any ports of call?"

"We hit the biggies: Hawaii, Tahiti, Fiji, like that. The empty quarter, we rendezvous with supply vessels. Everything is planned." He fluffed my pillow.

"I am impressed, Raoul," I admitted.

He ducked his head modestly and stood by like I'd asked him to wait. So I looked at my roll and found a crisp Benjamin for him.

"Thank you, Mr. Rutledge," he said.

port esteban

I thought I'd test drive Raoul's advice the next day when we pulled up in Port Esteban. Instead of going ashore, I decided to go to the gym, like probably I should have done sooner, to see what the ship's facilities were like. I slept in, since I had got an early start for the tenders the last couple of days and I wanted to catch up. Also that way I avoided everyone heading ashore with their guide books and sunscreen.

I put on dry weave shorts and cross-trainers right away, so that I was ready to work and no fooling around. And I took a towel from my room although I knew they would probably have some in the gym. I don't like to sweat without relief, because it gets in my eyes and stings. Also I find that the right equipment, the right clothes, and the right shoes help to set the tone and get me mentally prepared for an activity. I like to look the part, and I thought the towel around my neck helped.

I figured I needed a good breakfast, so I went down to the Big Banana. I had a smoothie with berries and yogurt, and a bowl of granola. Then I thought I needed protein, since I planned to do weights. So I had a plate of eggs and ham. I also decided to pick up some cash, since Raoul and the tour guides were making inroads. The *Mariola* had several ATM facilities, but I went to the one in the ship's mall because it was on my way and I hadn't looked at it before.

The mall was a big venue in the front half of the ship on decks ten, eleven, and twelve. It had a big atrium space and shops and salons and a food court and the Gallery. I looked around, and it was very complete. I bought water at TheCompanyStore, since the medic said I needed to stay hydrated. I kept one bottle with me, and told them to deliver the rest.

Then I found the ATM, and I took out my limit and checked my balance. Everything looked okay, but the receipt didn't give me a detailed history and I thought I should check. Probably I should have done it before. But I was on holiday after a lifetime of non-stop entrepreneurship and brinksmanship, so taking it easy the first couple of weeks was reasonable I thought. But on the other hand, I like to stay on top of my holdings, and I figured the time had come to look in on them.

So my next stop was computer services like Raoul said, which was nearly on my way to the fitness facility also. I had to go up to deck fourteen and then back to the aft section, and I met Brent who was the chief computer services officer, and he told me I should have set up my computer account day one or before I boarded even, and I told him I was on holiday, and he looked like he didn't think it was an excuse. He gave me a user ID, and I made a password that wasn't "password," and typed it in twice. Brent showed me how to log out and told me I could access the system from my suite now that I was set up. But I was already at computer services so I just stayed at the terminal and looked into my concerns.

I got online again after a couple of near misses. I'm a two-finger typist, and it slows me down. Plus the system was cranky. It reminded me of the old dial-up networks, and I was surprised that the *Mariola* had such crumby facilities. Finally the CruiseHomePage came up. It was busy and hard to follow, with pop-ups and promotions. I shut them down one by one and finally logged into my personal mail account. There were messages from the Company which I ignored. I found the picture of all of us with the minister of tourism in San Lazar, and the picture of me and Bailey and Teresa from Bud. I googled Laureen, like I sometimes do, and nothing came up, like always.

Then it was time to do some business and I logged into my bank accounts. Everything looked okay. I called up the exchanges and studied my holdings and browsed through a couple of online resources. I was mostly satisfied with my portfolio, but I was getting interested in a bond issue that was coming up, and I like to stay on top of high tech, pharmaceuticals, what have you. There was a biotech company I wanted to see about it. I looked at a few reports and I sent a note to my broker. It was a good day's work.

Then Brent came over again to offer his expertise. I asked him if I could print pictures, and he showed me. A pop-up told me I was in the print queue. It took several minutes, and I wasn't impressed that I had to wait around. It was getting late and I still wasn't in the gym.

"You've got a few bugs in the system, here, Brent," I told him.

Brent was the kind of guy who didn't blink or swallow. "We're researching upgrades," he said. "We have a policy of continuous renewal."

"That's the right perspective," I told him. "Because the set-up you've got now is hard to work with. I just got my mail, and the system's a dinosaur. It took me ten minutes before I could get in. It went to a blank screen twice before that."

"We're wonky today. All our users are getting blips. We've scheduled a review of systems for tonight."

"Why don't you do it now?"

"We don't want to inconvenience our users." He waved his hand around the room. Besides me there were two other passengers: an older woman I didn't recognize, and the J-kid, who was always turning up. He was wired up with the things in his ears, and rattling away at the keyboard like he knew what he was doing.

"You don't look really busy," I said, which was truthful, but tactless maybe. But it didn't worry Brent. He explained it all to me.

"Most of our users log on in their suite, or in other tech facilities, like the library or the board room," he said. "Our highest hits are in the prime time to midnight range, peak usage as per typical for entertainment and communications options. Second heaviest user fields are in the nine to five range, the old business paradigm. The predawn shift is our slowest time window. That's when we can shut the system down with minimal disruption to primary systems and secondary service users. Therefore our systems review is online for that era. It's the most convenient for the public we serve."

I felt that he was disregarding my concerns. "You're supposed to be serving me too," I told him. "It isn't convenient if the system comes down on me when I'm trying to get in. You should think about that, too."

Brent was all over it. "Of course, sir," he told me. "Our first priority is customer satisfaction."

They all said how dedicated they were to customer service whenever something went wrong, like saying they wanted to please me was supposed to please me by itself. It was getting old. I wanted action. I was just about to tell him so when I fell off my chair and he sort of folded down to the floor. The ship was pulling and leaning. An alarm came on and all the monitors went bright and then shut down to nothing.

We picked ourselves up and I hung on to the table. Brent staggered over to the old woman who was down on the floor too. He hauled her up and let her fall back into a chair. It was on castors, and she rolled backwards right away, and Brent pulled her up to the desk and tried to hold her steady. I went over and gave him a hand, and the J-kid drifted over near us and watched.

"What the hell is going on?" I said. I had to shout. The alarm was loud, and also it was my first time on a cruise and it was a strange thing, with the ship heaving and the computers shutting down. It wasn't what I expected and I thought we might be in some kind of a situation.

But Brent wasn't bothered. He said, "I don't know, Mr. Rutledge. Most likely it's some kind of drill." I think that was the gist — he didn't project, and the alarm was going. But he didn't look worried. So that was reassuring.

The old woman put her oar in. She couldn't keep a grip on the table, but she knew what was what. "The itinerary didn't mention a drill," she said. She shouted so we could hear.

Brent shouted back, "Maritime law requires a minimum of three unscheduled drills a year." And that also sounded reasonable.

The intercom came up. "Seven lambda. Seven lambda. Seven lambda. Code teal. Repeat. Code teal."

Brent made his way over to his station. He had to hold on to furniture to stay on his feet. When he got there, he hit a button on one of his computers and waited a minute and tapped at the keyboard and stared at the monitor. I couldn't see the screen but I don't think anything happened, because he did it all over again a minute later. Then he checked the connections for all the cords in his gear. There were several but he was efficient and it only took a minute, although it felt like forever to me, because I had nothing to do but hold on to the old woman's chair and wait for the word.

Then Brent tried the on-off switch again, but I don't think anything different happened. Finally he sat down at the desk and opened a drawer and squinted into it and frowned. Then he closed it and opened another drawer. He pulled out a red binder and started leafing through it. He still didn't say anything, and I went over to his station. It took a minute because the ship was lurching and throwing me around. The J-kid came too.

"So what does it mean?" I asked him. It put a strain on my voice because we were still shouting.

"We won't be able to get the computers up again for a while. Code teal means I should clear computer services. It's part of the drill. Passengers should report to the nearest secure area or you can stay in your cabin and wait for crew assistance if you have mobility issues."

port esteban

He was reading from the binder and I had to concentrate to hear. I didn't know what 'secure area' meant, but I didn't ask because he was giving his attention to the binder and the alarm was going off. Behind us, the old woman lost her grip and rolled around the aisles. The intercom came up again. "Eleven beta. Eleven beta. Repeat. Eleven beta."

"But what's happening?" I said.

"I don't know," said Brent. "I just run the protocol."

"But should I be worried?" I asked him. Because with the alarms and all, it felt like things weren't a hundred percent.

"Not if you follow the protocols. They're set up to meet contingencies. You don't have to panic."

"I'm not panicking."

"That's good. Because panic never helps," said Brent. I thought it was good advice but he didn't have to lean into it, since I wasn't panicking and the J-kid looked okay too. "We just follow the drill and we're fine," Brent said. He stood up and walked back to the old lady. We followed him. "I have to ask you to leave computer services now," he said. "Also, you should take the stairs instead of the elevator. You want a crewman to help you?"

The old lady took him up on this, but I passed and so did the kid. We headed out into the corridor. There were some stewards and cleaners around. They were stowing things and locking doors. The alarm kept it up, but no one looked worried. They looked like they knew what they were doing, and that was reassuring. We met a hospitality specialist who I think tried to herd us back to the cabins. She didn't project and with the alarm going also, I couldn't understand her, and she couldn't understand me. So we sort of signaled at each other and I nodded my head like I was listening to her, and then I kept going where I wanted.

It was a long way down to my suite from computer services, and the ship was manouevring with tilts and surges. I thought it would be work to go all the way back down to deck six, and pointless, since it was just a drill and there was no reason to panic. Also I was nearly at the fitness facility, and I decided I'd report there, since it was probably secure and it was closer. I thought anything I needed to know they could tell me there. Also, I wanted to do my workout, since I was mentally prepared for it. I'd been slacking off for a few days, and it was time to get at it. I thought I'd go up to the fitness facility and report for duty and when the drill was over I'd do a vigorous workout and salvage something out of the morning. Because so far it had been a loss mostly.

I tried to call the aft elevator beside computer services, but nothing happened. The J-kid was talking at me but the alarm was still going and the intercom came up again. "Seventeen epsilon. Seventeen epsilon. Seventeen epsilon. Code indigo. Code indigo. Code indigo." Finally I gave up on the elevator and went into the stairwell. The alarm was worse in there with the walls and the echo. I covered my ears.

The J-kid followed me and tapped my shoulder. He talked at me more and pointed down the stairs. I nodded at him but I don't take orders from a kid. He shrugged and put his jacks back in his ears and headed down, holding onto the handrail to keep steady. I went up. I don't like the stairs anyway, and the ship was unstable. I hit the wall behind me when the ship pitched forward and banged my knee on a stair when we tilted up again.

Two decks up, on deck sixteen, the stairwell opened beside a bunch of clubs I hadn't been to, the Quay Note, the Catfish Lounge, the Mosh Pit. They were closed and locked down and nobody was around to ask about them, but they looked attractive, with small intimate tables and a piano in the Quay Note, and tackle and nets on the walls of the Catfish Lounge, and a menu with oysters on the half shell, and I thought I should come back sometime and test drive them.

Then I went out onto the deck through a big set of doors facing the front of the ship and I came out onto the aft sports deck, another area I hadn't looked at before. It was a big open space all set up to be useful and attractive. The middle of the deck had sports facilities, beach volleyball courts and basketball courts and a lawn bowling green. Port and starboard of the sports area there were trees and flowers and vines

port esteban

planted in low beds and urns, and trellises and comfortable-looking benches. It was green and cool although it was under the sun and on a boat. Also on the sports deck, the alarm was still peeling but it wasn't as loud in the open air.

I worked my way forward, past the courts, up to the midship area where there was another indoor section that went up in a kind of tower. I went straight in through the big doors at the back, and I was in the fitness facility. There was a desk by the midship elevators, and in front of it there was a spacious area with racks of weights and state-of-the-art weight training equipment, and rows of stationary bicycles and treadmills. There were mats for floor exercises and exercise balls and big elastics for resistance. On either side of the room there were men's and ladies' locker facilities and showers and steam rooms.

It was a strange thing because it was a large facility and completely deserted. I had a good look around and there was nobody there. There were some towels lying around and water bottles. But there was no one at the desk and no one on the machines.

Then the alarm stopped ringing and we were sitting upright and I think powering forward. I thought there must have been a change of plan and we were leaving port, which was fine with me since I didn't think the ports of call had much to offer. The intercom said, "Ten alpha. Ten alpha. Ten alpha."

But I had my towel and my dry weave shorts, and the machines were all free, so I did a workout. I did some free weights and some sit-ups. I rode the bike for cardio. I rode twenty miles over hilly terrain and burned five hundred calories.

o o o

The change rooms were locked up, but I didn't mind since I like to be private, and the elevator was working again, so I went back to my stateroom. When I got there, Raoul came out of the closet and looked surprised to see me.

"You're safe, Mr. Rutledge," he said. "You made it. Am I glad." He looked weak and pathetic and his colour was bad, but he sort of bobbed his head up and down, and rubbed his hands. "That's one good thing today anyway," he said.

I didn't know what he was talking about. But I was happy to see him because I had time to think about the bad service I got while I was riding the stationary bike, and I decided I should register my issues. I didn't know if Brent would report the computer problems. And there were no fitness specialists in the fitness facility. Also, there were monitors in the weight room, but they were turned off and I couldn't watch videos while I was sweating on the machines. These are not small things. The facilities themselves were A-one, but I felt that the ship's staff had a bad day in terms of service, and if you put up with that kind of thing, you get more of it.

"I want to talk to you," I told Raoul. "Can you give me a minute of your time? Because this is important and I need someone who knows what's what."

"Yeah, sure, Mr. Rutledge, of course," he said.

I went back into the living room and sat on the couch, and Raoul came and stood in the middle of the room and listened attentively. He almost looked scared. It surprised me and it slowed me down, because I didn't have the heart to go straight into my complaints. So instead I started with the good news and I told him that he was right about the easy access to the facilities with most people ashore, and I told him about my long, vigorous workout on the stationary bike.

He cut me off. "You don't know about it," he said.

I don't like being interrupted. "What?" I said.

"There was an incident today."

"The alarms and all. I know. You couldn't miss it."

"But you're okay?"

"I hit my knee while we were manouevring. They shouldn't do that. People can get hurt."

Raoul nodded. "It's not the way we like to do things. It's an emergency posture. We had an ugly situation in Port Esteban. We had to leave in a hurry."

"I never liked the ports of call," I said. I had other things on my mind. But he wanted to talk about it.

"Many of them are very fine places," he said. "It depends on the geography and the economy and the particular individuals involved. There's a variety of factors. Port Esteban has been a cruise favourite for a long time for your high-end packages. It offers the standard beach and diving excursions and a number of exotic options that are popular with a sophisticated adult clientele."

It was beside the point, but got me interested. So I asked him, "Like what?" Even though I thought I had an idea.

"Port Esteban has an old culture, a high-spirited, pleasure-loving culture, with many traditional pastimes and amusements. It's not for everyone, but I say, live and let live. Different strokes for different folks. They've got a red-light district and a naked circus, a bullfight arena, various gambling opportunities."

I was impressed. "These sound like fine options," I said. "They sound historical and authentic. I wish I had heard about them."

"You didn't hear about them?"

"I only checked my mail this morning."

Raoul shook a finger at me. "We talked about it, Mr. Rutledge. You have to stay on top of updates."

"I'm ready now. I will in the future. Because I would much rather have signed up for one of those activities than banging around in the stairwell when the elevators went offline."

"You will enjoy some fine options in the future," Raoul said. "Although the way things turned out, it was a good thing maybe that you didn't go ashore today. Because we sent a gambling package in and things got out of hand."

"Bad luck at the craps table?" I asked him, because in my experience that is where trouble usually starts.

He shook his head. "Cockfighting," he told me.

I was surprised, and I let him tell me more.

"There's a consortium in the old city that offers a fine range of blood sports with associated gaming opportunities. They'll do you cockfighting, dogfighting, bare-knuckle boxing, what have you. A wide variety of traditional spectacles and contest-based wagering activities."

"It sounds like a fine slate of events," I told him.

"We had a good sign-up," he said. "Fifty, sixty people went for it."

"I've never seen a dogfight."

"They didn't have one on the program this time. It's a shame, because a dogfight is a fine show. It's a time-honored contest. You hardly see one now, with the animal lovers, but no matter what people say, nothing is more natural than two dogs trying to kill each other."

"Except you said they didn't have a dogfight."

"It was a quality menu still. There were cockfights in a variety of weights and classes, and then there was supposed to be a boxing match and a couple of girls going all out."

"It sounds like a well-planned event, with excitement and variety."

"It would have been a fine day. But things didn't work out."

"What happened?"

Raoul shrugged. "The consortium in Port Esteban. They're salt of the earth, and the Company has been dealing with them for years. But in their situation, with all the red tape and the high stakes, they're a no-nonsense group."

"They need to be, in that line of work."

"Plus their clientele has a rough element. Not our passengers, obviously, because this is an elite group on the *Mariola*. But the locals and the regulars. The consortium knows how to handle them usually, and they have to let them in. It's their bread and butter market."

"You want the crowd," I said. "It's part of the experience."

"It's part of the show," said Raoul. "But today, there were issues. I don't know the details. But our people got to the venue and the traditional activities were underway, and everyone was enjoying themselves. And then there was some kind of disagreement."

"These are high octane events," I said.

"It's a part of the experience, too. The crowd is lively and spontaneous. But you have to know how to handle yourself in that kind of group. In any group, really. You have to watch your surroundings and adjust yourself. When in Rome. You know how it is. I don't like to say it, but it could have been the passengers that started the trouble. People don't always know how to behave. And you don't want to get on the wrong side of these people."

"You need to show respect," I said.

"Whatever happened, it got out of hand. *Mariola* security was with our passengers. It's a part of the package, like we've discussed. And they made a decision to move the passengers out. I was talking to one of the security guys. He filled me in on events from his point of view. He said himself it was hard to follow from inside the crowd. But things were unpleasant in the venue and security made the call to move our people out."

"Safety comes first, even in a deluxe entertainment scenario."

"They were on top of it. But it's complicated rounding up several dozen people who are enjoying themselves. Plus they didn't have buses. They had to walk back to the pier."

"That's not right," I said. "What happened to transport?"

"The Company usually lays it on. But the cockfighting venue is right by the pier. It's an old warehouse facility that's been renovated to accommodate a variety of different activities, with a pit and a ring and a bar area and business offices and so on. It's conveniently located, and hospitality thought people would enjoy the exercise."

"Why would they think that?" I asked him. "People never enjoy exercise. They just want to fit in their pants."

Raoul nodded but he didn't answer my point. "They combined the gaming excursion with a short walking tour, and they pointed out the sights in the historic old town on the way to the match. It was an easy walk for the passengers, because they were mostly young and fit."

"It's a mistake," I said. "If people want exercise they can go to the gym and ride the stationary bike."

Raoul agreed. "It turned out to be a bad idea, although people were enthusiastic about it when they signed up, and apparently a lot of them enjoyed the exercise and the sun and the historic plaques. But when things got uncomfortable in the venue, *Mariola* security had to get all the passengers out and back to the pier, and the disagreement was escalating all around them. I don't know. I wasn't there. But I think there was a mob psychology aspect to the event. A bunch of the locals followed our people into the street and down to the checkpoint at the pier, and more people joined in, the kind of people who hang around the bodega looking for trouble. Then the checkpoint guards made a hash of it."

"They aren't always on top of their game," I said. "Although I've had good service sometimes."

"They didn't know their stuff at Port Esteban," said Raoul. "It's disappointing. They slowed down the legitimate passengers and it sounds like they didn't know how to handle the unsavory element. They lost control and it was a riot situation. There was gunfire."

"That sometimes happens," I said. "People get excited."

"The whole tender process was compromised."

I knew all about the tender process since I had tried it myself several times. I didn't whitewash it for Raoul even though I liked him. "That's just not a good system," I said.

"Plus they were taking pot shots at the ship."

"Now that is totally out of line," I said. It made me angry that people showed no respect. "Did they do any damage?"

Raoul looked serious. "Not to the ship. They only had little side arms, I think, and we were parked way out in the bay."

"You'd have to be some kind of sharpshooter to hit anything from so far away," I said. "Or have the right arsenal. A big gun or some kind of missile."

"Luck is a factor, too, even with small arms. People are out on deck. They can get hit."

I thought about it. It gave me a chill. I said, "I was out on deck. I crossed the bowling lawn to the fitness facility. I came up the back stairs instead of the midship elevator direct."

"You're a little bit protected there, because you're up high. People were more vulnerable on the starboard balconies or on the running track."

"We have a running track?"

"We have a great track. You access it from deck sixteen, where you were, from the fitness facility, or the pool deck in front, and it goes all the way around the ship's perimeter. You get sun and sea air, and it's professionally corked and sprung. So you never need to worry about shin splints."

"Just gunfire."

"Today, unfortunately, although it's not an issue usually. And even today, nobody on deck actually got hurt, since we were so far away from the dock, and the shooters didn't have the right weapons for a major offensive."

"Just enough to make trouble."

"Exactly. Passengers were mainly exposed to risk on the dock. The gambling party took some injuries, a couple of passengers and a security guy."

"Security runs a professional risk, but the passengers it should never have happened to."

"As soon as the gambling party got back to the ship, we left port."

"We ran away?" I said. "That's not right."

"We should have stayed to settle them. I was talking to a guy, Dean. He's part of the security detail, and he was saying the same thing. But we're a civilian outfit. We've got old people and children on board. We have responsibilities."

"Your passengers are a consideration. But sometimes you have to stand up and be counted. When you fly the flag you have to defend it. You can't let people take pot shots. They have to learn respect."

"This is true. Although technically we sail out of Liberia, so the flag isn't what you might think."

I was surprised by this. "You mean that first night in the Captain's Mess, I was raising my glass to the flag of Liberia?"

"Technically," he said. He put his hands up to explain. "But the toast is symbolic."

"Of what?"

"Freedom, independence, sailing under our own colours and setting our own course. The success and prosperity of the cruise."

"The Liberian flag symbolizes that?"

"It's the only nation of Africa that was never colonized."

"I didn't know that." I thought about it for a minute. "Although it's not really relevant," I said. "The point is, you defend the flag you sail under. You don't run away from a fight. It sends the wrong message."

Raoul looked serious and nodded his head some more. "It would have been better to stay and settle them. But we made the point before we got underway. Command sent out the Dragonflies to secure the tenders."

I felt foolish to ask so many questions, but there was a lot going on that I didn't know about. "What are Dragonflies?"

"We've got four Dragonfly X10s," said Raoul. "They're state-of-the-art military helicopters. The Company bought them at a government surplus sale. Good price and they never saw a lot of action. So the equipment is in practically mint condition. And we picked up the talent to fly them and maintain them. The birds are practical, and they look A-one. We use them for supply runs and deluxe passenger transport. You can book them by the day or by the hour from hospitality."

"So I could book a Dragonfly into town instead of the tender?" I said.

"You could do that," said Raoul.

"They sound like a fine option, Raoul," I said. "I am impressed." And I was. The Dragonflies sounded like a useful alternative to the tender process.

port esteban

Raoul nodded. "They're part of the security detail, too," he said. "They carry sidewinders and chickadees, and the gunner posts are manned and fully operational."

"It sounds like we have heavy, flexible firepower," I said. "I always think that's sensible."

"We have to be prepared," Raoul said. "Because some people would rather shoot first and ask questions later, and the *Mariola* has a comprehensive itinerary, including some hot spots where anti-patriot fanatics don't listen to reason. And if you don't have the firepower to back up your legitimate sightseeing demands, you might as well stay at home."

"Four Dragonflies loaded for bear are going to make an impression."

"It's a convincing display. Although we only got one in the air today."

"You said four."

"We have a total complement of four. But one of them was scheduled for maintenance, to change the oil and lubricate the parts. You have to be consistent with that kind of thing or insurance lapses and performance suffers. And one was doing a supply run, bringing in papaya from the Company plantation on the island. It's on the menu in the Captain's Mess tonight, and I guarantee it will be the best papaya you ever tasted. There's nothing like fruit right off the tree."

"I'll be sure to look for it."

"And the fourth was booked for passenger transport."

"To Port Esteban?"

"It was doing a pickup at Prince Clarence. A couple of passengers were having a good time and missed the sailing. That's another good thing about the 'Flies. You're enjoying yourself in a port of call and you lose track of time. No problem. You just get in touch with the Company and they coordinate with us for pickup. Very reasonable charge."

"So there was only one 'Fly on deck today?"

Raoul nodded. "It did the job, though. It strafed the pier and the locals took cover. That gave our guys enough time to get everyone onto the tender and back to the ship. And then we cut out."

"Problem solved," I said.

Raoul made a face. "We're still cleaning up the details," he said, "counting heads and trying to figure out who's where. It's one reason we run the drill, get the on-board passengers to a secure area, the Broadway and the Silver Screen, and do a roll call. We have to figure out who's here and who's missing."

"You lost some passengers, Raoul?" I said.

"Probably we didn't. We're still running the checks. I can take your name off the list for example. But beach excursions and the snorkellers and so on. They were still involved in their activities when we left port. We have to pick them up."

"We're going back to Port Esteban?"

"That would be easiest, tender-wise. But the harbour is still a no-go zone. So we changed the pickup venue. We're cruising to Callena, on the lee side of the island. The other tours will report there and we'll send the tenders in to get them."

"The guides know they should take their tours to Callena?"

"The guides are fully informed and up to date on the situation. All the tour information is cced to the Company reps at each port of call. They know where our people are. It's part of our service to you. Every tour operator has a cell and emergency contact info. The Company staff on the ground sends out the alert to the tours and brings them in safe."

"It sounds very well organized."

"It's a fine system. The Company has protocols for any situation."

"I'm glad to hear it, Raoul. I'm happy to hear it," I said. I was thinking about my own concerns again, because the riot and the shooting were unfortunate, but no one died, and it sounded like the Company had policies for everything. "While the Dragonfly was strafing the pier, I was on-board getting subpar service in a variety of ways. I can see that today was a day like no other. But I have to tell you, the crew and staff of the *Mariola* were tested today and in my opinion they did not pass the test." I said it firmly so he could see I meant it.

port esteban

He snapped to like he should and got on board to address my issues. "Yeah. Of course, Mr. Rutledge," he said. "You've got problems, I'm your guy. What can I do?" He leaned in like he was excited to help.

And since he finally gave me his good attention, I went over all my concerns, and Raoul agreed that Brent was a nice guy but useless in an emergency, and he said the fitness specialists cleared the fitness facility for code teal and code indigo, the whole green-blue spectrum, but they should have locked the door behind them. He showed me the in-house closed circuit where hospitality posted regular updates, and he showed me the Passenger Manual, which he pulled out of the desk, which had the ship's specs and evacuation routes and overviews of the amenities and switchboard extensions.

He said, "These are resources for emergencies and daily living. But any time day or night, if you need information, Mr. Rutledge, I want you to come to me. In an emergency posture, I'll be looking for you. This afternoon, I was afraid we'd lost you. You weren't on the roster for the Broadway or the Silver Screen, and I thought you'd be in your suite. But when I didn't find you here, all I could think was that maybe you went ashore, and I was kicking myself because I hate to lose a passenger I got to know and value, or any passenger at all if it comes to that, because passenger safety and comfort are my responsibility and the only measure of my job performance that counts worth a damn. I should have known you'd come through because you're a resourceful guy, and a riot on the docks isn't going to lay you low. But I want you to promise me, now, that if we have an issue or a crisis, you'll let me be your first line of defense."

He nodded hard and stared in my eyes, and again I was impressed with his initiative and the way he took his work seriously. It was a refreshing change on a day when other people let me down. So I didn't think twice. I said I'd take my problems to him at all times, and I got out my roll and found a c-note for him so he knew that I meant it. And he bowed his head, and slipped the bill into his pocket, and then he left.

amenities

CHAPTER EIGHT

After he left I had a shower and slapped on some aftershave, because so far my day had been only so-so and I wanted to get on with it. I figured chinos and a polo shirt for happy hour, and when I went into the closet to get them, I tripped on cases of water. They had sent them up from TheCompanyStore, like the clerk told me, and I was happy the water arrived, because at least one person was doing his job on the ship. But I had asked for six bottles and they sent six cases, and I wanted litres but these were single servings. It was sparkling and I wanted still. So I looked up the extension and called down to the store, and no one answered because they were still securing facilities, I thought. But I left a message and told them to take it back and bring litre bottles of non-carbonated water instead. And then I moved the flats so I could get at my things. They were heavy and in the way everywhere I put them. But I finally stacked three flats on top of the safe and three inside it since I wasn't storing valuables anyway.

The store really never should have mixed up my order like that. So it was another disappointment. I felt that the *Mariola* was not coming through for me. I wanted blue skies and smooth sailing. I wanted to enjoy the good things that I was paying top dollar for. The manoeuvres and the alarms and the no-shows in the fitness facility all put me off. They made me wonder about the *Mariola*, and whether I had made a good decision buying in.

But I decided to think about the good things that had happened too, like Raoul's attentive service and the store at least sending the order even if it got the details wrong. And it was early days still and every big enterprise has a few glitches. Finally I decided that things happen, and the trick is knowing how to roll with it.

So instead of brooding I focused my attention on where I should go for a cocktail. And I remembered that the Company supplied the Passenger Manual really so cruisers were fully aware of amenities, and I looked in the index under pubs and bars and found a long list, with many more facilities than I knew about. I'd only been to a few, and I made up my mind to check out more, especially since many passengers were still on the island and I wouldn't have to fight my way up to the bar. I had a look at the specs and I went down to the Hold on level minus one for my first stop.

It was a small operation with maps on the walls and barrels for tables. It smelled of tar, which I thought was authentic, maybe, but I didn't like. Also, there was nobody there, and while I liked it that I didn't have to fight for a seat, it was dull, and the bartender didn't have anything to say. So I finished my G and T and moved on.

Next stop, I went up to the Dexter, on deck three starboard side. It had an indoor section and a big patio outside, and it had business ongoing. So that was much better than the Hold. And although I didn't know anyone, I found a group of dedicated smokers on the patio and I bummed a cigarette and joined them. I met Poppy and Enright and Natalie and Ben and Saskia and Leanne.

When I came in they were rehashing Port Esteban. They had all been on the gaming excursion, and they were high flyers who liked action.

They were telling war stories and comparing notes. And although normally it is dull to listen to other people talk, I was interested to get their perspective on the venue and the riot.

"I had just put a hundred on a bird," Leanne said. "I don't know anything about birds, but I decided, 'I'm putting a hundred on this bird.' I liked its feathers. Then security said we had to go. They made me walk out on it!"

She was a nervous girl, very quick and jumpy. Her hair stood up on her forehead and she looked a little like a bird herself. She made a sad little face about leaving the cockfight behind, and her friend Saskia patted her hand and looked sorry for a minute.

Enright said, "You don't look at the bird. You look at the trainer. You see a guy who looks like a killer, he'll give you a bird worth betting on."

"I think security was out of line," Natalie said. "I told them, 'wait a minute,' and they didn't wait a minute. They grabbed my ass and hauled me out. I'm not paying them to grab my ass."

Natalie got to the point. She was tall and blonde and ready to set everyone straight, and she had a fine ass. She didn't need to pay people to grab it.

"I saw weapons, honey," Saskia said. "I think security was proactive."

"I tell security 'wait a minute,' I expect them to wait a minute," Natalie said. "They could have waited for the kill at least and let us cash out."

"They took care of us," Saskia said. She was a little older and relaxed. I could feel adrenaline coming off the others, but Saskia took it in stride. She leaned back in her chair, and half closed her eyes like a cat, and gave you a lazy smile if she noticed you. Of all of them I thought she was the girl who knew what was what.

"You think security came through?" I asked her.

She said, "They did their job. We all came home. They moved us out so fast, I didn't have time to be afraid."

So they enjoyed their day mostly, although Poppy lost a shoe on the docks, and Ben got shot.

amenities

"It's a flesh wound," he said. He showed me the gauze and the tape on his shoulder. "I didn't know I was hit till Tallie saw the blood," he said.

"I had hysterics," said Natalie.

"You don't notice the pain," I said. "You get a kind of high from the action. It's adrenaline."

"That's what Doctor Dan said," Ben said.

"They're very sharp in Sick Bay," I said.

"They cleaned me up okay," Ben said. "But they wrecked my shirt. They cut it off me." He was young I realized, not much more than a kid, and big and clumsy. He looked sulky and dim somewhat, with a little mouth on a big jaw.

"It had a hole already," Natalie said. "And blood never really comes out."

"It was my favourite shirt," Ben said.

"Ben lost his shirt gambling," Enright said, and we all laughed.

I said I didn't mind missing the riot but I was sorry I didn't know about the gambling opportunity, and Saskia said I could always go and lose a few bucks in the casino.

"I haven't been there yet," I told her.

"Oh, honey, you've got to see the Monte," said Saskia.

"We should go up and hit before dinner," Leanne said.

I told her sure. It was nice of her to suggest it and I wanted to see the room. But Ben said no.

"I don't feel like getting dressed," he said. "I think the dress code is bad policy."

"You love a casino," said Natalie.

"I don't like to tuck my shirt in every time I want to lose a couple of bucks."

Natalie said, "You have to dress for dinner anyway." •

She had introduced herself as Natalie, but Ben called her 'Tallie,' and I didn't put it together right away. Now it came to me all at once, and I remembered Natalie and Ben, the poor people who won the lottery and I got a very bad feeling. I was afraid that I made a mistake being friendly with this gang. Even though they went to the cockfights and had opinions about the security detail, Ben didn't want to go to the casino almost like he didn't like to risk his money. Plus he worried too much about a wrecked shirt. Also Natalie had a tattoo on her arm, and although it was artistic, I thought it might be somewhat low rent. So I did some fact-finding right away.

"Did I hear about you?" I said to Ben. "Are you the guy who won the lottery?" I tried to say it nicely, like I wasn't sure, so that he didn't know I knew all about him. People take offense sometimes if they think you gossip about them.

"Yeah. We won the lottery," Ben said.

"I won the lottery," Natalie said.

"Tallie won the lottery," Ben said. He rolled his eyes.

"It's an exciting prize package," I said. But there was no reason to flatter him. "It's too bad it was an interior suite."

"We bought a principal," Ben said.

"I bought a principal," Natalie said.

"We remodeled the prize suite for storage. Tallie needs good closets."

"It's tighter for a couple," I said. I felt I had good storage, and in a principal stateroom I thought they would have more extensive facilities. But women are difficult sometimes.

Still mostly I was relieved to find out they had money, because if they were poor like people said at Maromed, I would have had to cut and run, because it is complicated when you try to be friendly with people from a different tax bracket. So I was glad they had money and could pay their share, and it meant I could sit with the gang and enjoy a cocktail, which was my goal.

Ben kept trying to stay out of black tie. "We could go to the Local," he said. "Get fish and chips."

Saskia said, "But we'd miss you in the Captain's Mess, honey. And you look good in a tux."

Everyone was being very respectful of Ben since he was shot.

"I don't know if I can get into the jacket with my shoulder," Ben said, and I thought he was milking it, because it was only a flesh wound, like he said himself. But I figured he didn't want to break up the party, with the women making a big deal of him, and I could see his point of view.

Still, I was ready to move. So I signed for the next round, because I wasn't hurting for money, even if I bought a Balcony Stateroom package and not a Principal, and I told them I was going up.

"We'll meet you there," said Leanne, and I said I'd look forward to it.

So cocktail hour turned out okay, the way things do if you make an effort and know what you're looking for. The women were friendly and good-looking, and the guys had something to say, even though Ben was a little high on himself and Enright didn't fight me for the bill.

I went back to my cabin and put on my tux and then I checked the specs for the Monte. I took the midship elevator and I got off on deck ten, in the corridor behind the mall, and I went into the casino through revolving doors.

I should have gone there day one. It was a spectacular venue, going up three decks, like the mall, with a big open central area and galleries looking down from the floors above. Everything was elegant, with wood panelling and metal and glass and carpet and tile. It was a sophisticated space, not flashy and cheap like you sometimes see.

And although there were not a lot of people in the venue, with all the tours still on the island, the people who were there looked their very best. And no matter what Ben said I could see the formal wear policy was exactly right. Without a dress code, people start turning up in sweats and Birkenstocks, and the whole amenity starts to look seedy and desperate. So I was glad I had the heads up and changed into my tux, even though I still wasn't absolutely sure about the flared leg.

Again, since the venue wasn't crowded, I had the chance to look at everything and try things out with no lineups and no waiting. There were slot machines and a variety of games when you walked in: blackjack tables and roulette wheels and baccarat. In the middle of the main floor, there was a big bar area, in granite and steel, with leather bar stools. I took the escalator up to the mezzanine where they had craps and another bar area and an ATM and the casino manager's office and offices for the ship's bookies where they took bets and a couple of TV rooms where you could watch the race or the fight or whatever.

There was no escalator to the third level. So I got a G and T on the mezzanine and asked the bartender, and he said the third floor had private rooms for cards. They had a couple of bridge games, which the older passengers liked, and they ran several poker games. They had a penny ante game and a five K game and a fifty K game. If you wanted to play, the bartender said, you signed in with the casino manager, and he arranged everything and took you up to the third floor in the dedicated elevator; he had a key for it, but without it no one could get in, which I guess was secure and sensible, even though I thought it was insulting to the passengers somewhat, like we couldn't be trusted.

Saskia and Poppy and Leanne took their time, the way women do. I shot craps and lost some money, and I topped up my cash at the casino ATM, because I like to have a float in case of emergency. Then I moved on to roulette. The girls turned up finally, and Enright, who was with Poppy, and everyone looked good. Enright had put on his tux and the girls had put up their hair and showed some cleavage and thigh. We all had a drink and Leanne bet big and lost it all and looked like she was going to cry. And Saskia laughed her out of it so we could all enjoy ourselves. And Poppy let Enright do most of the talking until she had another drink and then she told me about losing her shoe, which wasn't very interesting.

Then I had a streak going for a while and I didn't like to leave. I stayed and kept playing when they went down to the Captain's Mess. I had a plate of sandwiches at the table, and I won some money and then I lost it all again. It was a good day.

o o o

I got into a good rhythm over the next couple of days. I'd get up and put on my shorts and trainers and go down to the Big Banana for breakfast. Then I'd go up to the fitness facility and work out.

The fitness specialists were back on duty the day after Port Esteban. There was a girl, Sarah, behind the desk, wearing yoga pants and a ponytail. I told her I'd been looking for her the day before, and she looked serious and told me they were running emergency protocols. She was young and not very bright, I thought, but I booked a consultation with her anyway since she had good muscle tone. But she had no cleavage, and I don't find boyish women attractive. So when she told me she'd look forward to working with me, I had to stress that it would be strictly business, and she nodded like that was what she was thinking too.

Every day for a couple of days in a row I went up to the fitness facility after breakfast, and Sarah put me through a set of presses and a set of crunches, and then she put me on the treadmill and monitored my heart and my breathing. She made a chart showing my progress and we talked about goals and visualization and how to do a proper cool-down after a grueling workout. She was very thorough, although I found the whole thing dull and tiring after a while.

Then after a workout I'd go back down to my suite and stand under the shower and drink water from a bottle. The store delivered still water like I asked in litre bottles, but I asked for half a dozen bottles and they gave me half a dozen six-packs of bottles. So again I was oversupplied. And they didn't take back the sparkling like I'd asked them to. I was disappointed they couldn't follow instructions, but I unpacked the big bottles and stacked them on shelves at the back of the closet and inside the safe because I knew I would drink it some time, and it was more work to explain again.

Also, I started restocking daily from the ship's ATMs, because they were conveniently located in the mall and in the Monte, and I like to have a reliable bankroll. So I counted out a float and kept it topped up and in my pocket, and the excess I put in the safe behind the flats of sparkling and the big bottles of still so the water covered my holdings. Then I chose a code for the safe so everything was secure and I locked it all up.

Other times after I finished my session with Sarah I'd roll up to the Slaker. It was the bar at the front end of the weight training area, and it had an indoor section and an outdoor section. It serviced the fitness facility and also the pool area at the front of deck sixteen. The bartenders made juices out of fruits and vegetables and grasses, and they had smart drinks and power drinks. They had a proper bar, too.

I'd get a bottle of water and a G and T, and I'd take some steam in the sauna, or else I'd go straight out to the pool area and sit in the hot tub, or walk a couple of laps on the running track, or sit in a lounger by the pool for an hour or two, taking the sun and passing the time with whoever was around.

There was always someone there, but it was never crowded, because it turned out we never made the pickup in Callena. I heard about it from Eddie. He was sitting by the pool wearing a hat and sunglasses the day after Port Esteban. He saw me and waved me over. I didn't recognize him when he was covered up, but he took his glasses off finally and I could tell who it was, and I was happy to see him, since I hadn't caught up with him since Maromed.

I shook his hand and asked him how he was doing, and he said he was doing fine. Nobody was sitting in the lounger beside him. So I made myself comfortable.

"Doctor Dan says you have to watch how much sun you take," he said. He put his glasses back on and pointed at his hat. He had a shirt on, too, casual and not buttoned up, but keeping the sun off him. And he was wearing trunks and he had a towel on his legs.

"I heard that," I told him. "You want a hat and some sunscreen. It's what people say."

"They overdo it," he said. "You hear too much about it, you get

amenities

cynical. I'm going to die of something. Maybe melanoma. Maybe a heart attack. I'm not fussy. And I'm not looking for it, because who wants to die? So I listen to what they say. But on the other hand, there's a limit to what I'm going to do. I'm not going to go overboard. It can suck all the pleasure out of life. And then, what's the point? I smoke a cigar and I want to enjoy it. I don't want to be thinking about lung cancer. I sit in the sun, I don't want to waste my time worrying about melanoma."

"But you have your hat anyway," I said. He was laying down the law. He made a very good case, but he was all covered up. Also he didn't leave a lot of openings for conversation.

"I don't like to burn," he said. "It gets itchy and it can be sore. Also it isn't attractive, and I like to look my best. But I like to get a bit of colour. So I take a few minutes in the sun. Then I put my hat on, to make sure I don't burn. And I have good sunscreen, 30 SPF, like they tell you." He showed me his sunscreen and then he put it back on the table between us.

"You're very well equipped," I said.

He shrugged. "I get hot sometimes, with my shirt and my towel. They protect me from sunburn, but I get too warm."

"You can move into the shade," I said.

"There is no shade by the pool," he said.

"You can move inside," I said. "After the sun, the a/c is very comfortable."

"I can't go running in and out of the a/c," said Eddie. "It's work. I need a hand getting out of the lounger. I'm not as young as I once was."

"You're young at heart," I told him, because I didn't want to be heaving Eddie in and out of his lounger. I was on holiday and it wasn't my responsibility. Also, he was cranky somewhat, and I don't like listening to people gripe. So I tried to emphasize the positive. But he was stuck in it.

"Eric usually helps," he said. "Or Dell. Someone is usually around to give me a hand getting into a lounger or getting back up. But they're stuck on the island. I had to get one of the waiters to help me today."

"It's their job," I said. I was glad he had someone else lined up to do the lifting.

"They don't have the training," he said. "So getting into the lounger is difficult, and getting out again. I'm not going to be jumping up and down all afternoon, five minutes of sun, then a trip to the bar, then more sun, then down to the toilet, and back again, more sun, then a dip in the pool. It's too much for me. It takes energy and flexibility. I get tired just thinking about it. I don't have the stamina anymore. I can't do all that jackrabbiting around."

I liked his style. He was old-fashioned sometimes, but I knew what he was getting at.

"That's why they have waiters at the Slaker," I said. "You never have to go up to the bar. They come to you."

"I'm just saying. I come out here to take the sun. I spritz myself if I get too hot." He had a sprayer with him, like for houseplants, and he gave his neck a spritz to show me what he meant. He put it back down again. "If I want more sun later, I take my hat off and enjoy it. But I don't go in and out of the a/c. Once I get here, I stay put."

"You take your time and enjoy yourself."

"I make it worth my while. It takes me twenty minutes, half an hour to get into my trunks, find a shirt. I have to get my things together, a towel, the sprayer, sunscreen, a hat, sunglasses. I put everything I need in a bag and bring it with me." He showed me a canvas tote he had beside the lounger. He put it down again. "Then I need five minutes to get into the chair. It's work. After all that, I want to make it worth the effort. I stay on deck for a couple of hours, until I can't take the heat anymore. Then I call it a day. I pack up my kit and go back to my suite." He thought about it for a second. "Or Sick Bay," he said.

It was an opening for me and I really should have asked him about Katherine. But he didn't say anything directly about her, and I hated to start talking about sick people, especially when it was a warm day and I was comfortable. So I ducked, and instead I just told him, "It's a good system." I really thought it was, plus he had put some thought into it, and I wanted to encourage him.

He rearranged the towel so his legs were showing. They were very pale and hairless. I tried not to look. He spritzed himself down, and then he put the sprayer on the table again.

"So you made it back from Port Esteban," he said to me, and I was glad we were moving on to other topics.

"I never went," I told him. "I've been disappointed sometimes by the ports of call. I decided to enjoy the amenities on the ship."

"It was the right decision," he said. "Although they did us proud in Maromed."

I didn't tell him about the bad water, because no one wants to hear about your intestines.

"The kids went over and they're still there," said Eddie.

"I thought I saw the boy around," I said to him.

"He stayed on board. He wasn't interested in the historical tours. Maromed was enough for him. He has other things on his mind."

"Kids," I said.

"They don't know how good they've got it," said Eddie. "But Steve and Eric and Lily and Della went on a tour of Port Esteban."

"They went to the cockfight?" I asked him.

Eddie looked surprised. "I don't think so," he said. "I didn't hear about that. It was a historical tour about pirates. They went to an old pirate fort that's been converted to a theme park."

It sounded like a scam to me, and again I was glad I had stayed on board, although I didn't say it to Eddie. Instead I told him, "That's not the gambling tour, then. It had a different profile. The pirate tour sounds very good, too," I said, because I didn't want him to think I was criticizing.

Eddie shrugged. "Della booked it for the boy. She thought it would be educational. She worries about him not being in school. She couldn't make up her mind about the cruise because she wasn't sure about taking him out of school and whether correspondence would be a quality alternative."

"With computers and the Internet, you don't need the classroom experience anymore," I said.

"That's what I told her. I went to the school of hard knocks, and I came out all right. Plus I told her to think about all the fine educational opportunities you get when you travel. So Eric told her the cruise would be okay. And then the kid wouldn't go on the pirate tour, even with the theme park. He missed out. Lily said it was a fine package. They had a good gift shop, too. But then things got out of hand. They didn't make it back to the ship."

"They didn't make the pickup in Callena?"

"There was no pickup in Callena," said Eddie. "They called out the army."

I was surprised they had an army.

"Or the coast guard maybe," Eddie said. "I don't know the details. They put roadblocks on the highway and made a curfew. The buses couldn't get through to Callena. The whole island is locked down."

This was all news to me, because I don't pay attention to world affairs. "I didn't hear about that," I said.

"Lily called me in the middle of the night."

I don't like that kind of thing. "It's a worrying thing when the phone rings in the middle of the night," I said.

"She called to tell me not to worry," said Eddie.

"They always say that after they wake you up," I said. "Your heart is racing by then."

"It depends where you are in your sleep cycle," said Eddie. "If you're in a deep sleep, it's disorienting when the phone rings. It takes you a minute to wake up and figure out what's what. But I was wide awake when Lily called." He shrugged like he was giving me the straight goods. "Old people don't sleep as much. I had the television on. Some crumby movie. Then Lily called to say that everything was under control."

"Still. She could have called earlier. Set your mind at ease."

Eddie wasn't bothered. "She called when she knew," he said. "All day they thought things would settle down and they'd open the roads. They gave up, finally, and she called to let me know they were stuck. It was a responsible thing to do."

"You had cell reception at least."

"Why wouldn't I?"

"They were having trouble before. The computers were slow."

"Was cell reception down?"

"I don't know. But it's the same set-up, I think."

He shrugged. "I don't know about those things. But they're staying at the Company compound until things settle down. It's a resort outside the city, with activities and accommodation."

"And it's part of the pirate tour?"

"It's not part of the pirate tour. It was the Company's fallback. It's a secure facility, with walls and gates and guards patrolling the perimeter."

"It sounds very well equipped."

"It was the smart move. They got everyone to a safe location, took them out of the line of fire. Plus the Company compound has tennis courts and swimming pools and restaurants. They put out a nice spread for lunch. Then they gave them a cocktail. Then dinner. There were fireworks at dusk, or crossfire outside the wall. Lily wasn't sure, but she said it was a fine display. And they found rooms for everyone, and handed out toothbrushes and floss."

"It sounds very comfortable."

Eddie was getting restless. He tried to sit up and couldn't. Then he settled back again and reached for his spritzer. He spritzed his face and put the spritzer down again and rearranged the towel on his legs. "I want them to get back to the ship," he said. "Mrs. Martin likes to have her family around her. She's fretting."

"They'll be back soon," I said, although I didn't know anything about it. "The Company will sort things out."

Eddie nodded and pulled up the towel and wiped off his glasses.

He put his glasses back on and spread the towel out over his legs again, and then he pushed it off.

"That's it for me," he said.

"You've had enough?"

"I've done my time."

"You want me to call a waiter over?" I said, because I liked Eddie, and I figured it was the least I could do.

"I'm ready to call it a day," said Eddie. He was trying to sit up again, but he wasn't making progress.

"I'll get someone to help you," I said, and I waved a waiter over. He had a tray with drinks and bottles, and he said he'd be back in a minute, and he went away again.

Eddie sat back and reached for his tote. He folded his towel and put it in his bag, and he packed up his sunscreen and his spritzer and his hat and his sunglasses. Then he sat in the lounger with the tote in his lap.

"How is Mrs. Martin?" I asked him, like I should have done first thing.

He shook his head. "She's a trooper," he said. "They've got her in Sick Bay. They put her in a private room. They keep an eye on her."

"They're very sharp in Sick Bay," I told him.

He nodded. "I think they're okay," he said. "Katherine's doing her best. She's tired and she's weak. She needs rest, regular meals. The medic keeps an eye on her. I go down in the morning, see how she slept, help her with breakfast. Lily spends time every day. She did. She will when she gets back. Or Eric. I take my dinner in Sick Bay. They send up a tray and I help Katherine with her soup. Sometimes we have a laugh." He stopped and thought for a minute.

"That's the way it should be," I said, because it sounded like love to me, and it was a beautiful thing, even though Eddie was old and pale and hairless and Katherine couldn't feed herself. It was the way I used to think Laureen and I would be at the end, looking after each other and loving each other. And that made me sad, too. So I didn't ask Eddie any more about it. But I told him I'd come down and say hello to Katherine sometime, and he said that would be okay.

The waiter came back again, and he gave Eddie a hand. It was a difficult operation, like I thought, because Eddie was weak and stiff, and I was glad I wasn't involved. But once he was on his feet, I got up, too, and shook his hand.

"You have a rest, kid," I told him. "Get your strength back. We'll see you later."

And he kind of waved at me and put his bag over his shoulder, and the waiter walked him to the elevators, and I didn't bump into Eddie again for a while.

○ ○ ○

I was still touring the facilities, trying to see all the sights. I kept the ship's specs in my pocket and I went to all the clubs and the lounges: the Bar Sinister, the Tropicana, the Geisha, the Local, the Catfish Lounge, the Quay Note, the Oasis. I skipped the Mosh Pit, which was a teen disco it turned out. Mature guests were welcome to stop by, but they only served soft drinks. So really there was no incentive. I went back to the Tropicana a lot. It was a crowd-pleaser. The waitresses wore grass skirts, and there was a big screen where you could watch the game. So I went there for a sundowner most days, and there was sometimes someone I knew hanging around.

One afternoon, Lou and Denise were at a table in front of the big screen and I hadn't caught up with them since Maromed. So I got a G and T and joined them. It was awkward it turned out. Lou was watching the ball game with intensity but the Bandits were embarrassing themselves. The bases were loaded and the Bandits' pitcher was throwing grapefruits. The a/c was going full blast, but Lou was sweating. And then the kid let a wild pitch loose and the runner on third walked home, and Lou made a little sound and put his head in his hands. After that it was difficult to get the conversation going.

Denise had paper with her and she was writing longhand. I thought she was sending letters to her friends, maybe, but she put me straight. "I'm writing a letter of complaint to the Company," she told me.

This was reasonable, because the buyer has the right to report back. But I thought she could be more efficient. "Why not send them an email?" I asked her, since it would be quicker.

"I'm drafting it," she said. "When I'm happy with it, yes, I will send it electronically."

So that was good. The pitching coach sent the kid to the showers and a relief pitcher came out. Lou lifted his head up like he had hope for a minute, and I watched, too. And then the next batter came up and blasted a home run out of the park. Lou put his head back in his hands, and I didn't like to watch, so I went up to the bar to get the other half, which I had to do anyway because they didn't have table service on. And then I came back and tried again with Denise.

"So what have you got to complain about anyway?" I said. I was trying to keep things light, because we were sitting on a cruise ship in the Caribbean with the a/c on and cold drinks, and things could have been worse. But Denise was in a mood.

"I am writing a letter of complaint about Port Esteban," she said.

"Don't get her started," said Lou. He still had his head in his hands.

"Well I think that's perfectly reasonable," I said.

"Thank you," said Denise, although she didn't sound grateful.

Lou didn't say anything and I had to keep the conversation rolling by myself. "Nobody signed up for a riot," I said. "And we aren't paying a premium to get shot at."

"I am writing to complain about the Company's participation in animal torture," said Denise.

This took me by surprise. "They torture animals?" I asked her.

"They took us to a cockfight," Denise said.

I laughed. "Oh," I said. "That."

Denise glared at me like it was my fault. "Yes," she said. "That."

"I told you not to get into it," Lou said.

"But that's cultural," I said. "Plus it's sport."

"It's disgusting," said Denise.

"And it's a gaming opportunity," I said.

Denise gave me a long look. "I don't think we're going to agree on this," she said.

I could also see that there was no point in talking about it. She had already made up her mind and wasn't interested in other perspectives. It was disappointing, because Denise had all her books and her notes and her cultural tours. She looked like a woman with an open mind. But when it came down to it, she couldn't see things from another person's point of view. She couldn't appreciate the culture of Port Esteban or the exotic entertainment opportunities the cruise director lined up for us. And frankly, if that was her attitude, I wasn't sure she belonged on a luxury cruise in the first place.

But I liked Lou and I liked Denise, even though I was disappointed by her attitude somewhat. So I finished my drink, and I watched the game with Lou. The Bandits went down in a landslide.

the captain's table

CHAPTER NINE

A few days after Port Esteban, I met up with Saskia and Leanne in the casino again. They had their hair up, and we were all in our best, and we had a drink, and I lost some money and refilled at the ATM, because I don't like to run low. Then I took them down to dinner in the Captain's Mess, one on each arm, like a player. And when we got out of the elevator in front of the Captain's Mess, Natalie and Ben stepped out of the elevator beside us.

It was good timing, and we were all happy to see each other. Ben had his tux on, sort of: he had the pants and the cummerbund like you would expect. But he left his shirt open at the top, and the tie loose around his neck, so no one would forget he got shot. He draped the jacket over his shoulders. It was a casual, elegant look, and I thought I might go for it myself sometime. In the meantime, I had a girl on each arm and cash in my pocket. I felt good. And the five of us made a big entrance into the foyer of the Captain's Mess.

Inside, there were only two hostesses, but they snapped to it. One girl picked up some menus, and Ashley was there and she was happy to see me.

She said, "Hey, Mr. Rutledge. You made it. Let me take you in." And she moved in to escort me. Right away Leanne dug in on my left, and Saskia kind of gripped also, and then she laughed and dropped my arm and caught up with Natalie and Ben. And then Leanne didn't like to be left behind and she let go of me and caught up with the others, too, and they all followed the first hostess into the dining room, and Ashley took my arm like she had planned at the beginning and pulled me in after everyone else.

It was irritating, because I was downsized from two to one. And although Ashley was younger, and in some ways much better looking than Saskia or Leanne, she was wearing her name tag, as expected, and she was only the hostess. So all in all, it just didn't make the same impression. But it turned out it didn't matter, because there was no one there to look at us, anyway.

Saskia and Ben and Natalie and Leanne all stopped just inside the dining room and looked around, and I caught up with them and looked around too. It was a strange thing, because it was usually so crowded and noisy, but that night, I could hear the waterfall running around the captain's table, which I never heard before when the room was full and everyone was enjoying themselves. Whole tables were empty, and other tables that were set for six or eight diners only had one or two people who looked lonely and sad.

Across the floor, I could see the J-kid at my table, rocking back and forth like always. But he was alone. Eddie and Katherine and Lily and Della and Steve and Eric were all AWOL. And although Lily was loud and obnoxious and Katherine had to be fed with a spoon, I thought it was better to sit with the whole family instead of just the J-kid. So I stalled, and I thought about what I wanted to do.

"Where is everyone?" I said.

"A lot of people are still at Port Esteban," said the other hostess. Her name tag said Jane.

"They still haven't sorted that out?" said Saskia.

"And some of our guests like to take advantage of the other dining options on board," said Ashley. "The Mariola has a variety of facilities, although the Captain's Mess is number one for fine dining." She smiled at me and squeezed my arm, and gave a little pull like she wanted to move me along. But I still hadn't made up my mind. So I shook her off, but nicely. I looked at Ben and the girls.

"Maybe we should take advantage of the other dining options on board, too," I said.

"It looks kind of quiet in here," said Saskia.

"It looks boring," said Natalie.

"I've had a plate of sandwiches in the casino sometimes," I said.

"I want a meal not a sandwich," Ben said.

"We could go to the Local, get some fish and chips," I said, because I thought it was a popular option with this crowd.

"But we're dressed now," said Leanne.

"You can wear what you want in the Local," I said, although I didn't know what their dress policy was.

Leanne frowned. "I never like to be overdressed," she said, and Natalie and Saskia nodded.

"I'm not changing again," said Ben.

"It took him an hour to get into his shirt," said Natalie.

"I had to take a painkiller," said Ben. He put his hand on his shoulder. "It's throbbing. I'm not getting good sleep."

"I don't want pub grub twice in a week," said Natalie.

"We have a great menu tonight," said Ashley. "We have a papaya theme."

I remembered. "I heard about that," I said. "I heard they flew the papaya in fresh."

"We did a special transport, from the Company plantation," said Ashley.

"Except." I had to think. "It came in a few days ago?"

"The 'Fly was at the plantation when the shooting started," Jane said. "They had to hold the transport and then redirect it. It made the ship finally."

"Chef Lousine designed this menu around papaya," said Ashley. "We had our fingers crossed the shipment would get through. Everyone cheered when the papaya landed."

"But it's not fresh off the tree," I said.

"It was harvested a few days ago, and we keep it in a controlled environment," said Ashley.

"We put it in the refrigerator," said Jane.

"It's the best papaya you ever tasted," said Ashley. "You get it at home, it's been in transport for two weeks, minimum."

"What's so great about papaya?" said Ben.

"It's an antioxidant," said Saskia. "They use it in facials sometimes."

"The salon took a crate," said Ashley. "It's a feature scrub this week. And the kitchen went to town with it. We have a papaya option in every course. There's a chilled fruit soup, a salad with papaya and almonds, ceviche cured in papaya and lime, lamb marinated in green papaya, and fresh papaya ice cream, made to order."

"I thought papaya was orange?" said Leanne.

"When it's ripe," Ashley said. "In the marinade, they use the unripe fruit. There's more acid. So it tenderizes the meat."

"I don't want to eat unripe fruit," said Natalie.

"It's only the marinade," said Ashley. "All the other dishes, the papaya is succulent. The compote, the ice cream. They're all made with ripe fruit."

"It sounds like a hell of a menu," I said. I looked at the others. "We could stay here. What do you think? Make our own fun."

"I don't like almonds," said Natalie.

"We have three salad options," said Ashley. "Only one of them has almonds. Or you can special order the salad with no nuts."

"Is there a charge for that?" I said.

Jane said, "Yes. Just like with any substitution."

"What if it's an allergy?" Natalie said.

"They need a certificate. You have to register with Sick Bay and the medic notifies the purser. Without the doctor's note, we can make the substitution, but we have to charge you." Jane was full of information for us, but all of it was bad.

"Even if it's medical?" said Natalie.

"It has to be documented is all," said Ashley. "But we can backdate it. You get the salad with the substitution now. Then you go up to Sick Bay whenever and register. The note goes into your account and the charge comes off."

Natalie thought about it. "Let's stay then," she said.

"Yeah. We'll have a private party," said Saskia. I was standing beside her, and she took my arm again, which was friendly. "You come and sit with us, honey," she said. "We've got a nice table up in the gallery. We'll pull up a chair."

This sounded like a fine arrangement. So I said okay, and we were ready to go. But Jane said no. "There are safety issues," she said.

"Eating with Rutledge?" said Ben.

I laughed like a good guy even though it wasn't funny. But Jane didn't budge.

"We can't put an extra chair at the table," she said. "It blocks the aisle. The waiters need unobstructed access. They're carrying big orders, hot food."

I looked around. There were about ten people in the restaurant. "There's plenty of elbow room, tonight," I said.

"It's workplace health and safety," she said. "Plus on a ship, with the surf and the movement." She made a face. "We have to be careful. People can get hurt."

I kept smiling even though she was making it difficult. "We made it through the riot," I said. "I'll take my chances with the soup."

"It's Company policy," she said.

I wasn't getting anywhere arguing with Jane. So I tried a different route. I said to Ben and the girls, "Why don't you come and sit with me? It's a table for eight, and there's only one guy there."

The girls were in favour. Leanne said, "That would be fun."

But Ben wouldn't go for it. "I have to sit in the gallery," he said. "I have responsibilities. I'm training one of the birds. It's tied to a tree beside our table. I'm teaching it to eat croutons out of my hand. Then I'm going to teach it to recite the Lord's Prayer."

"Honey, I don't think it's a talking bird," said Saskia.

"I've been working on it since we got on board," said Ben. "I'm making progress."

He nodded at Jane like he made up his mind, and he put his good arm around Natalie so we could all see he was taking her with him, and Leanne took his other arm that was bandaged up, and I noticed that he didn't flinch. He smiled at me, and Natalie smiled at me, and Leanne smiled at me, and they shrugged, like they wished things worked out better, but what could they do? I didn't care, because basically they were shallow, foolish people, but after all our good times in the Monte and the Dexter, and the drinks I bought everybody, I was not impressed that they cut me loose for a talking bird.

"But where is Rutledge going to sit?" said Saskia. She was still holding my arm. She was the only one of them who thought about other people sometimes. But it turned out Ashley was at the top of her game. So it didn't matter.

"Mr. Rutledge, are you still interested in sitting at the captain's table?" she said.

I looked over at the table. The captain wasn't there, but there were a couple of officers in their white uniforms. They looked sharp and professional in their kits. There weren't any other passengers with them, which was too bad, since I would have liked to sit with the movie star or the heiress or the entrepreneur. But it was still an attractive offer, much better than cramming an extra chair into a table for four and sitting with an unfriendly guy like Ben, who, you could tell, would want a lot of elbow room for himself, and would probably use his bum arm as an excuse not to pass the butter or pour the wine.

I gave it a minute, like I had to think about it, so that everyone had time to see what a good offer it was. Then I said, "That would be okay."

"I'll just check with the maitre d'," said Ashley.

She turned back to the foyer, and Ben said really fast, "I'd be interested in the captain's table, too." Because suddenly the talking bird didn't matter so much.

Ashley looked at me, which was only right since I was the one who took the initiative in the first place. And I took a minute to think about that too, because I wanted Ben to sweat. Then I was a nice guy, and I said, "Yeah. Sure. I'd like to take the whole party."

Ashley smiled and nodded. "I'll be right back," she said, and she went to take care of it.

I figured I'd have to find another tip for Ashley and something for the maitre d', and get a few bottles of wine for the table. So it was all going to cost me. But it was worth it to show Ben what a class act looked like. And the girls were excited.

"It's an privilege to sit at the captain's table," Saskia said. She gave my arm a squeeze.

Leanne was looking at the officers. There was the younger guy who was beside the captain the first night and another guy I didn't recognize.

"Hoss is here tonight," Leanne said.

She was pink and she made puppy eyes at Saskia, and Saskia took a second and then she smiled and nodded like it made her tired, and said, "You look good, honey."

"We might as well keep the officers company," Ben said. "Keep their spirits up. They've had some rough days." He said it like he'd looked at all the angles and decided finally.

Ashley came back with the maitre d'. He was solemn and impressive. He nodded at us and said, "Party of five for the captain's table."

"Party of five," I said.

He bowed us into the room. "Ladies, Mr. Rutledge, sir." Jane led the way and I let everyone get ahead, and I found a bill for the maitre d'. I slipped it into his hand and he pocketed it like he didn't notice, and then he went after the others.

I found a c-note for Ashley, too, and she said, "Thank you, Mr. Rutledge," like she should.

And I said, "No. Thank you. That was a very good suggestion."

And I didn't find anything for Jane, because she was looking for problems instead of solving them, and she needed to learn it wasn't how to do things.

I caught up with the group at the waterfall, and I said hello to the bouncers on duty around the space. They said, "How's it going?" and "Good to see you," and they waved us up the stairs. They were much more welcoming and friendly than they looked from across the floor. And then the officers saw us coming, and put down their cutlery and stood up, and a waiter rolled up and a busboy who rearranged the plates and the chairs while the maitre d' introduced everyone and we all shook hands across the table. "Mr. Rutledge, First Officer Hoskins, Chief Warrant Officer Warraich, Mr. and Mrs. Kozak, Ms. Guzman, Ms. Saunders." I was impressed that he knew everyone's name. It was just one more way the staff was coming through for me, and I had a good feeling again about the ship and the crew and the whole ball of wax.

"Now this is such a treat for us," said Saskia.

"No. It's our lucky day," said Hoskins, who was the first officer, so it made sense he was sitting at the captain's table. And although I would have been happy to get to know Captain Moncrieff, the first officer was an important man also, and the girls were tickled. "We don't see enough of you ladies," he said. He smiled and nodded at the girls. "Ms. Saunders, Ms. Guzman. I haven't seen you since orientation. I thought I scared you off." Although he didn't look worried. He smiled a big white smile and pulled out the chair beside him.

Leanne was first off the mark. She ran around the table faster than was sophisticated and got the chair Hoskins was holding, and Saskia went around the other way. She didn't look as motivated but she covered the distance and got the seat on his other side. The rest of us looked around for where we wanted to be.

The chairs were all in a row at the back of the table, with everyone facing the rest of the room, like the head table at a wedding. That way, all the other diners had a good view of the captain's guests, when there were other diners in the room to look at them. We ended up with the other officer, Warraich, sitting at one end, then Natalie, me, Leanne, Hoskins, Saskia, and Ben. I thought we made a good show, with the women looking their very best, me in my tux, the two officers, and Ben with his loose tie and his injury. Although the arrangement wasn't ideal for conversation.

"I hear there's a papaya theme tonight," I said. I wanted to open up a general topic, but nobody was listening. Leanne was all over Hoskins. Saskia was smiling and comfortable. She watched Leanne work. At the far end, Ben was consulting with the waiter, who was pointing out menu items and punching things into his handheld already. On my right, the other officer, Warraich, was working on Natalie. He got her going right away by asking about her tattoos. She had a vine or a chain tattooed on her wrist and up her arm. It was just the starter. Then she showed him her shoulder and her ankle. She gave him the tour. She was wearing a dress with no back and she sat on the edge of her seat and pulled her dress down at the waist to show him the tattoo in the small of her back. Warraich leaned in for a better view. They didn't care about papaya.

I told the waiter, "I'll take a G and T for starters." And he nodded and went off to the bar. I had a look at the wine list, and when the sommelier came, I ordered a magnum of Brut, because it was an occasion. And I got a couple of bottles of Chablis and a Malbec and a South African red I'd been wanting to try. "For the table," I told him, and he said, "Very nice, sir," and went to see about it. When the waiter came back with my drink, I ordered the complete papaya dinner.

the captain's table

"The kitchen will be so pleased," the waiter said.

Natalie ordered too. Warraich already had his salad, but he didn't go back to it until we all had something in front of us, which I thought was good manners. I asked him about his duties on the ship, and he started telling me about the engine and the crankshaft, but when Natalie finished ordering she yawned and played with her napkin. She was the kind of girl who needed to be in the centre of things, and if no one was looking at her she wasn't having a good time. But Warraich came through for her. He wrapped up the turbines and went back to tattoos, and this also impressed me. They moved on to henna and piercing. Natalie got started on a bad infection experience, and I didn't like to listen.

On my left, the waiter was trying to squeeze an order out of Leanne, but she was slow.

"I just need a minute," she told him.

"Of course, ma'am," he said, and he backed up and Leanne pretended to look at the menu, and then she put it down and went back to Hoskins.

"Oh, no, Leanne," I told her. "You look at that menu. Mr. Hoskins's soup will go cold if you don't decide soon."

"It's a chilled soup," Hoskins said.

"Or it will warm up," I said.

"How is the soup?" said Saskia. The waiter was hovering between her and Leanne, waiting patiently.

"Chef Lousine knows his fruit," said Hoskins. "He has the touch."

He was kind of laughing while he said it, and I didn't know whether he liked the soup or not. I thought maybe he was being sarcastic and I wondered if I should change my order. But that was a step backward, and I wanted forward progress. I wanted Saskia and Leanne to make up their minds so the kitchen could get on it and the waiter could bring out the appetizers. I opened the menu in front of Leanne and I leaned around her.

"What do you recommend for the girls, Mr. Hoskins?" I said.

He gave me a big white smile. "They call me 'Hoss,'" he said.

"What do you think, Hoss?" I said. I felt foolish calling him 'Hoss,' but I thought it would speed up the process. "What would the ladies like?"

Hoskins pulled the menu in front of him like he was willing to think about it, but he wasn't in a hurry. "What to do? What to do?" he said. "It depends. I need to do some research before I can answer the question. A little fact-finding."

I thought he probably filled up on rolls already. I took one myself and looked around for butter, and right away the waiter brought me a dish with little scoops of butter sitting on ice chips, and he got out some tongs and put two balls of butter on my side plate. And he snapped his fingers at the busboy who ran away and came back with baskets of more rolls that were fresh and hot. I took a hot roll and put the cold one back, and the waiter cleared the old bread off the table.

In the meantime Hoskins did his research. He sat back in his chair and looked hard at Saskia.

"Are you a girl with a sweet tooth?" he asked her. "Or do you like it hot?"

Saskia laughed. She was lazy and relaxed and she liked a little kidding around. Hoskins didn't wait for her to answer. He turned around to Leanne.

"Are you salty or sweet?" he said. He was smiling his big white smile. "You're not a sour puss are you? You're not bitter?"

"You mean what I eat?" Leanne said. She was thinking hard. You could see where the lines would set on her forehead.

Hoskins turned back to the menu and kind of scanned it. "I need honest answers, ladies," he said. "I can't proceed without them."

"I'm on the Jersey plan," said Leanne. She found her purse and pulled a little book out and tried to show Hoskins. He smiled at her, but he didn't look at it.

The busboy started handing out proper flutes, then, and the sommelier came back with a bucket and the Brut. He made a show with the wire and the cork, and he didn't spill a drop. I liked his style. He moved down the table pouring out the glasses. Ben poured the wine down his throat, so the sommelier went back to him once everyone had a glass and topped him up. I didn't think he took the right approach to an expensive bottle. And no one had said anything to me. So I said to everyone, "I thought we'd all enjoy a Brut."

"I always like a Brut," said Saskia.

Leanne looked up from her diet book. "Is this an occasion?" she said.

I held my glass up. "To the *Mariola*. Warm winds and safe harbours," I said. I thought it sounded large and good-spirited.

Saskia said, "Cheers, honey," and Hoskins said, "Calm seas," and Leanne said, "Cheers," and everyone went back to what they were doing before.

Saskia was smiling at Hoskins. "I'm a carnivore, honey," she said. "I like something robust."

"You like an intense dining experience?" said Hoskins.

"I like flavour, depth," said Saskia.

They had a good long look at each other. It put me off my hot roll. I liked Saskia, but I felt that Hoskins brought out a different side of her.

"The Jersey plan makes you rotate through the food groups," said Leanne. She was flipping pages. "I'm on week seven. Protein and unrefined carbs."

Hoskins said, "It sounds very scientific." He didn't look at her but she was reading and didn't notice.

"It *is* scientific," she said. "It's all based on kinetics. It's the first diet I've ever liked."

"You look good, honey," said Saskia. She looked away from Hoskins and smiled at Leanne. "You must have lost fifteen, twenty pounds."

"I feel healthy is the important thing," Leanne said.

"What's the holdup down there," Ben shouted. "Let's get a move on people. I want my dinner."

Natalie looked up. "You can wait," she shouted back at him. "You had a big pizza for lunch."

"I'm healing. I need regular meals," said Ben.

Natalie went back to Warraich. He had one ankle crossed over the other knee and his pants rolled up to show the tattoos on his leg. Natalie kept one hand on his knee and the other on his ankle while she checked out detail. Ben looked at her and shrugged. He looked at Hoskins and pointed at his shoulder.

"I took a bullet at Port Esteban," he said.

"You got caught in it?" said Hoskins.

"We were right on the dock," said Ben.

Hoskins raised his glass. "Men of the front lines, we salute you," he said.

I still wasn't sure about him. He didn't sound fully respectful. I didn't respect Ben, either, but he was a paying customer, and I thought Hoskins shouldn't laugh at him.

"We were there too, honey," said Saskia.

"And women," said Hoskins. He went back to the menu and ran his finger over the page, then stopped and tapped at it and gave Saskia a serious look. "For you, I recommend an appetizer of chicken livers, and the papaya lamb for a main course, with a side of basmati. Does it come with basmati?" he asked the waiter.

"It comes with basmati and a compote of papaya and tamarind," said the waiter.

"The basmati soaks up the juices," said Hoskins. "You get every drop."

"That's what I like, honey," said Saskia.

The waiter punched it into his handheld and Hoskins turned around to Leanne. He looked serious.

"I'm not familiar with the Jersey plan," he said.

"It's the island," said Leanne. "Not the state."

"And you want carbs?" said Hoskins. He took the book and opened it up, but he didn't really study it.

"I'm on week seven," said Leanne.

the captain's table

~ 133 ~

The sommelier came back, then, with the Chablis and the reds, and I had to check the bottles. The busboy put out more glasses, and again the sommelier made a fine show with the opener and the corks, and then pouring out the tasting glasses. It kept me busy for a few minutes, because there were several bottles, and I never like to take anything for granted. It keeps the service sharp. But eventually I gave the wine waiter the nod like he should offer everything around, and he went over to Saskia and Ben and started pouring. When he got back to me, I took a glass of the white for my soup and the appetizer.

Hoskins snapped the diet book shut and went back to the menu. He told Leanne a wheat berry salad to start and grilled swordfish for the main course, and she said okay, although she didn't sound enthusiastic. The waiter took the menus away, and the food started pulling up fast, like it should. The soup was cold and sweet, but I ate it anyway.

Hoskins looked down at Ben. "So you took a bullet in Port Esteban," he said.

"It's just a flesh wound," said Ben.

"Did you get a medical opinion on it?" said Hoskins.

"I went to Sick Bay," said Ben.

"Outstanding," said Hoskins. "You talked to the nurse?"

"The doctor looked at it."

"Doctor Dan is the best," said Hoskins.

"He cleaned it up," said Ben. "But he wrecked my shirt."

Natalie looked up from Warraich's ankle for a minute. "Would you please get over your shirt," she said.

"It was my favourite one," said Ben.

Hoskins kept smiling like he got a kick out of Ben and Natalie bickering. "Did you score any meds?" he said.

"Painkillers and antibiotics," said Ben.

"That's too bad," said Hoskins. "Antibiotics are no fun." He frowned. "Should you be drinking?"

"It's only wine," said Ben. "The percentage is so low you barely get a hit out of it." He was still holding the champagne glass.

"That's no way to talk about a good Brut," said Hoskins. But he laughed like he was just kidding around. "Are you going to have a scar?"

Leanne followed every word Hoskins said and Saskia was lazy and serene. But I wondered how long we were going to talk about Ben's bullet.

"I think so," Ben said. "I didn't ask the medic, but I think I will probably."

"Women go crazy for scars," Hoskins said.

"Oh yeah?" said Ben. He sat up a little straighter.

"I knew a guy who had fourteen bullet holes," said Saskia.

Hoskins whistled. "Fourteen?"

"Did you go crazy for them?" Ben asked her.

She didn't say. But she smiled and told us again, "Fourteen. I counted."

The busboy cleared away the soup plates. Then the waiter brought out the salads, and Saskia's chicken livers came up. The sommelier jumped up with the reds and Saskia took a glass of the Malbec, which I thought was a good choice. My salad was cold and sweet, like the soup, with fruit and sugared nuts. I thought I should have ordered the wheat berry salad, like Leanne, maybe, although I didn't know what wheat berries were, because I felt like I was eating candy for dinner. Natalie had the same thing, but she didn't complain. Warraich had his pants rolled down again, but his sleeve was pushed up as he showed Natalie his arm, and she was looking and laughing and eating her salad.

"I'm glad you counted," Hoskins said. "You have to verify a big number like that. You can't trust a man who tells you he has fourteen bullet holes. Not without an independent audit."

"They were all there," said Saskia.

"Where?" said Leanne.

"All over," Saskia said. She was concentrating on her chicken livers.

the captain's table

"These are wonderful," she said to Hoskins, kind of privately. Then, for all of us, she said, "Mostly on his legs. A couple on his hip. One on his arm."

"Was he military, law enforcement?" said Hoskins.

"Derek is a stockbroker," said Saskia.

"Disappointed clients?" I asked her. I felt like shooting my broker sometimes, although I always held back.

"His ex-wife," Saskia said.

I wished she hadn't. I thought about Laureen, and the cold hard look she gave me the last time I saw her. Not that I knew it was going to be the last time. If I had a choice, I'd wish she shot me fourteen times instead, because you get medical attention and you heal, and you can still talk and work things out and be a family together, instead of a pathetic loser buying champagne for strangers so he doesn't have to sit alone and think about all the people he loved who left him forever. I held out my glass and the wine waiter filled me up.

"That must have been some divorce," said Hoskins.

"We're all friends now," said Saskia.

I pushed my salad away, and a busboy cleared my plate.

Hoskins sighed. "Marriage is a minefield," he said.

Leanne looked worried all at once. "Are you married, Hoss?" she said.

"I'm married to the sea," said Hoskins. "She's wild and willful. I follow where she leads."

On my other side Natalie was looking around for the waiter, who stepped up right away. "Are these almonds?" Natalie asked him. She had an almond speared on her fork and she was holding it up to him.

"The salad is baby greens with papaya and almonds," the waiter said.

"I wanted it without almonds," said Natalie.

The waiter snapped his fingers and a busboy came to take the plate away. "I'm so sorry, Mrs. Kozak," he said. "We'll make a new salad up right away."

Natalie put the fork down, but she held onto her plate. "I ate it already," she said.

Me and Natalie and the waiter and the busboy all looked at the plate. There was lettuce still and spinach, and the almond on her fork, but you could see she had made good headway. For a minute, no one said anything.

Finally the waiter said, "I apologize, madam. I didn't know you wanted your salad without nuts."

"I told the other girl," said Natalie. "I don't like spinach, either."

"It was a procedural error," the waiter said. "The information was never passed along to the kitchen. I am so sorry."

Natalie made a snorting sound. She was unimpressed, and so was I. I was unhappy with the way things were working out, with Ben being ungrateful about the wine and Hoskins taking a disrespectful attitude to the passengers. And then Natalie's salad.

"Your staff needs to learn effective communication," I told the waiter.

"Yes, Mr. Rutledge," he said. "I'll take care of it personally."

"It's a medical issue," I said. "Allergies are dangerous."

"You have an allergy?" the waiter said to Natalie. He sounded worried finally.

"But I didn't sign up at Sick Bay so no one cares," Natalie said.

The waiter gestured at one of the busboys. "Get the EpiPen," he said. And the busboy went off at top speed.

"That's right," I told the waiter. "It's a serious thing."

"We'll make a note on your file, Mrs. Kozak," he said. He was punching buttons on his handheld, like the most important thing was getting his records straight. "This won't happen again."

"It shouldn't happen once even," I told him.

"It's regrettable, sir," he said. He signalled to the sommelier. "Let me offer you another glass of Brut," he said to Natalie. "To clear the palate."

Natalie didn't say anything, but she lifted her head like she might take an interest. For Natalie, the attention and special treatment mattered.

And the staff totally came through. The waiter nodded at the somme-lier, and the sommelier nodded back at the waiter and rushed away. The busboy came back with the EpiPen and gave it to the waiter. He held it out to Natalie like he was showing her a bottle of wine.

"Are you feeling any symptoms, Mrs. Kozak?" he asked her.

"Of what?" she said.

"Anaphylactic shock?" he said.

"I've got a little buzz going," Natalie said.

The waiter punched it into his handheld again. The sommelier came back again with another bottle of Brut. He opened the wires and popped the cork, and Warraich and the waiter and the busboy and me all watched him fill up Natalie's glass. She took a sip. Then she pushed her salad plate away.

"I don't need to look at this," she said.

She was giving orders again, which made me hopeful.

"Of course, madam," said the waiter, and he cleared it and handed it off to the busboy. He hung around beside Natalie. "I hope the rest of the meal is more satisfactory," he said.

"Me too," said Natalie.

Then she had another sip of the Brut and went back to Warraich, like she made up her mind not to let the bad service wreck her evening. And Warraich kicked in like a gentleman, and started telling her about historical tattoos and sailors in the South Seas.

The waiter brought out my seafood, then, and he leaned down between me and Leanne. "I am so sorry about Mrs. Kozak's salad, Mr. Rutledge," he said. He kept his voice down. "The meal is already a part of your cruise package, of course. But I hope that you'll let me take the wine off your bill, to apologize for the incident."

I said, "That will be fine," because it was a substantial savings for me. But I didn't crack a smile or say anything grateful, because it was only right and the least he could do. I started in on the ceviche. It had papaya in it, and I'd had enough fruit already. So I pushed it to the edge of the plate. Except for that, the dish was sharp with the citrus and the onions and peppers. It made a nice change.

The waiter stayed hunched over beside me. "I've got the EpiPen in my pocket," he whispered. "Just in case."

And I nodded again and he finally stood back and let me concentrate on my food.

In the meantime, the wine waiter went around with the fresh magnum and topped everyone up.

"Are we having another toast?" said Leanne.

She looked at Hoskins like he was in charge. He raised his glass. "To Derek and his full recovery," he said.

I was happy to go back to other topics. "So what happened to him?" I asked Saskia. "Was he injured?"

"He was shot fourteen times," Ben said. "It's got to hurt."

Saskia nodded. "He needed surgery, a transfusion, pins in his legs."

"I am in awe of the medical sciences," said Hoskins. "They can do anything these days. You talk to Doctor Dan sometime. He has stories to tell."

"Then he had physio for a year," said Saskia. "The only thing they couldn't fix was some nerve damage in his left hand."

"Was he left-handed?" I said.

"Doesn't matter," said Ben. He shrugged his bad shoulder. "You take a bullet in your wing, it doesn't matter if it's your main engine or not. You're not working at full power."

Saskia nodded. "His golf game never really came back. It was frustrating for him."

"But when you think about it," Hoskins said. "The wonder is that he survived."

"Was she really trying?" I said.

"She was trying, honey," said Saskia. "She never shot a gun before."

Hoskins made a clucking noise. "She should have practiced, taken lessons maybe," he said. "A little foresight yields significant results."

the captain's table

"It was a spontaneous thing," said Saskia.

I finished my ceviche except for the papaya, and I pushed the plate up, and the busboy took it away. The waiter came around again with the wine, setting everyone up for the main course. I took a glass of the South African red, because I was looking forward to trying it. And I was glad to see the girls take an interest. Saskia stuck with the Malbec and Leanne took a top up of the white. Natalie and Warraich were laughing and snorting. Warraich had his shirt out and the waistband of his pants pulled down, and Natalie was leaning in for a better view. But they both nodded at the waiter to fill them up when they noticed him, and I was happy that Natalie got over the almonds and enjoyed herself like she should.

But Ben and Hoskins disappointed me. Ben kept going with the white, even though he ordered red meat. He said it was a better fit with his meds. And he was glaring at Natalie and Warraich and not noticing his food anyway. And Hoskins put his hand over his glass, which I thought was priggish. I tried to encourage him, but he gave me his big smile and said, "I've got a duty shift coming up. I need to stay sharp."

Then the entrees came out, and I was happy again. Everything looked elegant and top of the line, and the waiters made a show, putting out the plates and grinding the pepper. We all dug in. The lamb was first-rate, but I didn't warm up to the South African red. It was pissy and thin, and I didn't feel like wasting my time on it. I flagged the sommelier down again, but he'd already poured out the last of the Malbec for Natalie. So I asked for the wine list again and I figured what the hell, because it was on the house after the spinach and the almonds and the EpiPen. So I ordered a Grand Cru and another Chablis, too, because Ben was knocking it back and Leanne was having fish.

"They're two different things, though," Ben said. "Taking a bullet from your wife and taking one in a riot situation."

"Statistically, you're more likely to take a bullet from a friend or family member," said Hoskins.

"You beat the odds, honey," Saskia told Ben.

The statistics troubled me. "It just doesn't make sense," I said. "The people you love should be the last people to hurt you."

"You spend more time with your family," said Saskia. "They have more opportunity."

"Opportunity, hell," said Hoskins. "They have more cause. What I find strange is that people don't see it coming."

"He thought she'd get a lawyer, not a gun," said Saskia.

The sommelier came back with the new supply and I had to check the bottles again and admire his work with the cork and taste it. I was getting tired of the whole process. But the Grand Cru was very fine, so I had a glass of wine to enjoy finally. The waiters topped everyone up, and even Hoskins took a splash. We were all pretty lit by then.

I said, "Would you rather be shot by a stranger or a friend?"

"It depends which friend," said Hoskins. "I have buddies on the security squad. I can't count on them missing fourteen times. I'd rather take my chances with a stranger."

"I'd have been safer if Tallie took a shot at me," said Ben. "I've seen her play darts."

The wait staff was circling around, clearing the plates. When all the dishes were gone and the rolls and the salt and the Parmesan, the busboy went around with a little brush and a pan and swept up the crumbs. We finished the wine, and I felt sleepy and relaxed. We were all starting to come down again. When the waiter gave us dessert menus, I passed. But I ordered coffee and a cognac, because it was the best part of the meal, when everyone is tired and happy. I wanted to enjoy the moment. The girls were studying the dessert cards. Leanne ordered papaya ice cream, made to order.

"Is that on the Jersey plan?" Ben asked her.

Leanne sat up taller. "It's fruit," she said.

Saskia ordered pear tart and extra plates and forks so she could share, and Ben and Natalie ordered trifle to split. Ben got up and walked

the captain's table

around the table and stood on top of Warraich, staring down at him, and Warraich stood up and tucked his shirt in and went around to Ben's chair, and Ben sat down beside Natalie. When it all arrived, Saskia asked who wanted pastry, and Leanne said yes right away. She took some on the plate with her ice cream, and ate it all in three bites. Then she said she had to go to the head, which she called the little girls' room, and me and Hoskins and Warraich stood up like gentlemen, and Ben didn't notice.

Saskia took her time with her dessert, eating little bites and enjoying them. She asked me if I wanted some, and I passed, and she said, "You've got to help me out with this, Hoss," and he smiled at her and said, "Twist my arm." She cut a little piece and put it on a plate for him with a fork, and they whispered together. I drank my cognac and Warraich drank decaf. Then Leanne came back and finally everyone was done.

I felt tired and full, but satisfied overall with the kitchen and the wait staff, because although there had been issues, everything was all right in the end, with the food and the wine and the sophisticated conversation, and that was the most important thing.

"That was a fine dinner," I told the waiter. "My compliments to the chef."

"I'll be sure to tell the kitchen," said the waiter.

"No. Tell the chef," I told him. "Tell Chef Lousine it was a fine meal." I had an idea. "Ask him to join us, if he isn't too busy. I'd like to say hello, congratulate him on his efforts. He did fine work with the papaya tonight."

"He'll be delighted to hear it," said the waiter, but he looked uncomfortable and he didn't snap to it. I thought I knew what he was waiting for.

"Invite him to the table for a cognac," I told him. I found a bill for him and he took it, like he should.

But then he said, "Unfortunately Chef Lousine isn't in the kitchen."

"He skipped out early?" I said. "What if someone wants a midnight snack?"

The waiter didn't say anything, and Hoskins said, "He's still at Port Esteban."

This was a bombshell. "We marooned the chef?" I said.

"He's at the Company plantation," said Hoskins.

"He was supervising the papaya," said the waiter. "They were supposed to do another run."

"In the end, we couldn't send the 'Fly back," said Hoskins. "We needed it for security."

"But is he coming back?" I asked them.

"We'll get him back," said Hoskins. "We're looking at air lifts."

"Will you air lift the passengers?" said Saskia.

"The Company has a top flight security protocol," Hoskins said.

"I saw the news last night," said Ben. He threw his spoon down. "Port Esteban's up in smoke. It was the lead story everywhere."

Hoskins didn't try to deny it. "It's a serious situation," he said.

"I'm surprised the tours are still on the island," said Saskia.

"Everyone's safe," said Hoskins. "The Company's on it, the island government, the relevant NGOs. It will be under control in a couple of days. Your friends will be back in no time."

The waiter brought me the damage and I signed without looking because there wasn't much for them to bill me for with the all-inclusive and the free wine. But I made sure I wrote in a decent tip because we had good service except for the nuts. I gave the chit back and the waiter said thank you and bowed at me.

And Saskia said, "That was a wonderful evening, honey. Thank you very much."

I told her it was my pleasure. "But it's early still," I said. "We should go for a nightcap." I looked around the table. "I want to try the Oasis. What do you say?"

Ben shook his head and stood up. "I need a painkiller," he said.

"He didn't sleep last night," Natalie said.

"I got a couple of hours," Ben said.

Natalie stood up and steered Ben away from the table. Neither of them bothered to say thank you, which I could have predicted, but it was still disappointing. Natalie turned around at the waterfall, and I thought maybe she remembered her manners.

"Mani-pedi tomorrow?" she said to Saskia.

"Two o'clock," Saskia said.

"See you there," Natalie said, and she followed Ben across the moat and down the stairs.

There was no one else in the dining room by then, and the waiters and busboys were standing around, folding napkins and blowing out candles.

"What do you say, girls?" I said.

"I'm done in," Saskia said. "A good meal always knocks me on my can, honey."

"Maybe Turkish coffee," I said. "You'll get a second wind."

"Another time, honey," said Saskia.

And Hoskins said he had to be sharp for his shift, and again I thought he was probably not as tough a man as he pretended. But Leanne said it was the best offer she had and Warraich said he'd come up for a hookah. So we all got up and crossed the moat, and security waved us out and the wait staff said good night, and Hoskins said it was a pleasure to see me at the captain's table and he hoped we'd do it again some time, which was polite and the way it should be. At the elevators, Saskia went down with Hoskins, and Warraich and Leanne and I went up to the Oasis.

It was a fine, exotic facility, at the top of the aft section of the ship, with an indoor area done up like a tent with low banquettes around the walls and low tables and cushions and carpets, and an outdoor section with a fountain and reflecting pools and sweet herbs growing in low beds everywhere. I had another cognac and Leanne had chai, even though it wasn't on the Jersey plan, and Warraich smoked a hookah.

The padre was there, looking fierce. He had a telescope and a note-book, and he took sightings and made notes. Leanne asked if he could tell her zodiac and he said he was charting our course. I was surprised because I thought the *Mariola* had GPS for that kind of thing. And he said, "The stars move constantly but they constantly remain." Again, I didn't know what he meant exactly, but I liked his style. And it was peaceful and the breeze was cool. So I enjoyed my drink and then I signed for everything and made a run for it before Leanne got ideas. Because she was a nice girl, but needy, and I wasn't interested.

the entrepreneur

After a few days, my new routine was wearing thin. In the fitness facility the novelty was gone. The exercises were difficult and they took a bite out of the day. Plus I saw no payoff. My shorts were binding around my thighs. They chafed me and I had to walk wide to avoid irritation. And at night, the collar on my dress shirt choked me still. I took my concerns to Sarah, my personal trainer. I told her about how sore I was, but she didn't take a hint and slow down. She had a drill sergeant side to her I didn't take to.

On the social side of things, I also began to feel disappointed in some respects. For example, I found Natalie and Ben on the pool deck in front of the Slaker one day. They were in the hot tub with other people and it looked like an attractive group. Everybody was noisy and talking. So I took my drink and climbed in. I figured Ben and Natalie would introduce me. But I was wrong. Natalie was bickering with a guy and didn't notice, and Ben was watching her and pitying himself.

"No, I didn't," she said.

"You said you did," the other guy said. "With a magician."

"He was a matador," said Natalie.

"Aha!"

Natalie splashed at him, and everyone lifted their drinks to keep them out of the wave while he slid under the water and surfaced again and sprayed us all when he shook his hair back. I smiled like I was enjoying myself, even though I had water in my drink and in my eye. Ben moved up to the ledge and checked the dressings on his arm. I could see the edges were green and crusty, and there was a pink foam sort of oozing through the bandage.

I said, "You want to look after that," and Ben nodded like he was listening, and he kept his eye on Natalie. She was showing the noisy guy the tattoo on her shoulder. And then Ben got out of the hot tub and walked away.

Ben and Natalie weren't good hosts. They didn't make you feel welcome and at home, which I thought was rude and ungrateful after I took them up to the captain's table and bought them wine and champagne and cognac. But people don't always come through for you, and that's why you should never depend on other people to make you happy, and you have to develop your own resources instead. So I made myself comfortable and enjoyed the scenery.

On the bench to my left, there was a girl with sunglasses. Her hair was slicked back, and she was sleek and tanned, and her bikini top was lying on the deck behind her. I thought with another good wave, I would get a fine perspective on events. Then she took off her sunglasses and reached for the sunblock, and one of the guys asked if he could have some, and she said, "Get your own." She sounded like she wanted to pick a fight, and I realized it was Jen, who I didn't recognize with glasses.

I had concerns on Maromed about Jen getting ideas about me, and I didn't want to give her false hope, but it's good manners and good policy to be polite to people, something Natalie and Ben didn't know. And Jen was young and entertaining, and she squeezed some sunscreen in her hand and rubbed lotion on her face and neck and her shoulders and breasts. So I was happy to see her and I asked her what she'd been up to.

"It's been crazy," she said. "I just got back on board."

"Is that right?" I said. "You got caught at Port Esteban?" I was interested because I hadn't heard anything for a while, and I was happy to get an update and hear some good news.

But she said, "Like I'd go to Port Esteban. It's a dump."

Natalie straightened up across from me. "The gaming tour was a laugh." She said it like she was hitting back.

"I heard it was a laugh riot. I was sorry I missed out," Jen said. She was fully sarcastic.

Natalie gave her the stink eye and sat up taller in the tub, although she had a bathing suit on, so there was no payoff for the casual observer. But you could see that she was ready to give it right back to Jen if it came down to it, and I thought it was strange that they didn't get along because they had so much in common. They were both young and attractive and they liked to lie in the sun and talk to people. But then since they lived on the same turf, I could see how they might fight and compete. It was too bad, though, because it was a sunny day and we had many good things to enjoy. So I kept talking to smooth things over, like it seemed I always had to do when I bumped into Jen.

"I wonder when the other tours are coming back," I said. "I never heard how they sorted it out, and I had friends on the pirate tour and the tour of the fort."

The kid splashing Natalie said, "Are they hostages?"

I don't like it when a kid with no hair on his chest interrupts me. So I didn't waste time. "The fort was a tour," I said. "It has a good gift shop apparently. When the trouble started the Company guides took all the tours to the Company compound in the interior. It's very complete, like you'd expect, with a pool and security and tennis courts." I smiled around at everyone so they wouldn't worry. "I just haven't heard when they're coming back to the ship."

"They aren't back yet?" Jen said.

I looked around the pool deck. There were dozens of loungers and just a handful of people taking the sun. "I don't think so," I said.

She shrugged. "I just came back this morning."

"I didn't know we made port," I said.

"We didn't," Natalie said. "We've been cruising too long. It's getting dull."

"You have to make your own fun," said Jen.

"But how did you get back on board?" I asked her.

"He chartered a helicopter," said Jen.

I didn't know who she meant, but I was interested in the transport. "You booked a Dragonfly?" I asked her. "That sounds like a fine option."

"Was it safe?" asked the splashing guy.

"It's top of the line technology," I said.

"We had blue skies," said Jen.

"I've been thinking of booking a 'Fly myself, at the next port of call maybe," I said. "I don't like the tender."

"It's hard for old people sometimes," the splasher said. I ignored him.

"So where did you go?" I asked Jen.

She smiled a little cat smile. "We took a few days in Martinique," she said. "It was Fredelle's birthday and he wanted to do something special for her."

I didn't know Fredelle, but I nodded anyway. I was impressed that Jen had been to Martinique. I didn't know she had such good connections and I was glad I was always nice to her, without encouraging her, because she was obviously someone who could go places socially.

I did a little digging. "You've got a place on Martinique, Jen?" I asked her.

"He borrowed it from Sam," she said. I also didn't know who Sam was, but there was no point in quibbling.

"And it was a birthday party?" I said.

"Fredelle turned twenty-one. It was nice."

the entrepreneur

"With all her friends around. That's nice."

"He likes to make her happy."

"That's the way it should be," I said, although I still didn't know who the hell we were talking about. "Did you do anything special?"

"Fredelle likes old dance music. He flew Beulah Jones in for a surprise."

"Are they still alive?" said Natalie.

"The ones who are," said Jen.

"That's class," I said.

"She'll always remember it," said Jen.

A big group of people came out of the Slaker then and started re-arranging the furniture. There were a couple of waiters and a steward and the cruise director with her clipboard. They folded up several loungers and hauled them away, and when they were done there was a little private island of four loungers by the pool and some side tables and several security boys hanging around in the background, looking large and keeping the gawkers away. And then the entrepreneur came out with a blonde and a brunette, and another steward behind them carrying a towel and a hat, and a waiter from the Slaker with a tray of drinks.

Jen said, "I should say hello."

She got out of the hot tub and patted at herself with a towel, but not too much, so she was still sleek and shining, and went over to the entrepreneur and his gang, and security waved her through. I finally put it together and realized that Jen went to Martinique with the entrepreneur, and I took my hat off to her, because he was certainly the guy to impress on the *Mariola*, and she got into his inner circle in just a few weeks, which was an achievement.

Natalie couldn't watch. She kept her eye on the horizon instead, like she was looking for land. But the other kids and I all watched Jen head over to the big man and say hello. He and his gang were all settled in loungers by then. He was in the middle with the blonde on one side and the brunette on the other. And Jen perched on the edge of his lounger and chatted for while, and then she jumped up and came jiggling back.

"So they're not such big pals after all," said Natalie, who looked after all and was satisfied Jen hadn't settled in.

But she was only back for a minute to pick up her sunscreen and put her bikini top on. She pulled the straps straight and said, "He likes it. But Fredelle doesn't."

When she went back to them, I thought she would stretch out on an empty lounger, but she made herself comfortable on the side of the entrepreneur's again and kept it up for the rest of the afternoon. Natalie couldn't take it. She left the pool deck, and the splashing guy went with her.

I sat back and enjoyed my drink and the sun. I concentrated on the good things around me, because I was paying top dollar and I had a right to pleasure, and I didn't need to waste my time on kids and their foolishness.

the purser

CHAPTER ELEVEN

After a few days like that, I was ready for a change. I wanted a beach or a quiet bar on shore and a pretty girl I could enjoy myself with for a few hours. In my room, I sat down at the computer to see what kind of options I had at the ports of call. It took me a minute to remember my password. The system was still slow. Finally the CruiseHomePage came up and I shut down the pop-ups and promotions one by one and opened the CruiseCalendar. It loaded at the monthly overview, but when I went in for a closer look the roster was disappointing.

The on-board activities were ongoing. There was a lawn bowling competition and yoga classes and tai chi, and intramural sports leagues, which didn't interest me because I was already tired and sore from Sarah; there was a Derek Jarman retrospective at the Silver Screen, and a midnight John Waters film festival; the Broadway was running *Annie* and *Jesus Christ Superstar* on alternating nights, with live music or comedians or ventriloquists or jugglers at the smaller venues. Then they had a slate of things for kids, crafts or raves or an Easter egg hunt. The ship offered a fine range of entertainment. But I was ready for something new.

But all the ports of call were cancelled. On the CruiseCalendar the items were struck out and faded, so you knew the activities weren't on offer anymore, but you could still read about all the interesting options they weren't letting you have. Underneath each item, it said, "postponed to next cruising season."

I scrolled back a few weeks to see if I was reading it right, and I could see all the activities that were scheduled on San Lazar and Prince Clarence earlier in the cruise. But after Port Esteban, all the ports of call were shut down. They had cancelled all the stops for the past several days, and they didn't have any scheduled for the week coming up. It was surprising, and even though I didn't like them very much, the ports of call were supposed to be a part of the cruise package, and I was paying an arm and a leg for the shore excursions, even if I didn't take advantage every time.

Then, since I was already in my account, I checked my mail. There were in-house notices from the purser and the cruise director and hospitality, and I skipped those because I wasn't interested. And I had spam and notes from my broker, and I ignored them, too. I googled Laureen, like I do, and nothing came up. And I had nothing else to do, so I decided to bite the bullet and talk to Raoul, and right then there was a knock at my door, and I said, "It's open," and Raoul stepped in.

"Speak of the devil," I said. "I was just going to call you."

He closed the door behind him, and said, "Great minds, Mr. Rutledge." But I let it pass because he tried to smile when he said it, and it looked terrible because he was so bony and green.

"Jesus, Raoul," I said. "You look awful. Don't they feed you?"

"I've got a fast metabolism, Mr. Rutledge," he said. He moved his arms like he was running or fighting, and then he dropped them down to his sides again. "Even when I get three squares, I still can't put it on."

"Even when?" I said. "That doesn't sound good."

Raoul shrugged. "Things get busy on the floor, with a private party, or an extreme clean after things get out of hand the way they sometimes do, or a double shift. We've all been pulling those lately. I miss my seating and my weight drops like a rock. I have to watch my blood sugar."

"You have a seating?" I said. It sounded funny coming from the cabin boy.

"We've got a big number of people, or we used to. The commissary puts us on a schedule so everyone gets fed."

"I've never noticed the commissary," I said.

"It's in the staff area on deck minus one," Raoul said.

"I thought deck minus one was the Hold and the hatches for the tenders?"

"There are passenger facilities in the forward areas, the bar and access points and an ATM, so that passengers can stock up before they go ashore."

"That's a very good idea," I said.

"But the aft section is crew quarters, with the commissary and a rec hall."

"It sounds very spacious," I said. I thought it must be stuffy and crowded but you don't insult people where they live.

"It's more spacious than ever," said Raoul. "We're short-staffed now with the people we lost at Port Esteban. We're scrambling to cover shifts and keep all the facilities up and running. Everyone's pulling doubles. The upside is, when you finally clock off, there's less competition for the ping-pong table in the rec hall. Not that people have a lot of energy left to play a game of ping-pong. But you've got a chance at the table if you want a game. Or for any purpose. Last night, Jimmy G stretched out on it and fell asleep. That would never have happened a month ago."

It was a lot to take in. I had to think about it. Finally I said, "We lost people at Port Esteban?"

Raoul gave me a hard look. "There were passengers out on various tours. We talked about it?"

"I know about that. But crew?"

"We lost staff and crew, say fifty hands all told give or take. People take shore leave if we're in dock on their day off. A big gang went into Port Esteban. It's a long time staff favourite."

"And they didn't report back?" I said.

"We cleared port in a hurry," said Raoul. He made it sound like it wasn't their fault, but you can't let it go when people don't show up.

"And now you're short-staffed," I said.

"We're stretched pretty thin," said Raoul.

"That isn't a good thing," I said.

"It's been challenging," said Raoul.

"The Company has obligations."

"Amen to that," said Raoul.

"Contracts have to be honoured," I said.

"You're a man of the people, Mr. Rutledge. I can speak for the guys I work with when I say we all appreciate your interest."

"It's my direct concern," I said. "I'm paying for the amenities. That includes a full staff complement. You can't run a luxury cruise on a skeleton staff. You want a drink and you have to go up to the bar, or if there's a waiter, he doesn't get back to your table when you're dry and the sun is beating down on you. It's uncomfortable. Or you need a hand getting up and the waiter has to clear his tray first. I've seen it happen. You're waiting and at the mercy."

"We're working round the clock to maintain service," Raoul said. "You know what my passengers mean to me." But obviously I couldn't let him off the hook just because he was trying. Important issues were at stake.

"Service still isn't up to standard," I said. "For example, Leticia keeps trying to clean my room."

"We talked about this day one, Mr. Rutledge," said Raoul. "I've been working on it ever since."

"But you're not making any progress," I said.

"It's in the planning stages," Raoul said. "Just as soon as we get the ramifications of Port Esteban sorted out."

the purser

He looked weak and tired, but I couldn't let it pass. "If you're going to use Port Esteban as an excuse any time something goes wrong, we aren't ever going to get anywhere," I said.

And again, I was happy when he shrugged and faced facts. "You have a point," he said. "Life goes on."

"Did you talk to Bobby?" I asked him. "About my idea?"

"Where we redistribute manpower?" Raoul said.

"That's it," I said.

"That was a very fine idea, and I talked to Bobby about it personally. He was definitely interested, and we floated it with the permanent stations and the C14 contracts. But the Brotherhood voted it down."

"Would it kill the union to get on side?"

"They look at life from the other end of the viewfinder. They had concerns. The guy who's out on rest, for example, he has no company. His whole squad is on duty and he's alone. It's not a holiday without a friend."

"But there'd be all the guys from the other service units."

"They're more like acquaintances. You don't really bond till you share a station with a guy, help him hose down a suite."

"So they ixnayed it?"

"We're still looking for the best option."

"I hoped we could resolve this," I said.

"We've got to find a better way, Mr. Rutledge," he said. "I am absolutely one hundred percent dedicated to improving service in this respect. We're lucky in a way, with the Port Esteban situation. We've got a window here. We're short-staffed and no one's had a day off for a while. It's testing us. But it also means old schedules are long gone. When we get the staff back, or replace them maybe, although I hope it doesn't come to that, we can come at the whole system with a better plan."

"So the Company's bringing in new staff?" I asked him.

"It's a possibility," said Raoul. "Although I'd hate to see it happen. We're a family, Mr. Rutledge. You lose a brother, you don't run an ad for a replacement. Plus, replacement staff." Raoul shook his head. "It's a complicated process, Mr. Rutledge. It's not an easy thing. The Company has to draft the ad and place it, check the resumés, and run the interviews. There are simulations and personality tests and a criminal background check and a Wassermann. And once they make the hires, there's a six-week training period, although a good steward is born and not made."

"They should hire ongoing," I said.

"It would be best, but management doesn't always take the long view. And even once they have new staff online, they have to manage delivery. We have a standard protocol for bringing replacement crew on board, because it happens — people jump ship or defect or get arrested. The Company flies new staff into the next port of call to meet the ship. But that is totally offline right now, because all ports of call are cancelled till we make the Pacific."

"I noticed that, Raoul," I said. I was still sitting in front of the computer and I nodded at the screen. "I was looking at the CruiseCalendar and I noticed that all the ports of call have been cancelled."

"Technically they're postponed," said Raoul. "We'll catch them on the flip side."

"To-may-to to-mah-to," I said. "You can call it what you like. It doesn't get me to the disco."

"It's a disappointment," Raoul said. "But the situation is out of our hands. It's an act of God out there, and the Company is trying to do right. When we get to the Pacific that will be our Shangri-La. You'll enjoy a fine tourist destination, wherever we dock, and God willing, my guys will come back safe from their ordeal, or worst-case scenario, the Company will bring in new staff and I'll get a day off, finally, or at least ratchet it back from the double shifts I've been catching for a while now, which would be a nice change also."

He was looking weak and hungry again, and I pitied him.

"Couldn't you chopper new staff over?" I said.

"In a crunch situation," said Raoul. "But the 'Flies are booked up, now.

They've got their usual routines, with private charters and the standard runs for the pharmacy and the Brinks guys. Now they added security tours and recon. And then regular maintenance ongoing. There's not much time left on the schedule. It's better if we hold on for the next few days. Then we'll clear the Canal and we'll have our choice of ports up the coast."

"Recon?" I said.

"With the ramifications," Raoul said. "The fallout from Port Esteban. It's not just a riot on the docks anymore. Now they've got a party."

I thought I knew about it. "I heard they called out the coast guard?" I said.

"The colonel called out the national guard. And then the guerillas came down from the hills and they burned down the government house and took pot shots at important foreign embassies. The Company compound was overrun. Neighbouring states saw their chance and sent in advisors, and other parties air-dropped private militias to protect their assets and their nationals."

This was all new to me. "I didn't know it went so far," I said.

"In a way it's a good thing," said Raoul. "Because it means the heavy hitters have to step up to the plate. They have interests to protect and their own people are at risk. They have to get involved. And once they're in the game, they like to take a leadership role. They're calling the shots now. The Company takes a back seat, obviously. We're a civilian outfit. We hand it over to the professionals and get out of the way."

"When the big guys get involved, things happen. They get their teams in place, and then they clean house," I said. I didn't want Raoul to worry. He had friends maybe who were still on the island. But then I thought some more. "I heard something about hostages," I said.

"We hope and pray that our people aren't in the fort," said Raoul.

"The theme park?" I said.

"It actually was a pirate fort back in the day. The troublemakers took it over, it's still very secure. They're holding foreigners there, making demands."

"But our people are okay?"

He thought about it for a second. "The Company compound looked very secure. At the last round of contract negotiations the Brotherhood pushed to get on the protocol for evacuation there. Although the way things turned out they were lucky not to be on the grounds when security failed. We don't know who got into the Compound exactly, or if they took our people to the fort. We can still be hopeful about passengers and crew."

"You think you'll get everyone back?"

"Oh yeah," said Raoul. He made a very firm gesture with his hands like he was laying the smackdown. "This is a blip on the radar. It's not a permanent situation, although the developments now aren't what people predicted at first."

He nodded at me and I nodded back at him. I wanted a minute to think about it, because I didn't know all the details before. I didn't know that security failed at the compound or about hostages at the fort, although I'd heard pieces of it. I took a minute and tried to calculate what it meant for Eric and Lily and Della and Steve. And I wondered also what the lookout was for Eddie and Katherine, if Lily wasn't there to lend a hand and they had to rely on the professionals in Sick Bay and the waiter at the Slaker who already had more on his tray than he could carry. And I thought about the J-kid sitting alone at the table for eight with jacks in his ears. And that was just one family group on the boat and there were many more who would be impacted by events. So I took a minute to think about all that. But I shouldn't have hesitated, it turned out, because Raoul took advantage, the way people do.

"I don't like coming after you with this, Mr. Rutledge," Raoul said. "But the purser says I have to." He pulled some papers out of his pocket. "It's about month-end. You have your fees and the charges for tours and rentals."

"I know about that," I said. I had to snap myself out of it and refocus. "It's in the ticket package. I looked it over when I signed up."

the purser

"So we've been at it for a few weeks now, and that first bill is over-due," said Raoul.

"It's pre-authorized," I said. "The Company has my signature."

"It looks like there's a problem somewhere in the line."

"A problem?"

"Something isn't going through somewhere. It's hard to say where the snag is. It could be a mix-up with your people, or it might be at our end, some kind of inputting error. We're getting more defaulters than you expect with this kind of clientele."

"You have to check your accounting, then," I said. "You run an audit and get back to me."

"I wish I could," Raoul said. "But we've got bills payable and we have to meet our obligations. So the purser sent me out to collect. You need to clear your tab with me and I can give you a receipt. The purser will send the paid-in-full note to the Company."

"You're kidding me," I said.

"It's the way they decided to handle it," said Raoul.

"Well it's the wrong approach," I said. "You're going around with a collecting tin? It doesn't look professional. It looks very fly-by-night. It doesn't build consumer confidence. I wouldn't do it if it was my business." Although at times I interviewed defaulters personally. But I enjoyed the interaction, where I had the right and the guy who owed me money apologized like he should and showed respect. But I didn't think Raoul would get that kind of response. He wasn't going to get it from me.

"It doesn't look professional," said Raoul. "I told them that in the purser's office. But they don't listen to service. They have their own way of thinking, and they don't take advice. What can you do?"

And he looked green and pathetic, and there was no point in taking it out on him anyway since he was just the cabin boy and he didn't have any pull in the purser's office, so I said, "You have my bill with you?"

He gave me the papers, and I put them on the desk and looked. "This is robbery, Raoul," I said.

"The monthly fee is standard, Mr. Rutledge," Raoul said. He sounded stiff.

"Yeah, the fee. Okay. Although it's a big number to start with. But what are all these other items?"

"They'll be for other services, extras."

"What is this 'energy surtax'?"

Raoul stepped up behind me and looked over my shoulder. "That's for the bar fridge," he said.

I checked the bill. "No. The bar fridge is a separate item here."

Raoul tried again. "That's the rental on it. The energy levy is the electricity charge."

"You're kidding me," I said.

"Because it's a scarce resource," said Raoul. "The ship generates a finite supply of power, and there's a lot of demand, like you expect. So you pay a premium." I gave him a look and he checked the numbers again. "It does look high," he said. "Although a refrigerator consumes a lot of energy. It can be responsible for up to a quarter of your household energy bill."

"It's a bar fridge," I said. "It barely holds a six-pack."

"You have other systems on your meter, too," said Raoul. "You run the a/c a lot?"

"We're in the tropics," I said.

"You've been closing the doors to the balcony like we talked about?"

I looked over at the French doors, which were open. I had the feeling Raoul already noticed, although he kept looking at me like I had his respectful attention. "I like a breeze," I said. "Fresh air is healthy."

Raoul nodded and looked over at the balcony finally. "You keep the doors shut, it'll take a bite out of that number." He went over and closed the doors and snapped the titanium bolt, and he started back over to me and then deeked past me into the bedroom. "Double the savings," he said. And he went in and closed the bedroom balcony access also. I thought he was being bossy again, like he sometimes was, but I was reading the bill closely, and I didn't say anything.

There was a charge for 'spa services,' which I figured meant Sarah. I decided right then that I'd cut out the personal training, because I wasn't enjoying it, and it was costing me an arm and a leg.

Raoul came back into the living room and starting fussing with the a/c settings. "It's a good habit to get into," he told me. "It makes a difference. You keep all the doors closed for a month. I guarantee that surtax will drop on the next bill. Plus the a/c is more efficient if you have the windows closed. It's more comfortable."

"And what's this 'pool amenity fee'?" I said.

"That's for the pool deck," said Raoul.

"The pool is free," I said. "Reliable people told me." But then I remembered it was Denise, and although she looked well-informed she had strange ideas.

"Swimming is free," said Raoul. "Any time you want, you can dive in and swim a few laps, or relax on a flotation device, although there's a rental charge if you want to use one of the ship's inflatables. But if you bring your own or do without, it's a refreshing way to spend a couple of hours. And that facility includes the hot tub. Absolutely no charge."

"Then what is this item?" I asked him.

"It's for the lounger," said Raoul.

"I have to pay for a lounger?" I said.

"It's a competitive rate," said Raoul. "Because it's a limited resource, too. We have several hundred guests, and only eighty-five loungers on the pool deck. We need a way to ration them, and an hourly charge makes people think twice. Otherwise people try to save one for a friend, or they put their magazines and their tanning butter and their hat on a lounger when there are tired people looking for a place to sit."

"Everyone has a lounger who wants one," I told him. "There's no one on the pool deck these days."

Raoul looked surprised, and then he made excuses. "I didn't know," he said. "I haven't had any time poolside to observe."

"It's a ghost town," I said. "There's just a handful of kids in the hot tub and the entrepreneur with his girls."

"When the commandos land in Port Esteban, the loungers will fill up again," said Raoul. "The beach parties will come home and demand will outstrip supply. You'll be glad that we have a pay to play system then."

"Yeah. But in the meantime, you have a surplus," I said.

Raoul looked at the bill again. "You make a point, Mr. Rutledge. They're charging you the standard rate even though our head count is down. I can take this up with the purser if you want. He might see reason on it."

He pulled out a pen and made a mark on the page. I felt like I was getting somewhere finally. The goal is never to pay the full markup because discounts and wholesale pricing can usually be arranged. I looked to see where else they were squeezing me.

There was a charge for laundry, and a big number for dry cleaning. There was nothing I could do about it, because you have to respect washing instructions. There was a bar tab from every facility where I had a drink or bought a round. There was a bill for water from TheCompanyStore, but it was for sparkling, and I told Raoul about the wrong deliveries and he made a note to look into it.

There was a charge for the tours on San Lazar and Itamar and Prince Clarence, and a charge for the tenders.

"You should pay me to take the tender," I said.

"On the other hand there's no charge for the land link at Maromed," Raoul said.

It was the only thing there was no charge for at Maromed. The Colonial Plantation package was a big ticket item, and the cognac and cigars were extra, it turned out. I didn't mind so much, because they were quality goods at least, and not plantation products like they kept trying to give me. So I knew I was paying for the best. And even though Eddie ordered them and really they should have gone on his bill, I decided I could eat it because with the Company compound compromised

the purser

and the hostages and the fort, I thought he had enough on his plate.

And there were fees for the driver and the dig excursion and the river rafting and the luau and the jump-up. And that reminded me, and I decided I wasn't going to pay for any of it since they gave me bad water and I was sick.

"I was in bed for a week after Maromed," I told Raoul. "I'm not paying for that kind of abuse."

Raoul made another mark on the bill and nodded hard. "It's a viable point, Mr. Rutledge," he said. "I can probably get you a discount."

"And what is this?" I said. There was a big charge from the Captain's Mess.

Raoul leaned in to look at it. "It's your restaurant bill," he said.

"It's all-inclusive," I said.

"Unless you order extras," he said. "A nice bottle of wine or a cheese course."

"A couple of bottles of wine should not run to this total," I said. "I need to see an itemized bill."

"It's on the back," Raoul said. I turned the page over. There was a column of numbers and I looked through it. They charged me for every bottle of wine I ordered with Eddie and the gang, and I had a G and T most nights. So that was fair. But then they included a substitution charge for taking nuts out of Natalie's salad, and there was a big wine charge for dinner at the captain's table.

"This is all wrong," I told Raoul. "They made a terrible mistake that night. They gave a girl almonds who was allergic. She had a seizure, and then they made up a new salad plate, but she didn't want it by then, obviously."

Raoul opened his eyes wide. "That's a serious error, Mr. Rutledge," he said. "We can't let it go. I'll see to it the charge comes off." He leaned over and made another mark on the page.

"And the waiter said he'd take the wine off the bill to apologize for the incident," I told him.

Raoul made another mark. "I'll look into that for you, too," he said. "There's a mistake there somewhere. I'll get it sorted."

So I figured I'd got the bill down by quite a bit. It was still sky-high, but I felt like I'd made a difference. Plus I like to negotiate.

"I tell you what, Raoul," I said. "There is no way you should even come to me with this bill, because, like I said, it's all pre-authorized. So home office is probably debiting my account right now, and when you come after me in person, you're just double-dipping, in my opinion. And also, this bill is wrong, as we discussed.

"But to help you out, because I don't like the purser leaning on you, I'll cut you a cheque for fifty percent of the total. That should cover the legitimate charges. You give me a receipt saying 'paid in full,' and then you get those mistakes off my bill and work out the proper total. If you get it down below the half I give you, and you probably will because that bill is mostly lies, you can keep the change for yourself."

Raoul nodded like he could see it made sense. "It's a good offer, Mr. Rutledge," he said. "But the purser's office is very sharp and I don't have a lot of room to manoeuvre. For one thing, we're operating on a strict cash basis right now."

"You won't take my cheque?" I said to him. I was insulted and I didn't try to hide it.

"It's because we have to meet our own payments, and the guys we're dealing with are looking for cash in hand."

"Isn't that unusual for a big outfit like this?" I said. My business had been mostly cash, but I had an idea that a large corporate concern worked on credit.

"Things are different sometimes in the tropics," said Raoul. "Although the Company completes many of its financial transactions electronically. They direct deposit our paycheques, for example. But we have to come up with cash right now, because our transit isn't prepaid like it should be and the Canal authority is squeezing us."

"Talk English Raoul," I said.

"We need cash to pay the Canal fee," he said. "When you cross the divide, you have to pay the man."

"Like a toll?" I asked him.

"A user fee," said Raoul. "It's an expensive piece of engineering, and there's maintenance and upkeep. They have to dredge the channel and oil the hinges on the lock gates. Also, they have a monopoly if you don't want to take the long way home."

"And they won't take a cheque?"

Raoul made a face like it stumped him. "I don't know the details," he said. "The purser's office didn't issue a bulletin. Normally the Company's agent would take care of the fees and we'd be good to go. But there's a hitch somewhere. It's an issue. I hope I'm completely off base on this one, but it may even be an indicator of financial concerns. When people don't take your cheque, you know confidence is weak. Creditors need to pay attention, and every employee is a creditor every day but payday."

These were worrying ideas. "You think the Company's in trouble?" I asked him.

He thought about it with his head leaning one way and then the other, and finally he said, "I've been with them a while, and so far they've come through for me and everyone I know, steady like clock-work. They've got a solid business plan, and they make payroll on the nail. I never heard a whisper about money trouble before. This kind of situation, it's not the usual thing for them."

"But they didn't prepay the transit," I said.

"And normally they would," Raoul said. "But then this isn't a nor-mal situation," he said, because he was looking at both sides. "We've got geopolitical ramifications coming up the spout. And we're running ahead of our original schedule, which might be a contributing factor. We were supposed to enjoy the Caribbean until July. Then when hur-ricane season starts up, we were going to make the Canal and begin our Pacific cruise. But the schedule's completely shot, and we're making the jump before we expected and the Canal fee is a big number. They maybe budgeted to have the money ready in July, and they have all their start-up costs now for the *Mariola*, and not so much income built up from the monthlies. Or the money could be tied up until July, or they have to organize a transfer. But the Canal is holding ships in queue until their cheque clears, so cash will take us pretty much to the front of the line. That's why the purser's collecting on the bills. All the bills and some money from petty cash will get us through the Canal pronto. That's got to be our priority right now. Bring the *Mariola* out the other side."

You could tell Raoul had no background in negotiation, since he told me his priorities up front. I let him get it off his chest because knowledge is power. And I sat back and enjoyed the leverage he gave me.

"I'm not in a hurry," I told him. "Let's pull into a nice port of call. I'll check out the local action and the Company can sort out its accounts."

"Are you kidding, Mr. Rutledge?" said Raoul. He looked scared. "We've got our backs to the wall. We can't sit around waiting for the financial office to check its sums. We've got to clear the region. This whole place is a powder keg."

"You said the outlook was hopeful," I said.

"In the long term," said Raoul. "They'll have it all sorted out in a couple of months. Next cruising season, we'll be back here enjoying the amenities, and when we pull into harbour in Port Esteban, if we bother to stop there and give them our business again, the troublemakers will row out to the ship and sell us their sisters. But right now, it's a concern, with Port Esteban and Santa Perdita and the Lower Harbour and Castillo on the Windwards all going up in smoke, and well-armed people all over the region, who don't respect standing conventions on war and the rights of foreign noncombatants. You don't want to stay in the same room as these guys. It's not a safe holiday destination. The major players, they'll go in and restore order. But we can't hang around while the marines do their thing. You don't want to get in their road either."

Once he got going he sounded desperate. It was like he was shaking his soft underbelly at me and daring me to ignore it. And even though

I cashed in my chips and retired and was no longer pursuing money-making or money-saving schemes as my vocation, I could still recognize a win-win barter opportunity when it came up. And you don't turn your back on those.

"So you need cash, then, Raoul," I said. "That's a lot to ask in the middle of the ocean. But I'll think about what I can do."

I reached into my pocket and pulled out my bankroll. I let Raoul see it was a decent supply, without fanning it out, because it's a bad idea to show your full resources when you negotiate.

"I maybe can't cover a big bill like this on short notice," I said. "And it isn't my problem if your guys can't run their own banking operations. But to help you out, and because I like you and I don't want to see you get in deep with the purser, I'll give you two K. That's ten percent of the bill, in cash, for a paid-in-full receipt." I started counting it out.

Raoul looked stunned. "We were talking about fifty percent before," he said.

"We were talking about a cheque before," I said. "Cash is a totally other thing." I kept counting.

Raoul took it all in for a minute. Then he picked his strategy. "There's no way that two large will cover it," he said. "Even when we adjust the bill downwards with corrections, I can't see knocking off more than three or four thousand, and that's only if the purser okays the adjustments. I can't speak for him, but I can tell you, the negotiation won't be a cakewalk. But I'll go to bat for you if you give me a cash payment of sixteen. I think I can sell enough corrections to the purser's office to get your bill down that far. It's twenty percent off your bill, a fine savings for you."

I laid the twenty Benjamins I already counted down on the desk in front of me. "It's your call, Raoul, if you want to take cash in hand to the purser, like he asked you to get, or if you want to go back with nothing. You made it sound like we had an issue with the geopolitical situation, and I thought a solid percentage of this bill might help you out. But if you want to sit around while the whole territory goes up in flames, it's up to you. To help you decide, I will sweeten the pot. I'll go up to five. That's a quarter of the bill. It's more than double my first cash offer. It's a large number. So I want you to think carefully before you decide."

I started counting. My bankroll was getting low, and I hoped Raoul was paying attention. It can be an effective technique if your opposite thinks that he's draining you. In the meantime, I had reserves in my other pocket and in the desk drawer and I had a large backup emergency supply in the safe. But I wasn't going to break into those resources in front of Raoul. I just counted out thirty more bills, and I laid them down across my first offer.

Raoul looked at the pile on the desk, and what was left in my hand. I thought he was considering my offer. But he had game it turned out.

"I hate to do it to you, Mr. Rutledge," he said. And he looked sad and sorry. "But the purser is turning the screws. If I can't show a good faith effort on your part, they're talking about sanctions."

"They're going to make me walk the plank?" I said. I wasn't really worried.

"They're talking about restricted access, limited menu choices, closing the bar," he said.

"They're going to cut me off?" I said. I was stunned. "That is the wrong approach completely. They're throwing away the goodwill of the consumer. It is guaranteed to cost you business in the long run, if I can be blunt, and you can tell the purser that I said so."

"I tried to reason with him," Raoul said. "You can't treat people like that I said. You spend weeks building a relationship. And then they throw something like this at you, and it wrecks everything. But if you can give me twelve thousand, I will do everything I can to sell it to the purser and keep your privileges intact."

I was surprised how far they would go just to squeeze some cash out of me. But also I was disgusted, since there are rules to the game and the purser was out of line. Because in the service economy, respect is fundamental. The help have no right playing hardball with the customer. It distorts the whole relationship. So I didn't waste any time making nice with my next offer. I checked the total again, and then I counted out thirty more bills. It covered half the balance almost, and I only had a few bills left in my hand. I pushed my offer over to Raoul.

"I've got eight GS right here. You can talk my total down that far and more now that I went over all the mistakes with you. I'll give you this, in cash, with my blessing that you keep any change left over once you correct my bill. I'll give you all that right here right now for a receipt that says 'paid in full.'"

Raoul thought for about one second, and then he nodded. "I'm going to try to swing it for you, Mr. Rutledge," he said. The sight of a large amount of cash is a powerful bargaining tool by itself. "Although I know I'm in for a fight with the purser," he said.

And he wrote 'paid in full' on the bill, and he gave me a separate receipt showing dollar amounts, and I gave him the cash, which he put in his pocket.

"I'm glad we took care of all this, Mr. Rutledge," he said. "It's an unpleasant thing and it hurts the client-steward relationship, another thing I told the purser's office that they ignored. Now that it's over, I hope we can move on." He stood in the middle of the room and waited patiently for me to make it all right.

I didn't mind really, except for the purser's office disrespecting me which I thought was insulting, because I figured I'd got a good discount on the first month of sailing, and I thought that was fair because the prices they charged were robbery. But I let Raoul make his apology, and then I unwound another Benjamin and handed it over to him.

"You were in an uncomfortable position, Raoul," I told him. "You were caught in the crossfire. I don't hold it against you."

Raoul took the bill and tucked it away. "It's a pleasure doing business with you, Mr. Rutledge," he said.

the canal

CHAPTER TWELVE

We made the Canal the next day. I got a G and T at the Slaker and climbed up to the running track and walked around it comfortably in the sun. From a forward position I could make out a blue-green patch of land on the horizon. So I stopped to watch, and we came in closer and then pulled through a breakwater and into a bay. There was land all around us with a city on one side and what I thought was maybe the main locks up ahead. And there were other ships in the bay, liners and tankers and small yachts and little speedboats, and we pulled up near the big ships and parked.

I felt excited, like we'd been down but we were getting up again, because there were vessels and a city with buildings and people and action all around even if we were sitting in neutral. And I went down to the pool deck to see who was around and to spread the word. I found a big gang, although it turned out everyone knew about it already.

"Hoss told me," Leanne said in a small, private voice. "He was in the Banana and he couldn't stay and have coffee because we were approaching. He had to be on the bridge."

Then there were Vance and Amanda, who I'd met before on the tour in Itamar. They travelled a lot. It turned out they'd done a loop cruise into the Canal and back out the same way the year before. So Vance had information for everyone.

"You don't just go waltzing in," he told us. He made a face like only an idiot would think there was an open door policy. "We have to wait in the bay till our ticket comes up. They have a system."

"Hoss says we go into the first locks tomorrow at dawn," Leanne told us.

I thought the timing was terrible. "Why do they do it so early?" I said. "It would be interesting to see, but no one will be awake."

"I'm setting my alarm," said Leanne. "Hoss invited me to the bridge."

"The bridge would be interesting," I said, mostly to be polite. It's a privilege when the captain asks you to the bridge, but the first officer was less impressive, and I never like to get up early.

Vance said, "That's a real opportunity. I watched our transit last year from the lock stations. The technical aspect is fascinating."

"They can't have a lot of guests," Leanne said, like she was letting us down gently. "There isn't room, Hoss says. And it's a work station."

"You let us know all about it, honey. We'll want to hear," Saskia said.

I didn't care about the bridge, but I was happy we were in the Canal. We were making a jump from one ocean to another, and I was feeling hopeful again.

"What the hell," I said. "We should celebrate. I've never made the Canal before."

"We have," Vance said.

I ignored him and talked louder. "We'll make the transit every year from now on," I said. "And in the future, we won't even notice because it will be ordinary to us. But we'll only make our first transit once. Plus we're getting out of the Caribbean with a whole skin, and right now that's saying something."

"Amen," said Teresa. I had to think. I met her with Bud and Bailey early on. She was a nice woman, older and good-looking.

"Let's make a night of it, up in the Crow's Nest after dinner. We can watch the sun come up on the Canal. What do you say?" Other people didn't always make plans and I was used to organizing things.

"I can't stay up," Leanne said. "I want to be fresh for the bridge."

"I never make it to the end of an all-nighter," Saskia said. And I believed her because she was fundamentally sleepy and relaxed like a cat. "But I'll come up tomorrow morning and see if you made it."

"It's a date," I said.

And Teresa said she was in, and Vance said they'd come, so I knew we'd get an education as well. And Tom couldn't decide. He was a good guy. He'd been on the tours while we were still allowed to take tours, and he had manners and sense and he was interested in things. He finally said he'd let us know, and I said that would be fine. And we said we'd meet in the Captain's Mess for the second seating, and head to the Crow's Nest after, and then Vance started in on the other cruise again and there was no stopping him.

I went back to my suite and put on my tux, not the one with the flared leg, which was at the cleaners. And I had my sundowner in the Monte, because I felt overdressed in formal wear at most of the other venues that were more casual. Ben was there, with his tux jacket draped on his back. He was lit, and in a funny mood. He bet like he was trying to give his money away and then we had another drink and talked about odds and luck and fate. He took the view that life was predestined, which I think is the excuse people make when they're lazy and unsuccessful, although I didn't say it out loud.

"You know when you're going to win," he said.

"I know when I feel lucky," I said.

"And you know when you don't," he said.

"If you know when you won't win, maybe don't bet," I said.

He made a face like I was dense. "We're in a casino," he said. "You have to lay your money down." Although no one forced him to come. "And the house always wins. I feel like I know it now. I feel like I'll never hit a big number again."

It's no fun gambling with a depressive. So I tried to buck him up. "What are you talking about?" I said. "Didn't you win the whole cruise package?"

"Tallie did," he said.

And I could see how he would feel like less of a man, riding around on his wife's ticket. I tried a different perspective. "It's not just what you win," I said. "It's what you do with your winnings. Like buying a better suite and turning the giveaway cabin into a closet."

"Tallie did that too."

"Or being shot and making it look good with your jacket on your shoulder."

Even that didn't satisfy him. He patted at his arm. "It hurts still," he said. "I think it smells funny." There was kind of a pong coming off him I didn't like to discuss.

"The important thing is you take your assets and you put them to work," I said. "In gambling terms, you make your best hand."

"Like stacking the deck?" he said. Beside us at the blackjack table the dealer pricked up his ears.

"No. Not like that," I said. "Using judgement and sense. Taking what's good and making it better, identifying losing strategies and retiring them. Sometimes not losing only means knowing when your luck has turned and walking away with your winnings in your pocket."

"You never do," Ben said.

It was true that I dropped a bill sometimes, but never more than I could afford. And I thought it was bad manners for him to say it, especially when I was trying to cheer him up.

"In the wider world, I mean. You look at your lie and you make your best shot. They call it luck, but it's something different."

Ben didn't want to believe it. He didn't like to take responsibility. He was happy to take credit when things went his way but he wanted to blame bad luck when things went wrong. And he wallowed in it also, like a mud bath. I couldn't talk him down, so I had to give up. And he went back to the table to lose some more and said if I saw Natalie I should tell her his arm was bad again. I restocked at the ATM like always and went to supper.

In the Captain's Mess, I met up with Vance and Amanda and Teresa, and Tom wasn't there and we didn't wait. Jane was guarding the door and she didn't want to let us sit together because it wasn't the seating plan. But Ashley took over and put us at a nice table near the moat. You could see Jane wasn't happy. She slapped down the menus and didn't tell us the specials. And then, when we looked, the menu was short and handwritten, with a lot of rice and perogies and pasta, and the girls shook their heads and said everything looked starchy.

The first thing I thought was maybe Jane was taking a shot at us for changing tables. But then I thought maybe she gave me the limited menu for defaulters, and that was worse. So I told Teresa and Amanda and Vance I'd be right back, and I went up to the balcony where I found Natalie, and I told her Ben's arm was bad, and she said, "Tell me something I don't know." And on my way back I pulled Ashley behind a palm tree and I told her my account was paid in full and I wanted to see the complete dinner menu for clients in good standing. But she told me I had the full menu, and I said I was surprised it had so many potatoes on it, plus Jane didn't tell us the specials.

Ashley listened respectfully. "The kitchen is working hard to maintain standards," she said. "We'll restock on the other side of the Canal, and things will definitely be back to normal when Chef Lousine comes home. But everything is very good tonight." She took my arm like always, and walked me back to the table and made me sit down again. "I can recommend the lemon risotto and the pureed yam soup. For a more traditional palate the kitchen has steak with potato and salad."

It was just the menu items, but she was telling us all about it, so it felt special.

"Is it tenderloin?" I asked her.

"It's a more robust cut," she said.

"It's all pretty heavy," said Teresa.

"We can do half portions," said Ashley.

"Is there a charge for that?" I asked her.

She made a sorry little face. "It's like a substitution," she said.

"So you get less and pay more?" I said.

"It's for the special order," Ashley said.

"They get you coming and going," I said.

Finally everyone decided. I had steak, and it talked back more than I like. But it was grilled right, and served with little smears of Dijon and horseradish and a chipotle sauce, and a baked potato in foil with butter and sour cream. The girls picked at their dinner, and Vance had an opinion about everything except the bill. The whole thing was more work than it should have been, the way events sometimes are.

Then we went up to the Crow's Nest, and Tom was there, and I was happy to see him because the evening wasn't totally panning out like I hoped and I thought fresh blood would help. He had a table by the window for us and I ordered espresso to keep me going. And then the elevator doors opened and Bud and Bailey stepped out. And that was even better because I hadn't caught up with them for a long time either. We waved them over, and Bailey held back beside the elevator. She looked like she wanted to cut and run. But Bud put his arm around her and brought her over.

"A nightcap," he said. "That's a good idea. I was saying to Bailey. It helps you to sleep."

We pulled up more chairs and they sat down. Bailey folded her hands on the table and looked at them, and Bud put his hand on Bailey's hands. The waiter came over.

"Two cognacs," said Bud.

"Me too," I said. "And another espresso."

The waiter took my old cup away.

"That won't help you to sleep," said Bud.

"I'm staying up for the transit," I said. "We all are. We're going to make a night of it."

"There. The transit," said Bud. He squeezed Bailey's hands. "Now that will be something to see. When do we get rolling?"

"Crack of dawn," Vance said.

"It's a long time to wait," said Bud. He was very interested and alert like he wanted to reach out since Bailey was folding up.

"It's easier to stay up than to get up," I said. "We're on a countdown. We'll stay here, kill a couple of bottles, watch the sun come up on the Canal."

"That's a very romantic idea," said Bud. "You're a sentimental guy." He looked at Bailey and held her hand. "You need a nice girl to share the moment. It makes everything sweeter."

My heart turned over inside me. Meanwhile Bud was looking at Bailey and holding her hands, but she wasn't giving anything back. Even when the waiter came up with the cognac, she sat staring at her glass and didn't talk. I never like it when people bring their troubles to the party. It's bad manners, and it makes things difficult for everyone else.

Teresa was sitting on her other side. "How you doing, Bay?" she asked her. She spoke quietly, like it was between the two of them. Bailey shrugged.

Bud kept trying to make the situation work, which I respected. "It'll be something to see," he said. "The Canal is one of the wonders of the world. We're very lucky to have the opportunity."

Everyone pitched in. We all found something to say so we didn't have to pay attention to Bailey's mood.

"It's a change to see dry land," I said. "We've been cruising for a long time. I feel salty and waterlogged. I'd like to go ashore. I wasn't always keen on the ports of call. But I like some change and variety."

"Maybe a nature walk?" said Amanda. "We did one last time."

"That's the sort of thing I like," Tom said.

"The lock facilities are more interesting to me," Vance said. "I asked about it, but they're not letting civilians into the work stations."

"It's security," Amanda said.

Bailey kind of whimpered and Bud put his arm around her right away.

"Are we stopping in the lake?" said Tom.

"Is it a lake?" I said. Because I thought it was a canal.

"It's a system of interrelated waterways," Vance said. "There's a bay, and some locks, then Lake Gatun, and more locks." He would have told us all about it but Tom got in front of him.

"We were supposed to stop in Lake Gatun," he said. "They planned some tours. I wanted to look at the birds. I'm an ornithologist. Amateur, obviously, but keen." He was a sweet kind of dopey guy. I had lots of time for him. "I thought I'd find something new to put on my life list," he said.

"Are they offering shore excursions?" I said. "I didn't see anything on the schedule."

"We took all the tours last year," said Vance. "We went to Barro Colorado Island and Orchid Island and a village of the native Embera people and the Spanish forts."

Bailey winced.

"No forts," said Bud.

"It was all well worth exploring," Vance said. "The Embera have a culture. Their canoes are elegant."

"I think you're right, though," Amanda said to me. "I didn't see any tours listed in the CruiseCalendar."

"And why didn't we go to town today?" I said. The Crow's Nest had windows all around. We could see the city lights. "We've got a few hours still. We should tender over, see some nightlife."

"Oh, no. Not here," said Amanda. "It's really dangerous. Except for the Free Zone, if you want to shop. You don't dare go into the city by yourself. They told us last year."

"And they're nervous since Port Esteban," Amanda said.

Bailey was crying. I didn't know when she started, but I looked over and her face was shiny. Bud had his arm around her, and he was kind of rocking her back and forth.

"It's okay, baby," he said. "Nothing bad's going to happen."

"We could have died," Bailey said.

"But we didn't," Bud said.

"They hate us," she said.

"Screw them," Bud said.

"They were so mean," Bailey said.

It was awkward. We all stopped talking except Vance who was clueless.

"They called me 'whore,'" Bailey said.

Teresa stepped up. "It's a long way behind us and we're not going back. Come on, Bay. Let's get our faces straight."

"Teresa's right," Bud said. "You go to the ladies', honey. Splash your face."

Bailey gave in, like she didn't have the spirit to say no. Teresa got up and waited for her, and Bud got up and gave Bailey a hand. And I got up of course when the girls did, and so did Tom who had manners, and finally Vance looked around and stood up, too. We all stood there while the girls went over to the ladies'. And then we all sat down again.

Amanda looked like she'd been slapped. "You were in Port Esteban?" she asked Bud.

Bud nodded.

"I am so sorry. I should never have mentioned a fort."

"She'll be okay," Bud said.

"I hear the riot was action-packed," I said.

But he wasn't excited about it the way Poppy and Enright and Saskia and Leanne and Natalie and Ben had been.

the canal

"It was a human tragedy," he said.

"Did Bailey get hurt?" I asked him.

He made a gesture like it wasn't the issue. "We got pushed around," he said. "Everyone panicked. But we only got bumps and bruises, thankfully. Still, Bailey saw a boy take a bullet. He was young. It shook her up."

"Poor kid," I said. Because it puts things in a different perspective when you come under fire, especially the first time.

"Also the crowd was mean-spirited. They called us names. Bailey takes it to heart."

"You got out safe is the important thing," Amanda said.

"The Company needs to rethink its policies and activities," Bud said. "They should never have let us in for that."

"I have reservations, too," I said. "Their billing policy is completely off base, for example."

"And the kitchen is floundering," said Vance.

Bud had no comment on these things. He sipped his cognac and thought for a minute and finally he said, "I'm thinking of taking her home."

"You're abandoning ship?" Vance said.

"I'm thinking about it. This whole junket was her idea, and now she's gone off it. There are bad memories."

"It's because they're fresh," I said. "Give it a few days. It will fade."

"I thought so, too," said Bud. "But she's still in it."

Bailey certainly was paying a price. Her makeup was running and her face was swollen. But it also wasn't a walk in the park for the rest of us.

"You have to get her mind off unhappy topics," I told him. "It was an unfortunate thing. But we need to get back into cruise mode. It's why we're here."

"That's the point," Bud said. "It's not a pleasure cruise anymore. That's why I'm thinking about taking her home. I have to do what's best for her."

I understood how Bud was feeling. When a man is in love, he wants to protect his girl and make everything right. Still, I felt that leaving the cruise was a bad idea, because when you get hit, the best thing is to hit back. If you fold and run away, you never stand up straight again.

Teresa and Bailey came back from the ladies. Bailey had cleaned up her face, but she still wasn't happy. We watched them coming back to us across the floor, and Bud stood up and I stood up and Tom stood up. And Vance stood up finally too. And Bailey dragged her ass over to the table. Teresa sat down but Bailey shook her head and said she was calling it a night, and Bud said he would too.

"No. You stay here," she told him. "You have a drink. Have a good time. You need a break." She was going to start crying again, you could tell.

"I don't want a break," Bud said. He put his arm around her and she leaned into him and Bud threw a couple of bucks on the table and hauled her away. And Tom and Vance and I sat down again.

It took a while to get happy again after that, which is why it's a bad idea to spend time with depressives, because it can spread and you can catch it. But we had some more drinks, and Vance drew a map of the Canal and explained it all to us, and Tom did some birdcalls, and the girls were warm and lovely. Eventually the sky got lighter. The ship powered up, and you could feel it humming like it was alive. And we pulled ahead across the bay and into the channel, just like Vance said, and finally we eased into the first locks.

There wasn't a lot to it, it turned out. They closed the gates behind us, I think. Then they opened the taps, and the boat went up little by little. I didn't time it, but I don't think it was too long of a process. Then they opened the gate in front of us and pulled us ahead into the next lock. We could see the little engines on the sides and the lines running to the Mariola. They pulled us up and closed the gates behind us again, and they raised the water in the second lock. We got a bottle of champagne and Vance told us about the trams and trolleys that pulled the boat. The sun came up beside us, where I didn't expect it. My head was starting to spin.

There was a third lock, and then finally we pulled out into a big lake and I thought we were on the road. But we went a few hundred yards and then parked it again beside some more ships that were already there, and we powered down again. And while we were wondering what would happen next and whether we should wait, Saskia came in looking rested and fresh and ordered coffee. And then Leanne arrived. Hoss came through for her and she'd watched the whole operation from the bridge. She was pink and very important with all her information.

"But why are we just sitting here?" I asked her.

"Hoss says we have to wait now to time it right at the Pedro Miguel locks."

And Tom said he'd enjoyed the show, and he left. And I asked Leanne what the Pedro Miguel locks were, and she explained it and Vance explained it also because he had a map. He showed us the locks we just cleared, and the lake we were in, which was Lake Gatun, and then the Reaches and the Cut going out of Lake Gatun on the other side, and then the Pedro Miguel Locks, and then more Canal, and then more locks after that. "It's narrow in the interior," Vance said. "Traffic is strictly one way at Pedro Miguel."

"We have to wait until the traffic going to the Atlantic clears," Leanne said.

"Who's going to the Caribbean these days?" I said.

"It's all military," Leanne said. She kind of whispered, "We're not supposed to know, really."

"When that traffic clears out, we'll get our chance," Vance said.

I could see it was a hell of a complicated thing. But I was fading, and we weren't going anywhere right away. I had a headache, from the espresso I thought or because I didn't sleep. So I said good night and left them at it. When I got back to my suite I realized I stuck Vance with the bill. And I didn't mind that either.

the divide

I slept past noon the morning after the locks, and I only woke up when Raoul brought in my laundry. I thought it was a good sign he wasn't palming Leticia off on me. So I said thank you. And he said, "Of course, Mr. Rutledge," like he hadn't shaken me down for eight large two days before, and I tipped him a c-note like I didn't hold a grudge. I had a shower and put on pants. And then I went out to restock, like I decided I should do every day.

I'd been thinking it over, and I didn't like the current state. The Company was leaning on the clientele and showing no respect. And Raoul was their bagman, so they didn't even have the muscle to do it properly. The whole thing was weak and unprofessional, and although I could see that it was difficult with Port Esteban and the Canal Authority and so on, I thought if the Company didn't have a better Plan B I needed to develop my own. And an important consideration in any plan is cash in hand. So I wanted to hit the ATM every day, to build up my reserves again, and to be ready just in case.

I went to the ship's mall, because it was on my way more or less. But the ATM there had a sign on it saying "out of order."

I asked at mall information, and the girl said, "Out of cash is more like it."

"Because of the geopolitical thing?" I asked her.

"Like that," she said. But that was all.

There was a machine in the casino and it was right behind the mall. But they had a dress code and I was in chinos. I thought I could sneak in, maybe, before the venue heated up. But I'd started late and it was getting on, and when I looked through the door I could see people at the tables already. Everyone was wearing their very best, and the casino manager was at his post, smiling and looking crisp in black tie. I thought about going back to my suite and putting on my tux, because coin and a lot of it was my first priority. But I had it on all night and it was a relief frankly to snap open the cummerbund and peel off my shirt after several hours of sophisticated entertainment. I wasn't in a hurry to suit up again. So I stood at the door of the casino considering my options. And then I had a good idea.

I went down to level minus one and looked around until I found the ATM near the tender bays. It was in a side room twenty paces ahead of the forward bay, with an ice machine and a first aid kit and a house phone. It still had currency reserves, because it was out of the way, maybe, and no one had a reason to go down there since they hadn't sent a tender out for a while. I took out my limit, because that was the point, and then I went back to my suite and pulled out the other cash I raised already and counted the total. It was getting to be a respectable sum again, although I felt I still had a long way to go. And then I stashed it all in the safe, and I stacked water on top to be discreet and locked the safe again also.

Then I finally went back up to the Crow's Nest, like I'd planned at the start. When I got there, Vance was gone, which was no loss, except Amanda was gone also. And Teresa just left, Saskia said, which I thought showed fine staying power. But there was new blood, too, and a big gang altogether, with Saskia still, and Leanne, and Poppy and Enright, and Lou and Denise, who I hadn't seen since the Bandits. He'd recovered. He was sitting up straight in his chair and talking and smiling. And Denise was also being sociable and not writing memos, which was a good thing. And a guy, Michael, who looked gay, not that I cared.

I pulled up a chair, and the waiter was right beside me like he should be, and it was Miller time. So I ordered a G and T and asked for an update.

"Honey, we crossed the Divide," Saskia said. She waved a napkin at me, and it was the map Vance drew.

"Is that reliable?" I asked her.

"I have the official version," Denise said.

She had a real map, laminated and in colour, that you could fold out and fold back up again. She let me look at it, and told me all about it also. There was the bay where we waited two days before, and the first locks, and the lake where we were waiting when I left, and the entrance to the Cut, and the Reaches, and the Culebra Slide where thousands of workers died when the walls of mud came down on them and three months of work were undone in a few minutes, and the Continental Divide, with Gold Hill on one side and Contractor's Hill on the other, and the Cucaracha Slide where more people died and more work was undone and then done over again, and the Pedro Miguel Locks that we just cleared, and the other lake we were cruising on when I pulled up. When she talked about it like that it sounded like we'd covered some ground. But I looked at the scale and the distances, and we'd only gone forty miles maybe. I was surprised. It took most of the day and we didn't get very far.

"We had to wait for the Pacific fleet," Michael said.

"That's need to know," Leanne said, because she felt she was in charge of tactical.

"They were in a big convoy," he said. "Everyone knows now."

"That will settle their hash in the Sargasso Sea," Enright said.

I agreed, and frankly I was surprised they didn't tell me first thing because it was a major development. But people aren't patriots now like they should be. They have their own concerns and they don't pay attention even though they wouldn't last five minutes without those brave men and women who make the world safe for tourism.

"It must have been something to see," I said. "I would have liked to watch the Pacific fleet power past in formation."

"They went single file," Michael said. "Gunmetal grey, and not a sailor in sight."

"Was it a big force?" I asked them.

"Twenty-two ships," Denise said.

Lou said, "There's more to come, apparently."

"We're not supposed to know that either," Leanne said, and then she told us so we could admire her depth of knowledge. "There's another flotilla, with surgical ships and support, but they're waiting for us to go through the Cut first."

"It's nice of them to let us in," I said.

"I'm guessing the Company pulled some strings," Enright said. He looked shrewd and satisfied, like he knew more than Leanne even.

"You don't think we're just taking turns?" Lou said.

Enright made a face like he pitied Lou for being dumb. "It isn't a four-way stop," he said.

"I'm just thinking," Lou said. "There are a lot of us. We're in a convoy with a bunch of other ships. I thought maybe Canal authority let twenty naval vessels go one way. Then it's our turn, and twenty liners go the other way."

Enright was very firm. "Canal authority doesn't tell our boys what to do," he said.

"But we're taking a turn now and they're waiting for us," Lou said.

"The Pacific fleet is standing down while we make our transit," Enright said. "It's not because they're weak. It's the most powerful marine task force afloat. They're only letting us take a turn because the

Company has influence. How many boats were there back at the starting gates, and there's a dozen in this run? We didn't move to the front of the line because of our good looks." He looked very satisfied. "The Company has connections."

I liked Lou, but I had to agree with Enright on the facts. "There were lots of people waiting," I said. "You didn't see outside the first locks, maybe. There were lots of boats waiting for a turn. And they're still waiting in the lake or in the bay. We're coming out the other end. The Company did all right on this."

Lou gave in like it didn't bother him. "That's one for the Company then," he said. He and Denise looked at each other and laughed without sounding happy.

"It's one for the Company," I said. "It's a change. The Company is not on a roll, in my opinion."

"Now there we do agree," Denise said.

I told them about the ATM in the mall being out of cash, and Denise said, "What about the tour?" I thought she was still mad about Port Esteban. But it turned out they organized a tender finally to look at the islands in Lake Gatun.

Michael took credit. "They weren't going to do any excursions. But I started a petition. I based it on the Geneva Convention."

"It might have been better if you knew the Geneva Convention," Enright said.

"I felt a thorough knowledge of Geneva was sufficient. And hospitality saw reason finally. They put people on a tender and took them around the lake."

I thought it sounded pleasant and informative, and I was sorry I didn't hear about it because I might have been interested in going, even if it was only getting off the big boat and onto a smaller boat for a few hours. I said I was surprised they didn't all take advantage.

Michael said, "They wanted us in the hatch right away. I had no sunscreen."

the divide

I said, "Did anyone go?"

"Everyone went," Michael said, because he started the petition and took pride in it. "It was a very popular option."

Saskia put her hands up and counted off. "Tyler and Philip and Hannah and Rom and Tom I think. Did Lissa go?"

"It was a crowd," said Lou. "I had a good view from up top. The tender was full."

"I was just down in the tender bays," I said. "I didn't see anyone."

"It was a few hours ago."

"And they enjoyed themselves?"

"They're still enjoying themselves," said Denise.

"Hospitality outlined risk up front," Enright said.

"We left them on the lake," Denise said.

And in all my life I never heard about such bad customer service.

"We're on army time," Enright said. "The clock is ticking. Hospitality told everyone the *Mariola* had to move as soon as it got the word. We couldn't wait around for sightseers."

"They couldn't hold the door for five minutes?" I said. Although I knew how slow and cranky the tender system was, and it would take more than five minutes to bring a tour party back on board. "The Company can't abandon its clientele," I said. "It isn't A-one service. In a war zone especially."

"They're not abandoned," Michael said. "They're doing the tour they signed up for. They'll see the birds, look at flowers, see the native way of life. Then maybe the tender will get a turn in the Cut."

"I don't see how," Enright said. He sounded fully satisfied. He wasn't put out by the complications other people faced. "The Company has pull but the fleet can't stand down for every rowboat and dinghy. They have a job to do."

"Or the Company will set up buses and take everyone across the Divide on the scenic route," Michael said. "We'll meet them on the other side."

And that sounded reasonable, too.

Lou said to Denise, "We should have gone. We'd be on our way."

Denise said, "Without our things."

And Saskia said, "I think the locks are coming up." She was looking ahead, trying to get a view.

"I'm going to settle up," Lou said. "You got everything?"

Denise looked at a stack of luggage by the bar and shrugged.

Lou said, "I'll finish moving it. They want us to be ready."

We'd been slowing down. Outside the window you could see we were pulling up in another lock. The mules and the towlines went into their routine. It was less interesting now because I'd seen it before.

"Are you taking shore leave?" I asked Denise, even though it didn't sound right. Lou was moving a big stack of luggage, and Denise was the kind of woman who travels light and thinks it makes her a better person.

She folded her map carefully, lining up the edges. "Just leaving," she said finally.

I got a very bad feeling when she said it. "Leaving?" I asked her.

Outside, they started draining the lock. Very slowly, we were sinking down, and the world was rising up around us.

"We're abandoning ship," she said. "It isn't what we thought it would be. It isn't what I thought it would be. I don't like it. Port Esteban clarified things for me."

"It was an unfortunate incident," I said.

"But there was a positive result," Denise said. "It brought things into focus for me. It made me decide what I wanted. I'd like to do the cruise. I've always wanted to see the world."

"That's what it's for. This cruise," I said. "You can see the world from your private balcony." And then I realized I didn't know what package Lou and Denise bought. She always talked like she had a superior package, but I thought if they were in some crumby interior suite with no view and no amenities, probably the experience was less satisfying. "You have a balcony, don't you?" I asked her.

the divide

She wouldn't tell me. "I don't like the view," she said. She was looking past me out the window and I didn't know if she meant the view from the Crow's Nest or the view from her private balcony, if she had one, or if she meant something else completely. "With things the way they are, I'm not enjoying myself," she said. "Call it consumer regret. Port Esteban shook me. There's trouble all over and I want to be at home with my family."

There was nothing I could say to that, obviously. When people pull family out it trumps everything. There were times on the *Mariola* when I'd have traded the elegance and the important people and the carefree lifestyle just to be at home with Laureen, eating a sandwich, or coming back from a job, or looking at paint samples, even. But that was all gone, and all I could do was google Laureen, and when I looked at it that way, I felt sad and angry at Denise for raising the topic.

Lou came back and sat down again. "Ready when you are," he said.

Over by the bar, there were only a couple of carry-on bags left.

"Did the Company give you your money back?" I asked, to annoy them.

"We'll eat it," Denise said. "I'm asking a lot of Lou."

"It's a big ticket to walk away from," I said. I enjoyed rubbing it in.

"Oh, the hell with that," Lou said. "We bought a deluxe stateroom. We'll keep up the fees. If things work out, we'll be back."

So they had luxury accommodations, and I was relieved I hadn't wasted my time being friendly with poor people.

"You're fair weather sailors," Saskia said, but just teasing, not mean.

Lou smiled. "It's the sensible kind to be," he said.

I was wondering. So I asked them, "How are you getting off the boat?"

"We're going to chopper off with the pilot," Lou said.

"You booked a Dragonfly?" I said. "I wanted to get a look at those. I've heard very good things about them."

"Come up top with us," Lou said. He looked at Denise. "We should go," he said. And she nodded and stood up.

Everyone said "Bye, Lou," and "Bye, Denise." The girls squeezed out a few tears and air-kissed each other. Denise gave Saskia the map of the Canal, to remember her by I guess. And then Lou picked up the carry-on bags and called the elevator, and we rode up one more level and stepped out on the flight deck.

It was windy up there, and I realized I hadn't been outside all day. There was a dirty smell of loam and mud, and a sound of fabric snapping in the wind. Lou had moved the bags onto the deck right beside the elevator, and there was another couple there too, and their bags, and an old babe sitting on a big suitcase, crying. A crew of guys in orange jumpsuits was jogging around, looking keen. They got in a line and started moving bags into the 'Fly.

I stepped out for a better view. The Dragonfly was parked in the middle of the deck, looking powerful. It was shiny with glass and polished metal, and it was all tricked out with features and accessories. I commandeered one of the jumpsuit boys to fill me in, and he walked me around the bird pointing out its features.

"The Dragonfly x10 is an assault gunship with modified transport and ordnance characteristics," he said. "It's got a maximum range of four hundred nautical miles, three hour endurance, and a two hundred and forty knot dash capability, with an external lift capacity of five tons. Modifications in the armament load can accommodate for passengers or cargo."

"Guns or butter," I said.

"Sir, yes sir," he shouted, and I liked that he showed respect and military discipline. "Each 'Fly in the *Mariola* fleet has a different weapons profile to cover a spectrum of attack configurations. Weapons complement includes autocannons, rockets, air-to-surface missiles, precision guided missiles, and depth bombs for anti-submarine scenarios. We've got sidewinders and anti-aircraft chickadees standard issue, and each 'Fly has two lateral flex-mount guns and a thirty mill helmet-mounted gunsight."

the divide

"It sounds like we have extensive resources," I said.

"Sir, yes sir," he shouted again. "Navigation and communication systems are fail-safed by component duplication and redundancy. The crew compartment is armoured against full-barrage ground assault and the fuselage is designed for progressive crush on impact."

"Does it increase survival rates?" I asked him.

"Eighty-seven point four percent in optimal collision scenarios," he said. You could tell he took pride in the numbers.

"Eighty-seven point four percent," I said. It was like nothing could kill them.

"Sir, yes sir," he shouted.

The crew was on board by then. I could see the pilots inside, running the preflight. The sun reflected off their glasses and they were reaching around inside the cabin. Lights came on and went off again, and the rotors came up for a minute and thumped and pounded, and then shut down again.

"It must be a rush to fly one," I said to him.

"Sir, no sir," he shouted. "I never had the pleasure. I keep the engine tuned, check the oil. Machine specialist, fourth grade, Delaronde, sir." He saluted hard and I saluted back. Then I gave him a c-note. I wasn't sure because he looked military, but he took it like an order and I sent him back to help with the luggage.

There were two other 'Flies parked on parking pads, and there were crews polishing them or loading them, or taking them apart and putting them back together. On one side of the deck there was a shack with equipment and a soda machine, and I bought a cold drink because it was warm even though there was a breeze. And then I heard a noise I couldn't place and I looked around and behind the shack I found the padre with a hose and a sack of corn. There were cages stacked against the back wall of the shack, and pigeons in them, and he was cleaning the cages out, hosing each one down, and filling up the water dish with water and another dish with corn.

"I didn't know people kept pigeons still," I said to him.

"We have always tended the dovecot," he said.

"Do you race them?" I asked him.

"Course and bearing matter more than speed," he said.

"The key thing is, they know how to get home," I said.

I respected Father McGrath because he was fierce and he knew what was what. But he wasn't an easy guy to talk to. So I left him with his birds, but nicely. And the flight group was nearly done.

"Ready in five," a voice said. It was amplified and coming from the 'Fly. A little group of officers came out of the elevator, Hoskins in his whites, and another officer, and a little guy in a bad uniform. You could tell it was a farewell party.

I went back to the gang and shook Lou's hand and Denise kissed me, which surprised me. I thought it was nice, and I was sorry I didn't like her more. I said, "Happy trails," but I don't think they heard me over the engines and the rotors and the voice saying "Good to go in three." Hoskins moved everyone over to the 'Fly, and he gave Denise a hand getting in and then the old babe and then the other girl. Lou shook hands with the officers, and he climbed in too, and the other guy. The runty guy went in last. Then Hoskins and the other officer and me stood back, and they saluted and I waved, and the 'Fly picked up. It hovered for a minute just above the deck. Then it pulled up and away. It flew into the sun, and then it circled back and disappeared behind us.

I watched it till it was out of sight and the sound of the chopper faded. And when I looked around again, I was alone.

news

CHAPTER FOURTEEN

I felt let down after Lou and Denise left, even though I didn't like her very much. It was more people who weren't around anymore to shoot the breeze with. And it was starting to feel like the end of the party, because you need a critical mass to enjoy yourself, and cruisers were dropping by the dozen. With Port Esteban and other considerations, it was easier to get a lounger by the pool, and this was good. But some nights at the late seating there were ten diners at twenty tables, and the girls only got two teams together for the beach volleyball tournament. So it was more of a beach volleyball game.

Staff issues were ongoing. They still didn't bring new people in to cover the crew they lost at Port Esteban. And we found out later more people jumped ship in the Canal. They opened the bay doors to load supplies at the last lock, and personnel made a run for it instead. It all made me wonder if Lou and Denise made a good decision and if I should check out of the *Mariola* also.

My gut told me, Denise is a bleeding heart and a do-gooder, and with that kind of attitude she had no business in first class. But Lou was successful. He bought a deluxe stateroom and he kept up the month-lies even though he might not come back. So he had money and he understood forward planning. And Bud was looking at his options, also, although he was whipped. There was no easy answer, but sensi-ble people, my kind of people, were leaving the *Mariola*, and I felt that I should consider my options too. So a few days after Lou and Denise flew out, I bit the bullet and got down to fact-finding. And the first thing I did was watch the news, which I hadn't done really since I came on board, to see what the world outside looked like.

There was a story on the new strategy in the oilfields. It looked a lot like the old strategy but with more private participation. Casualties were sky-high, and the pipeline was at risk. From North Asia there was footage of the rebels with their camps spread out across the steppe, and then a clip of the president speaking from an undisclosed location, shaking a fist at the camera and keeping the other hand on a button with a flashing red light. In a failed state in Africa, gangs of feral chil-dren attacked the local NGOs and made off with vaccine and rubbing alcohol. A coup in south Asia destabilized the region, and local govern-ments mustered conscripts. There were war games in the Balkans and civil disturbances in the South Seas.

Port Esteban got a mention, although there wasn't much new to report. The marines were mobilizing but they still weren't in position. There was footage of troublemakers with weapons, and diplomats duck-ing out of cars and in back doors.

Then they shifted to the domestic report and that was bad too. There was flooding in the heartland and drought in the Southwest. Wildfires on the Pacific coast took out acres of forest and a dozen mansions in a prestige community. The government imposed emergency water ration-ing, and the number for a tip line ran across the bottom of the screen so you could turn in your neighbour if he filled up his hot tub. In the south, citizen volunteers patrolled the border. Upcountry the Nazarene Secession called for spiritual resistance. They issued a communiqué calling public education the devil's playground, and they planted bombs in schools to discourage attendance.

There was a human interest piece about a guy that took the engine out of his car and harnessed a team of dogs to the chassis. He travelled across the nation, spreading goodwill and giving seminars on building dogmobiles.

I closed it down and thought I was right not to watch the news mostly. It was disturbing and it didn't show me an obvious next move. You could see the home front was no picnic. There was the environment and the economy and the local crazies. I had already known the domestic scene was unattractive on a personal level, with Laureen gone, but I also wasn't clear on my status with taxation and other government agencies. Before I left, people were taking an interest I didn't like, and it took initiative and planning to get out of the country and take my money with me. All these considerations made going home unappealing.

The rest of the world didn't look good either, with the war and suffering and refugees and death. That was the heart of the *Mariola's* appeal, that you could see the world, but through bulletproof glass, because the Company offered A-one security, and if things got too hot, you could sail away. It was a good idea in principle. And I hadn't given up completely on the *Mariola*, because it had fine facilities, and there were still venues I hadn't explored like the Gallery and the Humidor and the Arboretum. But with services curtailed and passengers jumping ship like lemmings, it wasn't like the brochure.

All I decided finally was that I should do more research, and not rule out any reasonable option, and that in the meanwhile I should continue to take full advantage of the amenities still available on the *Mariola*, because that was the point.

○ ○ ○

Then a few nights later I went to the Monte and lost some money with the high rollers, and when I went up to the mezzanine to stock up, the

ATM had a sign saying "out of service." So I had to go down to level minus one again, which was out of my way but at least the machine was still in business. And the next day I had breakfast in the Big Banana, like usual. I had eggs and sausage and toast. But I wanted fruit, because roughage is key, and they only had tinned fruit in syrup. They had a stack of single serving fruit cups on the table where the bowls of melon and berries used to be. I wasn't tempted but I was surprised, and I took a traveller as an example, because it went to the heart of the issue. Back in my suite, I turned on the computer but I couldn't get online.

I was disappointed because service was in no way back to standard even though we came out the other side of the Canal and they were running out of excuses. And I knew I had to call Raoul and register my concerns, even though it wrecked my day when I had to deal with this kind of thing. And right at that moment he knocked on the door and put his head in.

Even when I was disappointed with the Company and let down by every member of the crew, at the same time and against my will sometimes I was impressed by how Raoul turned up when I needed him like he read my mind. And while I was admiring him for it, he saw me sitting at the console and he nodded at it and said, "I don't think you're going to get anywhere with that Mr. Rutledge."

So I started in on it like I had to. "It's telling me to see my service provider," I said. "Should I talk to Brent?"

"Brent is on it," Raoul said. "The whole tech staff is. Something happened to communications. The net is down. Phones are offline. We don't get a TV signal."

"I noticed," I told him. "I can't get online."

"The tech boys will sort it out. They like a challenge."

I didn't lie to him. "It's not a good thing Raoul," I said. "I'm having doubts. I'm trying to make up my mind. Because there have been incidents and there have been problems. I'm looking for reasons to stick with the cruise and you're giving me reasons to pack up and go."

news

Raoul looked surprised. "Why would you go, Mr. Rutledge?" he said. "We're in the Pacific. We dodged the bullet. We're the lucky ones."

"The Company got us through the Canal," I said. "This is true. But it's old news. You can't coast on your laurels. You have to go back in the ring and earn your take-home every day."

"I know you're concerned, Mr. Rutledge. Speaking confidentially and as an employee, I can tell you I've had my issues also."

This was beside the point obviously.

"I was able to look into things before we lost contact," Raoul said. "I had an hour off finally and I dedicated it to research. The Company is looking steady. It's meeting obligations. I've got a good feeling about it."

I said, "Your people jumped ship in the Canal."

Raoul made a gesture like he was shooing them away. "Not everyone has what it takes. The stevedores are nothing new. They always jump ship. They think working a cruise line is immigration."

"Some passengers checked out also."

Raoul made a prim face. "They have the right."

"It makes me wonder," I said.

Raoul said, "Events arise and you assess implications. You think about your options and look at the public mood. But you don't have to follow the crowd. You can use judgment and sense. I did my research and I arrived at my conclusions. I didn't jump ship in the Canal."

I felt we were getting away from key issues. So I put the fruit cup on the table. "What's this?" I said to him.

He squinted at it. "I don't know, Mr. Rutledge," he said. "Is it peaches?'

"It's fruit cup," I told him.

"Fruit cup?"

"Tinned fruit cup, Raoul. We're supposed to get fresh. For the money I'm paying, the brochure says fresh fruit."

"If you check, it probably says 'when available.'"

"You're not going to give me the fine print."

"I haven't looked over that part of the contract, but Company legal is very sharp," said Raoul. "I doubt they left a loophole. But it's okay because Company outfitters know there's a customer preference for fresh fruit. They're on it. We have a supply run scheduled. It's what I need to talk to you about."

He pulled out some papers and I said, "We're coming into port finally?"

"We're not coming into port," Raoul said. I felt let down but he didn't give me a chance to develop it. "There are logistics with the area in flux, and the military passing through. They're locusts. They clean out the suppliers, and the Company is scrambling to find resources at a price."

"We're out of fresh fruit and they're haggling?"

Raoul looked hurt. "It's your dollar, Mr. Rutledge," he said. "They're looking for the best price for you."

"The monthly's a flat rate," I told him. "If the market surprises your guys, it's their problem."

"Everything ends up on your tab," Raoul said. "The Company could buy oranges at five dollars a pound, but you know they'll pass the markup on to you sometime. It's better for everyone when they look for the best price."

"It's a nice thought," I said. "But you pay what you pay in a seller's market."

"But if you're mobile, you take your purchasing power to a different market," Raoul said.

This was interesting. "Explain it to me," I said.

"I want to tell you about it," he said. "It's a good system. It's because we are buyers in motion, and because distribution is flexible also. You get a big service ship, or several, with holds for cargo and refrigeration and tanks for diesel and for fresh water. They pick up materials cheap on the Pacific rim and cruise to meet us. And we cruise to meet them. The Company calculates time and distance and the shelf life of the

news

produce and sends us the rendezvous coordinates. We're lucky in fact. We got all the details before communications went down. We have the timeline. It's just a few days now."

"How many days?" I said.

"I am not totally up on specifics. Within the week. You can count on it."

"And they ordered fresh fruit?"

"Crates of it."

"And for a better price?"

"A dollar fifty a pound. Less. We're talking wholesale, bulk, direct to market."

It sounded like they knew what they were doing. I was willing to give it my blessing in principle. I said, "This is encouraging, Raoul. If things work out, I'll have more respect. I can wait a couple of days for you to show me your stuff. But that is all. The Company is on waivers. It has to earn my respect every day."

Raoul nodded hard. "That's the way I look at my job, Mr. Rutledge. Every day is a new opportunity to satisfy the customer."

I felt relaxed and hopeful, and he was still holding papers in his hands. So I asked him, "What have you got there, Raoul?"

He looked surprised like he didn't know what he had, and he studied the papers to find out. Then he said, "I'm glad you asked, Mr. Rutledge. It slipped my mind totally, and this is important. This is your end of the resupply initiative." He held back just long enough for me to know I wouldn't like it. "The Company is still operating on a cash for service basis," he said. "I've got your latest monthly."

I was dumbfounded. "You've got my monthly?" I said.

"The last we heard from head office, we're still not getting any pay-down from pre-authorization. The purser can't explain it. But he has to plan around it."

"You're not here to shake me down again, Raoul." I wasn't asking. "I gave you ten large a week ago."

"Eight thousand, twelve days," Raoul said. "And that was late payment on the first monthly. It comes around fast."

"And it's not like the Company is supplying full service," I said. "We haven't had shore leave since I don't know when and they're serving tinned fruit in the Big Banana. You should be ashamed."

"I hate to do it, Mr. Rutledge. But the purser calls the shots. Also, this time, new factors are in play."

"New factors like what?"

"New factors like when we meet the resupply vessel, we have to pay cash."

"They still won't take your cheque?"

"The word is cash only."

"It doesn't sound to me like the Company has its financial house in order."

"My research says it's sound."

"But the suppliers don't think so."

"I can't speak to their reasoning. I only know the Company is meeting obligations."

He didn't look me in the eye and it made me suspicious. "You mean it's paying its suppliers?" I asked him.

"Paying for services," he said. "Personnel," he said. He held onto it for a second. Finally he said, "They deposited my pay."

"That's it?"

"It's an important consideration."

"For you," I said. "But there are other people to think about. It's personal and a little shallow for you to say that the Company has its finances under control just because you got a paycheque."

"It has larger implications," he said.

I said, "In the big picture it isn't worth a hill of beans, Raoul."

Then he was very dignified. "It's not a large amount of money, I know," he said. "I know it every time I see the total, and I see what my time is worth to the people who buy it. You don't need to tell me it's a pittance and an insult. But there is a big picture component. It says something about the Company. The working man is first in line for the shaft when a corporation goes into its death spiral. The CEO gets a golden handshake and major creditors strip the assets while Joe Grunt gets stiffed and the pension fund goes missing. If the Company is meeting payroll, then the Company is solvent. Meeting payroll is a reliable test of corporate health."

He took a cynical view of the capital risk taker, and it disappointed me. I filed it for future consideration. But I stayed on message.

"Not robbing your customer is a reliable test of corporate health," I said.

"No one's getting robbed," he said.

"You come around here waving bills in my face like a collection agency." This was a stretch. No self-respecting firm would hire Raoul to answer their phones, let alone deal with the public. But Raoul tightened up more. It was interesting to watch, like he might split his seams at any time.

"The customer has enjoyed a range of goods and services over the month and now the purser is asking him to pay for those items. It's not theft. It's consumer integrity."

"Except head office is already helping itself to my account."

"Our records don't indicate that."

"If you had reliable communications I could check it against my records."

"We've got a crack team of IT guys working around the clock."

"Let me know when they're done."

Raoul changed tack, because I had a viable point and he had to admit it. He thought for a second and then he said, "The purser is being flexible. He wants cash, but he'll take gold or precious gems, also. Although you sign a waiver agreeing that these aren't collateral and they become the property of the purser's office and may be used for barter or exchange. And people who choose not to pay will be put on a short leash in terms of shipboard services."

"He talks big, but is he really going to spank this clientele? I can't see him cutting off the entrepreneur." I thought considerations like this would keep the purser in line.

"He paid on the nail," Raoul said.

"Is that so?" I said.

Raoul dropped his voice because it was private. "I was just with him," he said.

"He's on this deck?" I asked, because I thought a big man like that would have something more substantial.

"He's on top, where the Admiralty Suites are."

"I thought you worked deck six?"

"I have an acquaintance with him from way back," Raoul said. "I worked a specialty line when I was a kid. Hard work. I couldn't do it now. But it was a solid education and I saw the sights from Micronesia to the Bay of Bengal. We have a rapport from back then, and the purser knows I can be tactful."

"And the big man ponied up?"

"A few large don't put him out."

"He must run up a bill," I said.

"He's got expenses. An admiralty suite is top of the line. So the monthly's substantial. And he has standing specialties, nothing in bulk but good quality. And some extras."

"I heard he booked a 'Fly."

"He likes to book a 'Fly. Last month he went there and back across a war zone. Extra security. Live entertainment. It adds up."

"And he paid the ante?" I said.

Raoul put his hands up. "No questions asked. He called his PA and told him full fare, carte blanche, no waiting. It's just business."

It put things in a different light when I thought about everyone on board doing his bit. Because it was united and democratic, and I liked it that we were all in it together. "The purser's going after everyone?" I said.

news

"I've been making the rounds all morning. Up and down the ship. Sometimes there are tears and sometimes there are scenes. Some people don't look at all the angles." He thought about it for a minute. "No offense," he said.

"Meaning what?" I said.

"Nothing, Mr. Rutledge," he said. "I just thought maybe you were feeling the pinch."

"I'm not feeling the pinch."

"Because some people think they can do luxury living on the cheap. They don't calculate sometimes the extras and the built-in costs. They get in over their heads, and then they have consumer regret."

"Money isn't an issue, Raoul."

"Some people just don't do the math. Or they aren't financially honest with themselves."

"I can cover my nut."

"Not you, obviously, Mr. Rutledge."

"You want to show me the damage?"

He brought the bill over, and I smoothed it out on the desk in front of me. Raoul hovered beside me while I looked at it.

It was a good idea, with everyone kicking into the kitty to get us over the hump, but the bill was still a sham and a disgrace. There were more charges from the Captain's Mess. I flipped the page over to check the details and I found the bill from the night we went through the Canal, with the drinks and the wine and the substitution charges for the girls' half portions. But the old charges were there too, for wine and for cognac from the night at the captain's table.

"We talked about this last time, Raoul," I said. "It feels like yesterday. They nearly choked that poor girl. Plus the captain wasn't there, just Hoskins and some guy. They put the wine on the house, to apologize."

Raoul nodded. "I looked into it," he said. "They took the substitution charge off for the salad without nuts."

"They didn't make a salad without nuts. That's the point."

"And they didn't charge you for it. They had a charge on the first bill. But I talked them down."

"So now they're not charging me for a plate they didn't give me?"

"It's straightened out is what I mean. And they took off the first bottles, the wine you ordered before the incident. And another Brut they gave you on the house."

"That's right."

"But they said you ordered more wine and then cognac after everything went down, and they had to charge you for those."

"Of course we ordered more wine. The entrees were just coming."

"You need a glass with your main meal."

"And they already told me it was on the house. They're welching."

Raoul shook his head. "I'm not explaining it right," he said. "They told you they'd cover the wine you ordered already to say, 'Our mistake, *mea culpa.*' And they popped another Brut in the same spirit. But that was the limit of their reparations. Because after that, and no one is accusing you, but an unscrupulous person might think, 'It's on the house. Let's try that '87 Grand Cru.'"

"Who would do such a thing?"

"You hate to think people could sink that low."

I flipped back to the main page and checked the other charges. There was a big number for the fitness facility.

"This is wrong, too," I said.

Raoul crowded in for a better look. He stood too close. It was his signature move. "It's your personal trainer and gym time," he said. "It's a monthly rate."

"I stopped going," I said. "I haven't been for weeks. I stopped cold turkey."

Raoul pulled out a pencil and circled the item. "I should definitely check it, then," he said. "There will be charges for a few days of use, because we were already into the current billing period when we looked at your last bill. But if you cancelled a few weeks ago, the number should be lower. This looks like a full month of service."

"I didn't actually cancel," I said. Raoul stood back to look at me. It was his other signature move. "I stopped going, but I didn't go up to the desk and say I'm not coming back. I don't rub it in. People's feelings get hurt."

"It can be emotional," Raoul said. "But they're professionals. They know it's business. Or you can tell me, and I can relay the message. I'll tell them now. It makes a difference, because if you don't cancel the booking, they hold the spot for you, and then they have to charge you."

"When I don't show up, they know I'm not coming."

"When you don't show up, they know you're not there. But it's too late by then to give the slot to another client."

"Don't they get drop-ins?"

"Not so much in the gym. Other venues, like Sick Bay or the salon, they can usually fill up a space on the schedule. They don't worry about no-shows at the salon. There's always a line."

"Even with so many people gone?"

"The ladies are getting ready for the Gala."

What with one thing and another, I got the bill down by a few bucks. But it was still a whopper, and I wasn't happy, even though it was a team effort and everyone was pitching in. I reached into my pocket and got my working cash, and I counted out the total, and Raoul wrote me a receipt. He put it on the desk in front of me and reached for the cash, and I blocked him and gave him a long hard look.

"I have to tell you, Raoul, this number is high for the services rendered. It makes a man think twice and wonder if there's a better place to spend his money." I said, "I've been thinking about signing out, calling the desk and booking a 'Fly."

"It has an appeal," Raoul said. "It's the wild blue yonder. I hope it isn't your decision. But I will personally let you know as soon as the 'Flies are back online."

"What do you mean back online?"

"They're impounded?" he said, like he was asking me.

"The Dragonflies?"

Raoul nodded. "Captain's orders. They're offline except for emergency transit until we meet the resupply ship."

"Lou and Denise just flew out."

"We sent a few people with the pilot. We had to send the pilot. It's protocol. He works for the Canal authority and he steers the ship through the Reaches and the Cut. We have to bring him on and send him off again and we supply his transport back to the authority offices. So the 'Fly was already committed, and it's no biggie to put a couple of civilians off with him. But we're in the open sea now. It's a long ride from here to the nearest rock."

"The Dragonflies can cover it. I was talking to a specialist. He said they could cover a distance."

"They can cover a distance. They're top in their class. But fuel is the issue. We need to conserve, and the Dragonflies aren't efficient. They burn diesel like hogs and we're running low. We have enough to get to our target coordinates, but no margin. Even when we sent the pilot home, we only put enough gas in the tank for a one-way trip and told them to fill up at the authority for the return leg. And now, all transport is offline until we meet the supply vessels and refuel."

"We're in lockdown?" I said.

"It's a golden cage, Mr. Rutledge, you'll see, with all the finest facilities most of which are still staffed and online. And the main gates will swing open in no time. If you're not fully satisfied in a week, or ten days tops, you'll have a range of options. You can chopper out on a refueled Dragonfly, or board one of the resupply ships and cruise back to port. But I'm hoping you'll choose door number three and explore the Pacific paradise with us. I honestly believe this is the best of all possible commercially packaged luxury worlds."

So I took my hand off the stack of cash and pushed it over to him, and he picked it up and counted it and straightened the bills and rolled it up and tucked it into an inside pocket in his jacket. And he stood waiting for a minute, and I thought it over and decided that on balance he gave me useful advice and he took my case to the purser when I was blatantly overcharged and he was going to tell Sarah so I didn't have to myself. So I peeled off another c-note and pushed it over to him too.

And he said, "Thank you, Mr. Rutledge," and I waved him away.

Right after he left, I checked the cash in my pocket and the cash in my safe. I recounted to get a current total, and then I looked at the bottled water situation too. I went back to the mall and ordered two more cases, and I told them to deliver. And then I went back to the ATM on level minus one and took out my limit again, because although I talked him down somewhat, Raoul still made significant inroads. And I went back again the next day, and the next. And then I went one more time, and there was a sign on it that said "out of service." So it was all over until the Brinks guys came back. Until then, I couldn't get any more cash. But no one else could either. And in the meantime, I figured, although some people might have better credit, no one had more coin. And I was satisfied with that.

the gala

CHAPTER FIFTEEN

The next concern was the Gala. It came out of nowhere, and it was a little strange, because it was scheduled for midsummer, but technically it wasn't even May. But hospitality made the call and moved it up on the calendar, because they knew that people are happier when they have something to look forward to, and this was a deluxe formal event in the Captain's Mess for all the cruisers still on board.

It would have been a zoo if they tried to put all the cruisers who started out on the *Mariola* into the Captain's Mess, but now they could accommodate all the guests since our numbers were down. Because Port Esteban was ongoing and it turned out the Canal tour never came home either. But no one was worried since fuel and logistics would sort them out, and the Company had a plan going forward to bring every-one back to the ship, although I never heard detail.

Most people were fully committed to the Gala. The girls went into high gear, getting waxed and sugared and trimmed. It was a pleasure to be around them, because they were happy and excited, and when they took time out for a drink and an hour in the sun, they had a good feeling about life, and we all laughed and joked together. Mostly they were busy, though, because they knew that pleasure doesn't happen by accident. It arises spontaneously only after careful preparation. So they were earning their happiness by making themselves lovely, sweating at the gym, and putting in time at the salon trying out new makeup and hair. They were in the mall, getting fittings and alterations and looking at shoes and jewellery and little purses. They were everywhere but the restaurants, because they stopped eating a week before the party, so they'd be fragile and petite when it mattered.

Some people will tell you that this is foolish. They will tell you that the clothes you wear don't matter and that it's what's inside that counts. But they are wrong, because everybody knows that better clothing leads to a higher quality of orgasm. So the clientele on the *Mariola* had the right idea when they invested time and effort in looks, and I was impressed with their hard work and looked forward to the good results we all earned.

I got into the spirit, too, because that was the point. I tried on my tuxes again, the one with the flared leg and the other one, and neither was as comfortable as it should be. So I bit the bullet, and I decided I'd finally take Raoul's advice and get a new one made up, and I went to Mr. Gualtieri, the ship's tailor in the mall, to see about it.

"For the Gala? No way," he said. "I'm swamped already. Look around."

There was a lot of action in the shop, with guys standing on stools getting their inseam measured, or in front of the three-way mirror in their boxers and garters with the tailor's assistants pinning the mock-ups.

"It's just that I'm not sure about the leg on my one tux, and the cummerbund is binding."

"A good cummerbund fits snug. It's a bad look when a cummerbund sags."

"My cummerbund doesn't sag."

"You've got no problem then."

"It cuts into me somewhat."

He sighed. "You want an opinion, you put on your cummerbund, come down here. You need the whole kit, the cummerbund and the shirt and the pants and the jacket. Shoes even. I'll take a look. See what I can do."

So I did that. He stood me in front of the three-way mirror and turned me around, with the jacket on, with the jacket off, arms at my sides, arms over my head. He was very thorough. Finally he took the cummerbund in both hands and tugged at it, like Raoul did, and pulled it around. Then he snapped it off me and checked the hooks.

"It's snug, not tight. It fits you right. I don't like to change it. But if you want, and I don't recommend it, I can move the fastenings. You've got a little play here, maybe a quarter, maybe a half an inch before it stresses the seam. If you want, I can move it over, give you a little more breathing space. Say the word."

So I said the word. And he nodded and put pins in the cummerbund to mark the spot and wrote out the work order. I signed it and he gave the notes and the cummerbund to his assistant. "He's very good," he told me.

"You're not going to do it yourself?" I said.

"Manny takes care of the fine jobs," he said. And he said it would be ready the afternoon of the Gala.

"It takes that long?" I said. "It's not a big job."

He shrugged. "There's a lineup ahead of you."

"But to wait so long for such a little thing," I said. "It doesn't seem right."

"First come, first served. It's the system."

"I'd hate it if there was a holdup," I said.

"You have my personal guarantee. Five o'clock the day of. No later."

I had my hand on my bankroll, and I thought about making him an offer. Because I'm not comfortable with suspense and I wanted the job done on time or before. But for a cummerbund it seemed like too much, and I was trying to watch my cash flow. So I just nodded and took my stub.

Then, because my tux was in for repairs, I didn't go to the Captain's Mess for a few days. I went to the Oasis, and had falafel, and to the Dreadlock for roti, and to the Local for shepherd's pie. Saskia called it low food and said it was a gourmet trend once. I didn't mind. I kept my main meal down to one course only for several days. And I felt this kind of restraint was a good thing, because it left me hungry, but fit, and I thought at the Gala I would appreciate the pleasures of fine dining all over. And it's a funny thing but true, that even though nobody wants to go without, a few days of small portions and holding back actually feels good. You more fully appreciate the finer things when they come to you. So I didn't mind so much that my cummerbund was in lock-up and I couldn't go to the Captain's Mess.

And then, the day before the Gala, they closed the Captain's Mess down totally to decorate the room and they put out all-day buffets in the Dexter and the Bar Sinister instead for lunch and for dinner. And the guys groused and the girls didn't notice because they were fasting. But I thought it was a good idea to let everyone take a day off and be impressed by the elegance and the splendour of the dining room all over again.

So all in all I was looking forward to it, and feeling prepared. And in the afternoon of the big day, I took an hour to lie in the sun poolside and relax. I was warm and comfortable and nearly asleep, and Jen pulled up beside me. She sat down on the lounger beside mine, and she didn't stretch out and relax. She sat on the edge watching me, which was the first bad sign.

"I've been looking all over for you," she said.

She sounded like she wanted to pick a fight like always. But mostly it was surprising that she was looking for me. Because although I always got along fine with her, without encouraging her, we usually just bumped into each other by accident.

"I like some sun in the afternoon," I said.

"I need some money," she said.

"Don't we all," I said. When a person is looking for a loan, it is sometimes a useful strategy to play dead and pretend you don't know what they're getting at. Although this is hard to pull off when they're direct.

"I'm not kidding around," she said.

"I thought you had money?" I said.

Jen said, "My parents screwed up. They didn't pay the monthly. I don't know. I can't get hold of them."

I sympathized. "It's the Company, I think. They aren't accessing the prepay. It's a problem."

"The purser says he'll cut me off."

"He said that?"

"Some weenie guy he sent to my suite."

It sounded like Raoul, although I didn't know where Jen's suite was or if Raoul and his team serviced it.

"Did you try to negotiate?" I asked her.

She made a sound in her throat. "He was staring at my tits," she said.

I thought it was a terrible thing. "You can't let that kind of thing pass," I said.

"I told the purser. He said to take it up with personnel. Then he wanted to talk about my account. He's got a one-track mind."

"He's a moneygrubber," I said. "It's his job. But he's unpleasant about it."

"So can you lend me?" she said. She had a one-track mind, too.

"Cash is an issue," I told her.

Another useful policy is to start by saying no. You can let yourself be talked around later if you want. But it establishes the fact that you are reluctant and only doing a favour.

Still I wasn't totally against it. For one thing, it was a while since I put a deal together, except bartering with Raoul, and I missed it frankly. It's a great thing when you have enough money and you never have to work again. But never working again can be restful or it can be dull. So the opportunity to put my skills and my capital to work was attractive. Also, like with any business proposition, there was risk, which made it exciting. I like action and the chance to beat the odds. It was the real thing, and it made the casino look like a game for girls. But I didn't rush into it either. Information gathering is an important first step. So I let the conversation spool out some more while I thought about things.

"The ATMs are down," I told her.

"I know that," she said. "So I've been asking all my so-called friends. They're all too cheap. So now I'm just asking whoever."

Well that made me feel warm all over. "They turned you down?" I said, to rub it in.

"Nobody came up with it," she said.

"Not even Fredelle?" I said.

"She's useless," she said.

"Did you try your friend the entrepreneur?" I said.

"He says he doesn't mix money and friendship." She thought about it for a minute. "He always stares at my tits too," she said.

Of course it was easier for him, since she sunned herself topless when she sat on his recliner.

"Another option is barter," I told her. "They'll take jewellery or gold."

"I'm not giving them my jewellery. They already have my clothes."

"They took your clothes?" I said. It was a strong-arm tactic, I thought, but creative.

"I took a dress in for alterations. They won't give it back."

"Did they do the work at least?"

"I don't know. They won't let me see it. They gave my appointment at the salon to Natalie."

I had never seen it before and it was strange to watch, but Jen was starting to choke. It looked to me like if she didn't stay angry she fell apart, and I don't like to see a girl upset, even Jen.

"Hold on now," I told her. "Let me get you a drink."

I waved the waiter over. It took him a few minutes, much longer than it should, and we sat there not talking, because she was trying to hold it together and I was thinking about if I wanted to do a deal.

The waiter pulled up finally. He was busy but completely on his game. "G and T, Mr. Rutledge?" he said. They knew me at the Slaker.

I said yeah, sure, and I asked Jen what she wanted.

"I want twenty thousand dollars," she said.

That was a surprise, too, because it was a bigger number than I expected, although I already knew you could run up a bill without really trying.

"Twenty thousand," I said. "That's more than a couple of bucks."

"I'll pay it back," she said. "It's not like I'm poor."

The waiter was still standing over us, looking interested.

"Are you sure you don't want a drink?" I asked Jen.

She said, "I'll take champagne cocktail," like she was doing me a favour. She glared at the waiter. "Easy on the bitters," she told him.

He jumped to it. And I kept my voice down while I tried to explain it to Jen, because she didn't understand private always and I don't like a scene.

"Twenty thousand dollars is a significant sum," I told her.

"It's chump change," she said, which was nice, considering she didn't have it.

"You're young," I told her. "When I was a kid and just starting out, twenty thousand was a stake."

"Times change," she said. "Catch up."

I didn't like her tone. "You want a loan from me, you need to show respect," I told her.

She opened her shirt and flashed me. "You want respect?" she said. "I have thirty-four double D respect."

"Do up your clothes," I told her. I hated it that she flashed me. It was one thing if she was taking the sun topless and I was attentive and on the spot and enjoying the scenery. But it was something else if she thought it was a commercial advantage. "If I want a dance, I don't have to pay twenty large for it," I told her. "Look around. There's a girl on every corner."

But it made me think differently about the loan. Because I have found by experience that lending money to people is sometimes a good way to get them out of your road. It depends on the dollar amount and the personalities involved. But for some people, if you pop them a couple hundred, and especially if they can't pay you back, they drop off the radar completely and you don't see them again for months, sometimes ever.

The waiter came back with our drinks and Jen did up her shirt and he made sure not to notice her breasts, and that was the way it should be. So I signed for the drinks and tipped high and in cash and he said thank you and went away.

Then I told Jen, "This is what I can do. I can't front you twenty large."

"Yes you can," she said. "You just gave the waiter big money."

"I gave the waiter a tip because he does an important job and I like to encourage him. You don't." Jen made a face like I slapped her. I kept going. "I have a lot of money. I have twenty large to spare, but I'm not giving it to you. It's too much. And I don't get anything I want for it. But I'm a nice guy and I know the purser's office. I'll talk to them. I'll give them a G in part payment of your bill, and I will vouch for you. They're hungry for cash. With a cash down offer, I think I can get you a ticket to the party."

"I'm not going without my dress."

She said it like I was begging but I let it go. "I'll throw in the dress," I said.

"There's a necklace in the pavilion I told them to put away for me."

It was like she was negotiating a whole other deal.

"I'll throw in the dress," I said. "A thousand dollars, your dress, and my support with the purser's office. All that will cost you two large."

"What?"

"That's the price."

"But you're only giving me a thousand."

"It costs two thousand. It's a flat rate." Because I didn't think she could calculate compound interest. "You pay me back first thing when your parents' cheque comes through and don't ever flash me again. That's my offer. Take it or leave it."

"Like I have a choice," she said.

"It's all on your say so," I said.

"Well all right."

She was mad and ungrateful even when she got what she wanted. And she jumped up and walked away. She didn't even finish her cocktail, and that kind of waste was a part of her problem, in my opinion. She wasn't nice about it, like I knew she wouldn't be, but I also didn't have to talk to her anymore, and that was positive. I lay in the sun and enjoyed my drink because I don't waste the good things I am lucky enough to have, and then I went back to my suite and pressed the call bell for Raoul and right away he knocked at the door. I told him come in and I sat down at the desk and pulled out my bankroll.

"There's a girl named Jen," I said.

"Miss Nickels. She's an eyeful," Raoul said.

I counted out five hundred dollars. "I don't think service should be looking at the girls," I said.

"You're right, Mr. Rutledge. I was out of line." He was watching me count.

"She's got an outstanding debt," I said.

"Twenty grand and climbing," Raoul said. "The purser asked me to have a word with her. It was emotional."

"She thinks the purser won't let her go to the Gala."

"It's a step the office took," Raoul said.

I pushed the cash over to him. Raoul put his eyebrows up. "I want a receipt," I said. "And I want the purser to let Miss Nickels into the Gala."

Raoul considered it. "I don't think I can swing it for you for five hundred," he said.

I counted out two more bills. "There is also a dress," I said.

"A dress?"

"In the pavilion. She took it in for alterations and they won't give it back."

"That is another fish to fry," Raoul said.

I put another bill into the pile. "That's the ticket to the Gala and the dress," I said.

"I might be able to get you one or the other," Raoul said.

"I want both," I said. I put another bill on the pile.

"The purser likes round numbers," Raoul said.

I put one more c-note in and pushed the stack over to Raoul. "Write me a receipt for a thousand dollars," I said. "Then talk to the purser and get the dress and show it to me."

Raoul wrote out a receipt and took the cash. "I'll be right back," he said.

But I thought it would take him a few minutes and I had things to do. I went to Mr. Gualtieri and got my cummerbund, and I picked up another flat of water at the store in the mall, since I was there and I thought I might be thirsty in the morning. When I got back Raoul was waiting for me. He had the dress. It was in a box and wrapped in tissue and ribbon. It looked all right.

"You need to take it to her suite," I said. "Do not look at her tits."

Raoul looked stunned. "I wouldn't do that, Mr. Rutledge."

I ignored it. "Did you talk to the purser about Miss Nickels going to the Gala?" I asked him.

"We sorted it out," Raoul said. "Money talks."

And he gave me his word that no one would harass Jen about her bill at the Gala. Although, after the party, he said, all bets were off. And I was satisfied with his work. So I gave him a nice tip, because that's how you keep service sweet.

o o o

And then it was time for me to suit up and have a proper cocktail. I put on my tux, and it was comfortable. Manny did good work with the hooks. And then I went down to the Dexter. They were packing up the all-day buffet, and it was nearly empty, which was fine with me because I wanted to ease into the evening. I spotted Bud. He was sitting at the bar, like old times, and I joined him. Except when I sat down I realized he wasn't really in a party mood and I'd made a mistake.

"All set?" I asked him, even though I could see that he wasn't.

"We're as ready as we'll ever be," he said.

I didn't like to be obvious, but I glanced around. "Is Bailey coming?" I said.

"She's on her way," he said. "She put on her dress and her makeup. The salon sent someone to do her hair. I arranged it. She couldn't make an appointment even. Doctor Dan gave her something and she's trying her best. But it's show time. If she doesn't enjoy herself tonight, I'm taking her home."

I didn't think he knew about the 'Flies being grounded, and I didn't tell him, since he had enough on his plate already and I didn't want to rain on his parade. And Bailey came in, and she looked lovely and sad, with good hair and bad energy. She looked like a strong breeze would knock her down. Bud got her a daiquiri, but we couldn't keep a conversation going, and I didn't want to stay with them, because they were depressives, frankly, and it was dragging me down. So I drank fast and said I'd see them up there, and I decided it didn't count as a cocktail, because it left me feeling flat and unhappy.

So I tried again, in the Oasis this time. But when I got up there, the barman was putting the chairs up.

"You're closing up shop?" I asked him. "It's the middle of the day."

"Nearly everything's closing for the Gala," he said.

"What if people don't want to go to the Gala?" I said.

"Everyone wants to go to the Gala," he said. He sounded bright but he was moving at speed and not giving me his full attention.

the gala

"But still," I said. "Free will and laissez-faire."

"We can't staff all the facilities. Manpower is stretched to breaking point. It's going to take all hands to pull off the Gala."

"The Dexter is open."

He checked his watch. "They'll be closing up soon. The only facilities online for this evening are the Captain's Mess for the Gala and the Mosh Pit for the kids."

"I wanted to open with a cocktail. To ease into the evening."

"A G and T?"

"That's it."

He went behind the bar. "I have to be in the Captain's Mess. I'm late already. But there's always time for a G and T." He was at it right away with the glass and the ice and the pony and the mix gun.

"That's my philosophy," I said.

He put a wedge of lime on the rim and pushed the drink across the bar. "But I have to lock up," he said. "Can I ask you to take a traveler?"

I looked across the floor to the open-air section of the venue. "I thought I'd enjoy the sunset," I said. But he pushed the chit across the bar for me to sign. I didn't like being rushed out of the venue. I worried about spillage in transit. But there was no one else in the Oasis anyway, so I said okay and signed for the drink, and I gave him a tip, but not a large one, because I was trying to conserve, and I didn't feel that he'd given me completely first-rate service.

"The Mosh Pit is open?" I asked him.

"One below," he said.

So I said thank you and I took a couple of long pulls to bring the level down, and then I called up the elevator even though it was only one floor, because I don't like the stairs.

On the next level, the doors to the Mosh Pit were closed, but I could feel the vibrations as soon as I stepped off the elevator. And when I opened the door to the club, it was like walking into a wall. The facility had state-of-the-art audiophonics, with priority to the bass end. I could feel it in my solar plexus. Also it was dark, with no windows and black lights and strobes and just some neon behind the bar where the staff poured sodas. There was incense in the air, or dry ice. I needed time to adjust. I stood by the door blinking and looking around.

I could see a DJ's booth in one corner and a bar on the back wall with retro neon signs for lemonade and granita, and around the perimeter there was a long banquette, like in the Oasis one deck up, with velvet upholstery and low tables and stools. There were kids slumped on the tables and sprawling on the banquette. The heiress was there, nodding somewhat.

In the middle of the room there was a dance floor, chained off around the perimeter like a boxing ring. And there were more tables ringside and across the floor, and there were cages on platforms in among the tables, and people were dancing in the cages and on the dance floor. There were a few kids on the dance floor but the cages were full, with at least one person in each, and many more in some, shaking it or showcasing it or just going at it.

Someone tapped me on the shoulder and it was the J-kid. He said something that I couldn't hear because the music was pounding, and I raised my glass at him. He looked at it and looked at me and said something else. I thought maybe he was ragging on me for bringing a drink into a dry venue, so I just laughed and patted his shoulder. And then he took me by the elbow and pulled me after him, and I figured what the hell. I moved my G and T to the other hand so I didn't spill and I let him show me around.

He pulled me through the tables and around the cages. He pointed at other kids and I smiled and waved too like I was happy to meet them. And he took me to the back and down a hallway and through a door marked "The Office." It was the can. It was dim inside, also, and the music was still loud. There was a row of urinals on one wall and some stalls and a row of sinks. A couple of young guys were hanging around, checking their look and dancing. And there were two comfortable chairs in the corner and a table between them.

The J-kid sat down in one chair and pointed, and I sat down in the other. Then he leaned over to me and said something else that I still couldn't hear. He snapped his fingers at one of the guys who jumped up on top of the sink and reached up to the ceiling. He pushed a tile out of the way and pulled himself up by the crossbar and disappeared. He was young and athletic and he could do that without breaking a sweat. And then his head came back into view, upside-down, and his hand with a bundle in it which he dropped down to the other kid, who caught it and brought it over to us.

The J-kid took it and opened it and laid out a tasting menu on the table between us. There were reds and whites and blues, greenies and pinkies. There were round pills and gel tabs and horse pills and time-release capsules and torpedoes that I didn't like the look of. There were little papers of powder. The J-kid unfolded them and showed me white powder and brown powder. There were rocks and resins rolled up in foil. He pulled out a little bag of herb and a little bag of seed. There was a baggie of mushrooms. And he had a couple of air mail stamps, the old-fashioned kind that weren't self-adhesive; he turned them over to show me the glue on the back and pretended to lick it, and we had a laugh about that.

The guy in the ceiling dropped another bag down to the guy at the sink, and he caught it and opened it and laid out the kit on the table beside the sample case. There were needles and a spoon and a lighter and a razor and a length of rubber to tie it off and a pipe and rubbing alcohol and cotton balls.

All in all, it was a very complete selection, and I had to admire the J-kid's thoroughness and the organization that he brought to his business. Also I had respect for his nerve and initiative, since he was taking risks like entrepreneurs do. All along I'd been thinking he was a loafer, the way the young and wealthy can be, just coasting and playing games on his personal device and listening to music. But all at once I found out he had work to do, with innovative and effective systems for storage and staffing and distribution. It was the kind of thing that makes you stop and re-evaluate. I was impressed.

And although normally I feel that alcohol is both legal and effective, I felt like I should do what I could to encourage the boy. Because he reminded me somewhat of myself at a younger age, although I never moved pharmaceuticals. It's a specialized concern, and while the rewards are attractive, the penalties are a disincentive. I wasn't sure what kind of laws applied on the high seas and I thought he might catch a break if we were between jurisdictions. But it was clear to me that supply was an issue, and that foresight and planning were key. So he was working in a challenging arena, and I did what I could to support him.

"What have you got in the way of pleasure enhancement?" I asked him. I had to shout because the music was grinding. "I'm thinking something upbeat and built for dancing."

The J-kid nodded hard like he could hear me, and just for a minute he reminded me of Raoul. He licked his little finger and picked up a yellow pill with it and held it out to me. There was a daisy stamped on it. So I took it off his finger and knocked it back with the rest of my G and T. Then I stood up and smiled at them all.

"I should get moving," I shouted. "The Gala's kicking off. Who do I see about my bill?"

The J-kid pointed at his associate by the sink. He was bigger and more muscular than the guy in the ceiling. And he stepped up to me and showed me two fingers. I thought it was steep. Some people would discount the first purchase or put it on the house even. But my guess was they had a monopoly aside from Doctor Dan, and that also gave them a business advantage. So I unrolled a twenty and the kid at the sink took it, and I patted him on the shoulder and went down to the Captain's Mess, because I'd enjoyed my cocktail finally and I was ready for the main event.

the gala

o o o

I was still early somewhat, one of the first, but the party was warming
up. From the door I could hear people testing mics in the room and see
the lights dropping down to a sophisticated party glow. The captain and
Hoskins and the hospitality officer and the padre were lined up at the
door, looking their very best and ready to shake everyone's hand when
they arrived. And I was happy that I got a chance to meet the captain
finally and say hello, like I'd wanted to since I came on board.

Hoskins stepped up and welcomed me like he should. He said, "Right
on time, Mr. Rutledge. It's good to see you." And then he made a wide
gesture like he was embracing me with one hand and the captain with
the other, and he said, "Captain Moncrieff was just saying he likes to
meet all the cruisers at the Gala." And the captain put out his hand and
gave me a big smile, and the hospitality officer stood just behind him,
whispering: "Mr. Rutledge. Six fourteen. Balcony suite. Interests include
social life and shipboard amenities."

I shook the captain's hand and pretended I didn't hear. "I've been
looking forward to saying hello," I said.

"It's a privilege," he said.

I didn't know if he meant for him or for me, and while I was wondering Hoskins butted in again to be charming. "Mr. Rutledge will get
the girls on their feet," he said. "He keeps the party humming."

"I like a good time," I said. "Good food and good people." I was
still shaking Captain Moncrieff's hand so he would know I had more
to say. I got to the point before Hoskins could elbow in again. "I sat at
the captain's table a while ago," I said. "It was a pleasure. I hope you'll
ask me up some time."

It is never a mistake to be direct because if you don't tell people
what you want sometimes they never know.

The captain looked happy to hear about it but he didn't make any
promises. "Your number's going to come up," he said. "Hospitality has

a system. They have it all worked out." I was still shaking his hand but he was looking at the hospitality girl. "Who am I sitting with tonight?" he asked her.

She whispered to him and I heard the names of the entrepreneur and the movie star.

The captain nodded. "Of course," he said. "Of course."

"Didn't they get a turn already?" I said.

The captain lit up. He looked like a little kid. "I've had the pleasure already," he said. "I've hosted them four or five times. Several times. I don't count. They hosted me back, too. People invite me to little suppers in their suite, just a few of us. And then I have them back to the captain's table. Turn and turn about."

"I thought we all took turns sitting at the captain's table," I said.

"We do," he said. The hospitality officer whispered to the captain some more. "Right," he said. He moved his other hand in for a double grip and squeezed somewhat. "We have to keep the line moving," he said.

I looked behind me. There was no one there. But the captain put another pulse into the handshake and dropped it, and he turned around to consult with the hospitality girl some more. I decided we had a good talk. I thought he'd remember me, and I let them know I wanted to be asked to the captain's table. So I accomplished my chief goal and I was satisfied with that.

I stepped along. I thought I'd say hello to the padre. But he slouched into a corner and lit a cigarette and glared at me like he dared me to talk to him, and then Ashley came up fast and took my arm. The maitre d' had the hostesses lined up at the door, and she took me past them into the Captain's Mess with individual attention like always.

As soon as I walked in the doors, I knew that they did the right thing with the timing and the Gala and even closing down the room the day before to decorate. The Captain's Mess was totally transformed. They took out the raised platforms and the sunken areas and most of the tables from the main floor, and they left the captain's table with the fountain and the moat and a few other tables around the perimeter. And the centre of the room was a dance floor, with the trees around it all lit with fairy lights, and still full of little birds and real butterflies, so it was like dancing in an enchanted forest. And Ashley whispered to me that it was a professional dance floor, corked and sprung and with an antiskid surface so no one would hurt themselves. The band was set up beside it with singers from the Broadway giving us standards and scatting. Already a few couples were doing their thing, older people looking happy and a little stiff, and some younger people too, fooling around and having a good time.

Ashley let me look for a minute, and then she pulled me ahead the way she did. "I want to get you to your table because it's all new seating tonight," she said.

It had to be since the whole room was rearranged. With the main level set up for music and dancing, they seated most of the guests on the mezzanine. So I wasn't surprised Ashley led me up one of the corkscrew stairs. She put me at a table for six and no one else was there yet. But the waiter came up right away like he should, and I ordered a G and T, and the daisy pill kicked in and I felt fine.

Soon the room filled up and Ashley seated Phil and Andrea, who I hadn't met before, and we shook hands and they were older and full of good feeling. And then Doug joined us who was also new to me, and then Candy and Belinda, who came together and I thought might be a couple, except they were both close with Doug, too. So I wasn't sure. But everyone was happy and attractive, and we had a fine crowd all together, and the band was playing, and the room filled up, and there was laughing and conversation. I had a powerful feeling of happiness again about everything because there were interesting people I'd never met before all around me and pleasure as far as the eye could see.

Our waiter came around at speed with flutes and all over the mezzanine corks were popping. Doug looked concerned. The waiter put a flute in front of him and tried to move on. He had his hands full, you could see, with a big section and glasses and drinks. But Doug caught his wrist and said, "We didn't order this."

"Don't interfere, Dougie," I said.

"I think it's a mistake," he said.

"It's a part of the Gala, sir," the waiter said. "All-inclusive in the ticket."

And then it was okay with Doug and he let the waiter get on with it. And the wine waiter popped a bottle for us and poured everyone out.

Then, just like that first magical night, the lights went down and everybody stopped talking and looked around, and a spot came up on the captain's table. And Captain Moncrieff stood up with a microphone in one hand and a glass of champagne in the other. Now that I'd met him and I'd seen him in action, I knew he was a climber and full of himself somewhat, but even still, he was the captain, and he looked crisp in his whites although his gut spilled over his belt. So I gave him my attention in spite of it all. And when everyone settled down he started.

"Well, we're not out of the woods yet in terms of supply and demand," he said. "But if we hold the course and stick to the plan, then it's under control and no sweat off my brow. And I'm not one to dwell on the negative, so I think we should all take the unhappy events on the other side and pay them no more never mind as my gran-pappy used to say."

He stopped and made puppy eyes around the room, and Belinda said, "He's a honey lamb," and everyone clapped.

"It was our first-class crew that pulled us out of harm's way, and the hand of Someone watching over us was clearly visible at our darkest hour. And on a side note, I'm sure Father McGrath would agree that we all feel safer knowing that Someone's got our back."

He looked over at the padre sitting near him at the captain's table. But the padre was looking down at his plate and I thought he maybe considered the captain wasn't respectful enough, although he meant well. The captain kept going.

"And besides our crew who were only doing their duty after all, it was you, our guests who stuck with us and are now reaping the rewards of this undertaking. Especially I raise my glass to our special guests at the captain's table who are a real honour and a pleasure for me as well as the rest of the cruisers. I'd like to say that you honour us and pleasure us with your continued presence and especially tonight at this elegant function which we hope you enjoy and treasure the memory of forever."

He stopped to let us show our appreciation, and we all clapped to show that we respected the entrepreneur and the movie star too.

"And to our other cruisers in the admiralty suites and the principal staterooms and the balcony suites, and all our guests, I'd like to thank you all for coming. I'm looking forward to cutting the rug tonight with all the beautiful ladies here."

He pulled some paper out of a pocket and his glasses. "A couple of housekeeping notices they want me to read." He put the glasses on and squinted at his notes. "The kitchen says the squab tonight is only partly boned. So cut and chew carefully. And they're asking you not to feed the birds. They're supposed to be on a special diet and cruisers feed them white bread and sugar and it kills them. So don't do that."

I looked around to see if Ben was listening but I didn't see him. Then Hoskins said something to the captain that no one could hear because he wasn't wearing a mic, and the captain looked at him and looked at us and kind of smiled again.

"Moving on then," he said. "I'd like to ask Father McGrath to step up now and say grace, to show our thankfulness for the good things we have in front of us."

But the padre had his head in his hands and he didn't look up.

"You'll come and say grace, Father?" said the captain.

The padre still didn't look up. He might have said something, but I couldn't hear.

"Won't you come and say grace?" said the captain. He was smiling still, but he looked confused. The padre shook his head some more. Then Hoskins said something else no one could hear. "Oh. I'll say grace myself, then," Captain Moncrieff said. "It's one of the things a captain does. I can marry people and bury them at sea. And I can say grace. It's part of the spiritual dimension of my job."

The padre put his head on the table and his hands on his head, but I don't think Captain Moncrieff noticed. He faced the room again and put his hands together around the microphone and the stem of his flute, and he closed his eyes tight like he was thinking hard. At my table, we all took each other's hands. It felt good, like a team before kickoff.

"Dear God in heaven," the captain said. "We thank you for the good things you rain down on us, for the food and the wine and the big band and, oh, the table service and real linen, too. We give thanks, oh Lord, for these great blessings, and we ask only that you keep it coming. Forever and ever. Amen."

Then he raised his glass but not the mic and we all did too, and we drank to the grace. And then the spot shut down and they gave us a bit of light around the room, but still subtle and magical, and waiters rolled out with the *amuse-bouche* and a basket of rolls, and we got on with the party.

It was a fine meal, although as Phil said, you could tell Chef Lousine was still AWOL and it would be a good thing when he got back and we got new groceries, too. But they made a better showing than they did for a while, and nothing too heavy. The girls didn't ask for half portions or complain about starch even though it was a fixed menu with no options and no choices.

They gave us olives and artichokes and sun dried tomatoes and slices of bread toasted and brushed with oil, and carrot soup with pepper, and a salad with noodles and cabbage and sesame seeds. Then the squab in a nest of wild rice, and no one choked. And a cheese plate with old cheddar and something blue and something creamy with herbs in it, and all with elegant crackers and figs soaked in port and with walnuts and candied orange peel. Phil ordered wine for the table, good bottles and several of them, and he wouldn't even talk about splitting the bill.

The waiter didn't stop to chat, but he kept the plates moving and the wine waiter kept us topped up and a couple of kids bussed. It was banquet service and impersonal somewhat, but efficient and the company was good so I didn't mind.

Between courses and while we ate, we had conversation, which I found difficult to follow sometimes, but smart and entertaining. And then after the cheese plate but before coffee and cognac, the tables broke up somewhat and people mingled more. The band gave us background through the main meal, and when the cheese plate was cleared they turned up the volume again, and the captain took the movie star onto the dance floor to open the dancing portion of the Gala officially.

I danced many different girls one at a time and they were all warm and beautiful in their way. I danced the girls at my table and then I branched out and danced everyone I knew. Saskia was lazy and lovely, and Poppy had a couple of drinks in her and she was friendly, and Amanda was warm and attentive. Andrea made me laugh although I couldn't remember the jokes after, and Belinda asked me about myself and admired my achievements. And Candy couldn't dance at all really. I wasn't completely steady either by then. So we did a slow number and she tucked herself into my arms and made little warm bird noises only I could hear.

As she nestled under me and we slow danced, a powerful feeling of happiness came over me. It came to me that it was all still possible. I could fall in love, and make love, and love someone and be loved by them. And I didn't have to be abandoned like roadkill on the highway, or watch the person I loved and leaned on disappear in the distance, and be alone all the time. All around me, the girls looked their very best, and with a pretty girl tucked into my arms, everything seemed possible.

I felt I could see other people arriving at their own conclusions. At the captain's table, the padre was gone and Captain Moncrieff complained to Hoskins, "Would it kill Father McGrath to thank God for the good things in front of us? Is it my job to mention the Invisible Guardian?" Hoskins nodded but he didn't say anything.

Across the floor Bud was dancing with Bailey. I was surprised since he didn't dance usually with his bad hip. But they were slow dancing too, just holding on to each other and swaying a little. I thought she was holding him up maybe. And then I thought maybe vice versa. They weren't finding the beat at all, and Bailey didn't have any fine, bold moves. But they held each other tight, and I thought it was for the best.

The entrepreneur brought Jen out on the floor. She was wearing the dress I got out of hock, and I thought he probably liked her better when she wasn't looking for a loan. She was dancing with the biggest man on the boat, so when they danced near me I smiled at her and told her the dress looked good, and she ignored me, which I expected mostly, although if she wanted to introduce me to her friend the entrepreneur I wouldn't say no. But she was dancing with the big man and she didn't notice me even though I bought her ticket to the dance.

Then Hoskins made a break from the captain and he danced with Saskia and laughed a lot. Natalie danced past with an officer looking sharp in his whites. I still didn't see Ben.

And then I saw Eddie. He was sitting alone at a table by the dance floor. I was surprised to see him, but happy, and when the song finished Candy went back to the table and I went over and said hello.

"I didn't see you before," I told him. "I'm glad you made it."

"They told me to come," he said. "Doctor Dan said I should come, and the nurses. They don't like me hanging around all the time."

"They think you need a break," I told him. "They're right. Doctor's orders."

Eddie shrugged. Then he said, "It hurts to love someone and watch them die."

It slowed me down. I said, "What are you talking about?"

"Katherine's dying," he said. "She's terminal."

I had no clue at all what to say. People were dancing all around us. The big band was playing.

"We got the diagnosis from a specialist, a good one. He told us six months or eight. A year at the outside."

It was a terrible thing for him to say, a terrible thing to hear. A part of me wanted to make my excuses and go away, but I also felt full of love and sadness for Eddie and for Katherine. And it was strange, talking about it while people were dancing around us, and when the band hit into the chorus I had to shout my sympathies over the brass. But I couldn't avoid it, because Eddie was a good man and my friend, and he had a right. I sat with him, and I said the things you say. I don't know if he listened. It didn't matter.

"When the doctor was telling us about it, Katherine was still with it," Eddie said. "We talked about it together, about what we would do. We booked onto the cruise. It was like we were sending it away or we were running away from it together. We brought the kids with us. I forgot sometimes her condition was coming too. Now I don't get away from it. When I'm in Sick Bay with her, I watch her slipping away. When I take a break, I think about it. Katherine's mostly out of it, which is a good thing in a lot of ways. But then I feel like I'm alone, and like I'm doing it. When she's the one who is actually dying."

I felt bad for him and I was going to sit with him and talk about it as long as he wanted. But I wished he wouldn't emphasize it. It was like looking straight at the sun.

"It's too bad Lily isn't here and everyone," I said. It was a way of talking around the worst parts of it. "They could help you."

"It would be nice to have their company," he said. "And I'm worried about them also. But I can't help them, and even if they were here, this isn't work someone else can do for you."

And I could see what he meant.

It was the saddest thing I'd heard for a long time, and it made it sadder with everyone looking their best and dancing. Then Eddie didn't have anything else to say and I didn't want to keep the topic going. So I just sat quietly with him. The band hit it up and up to a big finish and the dancers stopped dancing and clapped and Jen and the entrepreneur came out of the crowd and across the floor to us. I thought, this is the worst time for Jen to get friendly with me again. But the big man waved her away and he sat down with us.

"You look like you're running out of steam," he said. He was talking to Eddie.

"I get tired at night," Eddie said.

"You rest in the afternoon. Then you can go all night."

Eddie said, "I rest in the afternoon. I get tired at night also. But then I wake up, two o'clock, three o'clock in the morning. I don't go back to sleep."

"I figure out deals then," the entrepreneur said.

Eddie nodded but I didn't think he was listening. "Do you know Rutledge?" he said.

It was what I was looking for the whole cruise, but it came out of nowhere, and I wasn't totally at the top of my game. But I was completely where I wanted to be, sitting with Eddie and with the big man, and it made it better that Jen was on the other side of the room watching us all be friendly and comfortable. Not that it was an easy assignment in any way, and I thought Eddie turned it over to me because he had other things on his mind. For all these reasons and simple good manners I did my best.

I put out my hand and said, "Happy to meet you."

The entrepreneur shook me firmly. "It's a pleasure," he said. He turned back to Eddie. "You're coming up to the Gallery," he said. It didn't sound like a question.

"I'm going to pass," Eddie said. "I want to get back to Sick Bay."

The entrepreneur turned to me. "Help me educate our young friend," he said.

the gala

"What's the topic?" I asked him.

"I have something special laid on for dessert," the entrepreneur said. "I found an ambitious patissier in the kitchen. I'm giving him his big break." He pulled a card out of his pocket and said, "Let me tempt you."

He gave Eddie the card and Eddie sort of glanced at it. "I never liked that kind of cooking," he said. "I think it's show-offy."

"It's art."

"That's what I mean. I just like something to eat."

The entrepreneur gave him a hard look. "Shame, sir, shame," he said.

"I'd be happy with fruit cup," Eddie said.

"It's tinned," I said.

The entrepreneur looked at me like he was seeing me for the first time. "Exactly," he said.

Eddie said, "It reminds me. Tinned fruit in syrup was a treat, once. It was something special when I was a kid."

"We know better now," the big man said. "Don't you want to try something new?"

Eddie thought about it for a minute. "No," he said. "I don't want to try something new. I like the things I tried already. I want more of the things I already had, or I don't want anything at all."

The big man turned to me. "You'll join us for dessert, Rutledge? In the Gallery at the midnight hour."

He gave me the card. It was a menu. The big headings said things like, 'The Wages of Sin,' and 'The Flowers and the Fruits of Eden.' I couldn't make out the fine print. I was having trouble focusing with the low lights and the daisy pill and the wine. But I was intrigued.

"What's 'Billy's Bud'?" I asked him.

The big man shrugged. "I don't know the details," he said. "I leave it to creative because I like to be surprised. Here. We'll ask my event coordinator."

Beside me Eddie threw his napkin on the table. The entrepreneur put his hand up and a hospitality specialist rolled up instantly. I admired the big man's control of service because the waiter at my table was running a big section and didn't have time to chat. But designated talent still jumped up for the entrepreneur. He made a gesture to me and the specialist gave me his attention.

"What's 'Billy's Bud'?" I asked him.

He pulled out a handheld and started punching it right away. He read from the screen. "Billy's Bud is an infusion of green herbs served on the shaven pubis of a virgin," he said. He considered it. "It's conceptual," he said.

It sounded wrong to me, so I asked him, "Shouldn't it be 'shaved'?"

He checked his handheld. "It says 'shaven,'" he said. He looked at me and he looked at the entrepreneur. The entrepreneur gave him a steady look. "I'll make inquiries," the event coordinator said.

"You do that," the big man said.

The event coordinator went away and the entrepreneur looked at us and laughed. He liked being in charge, you could tell. And then Jen came back again and started pulling him out onto the floor and he let her. "I'm going to have 'Bitch's Brew,'" he said. "I'm looking forward." He pushed himself up and put an arm around Jen without looking. "I'll be expecting you boys," he said. "But we'll leave the chippies out of it. I lined up professionals." They got swept back into the crowd.

"God, what a parade," Eddie said.

"It was nice of him to invite me," I said.

"Katherine never liked him. He reeks of new money."

"What's wrong with that?" I asked him. "He worked hard."

"He's got a publicist for Christ's sake," Eddie said. "It's dessert not a chorus line. It used to be he'd have a dinner party and he'd bring out the chef for us to shake his hand. Our servants stayed in the kitchen."

"You want to get some air?" I asked him. "We could take a turn in the Arboretum, work up an appetite for dessert."

"No," Eddie said. "I'm done." He stood up. It was a bit of a process but not as bad as the lounger.

"I'll come back up to Sick Bay with you. Say hello to Katherine," I said.

And I would have done it, because he was my friend and I was concerned for him. But he waved me away. "You keep dancing," Eddie said. "You're young. I'll pass on your regards."

We shook hands and he shuffled off. I felt sad for him, but also grateful. I circulated to kill a few minutes. I didn't make a big deal telling people where I was going, because not everyone was invited, and I didn't like to rub their noses in it.

Afterwards in the lobby, Jen was making her case to the big man. She was holding onto him and saying, "Why can't I come? I want dessert."

He waved her away. "Chippies should know when they're not wanted," he told me. And we went up to the Gallery together where he laid it on for his friends and acquaintances. The food was so-so, but the presentation left nothing to the imagination. And I stayed until the chef came out and took a bow.

the blue pacific

CHAPTER SIXTEEN

The next day I crashed hard. I woke up late and thirsty and still wearing my tux, although the cummerbund had popped while I slept and the hooks tore the fabric somewhat. I threw it all in the laundry, and I got water and drank.

It felt like the days were drawing in. Communications were still down, though the tech boys were looking into it. We were close to the rendezvous point, but running low on all fronts. The purser sent a note around saying we had a good time at the Gala but now we had to economize. He asked for voluntary restraint. It was a low blow, after the dancing and the good food and too much to drink, but I was feeling sluggish and sad, and not in a mood to fight.

They shut down most of the bars. I found out the hard way, looking for dog hair the day after the party. I tried the Dreadlock and the Oasis and the Local and the Tropicana and the Bar Sinister and the Crow's Nest. No soap. Later on they put a waiter on at the Slaker for happy hour. But that was it.

Meals also were squeezed. They closed down every venue but the

Big Banana for breakfast and the Captain's Mess for lunch and dinner. The Banana kept its usual hours, but the selection closed in. They put weak instant in the coffee urns and where the eggs-to-order station used to be they had a guy with a pot of oatmeal.

Then the Captain's Mess was completely remodeled. The day after the party I arrived late because I wasn't moving fast and I had no luck with a cocktail and I wouldn't have come down to the dining room at all maybe if any other venue was still operating where I could get a ham sandwich and a beer. I didn't feel committed to getting into my tux and making chitchat with the J-kid at our big empty table. But I came down finally because I was hungry and had no choice, and it was a shock and a whole new thing.

They took out the dance floor, but they didn't put back the raised platforms and sunken intimate areas. They just lined the tables up across the floor. The birds were still in the trees, but the magic was gone. They roped off the mezzanine and turned up the lights so people didn't trip and hurt themselves carrying plates. And we were carrying plates because they closed table service and gave us buffet instead. Everyone lined up with a plate in their hands like we were in jail. All the waiters and bartenders still on board were reassigned to the Captain's Mess, and the hostesses put on aprons and worked too. But even still, once they cleared and brought ice water and ran refills of baked spaghetti or tuna casserole or jelly salad to the buffet, they didn't have manpower for individual attention. They didn't bring hot rolls or condiments around. It was every man for himself.

The only personnel still on task were the wine waiters, and diners could still order a bottle, and they cracked it for you like they should. But they were out of the most reliable table wines. So you either had to choose something very cheap or something very expensive. I tried both options at different times, and I felt regret either way.

It was hard to eat like a civilized person, because the hours were bad and the room was crowded, and if you wanted to get there before the main meal dried out in the chafing dish, you had to rush your cocktail or skip it or start good and early. The only good thing in the new arrangement was I could sit I where I wanted and Jane didn't stop me.

The day after the party, I rolled in late and hungover and tried to make sense of the new system. I followed Leanne down the buffet and looked around for a place to sit. There was a chair left at a big table where Saskia was, and Teresa and Enright and Vance and Amanda and Bud and Michael, and I thought Leanne would take it, but she went the other way and sat with Natalie and Poppy, and I brought my tray over and took the last chair, because these were people who knew how to have a good time, and who understood that pleasure is the goal and is always worth looking for especially when the situation is challenging.

The kitchen also was making an effort even though conditions were bad. They gave us hot hamburger sandwich on white bread with mushroom gravy. It was an honest meal, filling and like home, and I enjoyed my plate. But the girls fussed.

"It's the full fat special," Teresa said.

"And salt," Saskia said.

They split an order between them but neither ate really, not even the mushrooms. They cut it up and pushed it around with a fork. I thought they shouldn't waste since we were running low, but I liked them both, so I didn't say it.

We got more entertainment watching developments in the room. For instance, we had a fine perspective when the maitre d' hauled Jen's ass out of the room. She turned up later even than me and took a plate and got in line. She was complaining, for a change. And then the maitre d' turned up beside her and started talking hard. She ignored him. So he gave his team the nod and the minders who used to hold the perimeter at the captain's table rolled up and helped Jen put down her plate and cutlery, and they walked her outside.

"Wow. Don't criticize the cook," Michael said.

"They can't do that," Saskia said.

Everyone including me was sorry to see security taking the initiative, but I let them know it wasn't black and white either because Jen had responsibilities too.

"Don't get involved," I told them.

"She needs her supper," Bud said.

He was alone and I didn't ask about Bailey because you could see he was unhappy with things in general. But I said, "It's an issue with the purser's office." I kept my voice down because it was private for Jen, even if I didn't like her very much. Everyone understood what I meant, though, and people thought it over.

Finally Enright said, "She has to pay the piper. But they can't starve her."

"She won't starve," I said. "They just limit your options."

"But the Captain's Mess is the only option now," Teresa said.

"Can we call it an option if no alternative exists?" Vance said.

"It's not a full roster of choices," I said. "It's disappointing. The Company is letting down the consumer."

"Lou and Denise had the right idea," Michael said. "Who knew? I thought they were just being ethical."

"It's not ethics. It's business," said Bud. "The Company has to deliver on its contract."

"You can only say the Company broke contract if it didn't put a clause in the contract about it," Enright said.

"Did the Company put a clause in your contract about hot hamburger sandwich?" Vance asked him.

"The Company has a clause in the contract about nearly everything," Enright said. "It's probably covered."

Bud pushed his plate away and got up. He didn't say good night or goodbye, but we all liked him and felt bad about Bailey and nobody called him on it. And Vance and Enright kept at it like they didn't notice.

"They can't offer a luxury cruise without luxuries," Vance said. "It's a paradox."

"About Jen, I have mixed feelings," I said. "I don't like to see a customer strong-armed out of the lunch line. But there's another side to it. Nothing is free in life. She knows it. I know she does because we talked about it once."

Though at that moment, Maromed seemed a long way away.

The next day they drained the pool and the hot tub. They shut the steam room in the fitness facility and closed the salon. In a few days the girls started to look shaggy, and Hoss's roots began to show. The wait staff stopped bringing ice water around in the Captain's Mess, although that still didn't free them up for individual table service. The purser sent the stewards around to tell everyone about water conservation; Leticia came to my door, and told me not to flush every time and to shower every other day. I told her I'd consider it, although obviously I wouldn't, but I wasn't going to get into it with a girl.

o o o

The next thing was they ran out of tonic. I was in a lounger taking the sun by the pool, which was empty, and the waiter from the Slaker broke it to me.

"Maybe a martini, Mr. Rutledge?" he said.

I didn't like the idea. It's too much like straight gin, and drinking spirits neat is a sure sign of a problem.

"A Singapore Sling?" he suggested.

"Is that a girl's drink?"

"It's supposed to be garnished with pineapple and cherry. But we're low on fruit, so its profile is more masculine."

I asked for a Tom Collins instead, and he told me okay, and he went away for a long time and I was hopeful and then impatient and then he came back and told me they were out of lemons.

"How can a bar be out of lemons?" I asked him.

"It's the austerity," he said. "Citrus and tropical fruit are going fast."

So I sent him back to inventory the mixers they had left, and it turned out they had no fruit to spare but an array of lemon-lime drinks at the different venues and in the dispensing machines, and powdered drinks and frozen concentrates also, although they mixed these too strong sometimes, since the purser was rationing water. I tried them all over the next few days, and I found some things I liked, although it was pointless in the long run because I'd just get used to one and they'd run out. But at least they still had gin and refrigeration. So I had gin drinks that were too sweet sometimes, or thick like slush, but cold and refreshing.

Most days I'd get there early because service was slow. I'd take a lounger and sit in the sun beside the empty pool and I'd have a gin drink with citrus mix and shoot it with whoever was around, Poppy and Enright, Vance and Amanda, Andrea and Phil, Doug, Michael, and Teresa, and either Leanne or Saskia, one or the other, not both, because after the Gala Leanne wasn't speaking to Saskia. On the other hand, she had a lot to say about her. She didn't like that Saskia was close-dancing Hoskins at the party. So she was angry at Saskia and she had hurt feelings for Hoss. The whole thing surprised and disappointed me, because I thought he was flashy and cheap and not worth fighting over. And I thought Saskia had better sense even if Leanne didn't. But I knew enough to stay out of it and not give an opinion. And privately I thought Leanne made a mistake counting Saskia out in the first place, because it's a safe bet that a woman like Saskia, who knows how to take care of other people, knows how to take care of herself as well.

Most days, the entrepreneur showed up on the other side of the pool. A hospitality specialist came out first and rearranged several loungers in a group, and he came out with his girls and his security detail. His party had their own waiter dedicated, and once the party arrived, they sunned themselves in their private chairs with the hospitality specialist in the background and security on the perimeter and their dedicated waiter bringing drinks. By himself he had more service than everyone else on deck put together, and some people thought it was wrong, but I never criticized, because he paid for it and also he was my friend.

It was true that he never invited me to join his gang in their private loungers and enjoy a drink with speedy service from his private waiter, even though sometimes I walked back and forth past his group looking for a seat I liked. But sometimes he smiled or nodded or looked in my direction. And even though he never asked me to come over and take a load off, I didn't mind. Because he had his own agenda and so did I, and he had his girls with him, and big people are funny that way. They can be your pal and beg you to come to their party one day and ignore you the next. You get used to it the more you know them, and you don't let it bother you. So when people complained that he had special treatment, I stood up for him.

"He's in an admiralty suite," I told them. "It comes with extras, and it should. For his monthly alone he should get priority service. But he pays a premium on top also."

And people usually listened to reason. And it was warm and there wasn't much to do, and mostly people just felt lazy and relaxed.

○ ○ ○

Then for a while it seemed like the purser made a new rule every day about rations and limits. One morning I turned on the tap in the bathroom and nothing happened. I called Raoul and once again Leticia came instead, and she gave me a flyer about water, and when it was on and when it was off, and when there was hot water, and when I could flush. And there was a schedule for showers in the locker room in the fitness facility, which they recommended instead of washing in your suite. It made no sense and I wasn't happy about it but I didn't want to discuss it with a girl. So I told her to send Raoul to me, and she said she'd try.

I waited and he didn't turn up. Finally I gave up and went to the Banana before they closed the breakfast table. But I rang the call bell when I came back, and again after lunch, and before I went out to sit by the pool, and then before dinner when I was putting on my tux.

I was wearing the one with the flared leg again, and no cummerbund

the blue pacific

still, because it never came back with its hooks. And I put on a second-day shirt, like a lot of the guys were doing by then, because although I got some cleaning back after the Gala, it was unpredictable. I'd brought a dozen formal shirts with me, but after the Canal I never had more than two or three clean in my closet, and sometimes none. And sometimes someone cleared out my hamper, but sometimes no one did. And possibly the worst thing was I was relieved they left it sometimes, because at least I had a shirt even if it wasn't fresh. So I was going to have to ask Raoul what he was doing with my laundry, and that was another headache. And in the meantime the toilet didn't flush and I was concerned and I wanted to discuss that with Raoul too.

Finally, when I was tying my tie there was a knock at the door, and I said, "Come in," and it was Raoul. He came in and stood in the middle of the floor looking sad like he knew he was giving me terrible service. The timing was bad because we'd had the single seating in the Captain's Mess for a few days by then and I knew I didn't want to be late, but I had to talk to him anyway. There were too many issues and I'd let it go too long. So I had to go over it with him, and I sat down on the couch to hear all about it.

"You're wearing your tux still," he said. "That's nice."

"I'm going to dinner," I told him. I looked at my watch. "I can only give you a couple of minutes. I don't like to be late because food dries out in the heat tray."

"I understand," he said.

"Plus if you arrive late, you stand in line for a long time holding your plate. I run out of chit-chat for the people beside me. And you don't know for sure if you can find a chair."

It wasn't my main topic, but I let him know from the start I wasn't happy with the new system. There were problems everywhere. Raoul nodded hard like always to show me he fully agreed.

"It's an adjustment for everyone. Anything I can do to ease the transition?"

"I just want water in my suite," I told him.

"We're running a resource conservation program," Raoul said. "You got a copy?" He reached into a pocket and pulled a flyer out.

"I got the schedule." My copy was on the coffee table in front of me. I nodded at it. "I looked at it," I told him. "It makes no sense."

"It's an unfortunate development. It's temporary."

"Leticia says I can't flush?"

Raoul looked surprised and then angry. "You can flush," he said. He was very firm.

"It's not flushing now," I told him.

"You already flushed once?" he said.

"I don't know," I told him. "I get up in the morning. I flush. I don't pay attention."

"You can flush once," Raoul said. "You can flush many times when the water is on. Because when the water is on the tank fills automatically, and when the tank is full you can flush. But when the water is off, the tank doesn't fill. So when the water is off, you can flush once, but the tank won't refill and you can't flush again."

"And the schedule tells me when I can flush?"

"It tells you when the water is on," Raoul said. He opened out his copy and studied it. "The water is on for an hour in the morning and an hour at night. It's on a rotating schedule. I don't know the exact hours for this suite. It's what I'm looking for."

"And hot water?"

"That is another thing," he said. He pointed to a place on the schedule. "Deck six, port side, forward. You have water eight to nine in the morning and again at night."

"Eight to nine?"

"Morning and night."

"That's hot water?"

"That's running water. Hot water is a different thing. We'll go there next. For running water, you have two hours a day, from eight to nine

the blue pacific

in the morning and again at night. The taps are open and the toilet tank refills."

"So I can flush?"

"You can flush and the tank will refill."

"So I can flush more than once?"

"You could flush more than once, although the purser says don't."

"I'm not interested in the purser's opinion on this."

"It's not his business you wouldn't think."

"And hot water is different?"

"It's a subsection of running water." He went back to the flyer. "Hot water eight-thirty to eight-forty-five."

"That's too early," I said. "I'm not even awake most days."

He checked the flyer again. "PM," he said.

"That's too late," I said. "What am I supposed to do? Wash after dinner?"

Raoul agreed completely. "It isn't the best arrangement. I fought for my clients. In the end, it was the best I could do." He looked at the schedule in his hand like he knew it was garbage.

"Raoul, it's terrible," I told him. I didn't like to be harsh, but I couldn't pretend.

He agreed but he didn't answer my point. "Some people told me," he said, "and it isn't in the spirit of restraint, but they said they'd run the sink full of hot water, and the bathtub."

"I don't have a bathtub. Just a shower."

Raoul opened his eyes wide and looked around the room. "I forgot this is a balcony stateroom. It was deluxe staterooms and admiralty suites I was talking to." He looked around. "It's a challenge, finding the best option at your price point. But another possibility is, you can go up to the fitness facility. One client told me he'd use his fifteen minutes of personal hot water to shave, and take his shower in the facility."

It was the Company line and I didn't waste my time on it. "It's just not a good approach," I told him. "Plus you're backtracking.

You said before it was an honour system."

"It was a voluntary system," Raoul said. "It was the first plan. We tried it over several days. The feeling was we had to pull back more. So they made the water schedule and the laundry and the new dining room protocol."

"And that is another thing," I told him. "Where is my laundry?"

Raoul looked confused some more. I was getting tired of that face. "You lost your laundry?" he asked me. He made it sound like it was my fault.

"You lost my cummerbund," I told him. "And that's just for starters."

"They lost your cummerbund?"

"I haven't seen it since the Gala."

"You lost it at the Gala?"

It was one of those times when I didn't know if he was slow or if he was giving me the run around.

"I put it in the bag after the Gala. I tore the hook and I put it out to be fixed."

Raoul changed his face so he looked concerned. "Did you send it to laundry or the tailor?"

"I put it in the hamper, Raoul. I don't know these things."

He took out a notebook and a pen and wrote it down. "I'll follow up," he told me.

"And I don't have clean shirts," I said. I held out my arm. "This is from yesterday. You can tell by the cuff."

Raoul knew all about it. "It's the new laundry," he said.

"It's like no laundry at all," I told him.

"They have a new system," Raoul said. "There are bugs."

The clock was ticking and I wanted to go down to dinner. "Give me the short version," I told him.

"Dry cleaning is still absolutely online," he said.

"I'm glad to hear it. Where are my shirts?"

"Shirts are another issue." He gave me a hard look and I waited.

"The concept is simple," he said. "You need for background to know that we used to do laundry on demand. You put it in the hamper, we take it down and wash it. It comes back the same day."

"It was good service."

"Clean sheets and towels daily also and in a wide range. Flat sheets and fitted, matching pillow slips, shams, duvet cover, everything co-ordinated with the decor of the individual suite, redesign on line quarterly and at a reasonable cost so it never gets old. And face cloths, hand towels, bath mats, bath towels, and bath sheets in organic Egyptian cotton twill for premium absorbency. For private entertaining we have tablecloths, napkins, linen hand towels. Everything cleaned without phosphates or bleach and precision-ironed in the ship's laundry."

"I never said anything against linen."

"And fine linen service is still available, because laundry facilities are still online although in a more selective profile, and also because we have a large supply of items and less cruisers now who need them. So we can keep giving you fresh till the cows come home."

I looked at my watch again. "Shirts, Raoul."

He had his hands up. "We have to think now about resource allocation. Supplies are low. How do we deal them out?"

"I don't know, Raoul. Why don't you tell me?"

"To start, you need to take into account that *Mariola* laundry services has sizeable, commercial washers. It takes a large load to fill them up. In the old system, the laundry for each suite got done every day, even though the clothes from one suite in one day never fully fill up a machine, especially once the items are separated by colour and fabric into smaller discrete loads. So your clothes were clean every day but laundry services had the taps open twenty-four seven. So we developed different laundry scenarios to address new issues. We have three separate strategies fully developed and more still in the R and D phase. The first backup plan, which we tried for a week even before the Canal, was consolidation."

"Like a merger?"

"Exactly. But also like combining laundry from several separate suites."

Right away I was suspicious. "You put my laundry in with other people's?" I asked him.

"In essence. Because in the old system, each suite got a washer to itself, or several if they sent down darks and lights and coloureds and permanent press and delicates, because each subcategory has its own wash specifications. With consolidation, all the whites from several suites went into a pile, and when the pile was big enough to fill the industrial washer, everything was loaded in together."

It was a terrible plan and I was glad it was shut down. But now that I heard about it I had questions too.

"I guess it's none of my business," I told Raoul. "I guess you don't think it is anyway, since you never told me about any of this before. But if it's not a state secret, do you mind telling me whose laundry my laundry was consolidated with?"

Raoul looked sorry. "That's exactly the reason we moved to another laundry profile, because we felt there would be reaction. I can't tell you off the top of my head who you shared a washer with. But let's be reasonable. We know the quality of cruiser on board. So shared facilities are not a danger *per se*. And you share many other resources and facilities with fellow cruisers like the cardio machines and crystal, flatware, and china in the Captain's Mess, and no one gives it a second thought because we know that standard cleaning strategies protect your health and hygiene. And I can let you know also that your laundry was bundled with the laundry of other cruisers, not staff, since the laundry from service personnel was segregated plus we have different wash specifications and a separate laundry profile completely. But if you still need names and dates I can research it because they're professionals in the ship's laundry and I'm sure they kept records."

"I just think I should have a say when it's personal."

"I agree one hundred percent. We went over it. There was a long discussion about the best way of doing things, and we talked about asking people to choose their laundry partners. It was an approach that looked at the issue of intimacy and gave the customer choice."

"But you never asked me," I said. I tried to work out whose clothes I wouldn't mind washing with mine. Not Ben's, for example, if his arm was still green and tender.

"We decided against, finally," Raoul said. "There's the last kid to be picked issue. We didn't want to put a customer in the position where no one wants to go in with them. People's feelings get hurt and then the cruise director has a day."

"I don't know if you should make decisions based on staff convenience."

Raoul ignored me. "So we went with the party line model, where you share the phone with whosoever down the road. And you don't know them and they don't know you. It was better it turned out than sharing with friends. People are polite with strangers in a way they aren't always with the people they know best."

"But what about cross-contamination?"

"It was our biggest concern. Although when you think about the class of people involved and the exclusive and dwindling pool of potential hosts, you know contagions are limited in scope and variety."

"I still don't like the idea."

"It's less risky than you think. And in a hot water wash with a powerful detergent, your risk of parasites, fungi, bacteria is reduced to negligible. But it's irrelevant now because we stopped consolidation after a week."

"Because of cross-contamination?"

"Because we were looking for energy savings, and laundry services switched to cold water wash."

"You don't wash in hot?"

"Our head of laundry is a professional: degrees in household sciences and a doctorate in water chemistry. Twenty years experience. She can tell if your colours will run. She says a cold water wash is safe, and that's good enough for me. So we moved to cold water wash for the energy savings. But to address the contagion issue we switched out of consolidation and into amassment."

"Is that a word even?"

Raoul looked sensitive. "It's what they call it," he said.

"So consolidation is finished?"

"Its day has passed. We tried it. We moved on. It's no longer in play."

"I'm glad to hear it. Because if I'd known at the time, I would have had something to say."

"A lot of people feel that way. In retrospect it was a mistake."

So we agreed on that.

"And my shirts?"

"Amassment features individual laundry for the individual suite. We aim to cut the risks of misdirected articles and cross contact, especially in a cold water environment."

"Like before."

"Except we can't run small loads because we don't have resources to support it. So we have to wait until we get enough to fill the machine."

"Well that sounds reasonable," I said.

He wasn't sure. "The trouble is, they're industrial washers," he said. "It takes a lot of socks to fill them up." He looked over to my walk-in. "I'll tell you frankly, Mr. Rutledge, I don't know if you have enough clothes in your closet to fill a whole washer, even if they put dark and light and colour together. And they don't like to do that. The laundry technicians say you don't get a good result. So they separate the colours and hold out for maximum contribution. But it takes several days, obviously. Your sock drawer would be down to rock bottom before they had anything approaching a full load, and even then."

He stopped and let the idea hang. I had a think.

"Then how come I got any shirts back at all?" I asked him.

Raoul nodded like he does when he has no clue. "Again, I'll have to research the particulars." He wrote another note in his little book and studied it for a minute, and then he put the notebook and the pen back in his jacket. "Although now that you don't have to wear black tie in any venue, it means less."

Again, he took me completely by surprise. "And what is this?" I asked him.

He opened his eyes wide. "They suspended black tie?" he said.

"When?" I asked him.

"Yesterday?" he told me. He kept his eyes open very wide like he couldn't risk taking his eyes off me for a second. "Leticia didn't tell you?" he said.

"Nobody told me."

"They suspended black tie in the Captain's Mess and in the Monte and the Broadway."

"And it's because of laundry?" I asked him.

He put his hands out on both sides like he was going to make a speech. But he just said, "It's because of laundry, and the restraint, and the low supplies, and the new drill in the Captain's Mess. The purser thought it was better to relax the policy while we get through the challenges that lie ahead. Then we can go back to the way it's supposed to be and feel clean and refreshed when it all opens up again."

It was disappointing, but reasonable in some ways. "Because we all look somewhat crumpled these days anyway," I said.

"And the service staff don't have formal wear obviously. So they'll be in mufti or still in their kit if they don't have time to change. And it isn't anyone's first concern, but it would make a contrast if the guests were in their best and personnel came in wearing sweats and a T-shirt. It emphasizes the contrast, since everyone eats there now."

Again, and I was experiencing this too often, it was like he was speaking to me from a parallel universe where things looked the same and weren't. "Everyone eats where now?"

Raoul opened his eyes wide again and watched me with intensity.

"We've been running two kitchens up until now, with one servicing the clientele and one putting up staff meals in the commissary."

"You told me about that. It sounded like a good arrangement."

"Again, it's resources. We're going to amalgamate, to cook all the food in one oven."

"All the food in one oven?"

"I think it's a metaphor. I'm not sure. They have big ovens, industrial grade, like the washers. I don't know the specifics but it's an economy of scale. They only fire up one kitchen, and we all eat together in the Captain's Mess. There's a savings that way. The bean counters looked into it. And service personnel are committed to seating all paying customers before they line up themselves at lunchtime and at dinner. And they will leave a gap in time and in space between the last paying customer and the first service technician. Guaranteed." He nodded hard at me, like that made it all right. But he knew what I thought. "It's not what you hoped for," he said. "I know it. It isn't what we hoped for either. It isn't the way the *Mariola* was planned. But it's the way it is till we hit the rendezvous and start over. We all have to pull together. We're all in the same boat."

He smiled at me like it was funny. And I could not let it pass. I stood up finally and got my dinner jacket and put it on.

"We are not in the same boat," I told him. "My boat is a bigger boat than your boat. I'm on a boat that has a balcony stateroom just for me with hot water and laundry on demand and my own toilet that flushes any time I want it to. That's the boat I bought a ticket on, and I haven't forgotten even if you have."

Raoul went solemn right away. He knew he went too far and he tried to make it better but I had no time for it. He came over like he was going to help me straighten my jacket and I shook him off my arm and crossed to the door and he got out of my way and moved fast and got ahead of me to open the door, which was the least he could do in my opinion. But then he wrecked it again by blocking me slightly, with his hand out and ready to receive like in the old days when he actually gave me reliable service. And I could only look at him and shake my head in disgust. And then his feelings were hurt.

"I'm giving you the best I've got, Mr. Rutledge," he told me.

"It just isn't enough," I told him.

And I pushed past him out of my suite.

o o o

And a few days later Jen tracked me down by the pool, and I never had a peaceful moment again. I was dozing in a lounger, and she got between me and the sun, and then she sat down on the lounger beside mine and looked at me hard. I was disappointed she still bothered me even though she owed me money. It wasn't how I hoped it would work. But I was polite.

"You're up and at it," I said. "It's good to see you."

"Why wouldn't I be?" she said. "You think they locked me in my room?"

That was more or less what I thought, but I didn't want to insult her. "It took me a couple of days to put the Gala behind me," I said. "I thought you might feel the effects."

She ignored me, and she opened her own topic. "Can you do me a favour?" she asked.

"I already did," I told her. "I was happy to help. You pay me back when your allowance comes through."

She did not take a hint. "This is something else," she said. "Can you talk to him for me?"

The entrepreneur was set up on the other side of the pool with several girls and his own waiter like usual. The security guys covered his perimeter and the hospitality officer hung around in the background. When I walked past earlier he didn't smile or wave again, and I was beginning to wonder if we were still friends. But I thought he didn't see me probably or he had other things on his mind because the girls were topless and applying sunscreen or he was unreliable and didn't treat his friends the way he should, which was also a possibility. I thought Jen could tell me more about that. So I did a little digging.

"I thought you were pals again," I told her.

"For a little while," she said.

"Then what's the problem?" I asked her.

"He's not speaking again," she said. She started out strong, but her voice went down to nothing, and I thought she was taking it hard. I was sorry for her because young love is no cakewalk.

I told her, "You want my advice, there are other fish in the sea."

She rolled her eyes. "I'm not going to get with you," she said.

"I don't mean me," I said. I thought I made it clear from the start. But at least it gave me a chance to say it out loud and clear up any misunderstanding, and to give her advice, also, because she was a kid, and she made bad choices sometimes. "You need to look for someone your age who likes the things you like," I told her. "He's out there. You'll find him."

"I don't care about that," she said.

She sounded angry again, or else like she was going to laugh, and I was tired of trying to take her seriously because it was work and she was never grateful.

"Then it's not a problem," I said.

"He's leaving," she said. "He's choppering off and I want to go too."

Then I laughed. "No one's leaving," I said. "There's no way out until the fleet shows up."

"He booked a 'Fly."

"No one booked a 'Fly. They're impounded."

"He booked a 'Fly. Fredelle told me. He worked out a deal with someone in the flight crew."

Well, this was interesting and it took me by surprise. "He worked out a deal?" I said.

She nodded. "Fredelle told me," she said again.

"Your friend is reliable?" I asked her.

"She's a snake. But he was talking about it before. He was talking about it on Martinique even. Fredelle told me they were going. She rubbed it in."

"He's not waiting around for the resupply fleet?"

"He doesn't like waiting."

"No one likes waiting."

"He has cash. He can make other arrangements."

"I have cash," I said. "Maybe I should make arrangements too." I was thinking out loud.

"If you make a deal with the 'Fly guys, will you take me too?" Jen said.

Obviously I wasn't going to sign up for anything definite. I asked her instead, "You want to get off the ship?"

"Are you kidding?" she said. "They've cut me off. I have no Internet and no TV."

"None of us do. It's a technical glitch."

"And no music and no movies. They won't pour me a drink or let me into the clubs."

"Don't you have a personal music device?"

"I can't recharge the battery even or download new music. They won't let me see a show."

"Are the shows still running?"

"All the shows are running."

"That seems strange, while we're economizing."

"They have all those singers on board. It's their job."

"And at least we get something we paid for," I said.

"I don't," Jen said. "They won't let me into any venues."

Of course, she wasn't actually paying. But I didn't say that, either.

"They don't even let me go to dinner," she said.

"I noticed that," I told her. "I was worried about that. Are they feeding you?"

"They bring it up to my suite."

"You'd think room service would be more work."

"They do it for spite, like I'll cry if I can't go to the Captain's Mess."

"But you don't care?"

"Of course I care. It's boring in my suite all the time."

"But you get regular meals. That's a good thing."

"They give me Cheese Whiz sandwiches and beef stew from a can."

"They serve it in a can?"

"They heat it up in a microwave and put it on a plate."

"Well that's better," I said.

"It's disgusting," she said. "This whole deal is rotten. I want out."

She was tearing up again. It was uncomfortable. So I called the waiter over, the one who wasn't looking after the entrepreneur, and when he made it finally I ordered champagne cocktail for Jen, and I told him also to put Jen's lounger on my tab. He said, "Yes, Mr. Rutledge," and went out to take care of it like a good kid. And Jen looked surprised.

"The loungers are free," she said.

"The pool is free," I said. "Unless you rent a flotation device."

"There's no water in it."

"So you don't rent one now, obviously. But there's an hourly rental for the loungers, or there was when the ship was full. I don't know if they're still charging cruisers. They talked about a discount rate because there aren't so many of us now and they don't need to ration them, but I never heard the final decision on that. Still, I want you not to worry. If they're charging, it's my treat. And champagne cocktail too."

She wasn't grateful really because she didn't know how. But the waiter brought her drink finally and I thought over everything she told me. I thought things were worse than I knew if the entrepreneur was making plans. And I decided I'd try to talk to him about it myself, and find out what his thinking was, and if he had a seat to spare for someone who could pay his end.

But I figured Jen was out of luck, because she had no cash and he didn't care about her. So she couldn't buy a ticket off the boat for love or money.

the blue pacific

sick bay

CHAPTER SEVENTEEN

I had to think about how I'd approach it. So I decided I'd talk to Eddie first, because they were old friends and he'd have insight and some pull maybe, even though it meant I had to go to Sick Bay to find him. I don't like being around sick people. And also I said I'd visit and I never did. The longer I didn't drop by, the more difficult it was, because I was embarrassed for not going sooner. But I shouldn't have worried because everyone had other things on their minds.

Doctor Dan was in the front room. I hadn't seen him since he looked at me after Maromed, but I heard many reports of his good work with meds and tucks. He was slapping the computer when I walked in, and he looked unhappy generally. But I thought it would be unfriendly just to walk by. So I stopped to say a word.

"The system still has the tech boys beat," I said.

He didn't look at me. "I just need a couple minutes online."

"It's been a long time since we could go online," I told him. "I remember because I wanted to research alternative luxury resorts."

"I have important things to look up," he said.

He wasn't in a mood to chat, and I didn't need him to insult my concerns. So I said, "I'm looking for Eddie?"

He jerked his head behind him. "Ward two. Still."

And I went past the computer station into a big room behind. There were three doors along the left wall and another at the back, and in the middle of the room there was a pretty nurse standing at a counter counting pills into a dish and writing notes. She waved to me and pointed at a door and kept counting. And then a buzzer went off and she plugged her ears and it went off a few more times and she finished her counting and wrote something down and picked up the pills and put them on a tray with the notes and carried it all over to the first door on my left.

I looked in after her and I was surprised. Ben was sitting up in the bed with his head back and his mouth open. I went to the door for a better view, and he looked weak and clammy, and not really alert. He didn't look in shape even to buzz the buzzer. The nurse put the tray down by the bed and took a dressing off Ben's shoulder and you could tell she was working not to make a face. The smell was something else. I could smell it from the door.

"What's wrong with him?" I asked her.

She looked up at me and threw the old dressings in a can. "I'm sorry," she said. "I thought you were looking for Mrs. Martin." She came around the bed and straight at me very fast. I backed up.

"I was looking for her," I said. "It's why I came."

"Ward two," she said.

And she closed the door on me. Which was fine because I didn't like to look at Ben all clammy and knocked out and the smell and all.

The buzzer went off some more and then Bud came barreling out of another door. He looked at me.

"Where the hell is everyone?"

He said it like it was my fault but I didn't let it get to me. Everyone was having a day.

"The nurse is looking at Ben and Doctor Dan is out front," I told him.

Bud shouldered past me into the front room. I could hear him giving Doctor Dan an opinion. I didn't stay to listen because it wasn't my business. Instead I went over to the middle door and put my hand up like I was going to knock. The door was open partway and I could see Eddie sitting at the other side of the bed. And he looked up and saw me and got up and came to the door. I was relieved he didn't tell me to come in right away because I'm not comfortable around people who are dying.

"I didn't expect anyone," he said. "It's good to see you though. I'm glad you stopped by." We shook hands. "Katherine will be glad." He looked over his shoulder and kept his voice down. "I think she's sleeping. I was helping her with breakfast and she drifted."

It was getting late. I had already had a cocktail. It was time to go down to the Captain's Mess and stand in line for a plate. It made me sad to think he spent all day trying to give Katherine breakfast.

"We should let her sleep, maybe?" I said. "You want to stretch your legs? We can take a walk."

He shook his head. "I don't like to leave."

"I thought you liked to take a break sometimes?"

"I took some breaks. Now I'd rather stay. They set up a cot for me." He pointed to a little camp bed at the side of the room. It looked uncomfortable and I admired Eddie more for putting up with it. "They send my meals up," he told me.

"Beef stew?" I asked him. I was standing at the door. I didn't want to go in and discuss things across Katherine's sickbed.

"I don't notice," Eddie said. "But it's good service. I don't have to leave for anything." He went back into the room. "You come in now," he said. "Katherine will wake up and say hello. She'll be happy to see you."

He thought I wanted to see Katherine and I couldn't tell him no. So I followed him into the room and stood on one side of the bed, and he went around and stood on the other. It was sad and depressing and I felt low just being there.

"What's the news of the world?" Eddie said. I didn't think he was really interested, but he gave me the opening and I took it.

"It's going bad to worse," I said.

"It always is," he said.

He didn't sound interested and I respected it. But I wanted his help with the big man. So I kept going.

"I think we might be in real trouble," I told him.

"Probably," he said.

I asked him directly, "What do you think of getting off the ship?"

"What do you mean?" he said. He finished fussing with Katherine's blanket and sat down and I was happy I had more of his attention.

"I heard your friend booked a 'Fly."

"He loves that kind of thing."

"It's interesting because they're impounded now. The captain put them on hold because we're low on fuel."

"He doesn't mind the rules."

"I think he's going to cut and run."

Eddie shrugged. "It's the kind of thing he does," he said. "In business sometimes you cut your losses."

"You think it's time to cut our losses? On the *Mariola*?"

Eddie gave me a hard look. "It isn't really business for Katherine and me," he said. "We can't cut our losses. Not like that."

It was true and I didn't argue. But I still wanted his opinion. "For other people, then? What do you think?"

"I don't know," he said. He moved the blankets some more. He pulled them up over Katherine's hands, and he held her hands through the covers. There was a smell around her, not ripe like Ben, but musty and old.

"You think your friend knows the moment when he sees it?"

"He's got a nose for it," Eddie said. "He could always smell opportunity. He can see the financial shape and hear when key players are panicking."

sick bay

"He can assess risk?"

"Sure."

"Then I think we should follow his lead," I told him. "Talk to him maybe. You could get a couple of seats on the chopper, take Katherine to a top of the line clinic."

"They don't have anything for her," he said.

I let it sit for a minute. Then I told him, "You should maybe talk to him anyway? For yourself?"

"What do you mean?" He was holding Katherine's hands and looking at me across the bed. I sort of shrugged. He gave me a long look. Finally he said, "It's like this, Rutledge. I've lived my life the way I like. I had my way most of the time. Now I don't get my way anymore, not in things that matter. We heard the diagnosis and I knew that part was over. I can't keep Katherine alive. It turns out also I can't help Lily or Eric, although the marines are moving and they have a chance. My grandson is a lost cause. I wish I could say something different but he has no character that I see."

"He might surprise you," I told him. But I didn't go into specifics because Eddie was taking a hard line and I didn't know how he'd react.

"What I have to do now is be with Katherine. Everything else is out of my hands. You go to Mr. Moneypants, try to get a seat on his fly machine. You can use my name if you like but I don't think it will help. If you're still here tomorrow, come and have dinner with us. Katherine will be happy to see you."

Maybe because she heard her name, or because Eddie was speaking so firmly, Katherine came around then. She woke up with little low noises like she was angry or confused.

"There she is," Eddie said. He looked at her instead of me. He took her hand and bent over her, and his face opened up and he stopped speaking firmly, and was soft and warm instead. "There's my girl," he said. "You want some water?" Katherine made a weak kitten noise and Eddie got a glass of water with a straw that bent and he held it for her so that she could drink. "Rutledge came to say hello," Eddie said.

Katherine kind of looked around for me. She looked scared and confused. She didn't move her head but her eyes went all around the room trying to find me. I leaned in somewhat to make it easier for her.

"We missed you at the Gala," I said. "I was hoping we could cut the rug." It was out of the question obviously, but I had to say something. She looked at me like she was afraid.

"Rutledge says we missed you at the Gala," Eddie said. He said it louder like volume was key. But Katherine still looked out of it.

"Did you finish your breakfast?" I asked her.

"Breakfast?" she said. She hardly had a voice, just a breath.

"Will you try some more?" Eddie said. He reached for the tray right away. There was a plate with toast and jam. We all waited for a minute while Katherine thought about it. Then she shook her head. She closed her eyes and Eddie pulled the covers up some more. Nobody said anything for a minute.

"Well, we had a good visit," I said.

"You got to say hello," Eddie said.

"I'm glad I had the opportunity," I told him.

"It was nice of you to come," Eddie said. "Come again sometime."

I said I'd try, because what else could I tell him. And then I made a move. "You want me to close the door?" I asked him.

But he didn't hear me, or he didn't care, and I just left the door half open behind me, like it was when I got there. Eddie was fussing with the covers some more, and Katherine was looking at him, and looking scared and confused, and then she closed her eyes like it was too much work to keep them open. It was sad and private and not my business, and I left them alone.

I went through the big room and into the reception area in front. Bud and Doctor Dan were at it.

"Just talk to her," Bud said. "She's afraid."

"I can do a boob job in my sleep."

sick bay

"Don't say that to her. But you go in there now and use a bedside manner. Let her know she can trust you. Make her calm."

Bud was a large man although his hip was bad. He had a hand on Doctor Dan's shoulder and I felt that the doctor didn't have a choice really. But he talked back. "I have other patients on my caseload."

"You give them good attention once you've taken care of Bailey," Bud said.

He turned Doctor Dan around and helped him come away from the computer. The doctor shook him off and slouched into the back room.

Bud gave me a look. "He's got no manner," he said.

"He's good at what he does," I told him.

"So far he's useless. This is the very last thing he can think of trying."

I didn't like to ask because it wasn't my business. But I was there and I heard obviously. "Bailey's getting some work done?" I asked him. The timing seemed strange.

Bud nodded. He jerked his head after Doctor Dan. "He thinks her implants might have popped. He says leakage can have effects. Sometimes the immune system takes a hit and sometimes the endocrine system. She's sad. She cries all the time. He says he can see a rash although I don't see it myself, and her joints are sore maybe. She says everything hurts. He thinks this might be a way of dealing with it."

I wished him luck. But I don't think he noticed really. He nodded like he was thinking about other things and went back inside.

the 'fly'

CHAPTER EIGHTEEN

Since Eddie wasn't interested, I decided to talk to the big guy about transport myself, but I didn't know where to find him. I went back to the Slaker and his party was gone. And then I thought I'd see him at dinner, but he didn't show. I thought it over and I couldn't remember if I ever saw him in line at the buffet, and I wondered if he made other arrangements, even though we were all economizing together. Truthfully, it wouldn't have surprised me if he organized private meals in his suite, and not canned stew. Because if he could organize his own airlift, I thought he could probably organize dinner.

I got in line at the buffet anyway, because I was hungry. They gave me beanie weenies and jelly salad with carrots and peas. The jelly talked back somewhat, and Vance said he thought they didn't add all the water the recipe said. I sat down with him and Amanda, and he cut into his jelly with a steak knife to sample it.

"It's not sweet either," he said. "They're low on sugar, maybe. But there are vegetables in it, so that's positive."

"They're frozen," Amanda said. She sounded beat. She lost her spirit when they drained the pool and never got it back really.

"They're room temperature now," Vance said. He took what she didn't eat. Then he ordered cognac from the wine waiter and drank it with Postum because they didn't put out coffee, not even instant, or tea. I thought the cognac was the only luxury in a meal that should have been nothing but. And it made me sad.

After dinner, I looked in the Monte. The big guy wasn't anywhere. I was kicking myself because I could have struck up a conversation with him right away when Jen talked to me because he was still on the pool deck taking the sun. But I didn't like to in front of Jen in case it got her hopes up, and I wasn't sure if his security would let me in, although he and I had always got along. Plus I wanted to consult with Eddie first. So for many reasons I held off, and then I paid the price because I couldn't find him again. The easiest thing I decided would be if I dropped by his suite, except I didn't know where it was. Then I remembered Raoul knew.

I didn't like to do it because he gave me bad service the last time I talked to him. I didn't have a warm feeling for him. But then I thought it was a way he could earn my respect again, and I owed him the chance, really, because he tried at the beginning, when the Mariola first set sail and we were all full of hope. So I decided I could be the bigger man and give him an opportunity, and I went back to my suite and hit the call bell and sat back and waited. It took several minutes, which was another bad sign in my opinion. But finally Raoul knocked and I yelled for him to come in and he opened the door and held it in front of him and bent toward me somewhat, but he stayed in the hall and talked to me through the open door like he didn't like to intrude.

"Something I can do for you, Mr. Rutledge?" he said.

I was sitting on the couch, and I was settled in for conversation, because I was willing to try to repair our relationship and I knew it would take more than a minute. But Raoul just put his head in the door like he couldn't stay. He was sulking, and it was kind of entertaining except it wasn't a good time.

"Come in like I told you," I said. "I need to talk to you."

He thought about it some more. Then he took a step into my suite and kept the door open behind him like he might have to leave suddenly at any moment.

"Close the door," I told him. "It's private."

He looked over his shoulder into the hall. Then he looked at me again. He breathed out hard through his nose like he was just barely holding on. And he still didn't come fully into the room.

"I'm here to help, Mr. Rutledge," he said. "But you know. We have service issues ongoing and I have to cover an extended station. If you have a quick question, or a job you want me to do?"

I didn't like the way he was trying to own the conversation. And it was holding me up. "Close the door," I told him one more time.

He could see I was serious. So he closed the door behind him and stepped up. He still looked unhappy about it, however. So I waited a minute to show him I didn't mind about his moods. Then I told him, "You told me once you worked for the big guy, on a private cruise?"

"It was a public private venture."

It wasn't relevant. "You got to know him somewhat?"

"I had shore contacts already. I helped him out with some things he wanted. Some extras."

"A man remembers that kind of service."

Raoul shrugged. "I do my job. I do it right, I feel good about myself. I make an impression on a client, it's a bonus."

"Did you know he booked a 'Fly?"

"To Martinique?"

"No. Now. To get off the ship."

It was a second while he took it in. Then he cracked a smile and looked serious at the same time. "Nobody booked a 'Fly, Mr. Rutledge," he said. "They're offline."

the 'fly

"He booked a chopper. It's a public private venture he set up with the 'Fly boys."

Nothing happened for a second, and then his face changed. He looked like he hit a wall. It took another minute for him to put it in words. Then he said, "Those shits. You can never trust military."

"They're private security," I told him. "It's a grey area. They're mercenaries essentially and there's a higher bidder sometimes."

Raoul wasn't listening. He turned around like he forgot all about me.

"Where are you going?" I asked him.

"I have a job, Mr. Rutledge. I have responsibilities. I should look into it and find out. Probably I have to report."

"You're not going to turn them in," I said.

He turned around to look at me. "It's what a guy in my position is supposed to do, Mr. Rutledge. I work for the Company. I have to consider the Company point of view. The pilot is walking out on a contract and the big man is stealing Company property."

"Nothing's been stolen."

"It's conspiracy to steal."

"And really, so what if they do? The big man flies out. It's one less mouth to feed. No skin off my nose."

Raoul gave me his full attention for a change. But he talked very slowly and loudly and it was insulting somewhat. "If he takes the 'Fly, the chopper option is gone for good. It is potentially the only contact we have with the outside world at this point in time. We might want to hold onto it."

"We have four Dragonflies," I told him.

"We had four," he said. "Now we don't."

"What do you mean?"

Raoul put his hand out with one finger pointing. "We lost one Dragonfly at Port Esteban."

"On the docks? I never heard about that," I said.

"On the fruit farm," Raoul said. He shook his finger at me. "Chef

Lousine sent it back with a load of papaya, and then it went back again for another run and to pick up personnel and it never came home. We don't know what happened."

"So we lost it?"

Raoul glared at me like it was my fault. He put out another finger. "We lost another chopper in the Canal."

"There was no shooting in the Canal," I said.

"The transport never came home," Raoul said. This also was news to me. "They didn't have fuel maybe at the Canal authority, or the pilot did a runner. I don't know detail. But the 'Fly didn't come home and now there's only two on deck." He waved two fingers at me, and then he put his middle finger back down and held up his pointer again, which was confusing also. "If he takes one, we only have one left," he said.

"I can see that, Raoul," I said.

"And that one is scrap. They use it for parts."

"I thought they were top of the line?"

"Three of them are, and a spare."

He put his hand down again and scowled at me like it was my fault they bought junk. And I recalculated because it was worse than I thought, but it also proved the big man had a good instinct. He knew service was bottoming out and he made a plan. I admired him for it.

Raoul didn't admire him. He wanted to turn him in. He was jealous, like people are sometimes when they see someone who bats a higher percentage. But I don't feel envy like that. I wished I had insight like the big man's too. But I don't brood. Instead I looked into how I could use his insight to advantage, because that is enough for me. I tried to show Raoul that side of things.

"So this is the last 'Fly?" I said.

Raoul rolled his eyes. "This is the last 'Fly," he said. "And we have no communications and they're rationing water. We've been running laps in a holding position on these coordinates for three days, and I am not feeling hopeful. If the resupply doesn't get here soon, the 'Fly might be the only way we can send an SOS. If we can gas it up still, and if we have a pilot to fly it. It's our lifeline and he's stealing it."

"So we have one chopper and maybe enough fuel, today, to make it to the nearest landing pad?"

"They must think they can get there."

"And that leaves everyone else with nothing?"

"Squat."

"The lifeboats?"

Raoul made a sound like he was choking. "What about them? The fuel tank is running low and we're a thousand miles from land. You can't go anywhere in a lifeboat."

"So the smart thing is to be on the 'Fly when it lifts off?"

"If you don't mind about everyone else on the ship," he said. He made it sound ugly.

I told him, "It isn't necessarily selfish, Raoul. You said it yourself, it might be the only way to send an SOS. Why not send the message out. If the captain's only idea is to wait and hope, it's a good thing one person is making a plan. When he lands, I'm sure he'll mention that the *Mariola* is in trouble. And if he doesn't think of it, it would be a good idea if there was someone else on the 'Fly who was on top of it."

Raoul still looked mad. "And what do the rest of us do?" he said.

"I understand," I told him. "It's frustrating because you like to make a contribution. He shouldn't have to do all the work. That's why some of us should also travel with the big guy and help him out. Plus he might like company."

Then Raoul wasn't frowning so much. He looked at me with his eyes wide open and nodded somewhat like he was adding up the bill. "What are we talking about?" he said.

"You know all about him," I said. "He likes you, too. He told me at the Gala." I said it, although the subject never came up. "He had the after party and he invited me. It was a kick. We got along. Could you tell me where I could find him? I'd like to have a word with him and make an offer. There's room for several people and their luggage on a Dragonfly. I watched Lou and Denise load up in the Canal. They had all their bags with them and other people too. But there was still plenty of legroom. Plus I'm guessing he had to pay the pilots and the flight crew serious coin and the ground crew too, if he did things properly, to get the oil checked and security on side. I think he might appreciate a co-investor."

Raoul agreed. "I know the 'Fly boys," he said. "They don't get out of bed without incentives. They'll bleed him."

Again it sounded like spite to me and it was unattractive. "That is their right," I told him. "They have skills that are in demand and access. They can put a price tag on their assets in a free market. And it's a good thing because the higher they go the more he might want to take on a partner."

"You want to jump ship, too?" Raoul gave me a straight look again. It was a way I didn't think the help should look at a paying customer but I let it go because I could see he was having trouble learning a new idea. And he still didn't tell me where the big man's suite was. So I didn't get distracted.

"It's nothing personal, Raoul," I told him. "You do a very good job."

He thought about it for a minute. He still had a look on his face like he was working it out. Then he pulled himself together and stood up as tall as he could.

"Thank you Mr. Rutledge. I appreciate you saying it. Some people take all the work you do for them and don't notice it, or they complain about the little things you do wrong instead of showing appreciation. You always let me know when I did something right. It makes my job a pleasure."

"It's nothing, Raoul," I told him. I meant it too. We had our differences, but he wanted to make it right and I respected that. But I wished he'd get to the point and just show me where the big man's suite was.

"You're interested in buying in, and I understand your concerns," he said. "But it's a high-risk proposition. First because strictly speaking it's stealing."

I put my hands up. "We've been over that already, Raoul. It's for the best."

"I see that, Mr. Rutledge. I'm just saying. If the officers hear about it, they might get involved."

"I don't plan on telling them."

"Word gets around on a boat," Raoul said. "It's a small town that way." He wasn't actually looking at me. He was looking at the wall just beside my head, and his face was completely flat. "You heard about the plan," he said. "Other people might hear. Some people live and let live. Other people think they should take a position. It only takes one person talking out of turn and you have complications. The captain might try to put his foot down, or Hoskins. And there are security types on board with nothing much to do. It's not a problem if the big guy paid everyone off. But you don't know. If he cut corners, his team might have to work through resistance."

"The sooner they roll into action the less time people have to interfere," I told him. "That's why I appreciate it if you tell me right away where I can find him. The clock is ticking on the whole transaction."

Raoul said, "He's in fourteen oh four. It's a deluxe environment, indoor outdoor living room, private spa, fireplace. Plus he put some extras in himself. It's a stunner."

I stood up and stepped forward. I wanted to get on it and talk to the big man right away. Raoul didn't move.

"He's not there. I just saw him on the elevator."

"You rode the elevator with him?"

"I don't use the public elevator. We have service elevators and we ride up and down with the laundry and the cleaning supplies and room service meals. He was in the public elevator and I was in the hall when the elevator stopped. He was inside and the car was going down. My guess is he's going to the Broadway. His tootsie's in the show." He checked his watch. "She's on now. She's just making her big entrance and she's on for the next thirty minutes straight. Then she has a break, and she's back on at the beginning of the second half and again at the finale. He likes to watch the show. He doesn't like to be interrupted. So we have thirty minutes of planning time at least, eighty-five minutes if he stays for the last dance and he usually does. Can I show you something?"

I was hopeful, but he still didn't move. He was blocking me and he was too close. It was uncomfortable, but I wasn't going to step back obviously, and he didn't take a hint.

"What is it Raoul?" I said to him.

He hunched down and looked up at me like he understood I was the bigger man. He didn't back down but he showed respect. "I want to show you my station," he said. "It's nothing fancy. I don't have a fireplace or a spa. But I've been developing my own backup plan. I want you to look at it as an option for yourself as well."

I was impressed that Raoul was thinking about backup plans also. It was irrelevant to my concerns, but it showed foresight and I was happy someone on the boat was thinking. I liked to encourage it.

"What have you got in mind?" I asked him.

He looked me in the eye. "We've got a situation. We all know it, anyone who can think anyway, and that's a few of the crew and some passengers like yourself. We're out of everything, we've got no communication, and the captain is clueless. If the resupply doesn't make it soon, we are screwed. And although I have seen successful resupplies in the past, nothing we've done on the *Mariola* so far has gone according to plan and I am very worried.

"Ten years ago, fifteen, it didn't matter if the radio failed. The ocean was thick with liners and yachts. You lost a contact, someone pulled up to help you look. There was camaraderie and fellowship. Now with interruption in the supply side and a weak investment climate and so on it's the empty quarter here and we're lucky to see a spy drone pass overhead let alone see another boat in the vicinity. Even pirate vessels have thrown in the towel because there isn't enough traffic for them to make a steady profit. So we can't even count on a chance encounter with another vessel to put us in touch with civilization.

"The only thing we have going for us is our numbers are down. We lost a big percentage of passengers in Port Esteban and more in the Canal. I don't know the totals because the purser is a secretive man, but it's larger than you think. There are whole floors of deluxe living environments with no paying customers to enjoy them anymore. From that perspective alone it's a ghost ship.

"Also we lost staff on the island. They were very fine people who took a day to enjoy the sights and were never seen again. I don't know what happened to them and I worry every day. And many more ran away in the Canal. For them I have no pity. They had a contract and they ran out on it and left the rest of us holding the bag. Plus some of them owe me money, and I don't like a piker. But that's personal and beside the point, because again the upside is our total population dropped and we stretched our rations more than we could have done otherwise.

"But even with all the people who aren't here anymore, we're at the end of our rope now as far as I can see. We've blown through the whole bag of tricks. I ask the people I know in the kitchen, the ones who are left, and they tell me they're stretching the chicken noodle, and frankly the chicken noodle was thin from the get go. We're out of fresh produce and bottoming out on frozen. We have no white flour or shortening. We just finished the sweeteners. All of them, even the low cal kind. We're out of balsamic and wine vinegar and rice vinegar and cider vinegar. You eat at the Captain's Mess twice a day. You know which way the wind is blowing."

He was right about everything and when he lined it up like that it all sounded very, very bad. More than ever I wanted to get on the 'Fly. I wanted to go right away and find the big man, even if his tootsie was hitting the high notes. But Raoul was still blocking me.

"Food doesn't matter so much," he said. He was a runty guy.

"Food matters," I told him.

"It matters," he said. "But compared to water it doesn't matter at all. You can live without food a long time. Your body stores energy. You can live off the fat. For a healthy person or a fat one it takes a long time to die without food. But water is different. You need eight cups a day."

I put up my hand. It reminded me of something but I had to think. "I heard that was wrong?" I said.

Raoul shrugged. "Look at it this way. The *average* person gets eight cups of water a day, in beverages or in other foods, in soups or in sauces and fruit and veg and leafy greens. In an ordinary diet you get eight cups of water a day one way or another. But if we run out of food, you only get water in water and you still need eight cups a day. That's a minimum.

"We're in the torrid zone. The air temperature gets up to ninety-five degrees Fahrenheit, forty degrees Celsius every day, and the water temperature is high also, maybe seventy-five degrees Fahrenheit, twenty-five degrees Celsius at the surface. Right now, we have the a/c going full blast. But if we run out of fuel, and we will soon, the engines will shut off and the generators will fail. We'll lose the heat the engines put out, which is good. But without power, the a/c is gone, and on-board temperatures are going to skyrocket. We'll need water even more then, when it really starts cooking."

"You might want to stay on deck then," I said. "Or keep the windows open to get a breeze."

Raoul still didn't step off and I was tired of standing in front of him even though I was dominating him. So I pushed around him and walked over to the balcony doors. I had them open like always to let in the air. The sun was setting and a breeze was coming up. The sea was blue and calm. It was hard to believe anything bad could happen.

"I have a better idea," Raoul said. He turned around where he was and kept looking at me. "I've been making up my service station," he

the 'fly

said. "It's my safe house. It's got a single entrance, with a reliable locking system. There's a front room with storage and a tap and a back room with a cot. I moved some supplies in already: cup-a-soup and noodles. That kind of thing."

"I thought we were low on supplies?"

"Nobody misses a case of noodles."

It was good thinking. I told him, "I'm glad you've got a plan. Because it doesn't sound like the resupply effort is a sure thing, and even if I go with the big man and make sure he reports to the authorities, it might be a few days before a rescue party finds the *Mariola*. I'm happy you're taking steps. I'll know you're safe when I leave and otherwise I would have worried about you."·

Raoul nodded. "The thing is," he said. And then he stopped and I had to wait while he mentally fine-tuned his message. "What I really need is water," he said. "I've been bottling some when the pipes are open. But the ration is tight in the service stations too. They only turn the taps on for an hour four times a day, and we all have to share and it's earmarked for cleaning. Leticia fills up her pail and Horst fills up his and they clean the countertops and the fixtures in their sections, and then they dump it out and get fresh water for the floors. There's always someone at the tap. It's hard to find a time when I'm alone in the station and the water is on and I can fill up a jug. I've been working at it for a week now and I only have a couple gallons. And then I have to keep it confidential, obviously, and people don't respect your private space like they should." I didn't care about cleaning schedules. Like he knew it, he said, "You don't need all the detail. But the point is that water is hard to find, and that's where I think we can help each other." I didn't need his help, obviously, and I gave him a look. He nodded like he could show me. "You have water," Raoul said. "You have cases of water in the walk-in. I don't poke my nose. I saw them when I was bringing laundry. You could come in with me. I don't mean any insult by it but I think we'd be a good team. I'll share my safe house and the noodles, and you chip in with your water. We join forces. And that way we both have a better chance of holding on until the cavalry comes."

It didn't matter because I was going to chopper out with the big guy. But Raoul put some effort into his pitch. So I gave him honest feedback. "It's a plan and I can see you've been thinking," I told him. "But I have to tell you, I don't see the advantage. I could stay in my suite and have all the water for myself. Plus I'm not a noodle man."

"If you stay in your suite, I don't know if you'd get all the water to yourself. Worst-case scenario, you'd have to share with the whole cruise complement."

"It's my water," I told him. "I bought it." Although honestly The-CompanyStore never billed me.

"In emergencies, the captain can make new rules. He can tell people to share. Everyone puts what they have in the pot, and everyone takes an equal share out again."

"Communism's dead," I told him.

"We know how the story ends," Raoul said. "And it's fundamentally unfair, because you had the foresight and the wisdom but you get no benefit. Also it's a waste because nobody gets enough so it doesn't help anyone. But if we take it into my station and lock the door behind us, we're good to go for days, maybe weeks."

Twice as long, I figured, if it was just me. But I didn't say it out loud. Instead I told him, "If it comes to that, Raoul, I can stay in my suite and not share my water. I can lock my door. Plus I can open the windows and get a breeze. Does your service station have a window?" I thought it probably didn't. "It will get stuffy when the a/c goes down."

Raoul admitted my point. "Those are aspects of concern," he said. "In the station there's an issue with air circulation. But in your suite, there's a security issue. I have one exterior door and it locks automatically plus it has a professional dead bolt system operated by key or from the inside. You have multiple access points. If someone or a group of people want to share your resources, I don't know if you can say no."

"I can lock my door too, Raoul," I said.

"With respect, Mr. Rutledge, every guy with a cleaning cart has a pass-key, and the purser, and maintenance, and security. They all have overrides."

I walked back over to Raoul. I came up close and just stood on top of him. He still didn't move, and I was impressed with his nerve. But he was a runty guy and I dominated him fully. I could take care of myself. We both knew it and he nodded like I explained it to him.

"If it's an assault force of one, I know you can handle it," he said. "Even two, maybe three individuals, especially if they're hungry and tired. But you can't secure your perimeter alone. You've got a big balcony and two sets of French doors. A dedicated team can rappel down from the Arboretum and come in through the windows."

"There's a titanium bolting system," I said.

Raoul shook his head. "You and I both know it's not worth shit."

"I'll lock the water in the safe."

"They can ask you to open the safe."

"I can say no."

"We're looking at an end of days scenario here," Raoul said. "These guys are salt of the earth and good citizens and so on. But if the taps run dry it'll be every man for himself."

I thought some more. "The titanium locks really aren't secure?"

"They're a weak link. Whereas for my post hardly anyone has a key."

"Why do you have keys at all instead of swipe cards or chips or a biometric recognition system?"

Raoul nodded like he did when he didn't have a clue. "Not meaning disrespect, but the Company may have cut corners on security," he said. "But in my station it's irrelevant because nobody will come looking. In an emergency the crew will gather passengers in secure locations. They'll check the suites to find people who didn't hear the alarm. If order breaks down, God forbid, people will try the kitchens and the clubs and the commissary and the passenger suites. No one's going to search the broom closet. It's not the first place you think about."

He had a point and I told him so. "You make a good case," I said. "But I should see the space before I make up my mind. Let's go down right now. You can show me what you've got." I put my hand on his shoulder and turned him around, not in a mean way, but because I made a decision and I didn't like waiting anymore. "If the space checks out, I'll consider it as a backup," I told him. I got the door open and I was holding it with one hand and encouraging Raoul with the other. "But always remembering that my goal is the Dragonfly, and time is moving on." I looked at my watch. I wanted him to make a move. "I'll take a look at your station, and then I'll go down to the Broadway and talk to the big guy. It will be intermission by then and I'll bump into him casually and have a word. You can pack my kit while I'm at it. I'm not sure what I'll need. You can use judgment."

Raoul nodded like it was important. "Probably something light. It would be nice to take all your things with you, because if you get out you maybe won't be coming back, not in a hurry anyway, or at all, depending on the resupply and the Company's success in reassuring investors. But probably you can't take your full kit. Let's plan for limited baggage allowance. I'll get your twenty-one inch roller out of storage."

"I trust you on it, Raoul," I told him.

"I'll do my very best for you," Raoul said. He was still standing in the middle of the floor. "Since we're going down anyway, and we're here already, should we take some with us?" he said. He looked at my closet like my water was calling him.

"We should not," I told him. "I'm not moving a bottle until I decide where I'm going and what I'm doing. And don't even think about helping yourself," I said. "I counted," I told him, which wasn't true but I thought it hit the right note. "There won't be any missing if I come back," I said. "It's a deal breaker."

the 'fly

Raoul looked shocked. "Of course not, Mr. Rutledge," he said. "I just thought it would save time. It's your water. You make the call and no offense."

He came to the door right away like he was just waiting for the word, and we left my suite and walked up the corridor to a little steel door in the centre block at the front end. Raoul pulled a key ring on a chain out of his pocket and found a key he liked and unlocked the deadbolt, and then he found another key and unlocked the handle and pushed. He leaned in to hit the lights and then he held the door wide open for me, and I ducked my head a little and went in. Raoul came in behind me and the door closed on us.

It was a small room or a big closet with a concrete floor and a damp smell. There were lockers on the wall beside us, and a counter with a tap and a sink on the opposite wall. Carts for linen were lined up by the counter, with cleaning supplies and mops and buckets. At the front of the room there was another steel door. Nothing in the room looked homey.

"Can we drink this water?" I asked Raoul.

"It's potable," he said. "If it comes out of the tap, it's good to go."

"And you put some away already?"

He came around me to one of the lockers and worked the lock on it. He got right up beside it because the space was small maybe, and he kept his back to me and his shoulders up so I couldn't see detail. Then he opened the door and stood back. It was like a school locker and not big, but he had a couple of gallon jugs in it, one on top of the other.

"You think you can fill up a couple more?" I asked him. Because really there wasn't much there and I didn't see why I should kick in several cases of carbonated spring water with hint of lime if he only had two gallons of bilge water.

"I'm going to," he said. He closed the locker again and checked the lock. "I need more jugs, and I have to be careful. Leticia keeps putting her nose in."

"Women are like that."

"It's been an issue the whole time."

He walked up to the front and pulled the keys on the chain out again and unlocked the other door.

"Is that a good lock?" I asked him.

"Leroy," he said. "Top of the line. It's industrial grade."

"Not that titanium stuff," I said.

He made a face. "This is the real thing."

"I'll need a key," I said.

Raoul nodded and looked troubled. "They're staff only," he said.

"Are you kidding me?"

"I understand," Raoul said. "If you're going to ride it out here, you need your own key. But we're not supposed to copy them. The purser hands them out and he keeps track."

"If this is our default position I want access. I'm not going to stand outside scratching at the door and relying on your goodwill."

"Of course not, Mr. Rutledge, although my goodwill is dedicated as I've told you many times. But for your peace of mind and because it's only right, if it comes to it we'll find a key for you. I can get Leticia's or Horst's, maybe, when they're not looking."

He pulled his set out to show me. He had half a dozen keys on a ring and the ring was attached to his pants with a wire. "It's a tricky thing," he said. "Because the Company gave us good equipment. The ring is high-quality steel, and it's on a fully retractable spring-loaded steel wire with memory coil which is attached to a professional grade carabiner, Everest caliber." He stretched out his wire and pulled up his shirt so I could see the carabiner hooked onto his belt loop. "These babies hold. Even our most challenged staff don't lose them very much. So I'll have to have a think. Mostly I prefer stealth, but in the circumstances I might have to use force, and there can be repercussions. I have to time it right. Ideally I'd cut a new one, but maintenance has the key cutter, and they take orders from the purser."

the 'fly

"Can't you get a friend to help you out?" I asked him.

"Normally it's what I do. Get a friend in maintenance to lend a hand, or else go into town at any port of call, but I can't do that now, obviously. And a big gang of my so-called friends jumped ship at the last lock. You can't trust people it turns out." He was drifting off topic again. I checked my watch and I let him see it. "You don't need to hear my troubles," Raoul said. "But timing is important. We want to be ready to run but we don't want to tip our hand."

And that was true also. He pushed the second door open finally and reached in to turn on the lights and held it open and backed up against the lockers so I could get by. I went inside and looked. It was tight and small also, like a linen closet or an office for someone unimportant. But it had carpet, and behind the door on the left there was a little desk with a computer and a phone and shelves and cupboards over the desk. All along the wall on the right there were cupboards and open shelves with sheets and pillows. And at the front of the room and the front of the ship there was empty floor space and three high little windows like portholes. I stepped up to look, and the windows opened fine. Altogether the room was much better than the first room, and it reassured me somewhat. But it wasn't complete.

"Where's the cot, Raoul?" I asked him.

"I want to show you that, Mr. Rutledge," he said. Between the desk and the front wall with portholes, there was bare wall with no cupboards or shelves, just an attachment I didn't recognize. Raoul reached up and pulled on it, and a pair of legs folded out of the wall, and I moved out of the way and Raoul pulled some more and it was a cot or a Murphy bed and he pulled it out of the wall and lowered it down. It went from wall to wall across the room in the space behind the desk. It was a small space, maybe five foot, maybe six, from wall to wall, and the cot just fit. I had more doubts.

"It isn't big, Raoul," I told him.

"Cots are little," Raoul said.

"It's little even for a cot," I said. "Does it hold a person?" I asked him.

"It holds a person," Raoul said.

He was a little man and he didn't need a lot of mattress. I went around him to the cot and he squeezed against the desk so I could get by. I sat down on it and it heaved and there was a sound of metal and springs. I thought it might fold, but it didn't. I bounced a little, and it made more noises. I wasn't convinced.

"I don't know if I could be comfortable on this," I said.

"I have extra bedding." Raoul pointed at the sheets like they would help.

"And where would you sleep?" I asked him.

"We sleep in shifts," Raoul said.

I didn't like that idea, either, but I didn't say anything because I didn't want to insult him. He could see it in my face, maybe.

"We have to remember. It isn't going to happen really," Raoul said. "The resupply is going to work. Or it won't matter because in a couple of minutes, you will fly out with the big man to a tropical paradise. Or, worst-case scenario, the big man flies out alone and sends a squad in to get us and we're back on dry land in a week, ten days tops. And even if none of the above comes to pass, who knows? Another boat could be out there somewhere."

"Because the Company knows what it's doing, and if it doesn't, the coast guard does," I said.

"There are fail-safes all over the world," Raoul said. "People look out for each other, and if someone is in trouble other people help. It's human nature."

"And this clientele is very well-connected, which is another reason we'll all come out together on the other side of this."

"Can you imagine the lawsuits if the Company let things get out of hand?"

"I wouldn't want to be on that board of directors."

There was a noise and the door opened very fast. A guy came into

the 'fly

the office at speed, and Raoul turned around and backed up into me with his hands up like he was taking a bullet for me.

"Have I told you a million times to knock?" Raoul said.

He was backing up into me but he said it with authority and I was happy he took a stand verbally even if his hands were up like he'd surrendered.

"I need sheets," the guy said.

"Knock and I'll give you some."

Raoul was giving orders, but the other guy didn't notice. "I can get my own," he said. He reached for linen and saw me and his eyes popped. "Raoul, what the hell?" he said. He dropped his voice to be private.

"Horst," said Raoul. "This is not a good time."

"But what's he doing here?" Horst said.

Raoul put his hands down finally and took a little step back into the desk. "This is Mr. Rutledge, six fourteen," he said. He leaned into my name and suite number so Horst could see I was the big man in the room. But Horst still didn't take a hint.

"But what's he doing in the station?" he said.

"This is a private conference, Horst."

Horst made a face. "It's not my intention to intrude," he said. He sort of curtsied at me and he looked back at Raoul and dropped his voice again. "You got the cot down, Raoul?" he said. "You know what the purser said."

Raoul rolled his eyes. "You don't know what you're talking about, Horst."

"I mean it like a friend. There are twenty-four suites empty on this floor. You have a pass-key."

Raoul held fire for a second. Then he moved in closer to Horst, crowding him somewhat, and I thought he was going to dominate him physically. I had reservations. Horst was lean like Raoul, but tough and wiry. You could see it would be a fair fight if the two of them got into it, and I didn't want to get involved myself. But Raoul changed it up. He stayed close and serious. But he put his arm around Horst and started turning him around and giving him sheets at the same time like they were a team. I was impressed with his range of strategies.

"You want some sheets," he said. "Let me help you. You got, what, eight suites? Eight king-size?"

Horst took to the new topic right away. "Are you kidding me?" he said. "I got three twin, five double, nine king, and a custom. That's eighteen suites last time I checked, and I get more every day."

Raoul made clucking noises. "What are you thinking about," he said. "You can't handle eighteen sets of linen. The cart isn't made for it." He made up a stack of sheets anyway and loaded Horst up.

"I do the first eight suites," Horst said. "Two twins, the custom, and five kings. That fills the cart up. I do those suites then I come back and reload."

"You got four king-size already. Here's another." Raoul pulled more sheets down. "You got a cart?"

"I got a cart."

Horst nodded behind him and Raoul moved Horst and his sheets forward into the room and pulled the door open and held it and moved Horst back again. There was a cart parked at the door. It blocked the exit completely so we were all trapped in the office while Horst got sheets. Raoul held the door with his foot and turned Horst around to put linen on the cart. He kept reaching for sheets also.

"Here's two twin," he said. I wasn't convinced he was counting.

"I need four," Horst said.

"You said two."

"Two suites."

"I got you."

Raoul pulled out more sheets and Horst stood in the doorway and let Raoul load him up again. He followed his own thoughts.

"I started with eight suites," he said. "It's what I signed up for."

"There is dignity in labour," Raoul said.

"I got more dignity than I can use right now."

Raoul didn't let him start. "What's the custom?"

"For the extra-tall mattress."

"Is it ten-inch or sky-high?"

"Sky-high, for supreme support."

I thought it was for the McHuges maybe.

"I got you," Raoul said. He reached up to the top and pulled down some sheets with little birds on them and he gave them to Horst, who disappeared behind sheets but kept talking.

"Now I've picked up ten more suites and I haven't seen the beach for weeks. Every day I ask myself why."

"You're a thinker. It's in your character," Raoul told him.

"I don't mean philosophically. I don't understand the scheduling protocols they handed down."

"We've been over it. You grieved, you lost."

"I'm not convinced justice was served. I'm keeping records. I'll be taking it up with the Brotherhood when we get into port."

"I do my best," Raoul said. "But I've never yet been able to satisfy everyone."

"I'm not accusing you personally. Every rep has his own style. I feel you talk sense when the local meets but I notice you don't talk so tough when the purser's in the room."

"Some people want to pick fights with the purser. I favour dialogue. It's honey or vinegar. I don't judge but I'm true to myself." Raoul brought more linen down on Horst. "In the meantime you want to keep your nose clean so you can go into a conference with a sterling record."

"My record speaks for itself," Horst said.

"That's good. You don't want a note on your file."

"There's no note on my file."

"And this isn't the time to get one if you're taking a case to the next level."

"I work my ass off."

"That will look good in front of the panel."

"I'm working when there's no one to work for. I'm changing sheets no one is sleeping in."

"It is in no way your business what the paying customer does in their sheets or not," Raoul said. "Plus they'll be back any time. You mind your cart and do your job."

"And I'm covering sections for Jimmy G and Juan."

"It's an emergency posture."

"If I thought the burden was shared out equally," Horst said.

"The burden was never shared out equally," Raoul said. "Emergencies don't change fundamentals." He reached up to another shelf and counted. "You want sixteen pillow slips?"

"Give me some extra. And some bolsters."

"How many bolsters?"

"A lot. And some shams."

"Can you give me a number?"

"I don't have a firm number. I mix it up," Horst said.

Raoul shook his head, like he wasn't sure Horst's approach was fully professional, but he pulled out several armloads and loaded Horst up some more and then turned him around and pushed him out the door. Horst went quietly. I thought he got everything off his chest. I was impressed how Raoul took care of Horst and the variety of approaches he put into play. You could see he would be an asset in a situation. And I was surprised that Raoul ran the Brotherhood. It was something else to think about. Although I knew good men who came from that side of things, and knew how to put people and money together.

For a minute after the door closed we listened to Horst banging around in the locker room. "He's loading up," Raoul said. "Dusters and cloths. That kind of thing." And then we heard the other door open and close, and Horst was gone. Raoul shrugged and gave me a look. "That's what I've got to work with," he said.

the 'fly

I stood up. The clock was ticking. "It's not my business," I told him, and I meant I had no interest.

He snapped to it, the way I liked. "Exactly, Mr. Rutledge," he said. "And I apologize you had to see that. It won't happen again. But so you know, if it comes down to Plan B, Horst is not in on the deal and he will not be sharing space in the service area."

"It's good to know, Raoul," I said. "Although it doesn't matter anyway, because it isn't going to happen, really." I checked my watch. "It's getting late. I'm going down to the Broadway to have a word. You do your end. If things go the way they should, I'll be on my way any time."

"I wanted to talk to you more about that, too," Raoul said. He was standing in front of the door and he was blocking me again. "It's Plan A all the way and we should move on it, like you say. The very best thing, and I pray to God our Heavenly Father it works, is that you get on the 'Fly and chopper out. For you it would be a happy ending, and I can hold back my professional zeal and not go to Hoskins and explain the chopper or interfere in any way because most likely the resupply will get here any day now, and if that doesn't happen, at least you can alert the fleet and send a rescue squad. And even if that takes several days, and most of the people on this ship die because we run out of food and water and fuel and resources, I will probably land on my feet because I laid in a supply of noodles and tap water, and it will give me hope to know that you and the big guy are out there and working the problem. I'll have something to live for.

"So I am in no way pressuring you on this, and although I realize that space on the 'Fly will be limited, I want to tell you that I can be very helpful with languages and contacts in a number of different ports of call. And if you need me to come, I can be ready to roll in virtually no time flat."

He stopped then and let me think about the cost of doing business, and I didn't blame him, because the situation looked bad, frankly. It was tricky, because I couldn't make any guarantees and I don't like to make a promise I can't keep. But I didn't think it was a good idea just to tell him no, either.

"You took me by surprise, Raoul," I told him.

"I move fast. It's one of my qualities."

"And you want to abandon ship?" I asked him.

Raoul looked shocked. "I hate to abandon ship. It's the last thing I want to do. Never in my wildest dreams did I think I'd be choppering off the ship with you and the heavy hitters. But it isn't working out the way we hoped. All the things I planned, all the things I dreamed of. I don't think they're going to happen now. As a human being, I have to ask myself, what can I salvage from this? And as a committed professional, I want to know how I can maintain my identity as a personal service technician.

"You're the best client I have, Mr. Rutledge. You understand what I put into my work, and the satisfaction I get back. To maintain my identity as a professional, I want to guarantee your comfort even if you go away from the ship. If I could travel with you, I can help you, and I can hold onto that part of myself. Everything is better if I go too."

"What about your other clients?"

"Horst will look after them, and Leticia and Regina."

"What about Juan and Jimmy G?"

"They jumped ship. It's a reason Horst is so high-strung now, although he was always stretched too tight."

"And Ricky Rochelle?"

It wasn't important, but I remembered the beginning when I was keen and full of hope. Her name came back to me even though I never saw her.

Raoul shook his head. "We lost her at Port Esteban." He didn't say anything else, and I didn't like to ask because he was sensitive about the island.

"Horst will do his best, and Leticia," he said. "It won't be the same. They're second string essentially. My cruisers will feel the difference,

the 'fly

and they're good people, some of them. I'm running out on them. I know it, and I'm not proud. But it's a true thing, my other clientele, what's left of them, they never appreciated me the way you do. I don't know if they deserve my labour. It's a sad thing to say, but it's how I feel. My comfort is, a lot of my people deserted me first. They got off the boat in Port Esteban or in the Canal. There's nothing I can do for them anymore. And at least I could be looking after you still, and the big guy."

"You're sure about this?"

"If there's room for me. Could you talk to him about it? See if there's a place for me too? I don't mind if it's crowded." He hit his chest. "I never put a lot of flesh on my frame. I hardly take up any space. You'll be impressed how small I make myself."

"I can't guarantee anything, Raoul. And there's likely a cost." I shrugged. I couldn't pay for him, obviously, because if you start that kind of thing, where does it end?

"I have some personal savings, Mr. Rutledge," Raoul said.

"Oh really?" I said.

"It's not much. It's my rainy-day fund and my stake. But this is a crisis. If it comes down to that, I can make a bid and a good one. I won't embarrass you."

"Well, that's good." I told him. "You're a good kid," I said. "I hope it works out for you. I don't know how high the stakes are. There are factors. But I hope you can swing it." I thought for a second, because I wanted to make it very clear. "If you can't come up with the stake," I said, "you'll be okay. You've got noodles and the Leroy security system. And our mission is to send back the rescue squad." But I wasn't going to ante up to get him a seat on the 'Fly and I wanted him to know it.

"I'll make it through," Raoul said. "I don't want you to worry. Although, if you chopper out and leave me behind, it would be a nice gesture if I could have your water."

But I didn't want to move my water before I finalized my plans, because there was a chance I might want to be in my suite and alone instead of in a dead end with Raoul, and I certainly wanted a key in my hand when I moved my best asset. I wanted to keep my options open.

"You go down to my suite," I said. "Pack up a light kit for me, my toiletries and some fresh shirts. Nothing fancy. I don't need my tux, for example. On top of my safe, in the walk-in, you'll find several cases of water. There's three or four, I think, sparkling with lime." It wasn't the water I liked best, and I thought I could let him move it if it kept him onside. "You can bring them down here," I said. "It's a down payment and a stake, and I have more in the closet and the safe if I can still trust you by the end of the day. You take care of all those things. You don't have time to go running to Hoskins, and it isn't in your interests either."

"You make a sweet deal sweeter, Mr. Rutledge," Raoul said.

He stood in front of me and didn't move, like in the old days, and it took me a minute before I knew what he wanted, because as far as I was concerned we were exploring a whole new paradigm and the time for cash bonuses was past. I thought I made it clear last time, and even if we did have a more productive encounter this time, and Raoul was trying to optimize his stake for an auction with the big man, I still didn't feel that tips were back in play. You can't turn back the clock. So I stood my ground, and after a long minute Raoul came around to my way of thinking, and he sort of nodded and bowed and pulled the door open behind him and stood back to let me out.

"Where should I look for you again?" he asked me.

I checked my watch. "You think it's intermission now?"

He checked his watch. "Just starting. If they run it to time, and they usually do. They're professionals."

"I'll go down right now, catch the big guy, get an answer. He might be moving fast. We should be ready."

"I can meet you on the flight deck in ten," Raoul said.

And I told him okay.

the 'fly

But when I got down to the Broadway, it was empty. There was only a cleaner in the foyer. He was an older guy with no puff, and he was pushing an old-fashioned sweeper, rolling it back and forth on the carpet. It clicked and popped. I looked around and there was no one else. The doors to the theatre were wide open but the house lights were up, and I didn't see anyone in the seats or on the stage.

So I asked him, "Did the show end early?"

"The show?" he said.

He looked straight at me but he kept running the sweeper back and forth between us. I didn't think he was a very bright light.

"Is it over already?" I asked him again.

He gave his attention to the sweeper and I thought he wasn't going to tell me. Then he said, "Closed the show."

"They didn't do a show tonight?" I said.

It took me by surprise after all my careful planning. I was counting on having a word with the big guy casually in the lobby. I couldn't believe I missed my chance.

The guy stopped his sweeping and looked at me again with his mouth open. It took him a minute. "Did a show tonight," he said finally.

"Then it isn't closed," I said.

Then he got back to it and I had to wait while he pushed the sweeper under a bench against the wall and ran it back and forth. It took all his concentration. Finally he took another breather and he said, "Closed it down at halftime."

"Just like that?" I said. "In the middle of the show?"

"Surprised the audience."

"Why would they do it?" I said. Because it wasn't what you expect.

"Union," he said.

I thought I should have known the union would put its oar in, although I never in my life thought the tap dancers would be the first ones to down tools, and I thought it showed character that Raoul didn't lead the strike and used his position instead to keep the Brotherhood up to the mark. But it was definitely time to get off the boat if the bit players weren't doing their walk-ons anymore. I wanted to catch up with the big guy right away even if I couldn't make it look like I just bumped into him by accident. Sometimes you have to be direct.

I went back to the elevator. It took a minute to come up and then it was full of people dressed in their very best even though dress codes were relaxed all over the ship. Enright was there and Poppy.

"Come and hit for a while," Poppy said.

I was still in my shorts and a polo, and I said I didn't like to since I wasn't dressed.

"Black tie is optional," Poppy said. "Come as you are." She was lit somewhat and friendly like always when she'd had a drink or two.

"I don't know if it's good policy," I said.

"It's the thin edge of the wedge," Enright said. "The slippery slope. First it's casual Fridays. Then sandals with socks."

He was lit also, and he always liked to lay down the law. I thought I wouldn't necessarily miss him.

"Then put a dinner jacket on," Poppy said. She kept trying too when she was lit. "We'll hold the elevator. Nobody minds," she said.

"I'm going to the Arboretum," I told them, "to get some fresh air."

There was no point in telling them how bad things were. The 'Fly had limited space, and they were happy wearing black tie and playing games of chance in the Monte.

"No one wants to hit anymore," Poppy said. "No one likes a game of chance. Ben used to hit every night. You never see him now."

"The Arboretum?" Enright said.

"On deck sixteen," I told him.

"That's the lawn bowling green," Enright said.

"It has vines and trellises," I said.

"Pergolas," Poppy said. She couldn't put the whole word together but she enjoyed trying.

the 'fly

"Sure. But it's not an arboretum," Enright said. "That is something completely different."

The elevator pulled up at deck ten and the bell sounded and the doors opened beside the casino. I stepped to the side so people could get off, but Enright was at the front, and he put his arms out wide and held the doors open and everyone had to wait behind him. He turned around and looked stern.

"It isn't even a greenhouse," he said.

Then Poppy took his arm and pulled him away and they all went to gamble. I went up to deck fourteen, and I got off the elevator and ran down the corridor to fourteen oh four. I took a second to pull myself together, because I didn't want to look desperate and worried. Presentation matters. And then I knocked. I was firm but polite. There was no answer. I waited a minute and then I knocked again. Nothing. I tried a third time, and I still didn't get anywhere. So I figured he was probably already on the move with his whole staff, or at least I'd be a fool if I didn't explore the possibility.

I ran back to the elevator again and hit the call bell. I had to wait some more, and I was even thinking about taking the stairs although it was four floors up to the flight deck. But the elevator came finally, and I took it up. I crossed my fingers and hoped Raoul had packed my kit and was waiting for me topside, because I didn't think I had time for long goodbyes.

When the elevator doors opened for me on the flight deck someone had a light in my face right away. "We've got you covered," a voice shouted. "Get down. Get down." He was standing close to me and yelling, and he had supporting armament, a semi-automatic, clip in and safety off, three feet from my face. I couldn't see much else because of the flashlight in my eyes, and I wasn't completely expecting a high-voltage situation. But I have experience and I know how to handle myself. I put my hands up high and kept them there. I didn't want to spook anyone.

"It's just me," I said.

"Get down on the ground," he yelled.

It was one guy shouting all the time. He had big lungs and he used full force. Some people think they look big if they talk out loud but usually it means they're young and don't have experience. You want to step carefully around that profile. I kept my hands up and I took a step onto the deck and started to kneel down. The tarmac was uncomfortable under my knees which gave me another reason to move slowly. Plus I wanted to look around. There was commotion everywhere.

"Good to go in five," someone said in the background.

The 'Fly was parked on the bull's-eye in the middle of the deck. The rotors came up and went down, and lights went on and off, just like with Lou and Denise. I figured they were going through their pre-flight. People were jogging back and forth in squads of two and three.

"Come on come on," the kid with the big voice said, and I kept lowering myself down like he wanted.

Then another voice came in. "What is it?" he said.

"It's some guy," said the kid.

"It's me. Rutledge," I said, because I like to speak for myself. "I was looking for the big man."

"Now is not a good time, Rutledge," the new voice said.

And I realized it was him. "Oh, is that you?" I said. I couldn't see really. I was kneeling by then and the kid still had a flashlight in my face. But I smiled in the direction where I heard the big guy's voice like I was happy to bump into him. "Are these your boys?" I asked him. "Could you tell them to lay off a bit?"

"They're professionals," he said. "I don't interfere."

"I understand," I told him. "You have to trust your crew." Although I thought it wouldn't kill him to say a word since I was on my knees and we'd always got along.

"Face down on the tarmac," the kid shouted. "Move it move it move it."

I thought he was hopped up. Some guys do that before action to get an edge although it never was my style. But it gave me another reason to follow instructions carefully. Also the light in my eyes was less of an issue the lower I got. I had a clear view of boots running back and forth around the 'Fly, and people stepping up and in. And I kept talking, because I had a goal in mind and you only get the job done by doing it.

"You're heading out then?" I asked the big guy. "I think the rental on the 'Fly is going up these days. I thought you might like a co-investor, someone to split your costs with." I was spread out on the tarmac and it dug into me, plus I had to hold my head up and look happy while we negotiated since I didn't have leverage. It was a challenging position overall.

The big guy laughed. "I'd love to unload some of my costs. But I have nothing to sell you."

"I'll take a seat on the 'Fly," I told him.

I didn't see Raoul anywhere, which was disappointing because I thought he could have packed a bag for me at least. But since he didn't make it to the flight deck I didn't even ask about a ticket for him.

"Sorry, Rutledge," the big guy said, and I was happy he remembered my name. "The manifest is full. These boys are working their transit. They're buying in with their skills."

"Good to go in four," a guy said in the background.

"That's the way," I said. "It gives the kids a chance." I wasn't going to tell him not to when the boys had guns. "All I'm saying is you don't need to carry the whole financial burden yourself."

"There's no room at the inn. I'm running out on a lot of people. I'm all torn up about it but I have to make decisions."

"I travel light. I don't have a kit or dependents."

"Are you dense? I told you no. I meant no. I told no to people I like." He was starting to get sore.

"Elevator up," the kid with the gun said.

I didn't know what he meant and I figured it was now or never with the big guy. So I went for broke. "What's going to happen to the rest of us?" I said.

"It's the Company's lookout," he said.

"You'll be in touch with them?"

"Or my legal team."

"You'll tell them our status?"

"Don't they know it already?"

"The way I see it, you're leading a rescue mission."

"If you like."

A bunch of things happened at once, they way they do in these situations. First, the welcoming committee moved off me. I looked up and there was no flashlight and no automatic. I thought the big lung kid maybe realized I was in no way a threat since I was having a nice conversation with the man. Then the elevator bell sounded and I looked back and I saw that the kid had stepped up and was covering the door. I thought for sure it was Raoul with my flight kit and although it didn't look like I would need it I was happy he had come through for me, and I appreciated the diversion. Then the doors opened, and the light from inside the elevator spread out across the tarmac. And since the kid with the gun moved off, I rolled ahead of the light and got behind some crates at the side while the kid was shouting at the new person.

"Put your hands up. Put your body down. We got you covered. Do it do it do it."

Then a girl said, "Why are you yelling?"

I peeked around the crate. It was a blonde. Not Jen, although she might have been one of the girls the big man kept around. I wasn't sure. She stepped out of the elevator like guys yelled at her and waved guns all the time. Maybe they did. Pretty girls sometimes live in high action worlds. Behind her, the elevator doors closed and it was harder to see with only the flashlight on her and the lights from the 'Fly going up and down.

The kid with the gun kept shouting. "Get down on the ground. Get down on the ground."

the 'fly

"Don't yell at me," she said. "Tell him not to yell?"

She was looking over at the 'Fly, and I thought the big man would look after her if she was one of his girls. But he wasn't in a loving mood.

"What are you doing here?" he said to her.

"Are we leaving?" she said.

"You can't come," he said.

"You said I could," she said.

"Well you can't," he said.

"You said you had a seat for me," she said. She took a step forward.

"Good in three," the countdown guy said.

"Stay where you are. Get on your knees," the kid shouted.

She shrugged at him and kept going.

"Do it now," he said.

"Yeah. You scare me," she said.

He moved in to block her and she tried to push past him. He used his flashlight hand and caught her by the arm and he pushed her down on the tarmac. I think she didn't expect him really to go after her. She made little screaming sounds and slapped at him like girls do. He applied more force.

"Get off me," she said. She looked over at the 'Fly. "Get him off me," she said.

"I don't micromanage my people," the big guy said.

And then the elevator opened again, and the kid kept his flashlight hand holding the blonde down and pointed his gun at the elevator. I thought for sure it was Raoul this time, and the kid shouted into the elevator, "I got you covered. Step out of the doors. Get down on the ground. Do it now."

He sounded like he was coming undone, and the girl was resisting, and the rotors were thumping.

And then I heard the captain. "Jackson?" he said. "Is it Jackson? What are you doing with that gun?"

I leaned out again to get a better view, and when the lights on the

'Fly came up again, I saw the captain and Hoskins. They were standing just in front of the elevator looking sharp in their whites, with their hands in the air.

"It's Wobanski," Hoskins said.

"I don't give a rat's ass who it is," said the captain. "Why are you pointing a gun at me, Jackson?"

The big lung kid gave up trying to hold the girl down. He pulled her up on her feet and held her across his chest where he could control her and she could be useful as a shield. I thought he had better skills than he showed at first. Then he stepped up to the captain and cold-cocked him and stepped back again. The captain dropped like a rock.

Hoskins looked down at the captain and then up at the kid. "That's mutiny, Wobanski," he said.

"You got that right," the kid said in his big voice. "Now get down like I told you."

Hoskins wasn't an idiot although his whites weren't their whitest anymore and his roots were showing. Very slowly he started to get down beside the captain, and the captain came around and kind of moaned and felt around the tarmac. The kid with the gun watched them hard and the girl squirmed around and told him, "Let go of me. Let me go," and the countdown voice in the 'Fly said, "Good in two." And then the kid with the gun looked up and around fast, and everything changed again.

Beside the elevator, the door to the stairs opened and a team ran out at speed, body armour on and safeties off. I could see an array of armament: AKs, and light machine guns, and a couple of RPGs. So it turned out the big guy didn't nail down the whole force, I thought, or security took the incentives and double-crossed him. Either way it was messy and not fully professional the way things should be. I knew if he had my capital and my advice he could have done better, but it was too late for regrets.

For a minute everything was in motion. The captain's boys came out laying down cover fire, and they fanned out fast and took up a

the 'fly

variety of defensive postures. The big man's team returned fire and retreated to the 'Fly. Hoskins took the opportunity to find cover. When the smoke cleared, Hoskins was near me beside the elevator stack, and the captain was still feeling around the tarmac like he lost his glasses. The big lung kid was bleeding beside him, and the girl was under the kid, not slapping at him anymore or whining. The big guy and most of his team were in the 'Fly. One of the big man's security guys was still on the tarmac behind the bird crawling toward it and dragging his leg. He shouted to his buddies and reached his hands to them but nobody was looking out for him. The rotors on the 'Fly were picking up and a defensive contingent was in position at the door. The captain's boys were all around it covering the angles.

Everything hung fire for a second, and then the countdown guy said, "Good in one."

"You can't take Dragon Three," shouted one of the captain's boys. I couldn't hear well over the rotors, but I thought I recognized Delaronde, machine specialist fourth class, and I was happy there was one guy on the 'Fly squad who didn't sell himself to the highest bidder. "It's due for maintenance," he shouted.

"Stand down rotors and step away from the bird," Hoskins shouted. I was closer to him but it was still hard to hear.

"It's not fueled up," Delaronde shouted.

Someone found a bullhorn for Hoskins and he gave more orders, but amplified now so everyone heard. "For the last time, sir, step out of the 'Fly," he shouted. "Instruct the mutineers to lay down arms. Power off and come out with your hands in the air."

There was a burst of gunfire from the 'Fly and a line of dust shot up on the tarmac establishing a perimeter all around the bird. The guy with the leg cursed some more and stopped trying to move in and the guys in the bird closed the door. The 'Fly lifted up, just like with Lou and Denise, except no one saluted. It went straight up about six feet and hovered.

Hoskins shouted into the bullhorn, "Fire at will." And his boys squeezed off a couple of shots. And then when no one expected it, the captain hauled himself up. He was nearly under the bird and he was weaving and bleeding from the head, but he waved his hands like his guys should hold up and they held up.

"I said fire at will!" Hoskins shouted with his bullhorn. The captain's boys looked at Hoskins and at the captain and at each other.

"We need the 'Fly," the captain shouted back. He didn't have a bullhorn and it was hard to hear, but he was firm.

"With respect, sir. That's why we need to shoot," Hoskins said. He was talking through the bullhorn, so his voice had more authority.

"We can't use it if it's damaged," the captain said.

"We've got a team of mechanics," Hoskins said. "They can fix anything."

"They can't fix Dragonfly Four," the captain said.

"No one can," machine specialist Delaronde said. "We stripped it for parts."

"Which is why we needed Dragonfly Three," Hoskins said.

"In working order," said the captain.

Above us the bird lifted and torqued. The security boys shifted their cover to adjust for the new angle.

"Also, he's an important man," the captain said.

"Bring it down!" Hoskins shouted.

"I'm captain here."

"It's really an honorific, sir."

And then the 'Fly lifted up and away. Hoskins threw down his bullhorn and grabbed an AK from one of his guys. He shot at the bird, which as far as I could see didn't help us at all, because there was no advantage if he shot it into the sea. But I couldn't tell if he hit it. The pilot didn't have lights on and the sound of rotors died away.

Hoskins kept shooting for a bit anyway, and then he threw the weapon down, and Captain Moncrieff staggered over and slapped at him. He was bleeding and weak and he couldn't put a lot of force into

the 'fly

it, but he kept at it, even though slapping Hoskins was as pointless as shooting the 'Fly. The security guys stood around watching them and looking at each other.

I felt it was the moment when I had to choose. I thought for a second whether I should throw in with Captain Moncrieff, or with Hoskins, or with both of them if they shook hands and called a truce and worked together for the good of the passengers. But that didn't look likely and I didn't see that either had a lot to offer, separately or even if they worked together, since the 'Fly was gone and supplies were low and neither had a strategy that I could see. The only thing going for them, I thought, was that security was well armed, but I didn't see how that worked to my personal advantage.

On a practical level, even though he was unreliable in some ways, Raoul offered the best combination of resources and creativity. I felt I had the best chance of long-term success if I went in with him. Plus we already came to terms. So while the Captain and Hoskins bitch-slapped each other and the security detail watched them and waited for orders, I slipped quietly through the door to the stairs. It wasn't a time to wait for the elevator. So I took the stairs two at a time all the way down to deck six.

the station

CHAPTER NINETEEN

When I got back to my suite, Raoul was in the closet.

"There you are, Mr. Rutledge," he said. "I was getting worried."

The cases of water were gone from on top of the safe, which was okay because I told him to move them. But several litre bottles of still that I didn't okay were gone also.

"Give me the key," I told him.

"The key?" he said.

I hit him once hard across the face. "We don't have time to play games, Raoul. We've got a situation here and we have to move fast. I have more water in the safe and we'll need it, but we're not moving anything else until you give me the key to the station. I like you and I respect you, but I don't trust you. You want me to open the safe, you hand over the station key now."

Raoul thought about it a half second longer than he should, and I knew I could never turn my back on him again. Then he tried to make a better impression by being busy. He reached into his pocket and pulled his key ring out on its retractable wire and found a key he liked and started to work it off.

I put my hand out. "Give me the set," I said.

He didn't stop. "It's better this way, Mr. Rutledge," he said. "I'm a pack rat. I keep everything. You don't need the key to my bike lock at home or my mother's apartment."

He didn't give them to me, so I reached out and took them. I grabbed the whole set and pulled them to me. The wire played out to its limit behind the keys and then pulled Raoul a step into me. He put his hands up like I shouldn't think he was trying to dominate me. But he still didn't help.

"You're a strong man and I respect that, Mr. Rutledge," he said. "But it's steel wire, twenty mil gauge, precision ground and tempered to high tolerance."

I reached to where the keys attached to his belt loop and pulled them off his pants. Raoul looked down and picked at the loop. There were threads hanging from the end and a hole in his pants where I pulled it off.

"You didn't have to do that, Mr. Rutledge," he said. "You could have just opened the carabiner. It's how it works."

"Or you could have," I told him. I let the wire snap back, and I folded the keys and the carabiner and put it all in my pocket.

"You tore the fabric," Raoul said.

"Send it to laundry services," I told him.

I had to push around him to get to the safe. I worked the combination with my shoulders up so he couldn't see, because although I didn't need it right away, I thought it was possible I'd want a secure lock box again some time in the future. I opened it and pulled out half-litre bottles of water, and I loaded Raoul up. I gave him twelve half-litre bottles, and I left eight litre bottles on a shelf to take with. All the other water still on the shelves I moved into the safe with my cash neatly stacked behind it, and I made sure Raoul saw all the water in the safe before I closed it. He hated to leave it behind.

"Why don't we take it all, Mr. Rutledge?" he said. "While we're here."

"It's heavy," I said.

"I can take more," Raoul said.

He had many bottles already. He arranged them in his arms. But I closed the safe and spun the dial.

"It's better here," I told him. "It's waiting for us and no one else can get it."

I was nice about it but Raoul could see I wasn't going to budge and he could also see I had a private line on a valuable resource. I thought it would keep a leash on any funny business for a while. I picked up the litres and waved him out and he gave in and went first and I closed the closet door behind me. Then I made sure the balcony doors in the bedroom were locked, and I went into the living room and closed the door to the bedroom and closed the doors to the balcony from the living room and locked them even though it was only a titanium bolt, and I pulled the door to the suite shut and it locked behind me. I locked everything I could.

Outside my suite, things looked different. There were bright lights and long shadows in the hall, and Raoul was running down the corridor. I thought for sure if I didn't have the key he would lock me out, and I thought he could still have an alternate plan. So I went after him fast, although not running, because it was dark in places, and the water was heavy.

But he had no options, and when I got to the station, he was waiting at the door, kind of nervous and pacing. I put my litre bottles down and pulled the key ring out and looked for the key. It was hard to see, and Raoul was impatient. He put his water down and tried to show me. I slapped his hands away. Then the door opened and Horst stepped out. He looked at me. Then he looked at Raoul. I thought he was going to ask what we were doing. But he had other things on his mind.

"You hear it?" he said.

"Hear what?" I said.

"Nothing," Horst said.

the station

Raoul gave Horst his full attention. He stepped up and nodded hard and looked at him seriously, while Horst waited patiently to find out what Raoul had to say on the topic. Then Raoul hit him. Horst wasn't expecting it and his head snapped back and hit the door frame behind him, and Raoul hit him again and he folded, and Raoul followed him down and hit him several more times around the head and the neck. He hit him till Horst stopped reacting in any way. Then he reached into Horst's pants and felt around and took the keys off his belt loop. He stood up again with them in his hand.

"Now we both have access," he said. He thought about it. "You take these," he said. "I'll keep mine. There's less confusion."

He held Horst's keys out to me in one hand and put his other hand out like he wanted a tip. I ignored it.

"I have keys already," I said. "You keep those."

Raoul kept his hands out like he didn't know what else to do with them.

"And Horst is just lying there," I said.

He was spread out along the wall. There was blood where he was bleeding from his nose and mouth.

"Someone's going to notice, maybe ask questions."

Raoul gave it his attention. "Mr. Rutledge. Please. I understand the situation," he said. He looked at Horst's keys and pulled one out and opened the door to the station, and he leaned in to look around and leaned back out again still holding the door. "You go inside. Take care of the water. Get comfortable." He held the door for me and put Horst's keys in his pocket, and he kind of kicked at Horst. "I'll take care of things. I'll be back momentarily. I have a key now. You lock the door. It locks by itself. But you close the dead bolt also. You want to feel safe."

I stepped into the station and Raoul said, "I can help with these."

He ducked down and picked up bottles of water and held them out to me. I went into the station and opened a locker, an empty one with no lock on it, and I started stacking bottles inside. Raoul moved them to me two at a time. It didn't take long and no one came around while we were working.

"Really. I'll be ten minutes," Raoul said. He pulled the door shut, and I locked it like he said, because it was why I was there after all. I wished I had a lock for the locker, too, but I didn't. So I just closed the door securely. Then I moved quickly because I knew that Raoul would be working at speed also.

I looked in all the other lockers that didn't have locks. It was difficult to see because the lighting was bad in the station also, high and bright with dark shadows in the corners, and not how I remembered it. But I felt around all the shelves and looked as well as I could. Two lockers were empty, and then another one had cleaning products and rags. Also hairnets and rubber gloves and economy size bottles of antibacterial hand sanitizer and vaseline and lip balm and lotion with aloe for chapped hands. I took a can of aerosol cleaner and a jug of bleach and I moved them to a separate location, so I knew where they were and Raoul didn't.

Then I tried the keys in the lockers with locks that locked with keys. There were three of them and I found all the keys on Raoul's set. One locker had personal portion noodles and noodle soup. There were cups stacked up from the floor, three across and three deep and up to my waist, and there were single serving packages of noodles without cups stacked on the shelves. I felt that when it came to noodles at least, Raoul told no lie. I put the lock back on the locker and memorized the key.

The next key-locked locker had tinned goods. There was more soup, but condensed, and there were tins of pork and beans and chili and beef stew, which I didn't have a taste for right then, but I thought I might be grateful for sometime in the future. There was a good supply of food in the two lockers, more food than Raoul mentioned, really, which again disappointed me somewhat. But I was getting used to it and knowing was better than not knowing.

In the third key-locked locker there were four flats of water. They were stacked sideways, two on the floor and two more on top of them. Also several bottles of still that I didn't authorize. I was happy we had a good supply but disappointed Raoul took initiatives with my property. Also in the locker there were more tinned goods on the lower shelf, though a smaller selection, and on the top shelf there were more shammies and rags for cleaning and several formal shirts, washed and starched and ironed, with their ruffles standing at attention. It was another let down when I found them. And it was a strange assortment of things for Raoul to lock up. So I checked the space carefully, feeling behind the tins and patting down the shirts and cleaning rags.

Under the shammies I found a hunting knife with a fine edge in a leather sheath with a strap. It was stored handle forward for easy access. I considered leaving it, so Raoul didn't know I knew about it. But I didn't see an advantage, and I decided safety first. I took my shirt off and hung the knife in its sheath across my chest and tucked it inside the waistband of my shorts. Then I put my shirt on again and adjusted it to cover things. I closed up the locker again and memorized that key also.

All the other lockers had combination locks. I knew one had jugs of Raoul's water that he showed me before. And I figured the other lockers were Raoul's or Horst's or Leticia's or even Jimmy G's or Regina's, and I couldn't get into them right away, although I certainly planned to try. The locks were nothing special and standard bolt cutters would open them, I thought, although I didn't have bolt cutters. But I thought even a good quality can opener might give me access. I kept it all in the back of my mind.

And Raoul still wasn't back. So I found the key to the forward room, and I took another can of aerosol with me and went in. I found another good place for it at the top of the linen shelves beside the door behind sheets, where it was out of sight and I didn't think Raoul could reach it.

Then I did an inventory of the rest of the cupboards and shelves and the desk. There was a computer and a house phone. I didn't think that either had anything to offer at that point, and also I didn't want in any way to tip people off we were in the station. So I left them alone. The desk had three drawers. One had office supplies I didn't think I would need. Another had spoons and forks and a flashlight and a box of candles and a box of matches and a lighter and several emergency flares and a deck of cards. The last one had pins and safety pins and a pincushion and needles and thread, and again, I thought probably I didn't need any of it. In the cupboards over the desk there were several large binders on one shelf, and a kettle and an iron and a bottle of starch. Also there was a first aid kit with bandages and rubbing alcohol and Polysporin and peroxide and eye drops and cotton swabs and hypodermics. There was Aspirin and acetaminophen and ibuprofen. There were no really effective meds, but I thought in an emergency Sick Bay probably had stock left, or the J-kid's stash even.

And then I looked at the windows again. The cot was still down, and I stood on it to get a good look, and the springs complained, but it held. I opened the windows wide, and I put my face right up to the frame and breathed in fresh air. It was cool and dark outside. I thought I should see more light from other rooms on the boat, but nothing was bright.

Then I heard noise in the first room, and a second later Raoul rattled the handle and came in dusting himself down. He was still in his whites but looking grubby with a dirty collar and blood on his cuffs. I thought, better him than me.

"You got some air, Mr. Rutledge," he said. "It's a good idea. Although we'll have trouble making a through-draft, like we discussed."

"We'll close it in daytime," I said. "Maybe block it with sheets."

"Try to keep the heat out," Raoul said.

I stepped off the cot and sat down on it. "You took care of it?" I asked him.

"He won't make any trouble," Raoul said.

"He won't file a complaint?" I said.

the station

~ 309 ~

"Mr. Rutledge, please. He's not in a position. I took care of it."

I thought I understood him but he didn't say anything definite, and although that left me somewhat in the dark, I appreciated it, because nobody wants to be an accessory.

"Will the purser notice?" I said.

Raoul made a firm gesture. "He has other fish to fry," he said. "He should sound the alarm any minute."

I wasn't sure what he meant. "For Horst?" I said.

"For the outage," Raoul said. "We've got no power. The engines cut out."

I looked up at the light. It was blinding. "We have lights," I said.

"They're emergency lights," Raoul said.

I looked more closely. I had to squint. And I could see it was only a couple of bulbs attached to a pack. I looked up at the fluorescents in the ceiling, and they were off. Raoul jiggled the switch. The fluorescents stayed off.

"When did this happen?" I asked him.

"We were leaving your suite," he said.

I couldn't remember the exact moment, but I knew he was right. "I thought it looked different," I said.

"Lighting is an indicator," Raoul said. "Also you can hear. The background is gone."

"That's the engine?"

"The engine, central air, the bar fridge in your suite. All the machinery is offline and everything that draws power isn't drawing power anymore. It's the end of the line from a power perspective."

"Why did they do it?"

"We're out of fuel."

"Are you sure?"

"They wouldn't cut engines otherwise."

He was calm, and I liked it that he could hold it together. Because I expected him to cheat and to steal and to stab me in the back, but at least the way he talked I didn't have to worry that he'd crack. Also he knew the drill and I needed to hear.

"What's coming up?" I asked him. "Outside this room, what's going on?"

"First thing, they secure tactical stations."

"And what are they?" I said.

He held up his hand and counted off. "Engines, bridge, communication, technology, security. Also kitchens, pantries, water."

"The kitchen is tactical?"

"Food supply is critical."

It made sense, although it was strange to imagine a security detail guarding the buffet. The food lately was so-so at best, and portion size was dainty.

"There isn't much to secure," I said.

"It's the bottom of the barrel," Raoul said. "They have rice left and pasta. But sauce is hard to find. Vegetables are tinned. Milk and eggs are powdered only. For meat we're down to sub-prime cuts and offal. Mostly they grind it for shepherd's pie or boil it for stock."

"I'd rather have beef stew from a tin," I said.

"Also stock and powdered milk and rice and pasta raise a red flag," Raoul said. "Because they need water to cook in or as an ingredient, and water is the key issue. I don't know details because the quartermaster was very protective about numbers and volumes, but I think supplies are failing. My guess is they're drawing water from the bottom of the well. And I don't know how they're going to access anything that's left in the tank without electricity to work the pumps. So that is another consideration.

"The bottom line is, leadership, if it can, has to secure water holdings and maybe set up water recovery systems like barrels for rainwater and solar stills. But these make small contributions only and I can't see them servicing several hundreds of people once the water tank is completely drained. So my guess is the ration will be tight, and strictly for drinking, no washing and no flushing. And even still, I think they have three days maybe of drinking water and then they are at the very end of their rope."

"Three days?" I said.

Raoul said, "Three days." He was solemn. We both knew it was the real thing.

"Are we in the right place?" I asked him. In a crisis you have to test every angle. "Should we be with the group until the taps run dry and then move down here? We could save three days of our supply."

Raoul looked concerned. "I thought you thought it was go time, Mr. Rutledge," he said. "I thought you wanted to set up in here. It's why I took Horst down. I misunderstood. It's awkward, but we don't have to stay. We can go to the collection point when the klaxon sounds. We have the option. The issue is, can we get back? They'll take a head count and keep track of people from here on in, for rations and for public safety. In a couple of days, when we run out of food and water, I think order will break down and we can probably come back down and no one will notice in the confusion.

"But it's iffy. Security will run patrols. Looters or desperate people might get here first, service technicians with pass-keys and a self-help philosophy. Our stock is locked up. It's probably safe. But people might have bolt cutters. We could lose control of our resources. That is the risk. Also power will still be off. Depending on the time of day we might have to find our way in the dark."

"It doesn't sound safe," I said.

"Think of it this way. If we join the group, we take on risk. What is the risk to staying here? We lose three days of water from the public trough. Otherwise there is no downside. If a resupply heaves to, we join the gang, tell them we got lost. What are they going to do? The Company should be happy they recovered a customer. So that option is still totally on the table. But in the worst-case scenario, if the ship drifts and we wait for a resupply that doesn't come and we run out of water and food, and panic and desperation set in, where do you want to be? Up top with the hungry, thirsty masses, or tucked in safely down here, riding out the storm and holding on a few more days hoping for help and a happy ending?"

He made a good case. I felt sorry too about other people suffering if a resupply didn't roll up right away but I felt a powerful respect for the stock that Raoul and I laid in. I was satisfied with our planning. I thought about the flats of water Raoul moved and the half-litres and litres we brought down together and the jugs of water he locked away before. We had more than a three-day supply. We had many days each of water, and I had more still in my safe. We were outfitted to outlast everyone on board and if anyone could hold on until help arrived it was us.

"Let the purser lock up his powdered milk," I said. "I'd rather dig in here."

Raoul nodded like he thought it was the right plan, and he kept going. "They'll lock down every strategic concern," Raoul said. "Food, power, IT." He held onto it for a second. "Transport."

"You mean the 'Flies?" I asked him.

Raoul gave me the fish eye but he didn't ask right away. Instead he talked around it like people do. "They'll check the lifeboats and the tenders," he said. "The ones they still have. They need to test the manual override on the davits with the power down, and they'll inventory lifeboats for first aid kits and oars and emergency rations." He stopped and looked sideways like it was a thing he just thought of. "And the choppers," he said. He tried to sound casual. "Did you get up to the flight deck?" he asked me.

"I got up to the flight deck," I told him. "I stuck with the plan."

I didn't say anything else for a minute, because I was deciding if I was going to follow up. I didn't like to, because we were in a difficult situation and all we had was each other. But I decided I couldn't let it pass that he didn't bring my kit. Although we were in a situation

the station

and we didn't know if we would come out the other side, if we did I wanted to live in a world where people understood service. So I went into it.

"You didn't make it," I said. "I was looking for you like we said. I was sorry you didn't come through for me."

Raoul knew it mattered. He put on a sincere face. He was still standing in front of me and he hunched and looked humble and put effort into his excuse. "I was afraid he might not see reason," he said. "It was unorthodox, but I decided on balance the percentage move was to stock us down here. I want you to know I didn't make a snap decision although I acted at speed. I knew you'd be disappointed if the big guy took your offer and you had to book out without your kit. But I've seen him in action many times and I read the unauthorized biography. I didn't like your chances. I thought you'd end up back here and the best thing I could do was set us up for the long haul."

"You thought he'd turn me down?"

"I thought it was a possibility."

"You didn't mention that when we were discussing."

He opened his hands like he was showing me his heart. "I don't like to think bad about people. I have an instinct and I know people have areas of weakness. But I like to think they grow and become more than they were. Also, you were hopeful. You had a good feeling about your chances. I didn't like to jinx it."

And that made sense to me, because no one likes a killjoy.

"The thing about the big man is he made his pile and he has business sense," Raoul said. "But he lacks the human touch. It isn't something you like to see in your friends."

"It's disappointing," I said.

Raoul said, "But I'm assuming. I don't know facts. What happened? Did you find him? Did you get a chance to talk?"

"We talked," I said. I didn't like Raoul standing over me, asking questions. I didn't want to think about the flight deck. It was ugly and unhappy. And I felt that Raoul didn't earn the details when he didn't pack a kit and follow through for me.

But he wouldn't take the hint. "Did you ask him about transport?" he said.

"I asked him."

"What did he say?"

"He said no."

I didn't feel like telling him more, and he respected it for about ten seconds. Then he asked, "And did he book a 'Fly?"

"He took one," I told him. "He faced strong objections."

"You told him what you thought?"

"I said my piece. And then the captain turned up and Hoskins?"

Raoul looked interested. "Trying to abandon ship?" he asked.

I had a good look at him. I thought he was taking a shot at the brass, and when little men like him step out of line you have to show them their place again right away or you have chaos. And especially I thought he had no right to criticize when he was laying low in his station while Hoskins and the captain were taking risks for all of us and personally leading the defense which was more than Raoul did.

"They were trying to correct his point of view," I told him. I kept my face hard.

He put away his disrespect and focused on facts like it was his only concern. "Did they educate him?" he said.

"He didn't listen."

"Did they at least contain the 'Fly?"

Again I thought I heard criticism creeping in. I laid out the facts. "They brought support and they tried reasoning and force," I told him. "But he insisted. He made up his mind and he authorized his people to resist. He took Dragonfly Three." I thought about it for a second. "We have Dragonfly Four still," I said.

Raoul summed it up. "So the power is out and we have no operational fly machine."

the station

~ 315 ~

I had to admit. "The big picture is unhappy," I said. "There was shooting. There may have been fatalities on the flight deck. Also, I'm not sure but Hoskins might have hit Dragonfly Three. They had armament to bring it down. But there was disagreement about the order to shoot. All I can say is, the bird may have taken fire as she flew."

Raoul rolled his eyes. "It's worse than I thought," he said. "There was some doubt in my mind up until this point, but there's no question now. We are definitely better off down here."

I had to agree. "We're in the best place we can be, the best place anyone can be on this ship unless someone else made a better spider hole than this and good luck to them," I said.

Raoul clapped his hands together. "On that topic, I'm going to suggest we take a moment now to organize the station."

I looked around. I didn't see anything we needed. "What do you want to do?" I asked him.

"We should set up for when the lights go out," Raoul said.

This surprised me. "Are they going out?" I said.

"Emergency lights have a limited battery."

I didn't like the sound of it. "How limited?"

Raoul said, "It depends. Emergency lighting is calibrated to the needs of different stations and amenities. The light in nonessential stations and passenger areas lasts ninety minutes I think. Two hours maybe."

"Passenger areas are nonessential?" I said.

"Strategically nonessential."

It sounded insulting, but I was also trying to calculate. "How long has it been?"

"Between forty-five and sixty," Raoul said. "I didn't check my watch. I'm estimating. But my guess is we have an hour left at most, and probably less depending on the power pack design and battery freshness. So I don't want to disturb you, but I think I should set up the location so that we're ready when the lights go out."

It made sense. And I didn't want to be alone in the dark with Raoul without some mental preparation also. So I gave him the nod and he went into action.

"First thing, Mr. Rutledge. I'm going to ask you to come over here." He pulled the chair out from the desk and held it for me like we were in the Captain's Mess. "You take a load off and I'll make up the bed."

He took a step to me and I brushed him away because I didn't want him anywhere near the knife or the sheathe, or any part of me that he could hit or head-butt if it came to it. And I stood up and he waved me into the chair. "That's right, Mr. Rutledge," he said. "You be comfortable." I got around him and sat down on the chair and he looked at the cot and pressed the mattress firmly like he was making sure it was stable which wasn't necessary after I stood on it and sat on it. Then he turned around for sheets and I thought about how I didn't want him reaching for the sheets on the top shelf where I put the aerosol tin as a precaution. But he took from a lower shelf and spread it on the cot. And then he put on another sheet and a blanket and tucked everything in.

I went after more detail while he worked. "You said they take a head count?" I said.

Raoul got pillows down and pillowslips and pushed the pillows in the pillow slips and beat them up so they were light and fluffy. "When tactical is secure they'll sound the klaxon. Hospitality and service will help passengers find secure areas."

"They'll go back to the Broadway?" I said.

"They can't go to the Broadway," Raoul said. He looked offended.

"It was the secure area at Port Esteban," I said.

"It was daylight and we had power," he said. "You can't make people climb stairs in the dark."

And I could see his point.

Raoul pulled the sheet back a half-fold for easy access at the top of the cot and put the pillows on top and arranged them. It was a small cot and not comfortable but Raoul made it look like the bridal suite. "Mr. Rutledge, I'm going to ask you to move back over here," he said.

He put his hands out for me again and I dodged him some more and protected my knife side. We squeezed around each other again and I sat on the cot and leaned back against the pillows. The window was open and the air was a little cooler near it and the sheets smelled clean and fresh.

Raoul looked up at the emergency light. Then he sat down at the desk and opened a drawer and closed it and opened another one and pulled out a flashlight and a candle and a lighter. "What do you think?" he said to me. "Candle or flashlight?"

I thought about it. "Are we worried about oxygen?" I asked him.

"Not in a critical sense," he said.

"I like a candle for a steady light," I said. I thought some more. "But I don't like a fire hazard."

"I hear you," he said. He kept the flashlight in one hand and put the candle and the lighter back, and he rooted around in the drawer again and came up with another flashlight and threw it to me. I checked the on-off switch and kept it in my hand for convenience.

"We can each have one," Raoul said. "We can light up anything we need to see."

He reached into the drawer again and pulled out a box. "We have extra batteries," he said. He weighed the pack in his hand. "Some. We should think of flashlights as emergency lights also. We don't want to waste."

I agreed. He put the extra batteries back and put his flashlight on the desk very firmly. "Now I have a thing I want to get for you," he said. He had a big smile and I was suspicious right away. "I'm not going to tell you," he said. "You be comfortable and I'll take five minutes." He rubbed his hands together and bowed at me sort of and went to the outside room.

I got up right away and listened at the door. I could hear him at a locker. I put one hand on the handle of the knife and kept the flashlight in the other, and I used my flashlight hand to open the door and peeked.

Raoul was working at a locker with a combination lock. He heard me, but he didn't show fear. Instead he looked over his shoulder at me and smiled some more and moved in front of the locker more so I couldn't see detail. I didn't like to leave him alone, but I had the knife and he wasn't at the locker where I found it. So I went and sat on the cot.

A minute later Raoul pushed the door open and stood in the doorway like a picture for a second so I could appreciate. He was in his whites still, and even though they were grubby and stained with blood they held their shape. He had a tray in one hand with a glass and a sidecar on it. He brought it all over to me and stood beside me and held it in front of me and sort of bowed again.

"A G and T, Mr. Rutledge?" he said.

I was astounded. "You have tonic?" I asked him.

"I have tonic. I found a couple of bottles of tonic in a place I know, and a plastic lime. So you don't have to worry about scurvy yet. There's no ice is the downside. I feel bad about that."

But the tonic was lively and he poured it over the gin and the drink sparkled in the glass on the tray. It was hard to hold back. It took all my control. I had to dig in and focus like an elite athlete, because I wasn't going to be undone by a G and T on a silver tray.

"Raoul," I said. "This is the best thing a person ever did for me. And it would be even better if you would share the moment with me. I don't want to drink alone at the end of a day like this letting you wait on me hand on foot. Go now," I told him. "Get another glass. Bring the gin in and the tonic and the plastic lime and I will pour you a drink and we will drink together and toast the future in fellowship. I'll wait for you."

I took the drink off the tray and held it and nodded at the other room. And Raoul thought about it for several seconds, which made me happy I did it, and then he nodded and said, "Mr. Rutledge. You are a prince among men, and if I may say, if I had to be trapped in a service station in the south seas while several hundred people slowly starve

the station

~ 319 ~

and suffer heatstroke and die of dehydration maybe, while an uncertain future lies ahead, I cannot think of anyone I'd rather pass the days with, and I will take you up on your offer and share a drink with you, and we will toast the future and whatever it brings."

He went back out and rummaged around for things quickly, and it hurt me right down to my root, but I got up on the cot and poured my drink out the window. And when Raoul came in again with a glass and a bottle of gin and a bottle of tonic water and a plastic lime on a tray, I put the flashlight in my pocket and took the tray and told him, "Now you have a seat. You take a load off. You worked hard enough."

And I pushed him into the chair and put the tray down on the desk and put myself between him and the glasses and poured a drink for him and another one for me, fast and with my shoulders up so he wouldn't notice that I'd emptied my glass. And I turned around again and gave him his drink and held up my own and we said "L'chaim" and "Prosit."

The lime was bitter and not the real thing, and there was no ice and all the materials were room temperature or better. But none of it mattered. It was a drink to savour, and I got my flashlight out again, and settled back on the cot with the flashlight in one hand and my drink in the other, and took slow sips and tasted each sip with my whole tongue before I swallowed. Raoul also sipped quietly for a few minutes.

The alarm came up then. It was a long way off, but persistent, and it wasn't the voice on the intercom calling codes like I expected. It was an old-fashioned handmade sound.

"That's it?" I said to Raoul.

He nodded. "It's the klaxon," he said.

"It doesn't sound serious," I said.

"It's the real thing," Raoul said. "It's hand-cranked. That's a feature, because it's off the grid and good to go under nearly any circumstances."

"And it means security has locked down its targets?" I said.

"It's safe to assume," Raoul said. "It's the signal that personnel should move guests to secure locations."

"What were they doing before?" I asked him.

Raoul sighed. "Keeping the peace," he said. "It's the hardest assignment. While security is mobilizing, the priority for service technicians is keeping passengers calm. You can imagine what it's like in the Broadway when the lights go out."

"The lights were out already," I told him. "They shut down the show."

"They closed *Annie?*"

"The other one. The tap dancers' union got involved."

Raoul stared at me. "They have a union?"

"Something like that."

He shook his head. "Not in the Broadway, then. But everywhere else in the ship the crew was doing its job ongoing in spite of challenging conditions. When the power shuts down and emergency lights come up, the dedicated men and women of the *Mariola* pass information to the passengers. They take a head count and make a list of names to check against the manifest. They lock the doors. No one leaves the venue because you don't want people wandering around in the dark. Then you have to deal with questions and complaints: What's going on? How much longer? Why can't I go to my suite? You make a general announcement and people don't listen. Then you have to explain it again to everyone individually."

"We pay for personal service," I said.

"In an emergency configuration it's one more thing," Raoul said. "It taxes the service providers. And the drunks want to fight and children have to use the washroom and the hysterics are panicking. Personnel have their hands full keeping the atmosphere upbeat although they have some options. They can open the bar or organize games or start a singalong. But no one is really happy till the klaxon sounds and they take the customers to the gathering point."

"And they're not going to the Broadway?"

"Without lights and power, the default facilities are the aft sports deck or the fitness facility in inclement weather. They're large spaces. They can hold a few hundred customers and crew. And they take advantage of natural light. Is there a moon tonight?"

I tried to remember but couldn't.

Raoul shrugged. "It doesn't matter," he said. "You want to be on deck, out of doors if possible, ready to abandon ship if it comes down to it, lit by the stars if they're out. Personnel have flashlights also. They call the roll again."

"And then people go back to their suites?"

Raoul looked at me and kind of laughed. "The suites are totally out of the question, Mr. Rutledge. Private living is gone for good, and individual initiative. To simplify things and keep everyone safe, they'll set people up on the top deck, indoors or out. They'll sleep and hand out rations there, and wait to be rescued. No one goes below decks alone. You can't have people inside without light. Letting people below decks is a recipe for disaster when the power's out," Raoul said. "They'll keep everyone corralled on deck until things resolve themselves one way or another." He drained his drink and put his glass on the tray.

"What about people who were in their suites when the lights went out?" I said.

Raoul nodded. "Most people are out at night, dancing or gambling or seeing a show. Even now, with many venues closed, people are enjoying all the facilities still up and running. But some people take a quiet night in their suite, a romantic evening or a private party. Usually they notice when the power goes off. They want answers. They call for the steward. And if they call or not, service technicians are detailed deck by deck. They go door to door alerting people and gathering them on the floor. When the klaxon sounds, they lead the shut-ins to the rendezvous point also."

And at that moment the emergency lights faded and failed. I had my flashlight on and pointed where Raoul was very quickly, but he got there first, and he shone his light effectively in my eyes. Truthfully, he won the draw and if he wanted to take advantage he had the chance because I gave it to him. It reminded me I couldn't be comfortable. I acted right away to take back control.

"What are you doing, Raoul?" I asked him.

"What are you doing, Mr. Rutledge," he said to me.

I didn't like his tone. It was halfway between a challenge and a sneer. I pretended not to notice and filed it for future consideration like always. But I just said, "You're going to make me blind," like it was an inconvenient thing I didn't expect. I squinted and turned my head away like I didn't know why he was spotlighting me but I wished he'd stop, and I pointed my light at the door behind him.

Raoul thought for a second. "I thought we needed some light is all," he said.

He lowered the beam. I could look at him again and I stayed very sincere. "But we don't want to waste battery," I said like it was my only concern.

"This is true," he said.

"And we don't want anyone to see a light in here," I said. "If emergency lights are drying up all over the ship."

"It would be a tipoff," he said.

We both kept our lights on though. No one wanted to be the first to lose sight of the other. But slowly and together more or less we let the beams drop down to the floor, because we both knew that less light was safer.

"Although from this room to the locker room to the corridor is a long way for a weak beam," I said.

"And through two doors," Raoul said.

"Do you think people could see light coming from our portholes?" I said.

"We're safer from security if we keep dark," Raoul said. He looked like he made a decision, and he stood up. "Mr. Rutledge, you had a day," he said. "The big man and the flight deck and up and down the stairs.

the station

~ 323 ~

You take first shift on the cot. I'll take a shift in the room outside. I'll sit by the door, keep my ears on. Other people have pass-keys although no one should come around. It isn't in the drill and there's no reason. But we know customers can get lost or disregard instructions from the crew, and personnel sometimes improvise. Especially the next couple days, with supplies going down and people with access looking around maybe. We have to be ready. We may have to take action."

"I'm with you on that," I said. And I was, because we sacrificed and prepared ourselves and it wasn't right if someone else got the benefit of our forward thinking.

Raoul opened the door behind him. He made a pass with the flashlight, and truthfully the room looked bare and uninviting. But Raoul came through. "I'm going to set myself up here," he said. He pulled the door wide and thought about it. "I'll prop the door for air," he said.

But I said no. "I'm a light sleeper," I told him. "I don't like to be disturbed."

He put up a fight. "I'm not completely satisfied with this arrangement," he said.

But it was a long day and I was tired and didn't have time for complaints. "We'll test drive it now," I told him. I stood up and dominated him fully so that he had to back up through the door. Truthfully I could feel the temperature going up as we got further from the window. But I couldn't have him near while I slept. "You let me know tomorrow how it went. I want to take a shift in the morning. Wake me up at dawn," I said.

I closed the door on him and the lock clicked shut, which was reassuring even though Raoul had a key. And I jammed the chair under the handle which I thought wouldn't stop Raoul if he decided to make his move but would slow him down and give me a few seconds that might make all the difference. And it was the best I could do.

I lay down facing the door, with one hand on the knife and the other on the flashlight. And although I was afraid I might not sleep, I dozed off right away, I think, because I don't remember anything else and then sunlight was streaming in the windows and Raoul was scratching at the door and rattling the handle.

○ ○ ○

On the first day, when I went to the door to see, Raoul had unlocked it and tried to push it open. But the chair kept it closed nearly, and Raoul was too weak or polite to push past it. He just stood at the crack between the door and the frame and whispered at me.

"You had a good sleep then," he said. "I'm glad. You're fresh now. You can hold the hall door. I'll show you how I set it up and you can take a turn."

He pushed against the door again, but I put my foot in and kept the chair in place while I woke up more. I checked my watch.

"It's late," I said. "You were supposed to get me when the sun came up." I could hardly see Raoul through the crack in the door, but I could see he didn't look me in the eye.

"I might have dozed," he said. "It wasn't comfortable. I have a crick." He put his head on one side and then the other like he was stretching his neck.

"You left us at the mercy?" I said, and maybe I raised my voice somewhat. "I was counting on you to cover the entrance." I was disappointed he didn't come through even on little things.

"We want to keep our voices down," Raoul said. "Security is running patrols. We need to be careful."

"It's another reason to be alert at your post," I said.

"I was beside the door all night," Raoul said. "Nothing happened. I was ready if anything came up. I can show you. But nothing did."

He pushed some more at the door and I held it up another second and thought. But when I pressed my arm against my side, I could feel the knife, and I was rested and ready, and I needed water and food anyway. So I moved the chair out and opened the door wide and stood back like I was welcoming him home, and he took a step back into the mop room like he didn't like to crowd me or he didn't fully trust me. The daylight from the cot room lit the mop room somewhat and Raoul looked strange to me. He was in his briefs and holding a stick and he whispered so I had to lean in to hear.

"I made some arrangements, Mr. Rutledge," he said. "You can set yourself up so you're comfortable, but I'll show you my defensive posture. It might give you an idea." He pointed at a bucket upside down behind the door to the hall. "I turned a bucket over and used it for a chair," he said. He sat down on it and showed me. He had the stick in his hand and he held it like a baseball bat. "It's warm in here, like we thought," he said. He had a half-litre of water by the bucket and he picked it up and drank. There were two empty bottles behind him also. I thought three bottles of water was a lot for one person in one night when the ration was short and all I had to liquefy me was a gin and tonic that was gone before the lights went out. So to keep things even, while he drank and put the lid back on his third bottle, I went to the locker where I put the last bottles we brought to get some for myself.

I had to step fully into the mop room, and the door swung shut behind me. But I had my flashlight in my hand and I was alert and turned it on instantly. Raoul had his also. But I hit the switch first which satisfied me. And then we were both polite and shone our lights around the room only and away from each other's eyes. And I carried on like I trusted him fully and reached at the locker for water.

Just before I opened it I wondered if there would be any, because Raoul could have moved it all into his jug locker with a combination lock at any time during the night. But I opened the door and there were still many bottles. I thought it showed character that he didn't stash it all for himself. Or he was afraid to make his move yet. I filed it away to think about and took three half-litre bottles because it was only fair. I put two under my arm for later and cracked the last one and had a long pull. I never liked water and it was warm and flat. But I felt refreshed when I drank and I drank some more.

Raoul kept the beam low but he watched and nodded at me. He said, "We were thinking straight when we laid in water. We're going to have to talk about a ration, how much is right. But regular hydration is key. Also I found I was more comfortable with fewer clothes on. So I stripped down to my briefs."

He spread his arms so I could get the full effect and he nodded hard like he thought I would want to follow his lead. I just looked back at him because he didn't know anything about me if he thought I was going to take my shorts off on his say so. After a minute he moved on and talked some more about his set-up.

"Sitting on the bucket, I can lean against the back wall." He showed me. He stretched his legs out in front of him. "It's not so bad and you can take a load off when you're tired. Also the room is a sauna. You can feel it yourself."

I nodded. It was dark and hot and I understood how he could doze off and sleep most of the night. I didn't think it was an A-one defensive strategy, but I also didn't feel so bad about taking the cot for myself, because it was small and I was cramped. So we both got rested as well as we could in conditions that weren't ideal.

Raoul stood up then and tried to wave me over to the bucket. "You have a seat, Mr. Rutledge," he said. "Test drive the system." He held the stick out for me and I took it because it was better if I had it than if he did. It was the handle of a mop or a broom and sturdy. You could do damage with it if you needed to, and I thought I should keep it with me in future. But I wasn't going to sit on the bucket and hold the door, obviously.

"I understand the concept," I told him. I kept my voice down to make him happy. "I don't need to practice holding a stick. I think we don't need to watch the door during the day. We'll hear if anyone tries anything. And it isn't safe to spend long hours in here when daytime temperatures are in play. It's hot in here already and it smells."

There was a stink in the room. It was background but unpleasant.

It had been worrying me since I first stepped into the mop room, but I only just then put my finger on it.

"I set up our latrine," Raoul said. He shone his light at another bucket on the floor beside the trolleys. It had a lid. "Also paper and hand wash." He pointed at a roll of tissue and a bottle of antibacterial hand sanitizer on the counter.

"Do we have air freshener?" I asked him.

Raoul thought about it and nodded. "We have alpine or citrus air deodourizing spray. Also plug-ins, but we don't have power." He shrugged. "My vote is we should think twice about air care products. Anyone coming down the corridor who gets a whiff of mountain fresh pine will know it for what it is, especially if that person is in any way connected with cleaning or personal services on board. It could be a red flag and a giveaway."

He had a point.

"But if they smell a latrine that will be a giveaway also," I said.

Raoul thought for a minute. We both looked at the bucket. "We'll burn matches," Raoul said finally. "I'll leave a box out. It will only be an issue for a few days I think anyway." He didn't say, but I knew he meant not because we wouldn't last but because other people might not. And it was sad and unfortunate but true also. So I agreed.

Then he went past me to the door to the cot room, and he pulled out Horst's keys also on a retractable wire and attached to his briefs, and opened the door and ducked inside and rummaged in the desk and came out with a box of matches, which he put on the counter. He waved his hand at the tissue and hand sanitizer and the matches. "We have a good paper supply," he said. Then he kind of bowed at me and went into the cot room and closed the door so I could be private which was polite.

Still I didn't spend that day or any other in the mop room. It was stifling and the matches didn't kill odour on a long-term basis. Instead, for the next several days, we holed up in the office during the day, fanning ourselves with file folders and taking shifts in the evening at the outside door. I took a couple of turns in the mop room for an hour at a time maybe to chip in with security. But I detailed Raoul to cover night watches mostly, and he moved the upside down bucket to one side and pulled out a stack of sheets and piled them up to make a mattress, and he took pillows also. I thought he was probably more comfortable on the floor than I was on the cot, which was small and the springs needed oil. I kidded him about it and he smiled his terrible smile and nodded. I still kept the door closed and jammed while I slept, because there was no point in taking risks when we had come so far.

Food was abundant. But Raoul didn't think through the full effects of power loss. The first day I came back in the office after I used the latrine, and Raoul was straightening the cot. When he finished I pushed around him and sat on the cot again, because it was better than the chair. And Raoul looked at me like he might say something, but I didn't encourage him and he swallowed it. He clapped his hands together instead and moved forward.

"Something to eat, Mr. Rutledge?" he asked me.

I hadn't had anything to eat since supper the day before, when I only had beans and jelly salad. So the answer was obviously yes. He reached up and pulled the kettle out of the closet.

"I'll make noodles," he said.

I looked at the kettle. It had a cord and a plug. "How is that going to work?" I asked him.

Raoul looked at it again and reflected. He put it back in the cupboard. "The noodles are precooked," he said. "Water softens them, but they don't need to be boiled."

"I don't know if I feel like noodles," I said.

"I can open beans," he said.

"I had beans last night," I said.

"Chili? Beef stew?"

"It's a hot day," I said. "They're heavy."

the station

Raoul nodded. "What you really want is fresh fruit and salad. A little seafood maybe. A cold vichyssoise."

He meditated for a minute on all the good things to eat we didn't have. I felt it was a mistake and focused on the available food options instead.

"Maybe soup," I told him.

He pulled himself together. "I'll bring a couple. You can choose." He put his hand out. "Could I have the keys?"

He never stopped trying to get back his keys, but I didn't let him have them, obviously. Even though I was comfortable I stood up. And he accepted it and put his hand down and opened the door and held it for me. I pulled out the keys and found the ones I wanted and took my flashlight and went into the mop room and opened the two lockers with most of the food supply. Raoul took noodles in a cup for himself, and I took a tin of beef barley soup for protein and carbs and a tin of minestrone for vegetables. Then I closed the lockers again and Raoul took another run at it.

"You don't have to do that, Mr. Rutledge," he said. "We can leave them open. It will save time in the long run. I can just come out and get supplies. I don't have to ask you for keys."

But of course I didn't trust him. He could still at any time move everything into a locker he had a combination lock on, or move the combination lock onto the food locker, although if he did that, I would have access to his jugs of water maybe instead. But I didn't say it out loud, because we were still pretending to be a team. Instead I told him if a patrol got in and found us, it didn't matter if they hauled us away to the top deck as long as our food supply was locked down for later. Because we would likely outlast other people and we could make our way back down when order crumbled on the bowling green. But if the patrol also found our food and took it, then we were screwed, and they were more likely to do that if we left the lockers open. So as a safety precaution I wanted to keep the food in lock-up at all times. And Raoul had to agree.

We took our selections back into the cot room and Raoul pulled a can-opener and spoons out of a drawer. But we couldn't heat anything up and we had no plates and no bowls. Raoul poured water into his noodle cup, like it was designed for, and he let the noodles sit for a minute and said they were fine. I ate some concentrated soup and added water when I brought the level down. I was hungry. So I didn't mind. I ate everything and licked the tin after.

And then we talked about water and the daily ration. We started by trying to figure how much water we needed to drink every day, and we decided a litre a day was close, and a generous serving in our situation. So after the first night when Raoul drank three half-litres of water and the next morning when I took three half-litres to keep things even we decided we'd try to hold ourselves to a litre a day each.

Then we talked about if we should take a litre to drink plus some extra to make soup, or if we should make soup or noodles out of our daily litre. At the beginning we both made the case that we needed a litre of water to drink and then more to make the meal also. But we both knew in our hearts we were wishing. So we admitted it and agreed we'd use part of our ration for soup or noodles if we had them. It was a hard thing but the right thing and a part of our restraint, because we were in a difficult position and we had to use discipline if we were going to survive.

Then we tried to calculate total supplies. In my mind I counted it out and with the half-litres and litres still in the locker and the jugs and the flats of sparkling and the water I left in my safe even if we split everything straight down the middle, and at no time was I totally convinced that our partnership would hold, we had enough water to last twenty-five days each, I figured, up to thirty maybe. Raoul couldn't remember the volume on his jugs and he made excuses not to open the locker and check. So I had to estimate somewhat. But I summed it the best I could and divided by two like we would hang together for the duration and came up with a thirty-day maximum.

From one point of view it was a death sentence, since it was thirty days only and then we'd be at the mercy of the hot tropical sun and a rescue squad that might never arrive. But from another point of view, it was a blessing and salvation, because it was more water than anyone else had on the boat, and more time to hope for the best, to look for a ship on the horizon or a plane in the sky, or even a storm cloud that could fill a cup with rainwater and keep us liquid and hopeful for another day still.

o o o

We waited in the station many days. They were the longest days of my life. At first it was boring and uncomfortable. Then it got worse. We had nothing to do and no room to do it in. Also we had to be quiet, because security and then other people who shouldn't have came down the hall sometimes and tried the doors. As far as we could tell the ship's crew followed protocol and brought the guests into a central location where they could service them all together, but people wandered sometimes.

On the first day we heard people walking down the hall and opening and closing doors to suites and calling names. They called my name over and over. It was a roundup, and they were persistent, although it also sounded calm and orderly.

When the last footsteps walked away, I said to Raoul, "They didn't look in here?"

"It isn't part of the drill," Raoul said. "The lights are out and there's no power. On these rounds they're double-checking for people who were passed out maybe, or getting some action when the klaxon sounded. They're looking for people who are confused now, or maybe in trouble, because accidents happen in the dark."

And that made sense. But discipline slipped very quickly. Because later in the first day when the cot room was just getting dark, Raoul took up his station on the upside-down bucket, and someone else came down the corridor, but quietly, and hurrying and light on his feet, with long pauses sometimes between sprints, and not calling people by name. I was wide awake still because it was early, and lying on the cot with the knife tucked in my shorts and the stick beside the bed and the flashlight in one hand. And I left the connecting door propped open while I was still awake so Raoul could get air for a little while and I could see what he was doing.

We heard someone scurrying in the hall and making metal key sounds at the doors and shaking them. And we heard doors open sometimes, and close again, and then quiet for a while, and then more rattling at other doors. It came closer and I stood up and brought the stick and stood at the door to the cot room and Raoul stood up by the door with hand sanitizer in his hand. We both listened hard and didn't breathe.

The handle to the station rattled. Someone tried a key in the lock. We could hear it clicking and scratching. But it didn't fit, and whoever it was went away and we could hear them trying other doors up and down the hall. Finally we relaxed our posture and Raoul sat down again on his bucket and I went back to the cot. But I gave Raoul the stick again, so he could hold it while he watched the door. I didn't feel totally comfortable giving it to him, but it made sense he should have it if people were coming right up to the door and testing it. And another person might have the right key.

On the second day someone came down to our deck and kicked up a fuss. I didn't recognize the voice, though you could tell it was a guest. He was complaining in the hall and a service technician I didn't know was talking back.

"It isn't what I call all-inclusive," the guest said.

I thought he had a point. And to increase his concerns, personnel didn't take up his issue. "I have to ask you to return to the central service location," the crewman said. I didn't recognize his voice either. "This is a non-serviced area, off limits to guests at this time."

"I own this suite. I paid for it."

"Ownership is contingent. Please follow the flashlight."

the station

~ 333 ~

"My property isn't safe. My watch is missing and a gold chain. Someone's pilfering."

"With respect. You might have misplaced it. It's hard to tell in the dark."

"I know where I left it."

"We'll report to security."

"Security probably took the damn thing."

"All our agents are fully bonded."

It didn't reassure the passenger. Plus it turned out he had gum and the service technician wanted to confiscate it for supply central. The customer stood his ground on all points. And then the service guy went away and came back with support. We heard it all. It was disrespectful and not the way to treat a client.

In the station, the heat went up to the top of the tree. The office was bad even with the windows open at night and then blocked in the day to keep out the sun. After two days or three we gave up on that and kept the windows open at all times and took turns standing on the cot and breathing fresh air.

Raoul took off his whites the first night and never put them on again. He sat behind the door in the mop room holding the stick in his briefs. But I kept my shorts and shirt on so he didn't see the knife. I made a fan out of file folders from the office supply drawer and waved air on myself. It eased me somewhat, but I smelled like a zoo animal.

To pass time in the afternoons we played cards and used pins for markers. I kept mine in the pin box and Raoul kept his in the pincushion. It went back and forth for several days and then my luck turned and Raoul cleaned me out. He made a porcupine out of the pincushion and kept it on the desk as a trophy.

Off and on we debated going out and scouting. We wanted to assess conditions and empty the bucket. But it was risky.

"They've been on a ration several days now," I said. "They're weak and drying up. We're stronger and sharper."

"That's our theory," Raoul said.

"It's your theory," I said.

"I stand by it. I'm just saying we haven't tested it."

"It's why we need to go out," I said.

"But they could be getting desperate."

"I think we could take them."

Raoul nodded. "Okay. If somebody tackles us head-on," he said. "But what happens if someone follows us back? Maybe they turn us in and confiscate our rations for the ship's company, or maybe they're in it for themselves or working with a service technician with a pass-key? Either way, all our preparation and restraint go up in smoke if they come in a gang and take us out with bigger numbers.

"If you want to dole out your portion of water, it's your call. But I laid in my water for me and I don't want to share with everybody. I like people. I'm a people person. I'm broken up about what's happening," he said. He meant it too. I felt the same way. "If it would help, I'd share my last cup of noodles with them. But there are hundreds of people on this boat, and all the noodles we have in the whole station divided for all the people out there wouldn't keep anyone alive for a day and a half. It's a terrible thing to know and not do anything about it, but they are doomed and there is nothing practical you and I can do to save them. The best thing we can do is look after ourselves and try to hold on until a rescue squad turns up."

And when he put it like that I could only agree.

Then we finished the water in the open locker and we had to decide who would open his private stock. I had the key to the lock on the locker with flats of sparkling and Raoul had a combination lock on the locker with water jugs. I didn't see why I should break into the sparkling water when I already shared many bottles of still, but Raoul made excuses about getting his supply of tap water. We argued it out for several hours while we got drier and drier and the room heated up.

"It's completely potable, and we will be happy we have it," Raoul said. "When it comes down to it, if help doesn't arrive first and rescue us, I will pull out the jugs and crack them and together we will drink the water that I poured out and saved for us. But I moved those flats of sparkling for you." I enjoyed the way he made it sound like he did me a favour and didn't stand me up on the flight deck and try to steal from me at the same time. "They're a better resource, and sparkling is actually more refreshing than tap water. It's the carbonation. Plus the citrus has flavour and nutrients."

"Tap water is tested and filtered more."

"At home it is. The ship's tank was filled on the islands. We don't know what their standards are."

"Didn't the Company ask?"

"I think we know the Company didn't do due diligence in all respects."

"I was drinking water from the *Mariola*'s tank for weeks."

"Under ordinary conditions there's no issue," Raoul said. "But living like this we need to watch our immune systems. I think the sparkling water is healthier. They sterilize the bottles."

"So we should save it for when we're weakest."

"We've been underground for a week and it's a hundred and ten degrees, Mr. Rutledge," he said. "Our need is pressing now."

Finally I came at it from a different angle and changed his way of thinking. I took a shift in the mop room and closed the door between, and I unlocked the locker where the flats of sparkling were, and got one flat with twenty-four bottles of sparkling water with citrus accent, and brought it back to the cot room with me.

Raoul rubbed his hands and said, "I knew you'd take the right view, Mr. Rutledge."

I didn't say anything. I sat down on the cot with the flat on my knees and I used my keys to split the plastic around the bottles, and I pulled a bottle out and broke the cap off on the side of the desk and took a long pull. Raoul watched me. He started to look nervous.

"Can I have a bottle too, Mr. Rutledge?" he asked me.

I had another long drink. I'd drunk most of the bottle by then, but they were little, not even a half-litre.

"Cooperation is key, Raoul," I told him.

I gave him a hard look and let him think about it. He understood me, and he knew he was beat. He went out to the mop room, and I let the door click shut between us so he knew I wasn't watching him at the locker and trying to pry into the combination. And he took a few minutes and then he came back in with a jug. It was large, at least two gallons I thought, and I was impressed that he could carry it. And we talked it over and decided to bottle it in the empty half-litre bottles, so we could measure and watch our ration. We filled them all up and had more water still left in the jug. And we marked the level so that we could continue to trust each other fully.

Then we decided our ration would be one half-litre bottle of jug water and two smaller bottles of sparkling citrus a day while the supply lasted. And I was happy that Raoul was reasonable about it all, although I had to take a risk to bring it forward. But I came out on top, because I only brought out one of the four flats in the locker and I had my other stash, but Raoul had to give up a whole jug, and I thought he only had two.

o o o

On the fifth day order broke down in a bigger way. We heard more people moving down the hall, and they weren't careful anymore not to be noticed. People working in teams called to each other and cursed. We heard a girl sort of whining and somebody hushing her. Later people rattled doors or shouted short, angry directions at other people. Someone gave an order to halt, and we heard people talking back and running.

It was a strange thing because we couldn't see anything and we could only try to piece together what was happening. But we also couldn't ignore it because there was nothing to take our minds off it when we heard voices in the hall. We sat in the dark in the station listening to people shout at each other, trying to get the gist. There were long stretches when it was quiet, but you never knew when you'd hear someone, or someone would try the door to the station and we'd have to stand guard in case it turned out to be a service guy with a key who was searching the ship deck by deck looking for water and food.

By then we figured they were out of everything and everyone knew it was serious, but people still had energy to forage. They didn't worry about noise and we would hear three or four voices together sometimes and a racket of footsteps and pounding on doors. It hit a peak on the seventh day or the eighth. I was having trouble keeping track. We heard people angry and yelling. And then there was gunfire from up top and other places on the ship and once very close, in the hall outside the station, which was dangerous obviously, and there was nothing we could do but stay low and pray.

Then the big activity died back and the crying started. It was three days after the shooting in the hall. Someone parked it close to us and howled. He was raving and out of his head and he set up shop right by the station and wailed for an hour. When he stopped it was a relief. And then he started again.

Raoul said it was dehydration taking its toll and it was a terrible thing but he thought it wouldn't be long.

"It's been an hour already," I said. "It feels like forever."

"It'll be over in a day."

"A day?" I said. I didn't know if I could take it.

"Convulsions stop. The tongue swells. They aren't dead yet but they don't make so much noise."

I hoped he knew what he was talking about because the crying was terrible to hear. It didn't sound human. It sounded like an animal in pain and if it was an animal any person with morals would put it out of its misery.

When we heard a person crying like that and in pain and we had a gallon of tap water and several bottles each of sparkling water with citrus also, it took control and discipline not to open the door and share. First we sat straight in the cot room looking hard at each other. Then I had to cover my ears. I bent over with my head down and my hands on my ears. Then Raoul made a move like he would go and see about it, and I grabbed him by the wrist and pulled him down again. He sat on the edge of his chair and I sat on the edge of the cot. We put our heads together and held onto each other, although I was careful not to let him touch me anywhere near the knife. I put my arms around him and he put his arms around me, because you feel safer and have hope if you're close to a warm, breathing person when that much suffering is happening outside your door.

We both thought about opening the door and stepping back into the halls where people were desperate and doomed. We thought about it even though if we did, we could only haul a dying person into our safe place and make it a little less safe that way, or else leave the safe place behind, maybe forever. Neither was a good option but it took both of us working together to hold ourselves back and hold on for a better day in the future when the crisis was behind us and good prospects rose again. I held onto Raoul and he held onto me, and we both held each other back. Because both of us wanted to go out and help anyone we could find, and both of us knew it was the end for us if we did.

And truthfully both of us were also afraid because the people outside sounded like they suffered so much they weren't human anymore, and both of us wanted to stay very still and hide from everything that was lurking in the shadows. And if any suffering, howling person came through the door, I thought both of us would hit them with a stick until they stopped moaning and raving and making us suffer by suffering themselves.

I lifted my head and looked at Raoul, and it was blurry and hard to see but he was crying also, and we listened to the person raving in the hall, and wrapped our arms around each other tight and cried and prayed until the raving stopped again, this time for good.

the station

o o o

I killed Raoul on the twelfth day I think. It wasn't my choice, and for practical reasons and sentimental ones, I would have been happy not to do it. But the crying in the hall pushed him over the edge, I think, and he moved forward any plans he had, to get it over with and embrace whatever future was left.

I went to sleep like usual on the cot with the door closed and the chair jammed against it, and Raoul in the next room with the stick. But I woke up to an ugly world with Raoul trying to garrote me, and I had to act quickly. He had a wire on my neck, but I got a hand in before he twisted, which gave me a little more breathing room but also took that hand out of play. With my other hand right away I found the knife still in my pants, and I got it out of its sheathe and hit Raoul hard and full in the body, twice, before either of us could stop and assess.

It didn't finish him. But he staggered back and released the line, and I let the knife drop and worked on the wire, untwisting it, which thankfully I could do, or it would have been all over for me in the station right then. It was Horst's key ring on its retractable wire I found out later, and the keys and the carabiner were still on it, which gave me purchase for twisting it off. I got the wire away and had a breath in my lungs before Raoul came back in to try again, which he had to do, because once you start that kind of thing you're committed.

It was dark in the station, with just a little moonlight coming in the portals. I'd lost the knife and Raoul fought dirty like I expected. He'd brought the stick as well as the wire, and he swung it around, but he couldn't get a real backswing in the little space, plus he lacked power generally. We wrestled for it, and I got it away from him, and then he scratched and pulled linen down on me. We banged a cupboard open and he grabbed the iron and swung at me with it.

Finally I came up beside the shelves and reached for the aerosol I put up top. I gave it to him in the face full on. It was mountain fresh pine room deodourizing mist it turned out, and it packed quite a punch. Raoul choked and laid off for a second, and I held my breath and hit him with the can, and then I got the iron away from him and I hit him with it and hit him again. He went down finally and I climbed over him to the cot, and I found the flashlight on the pillow where I left it when I fell asleep, and I shone it around and found the knife also. Then I went back to Raoul to see.

He was still alive but fading fast. There was blood everywhere, and he was bleeding from his chest and from his gut. Blood was soaking into his briefs and the linen underneath him, and he was bleeding from his mouth and his nose also.

"It isn't how I wanted it to end," I told him.

He tried to say something and I had to lean in to hear. He had trouble speaking with the blood and the hole in his lungs. It was more of a wet gargle. I kept talking to ease the moment.

"I thought we might make it, you and me together," I told him. Which wasn't exactly true, but wasn't completely untrue either. And he was dying so I didn't see any point in insulting him. Also, I had a last request, and it was worthwhile keeping him sweet. "I've got a ways to go still," I told him. "Do you want to tell me the combinations on those lockers?" I pointed to the outer room. "There's no advantage to you if you keep it. You might as well share."

He made a funny sound and I leaned in some more. I was hopeful, I admit. And he made an effort. But it was disappointing.

"I don't mind dying," he said. "Everybody's got to go. But I'd be happier if I watched you go first."

It was work for him to say it, and I felt sad that he put his last energy into hating me. He rattled some more and fought to breathe for a long minute. And it was awful to watch, and then he was dead.

o o o

the station

~ 341 ~

I didn't do anything for a while then. I didn't feel energized and I had no reason to hurry. I waited for the sun to rise and I thought about moving out, because the halls were quiet and the station smelled. But in the end I decided to give it more time, because if someone else was hiding out like me, they might come out, and it could be awkward or dangerous.

I had to organize the cot room again. All the linen on the floor I moved out to the mop room and put it in the pile behind the door with the other linen Raoul used to sleep on. I put Raoul in an empty locker before he stiffened. He was little and lean, and I folded him up, and he fit under the shelf. I remembered he told me once he could make himself very small, and it made me sad to think about. But I put him in the locker and closed the locker door securely. And then I stayed in the cot room several more days and only went into the mop room to get supplies and for the bucket.

I decided I'd give it three days. In the end, I waited nearly a week until I didn't hear anyone moving for many days in a row. All I heard by then were strange sounds coming from the bottom of the boat like something was jamming or meeting resistance. I started to wonder then, what happens to the turbines when the guy who's supposed to oil them doesn't oil them anymore? I didn't know, but I didn't like the machine sounds, and I didn't hear people around, and by then the station was too much for me. It was a mess and it stank from the bucket and Raoul's locker, and there were flies.

I took both flashlights and the extra batteries, and a flat of sparkling with me, and I left the last flat of sparkling water and some bottles of still locked up in their locker where they were secure. I had an idea it might be a good thing to have different stashes around the ship. Then I opened the door to the hall.

It was dark and the flashlight only lit up a few feet around me. I stepped out of the station and tripped right away on a body. It was facedown in the hall and giving off a stench. I closed the door to the station behind me and made sure it was locked, and then I covered my mouth and went around the body, back to my suite.

There were issues. The door was open. In the big room the furniture was still nailed down but the soft chairs were cut open and the monitors were broken with their knobs and wires torn off. In my room, the bed was untucked and everything was thrown around. My clothes were all over the closet. Things were missing from drawers: cufflinks and a watch. It was the least of my troubles with the ship making sounds like a dying animal, and low rations, and corpses in the hall, but it shouldn't have happened, and I was unimpressed.

I closed the door to my suite behind me and it still locked so I locked it also. And then I opened the doors to the balcony and stepped out for a long breath. It was hot, but fresh, and it was a relief after so many days in the station. Then I went into the closet and opened the safe and everything was where I left it, the water and the money. And that was a relief. I took the sparkling I brought with me out of the flat and put it in the safe one by one. And I took out two big bottles of still and went into the bathroom and plugged the sink and filled it with water, and I washed my face and my hands, and then I stripped out of the clothes I wore for many days in the station and cleaned myself all over. It was only a sponge bath, but I felt like a new man when I was done. Then I put on something fresh, even though it was wrinkled from lying on the floor. And I locked the safe up again.

Next, I went out again and reconnoitered, because I had to. The whole ship was dark, and I had to take the stairs, and I only had the light from the flashlight which was weak. Every now and then I found a body in the hall or in the stairwell, rotting and smelling and breeding flies.

My first goal was Sick Bay, because I wanted a mask, and I thought I'd look into meds while I was there. The first room was empty and so was the big room behind it. There was no sign of Doctor Dan, but I didn't expect him to die at his post really. I opened cupboards and looked for supplies. And then I heard a sound that wasn't flies or the boat, and it was dark and I only had a flashlight, but I had to find out because I couldn't afford to be surprised.

I looked in the first ward, and I found Ben, who was dead. He was green and rotten all over, not just on his arm, although that was the only place he had a dressing. But the only sound in the room was flies.

In the second room, Eddie was with Katherine. They were where I left them many days before, when I went to find the big man. And I looked at them and wondered if Eddie ever left the room even when the klaxon sounded, or if he just sat with Katherine and held her hand until they both drifted and passed. I admired him for being with her and loving her to the end. It gave me hope that a person could make a happy ending. And I was sorry that Ben died alone and Natalie was nowhere near, but she was young and looking for action, and not every heart is true.

Then I heard the sound again, like a frightened animal, and I had to go into the last room. I shone the light around and I found Bailey sitting up in the hospital bed, and she put a hand out to me and stretched her mouth out wide. I saw corpses in the halls and in the stairs and I was getting used to the dead. But Bailey was alive and it was horrible to see. She had no lips, but her tongue was swollen and dry and her eyeballs were standing out and her skin was stretched over her bones like it might snap. She lifted her arm at me and knocked over empty water bottles on a tray in front of her, and she made a face like she would cry if she could, and she moaned like an animal in pain. And it was frightening and hard, but I did the thing I had to do, and brought a pillow over and held it on her until she stopped fighting. I didn't like to do it but it was a last resort and a desperate situation, and it was the only thing I could do, really, to help her.

Then I went back to the big room and found a mask finally and some pills, and I put the mask on my face and the pills in my pocket and I took a moment to steady myself. But just a moment, and then I straightened up and got to work, because if you don't get back on the horse right away, you don't at all. I wanted to check out the whole ship, to gather up anything that would help me survive until a rescue team came, and to see what kind of world I was living in.

I went deck by deck, checking out the public rooms and also suites where the door was open and service stations and storage areas. I went into every bar and restaurant, and I saw wreckage everywhere. The venues had all been opened up and pillaged. Tables were turned over and glasses broken. But there was nothing to drink or eat. No bar snacks or soda. There were corpses sometimes, people who died looking for food, or who wandered off delirious and died alone in the Voodoo Lounge or the Bar Sinister or the Dreadlock. I got to know the sound of flies and the smell of bad meat, and I stepped carefully when the warning signs came up.

In the Captain's Mess, the trees were dead and the little birds were dangling by their feet from their little gold chains. The carpet was littered with dead butterflies. Their wings were still bright, but they crumbled to dust underfoot. The chafing dishes were empty. The buffet was closed and the cupboard was bare. I went into the kitchen and checked the pantries and the walk-in refrigerators. Everything was empty and the power was off.

I got up to the upper decks while there was still some day left. I held my nose and went up to the Mosh Pit and, like I was afraid, a lot of kids holed up there to die. They were dead on the banquette and in the cages and on the dance floor, and there was a stench my mask couldn't filter. Still, I came that far and I had a goal, so I flashed the light around and found my way to "The Office," and I was lucky there, because I wasn't sure how I would get up to the ceiling. But I didn't need to because the kits were open on the little table. The J-kid was in a chair beside it, dead and fly-covered, with a strap on his arm and a needle in his hand. So he died happy. I checked the samples on the table, and I took one with a flower on it, and one with a happy face, because I was having a day. And I wrapped the rest and took them for later.

the station

Not that I thought I would find anything, but I went up the stairs to the Oasis. It was empty and wrecked with cushions ripped and glasses smashed. Outside on the patio, the reflecting pool was dry. I recognized the padre by his collar. He was dead, sitting by the stone basin with an empty bottle in his hand. His face was black and fierce, but that was always his style.

From the patio I had a view of the sports deck, and it was terrible. All along the beach volleyball court and the basketball court there were corpses, all collapsed and burnt black in the sun. There were passengers in expensive cruise wear and crew in whites and security in jungle camouflage. I could tell by the pips that some people were officers, but from a distance I couldn't tell Hoskins from the guy who greased the turbines, and I didn't want to go in for a closer look. Some people died on their backs like they went gently in their sleep, and some people died on their hands and knees like they were trying to crawl away when death caught up. Some people were sitting on the benches in the Arboretum under the dead trees. They were all dead.

I went back through the Oasis and down the stairs and across the sports deck. The flies and the smell were bad even in the open air, and I tried not to breathe and I tried not to look. And I went through the fitness facility and out through the Slaker and there were more people in loungers around the pool, and the pool was still empty, even if the loungers were free. And although I spent time with them and knew their qualities and liked them more or less, I didn't recognize anyone.

The sun was setting by the time I got up to the flight deck, which was my last stop. The elevators didn't work of course, so I climbed more stairs. I was finding them difficult, and I wondered if the heat was getting to me. But I held onto the handrail and pulled. The Crow's Nest had been tossed around and I didn't stop to look.

On the flight deck, Dragonfly Four was parked on its pad. It looked powerful and gleamed in the sun, even though it was crippled and there was no one alive to pilot it. The big lung kid and the blonde and the big man's guy with the leg were lined by the elevator, what was left of them, like someone thought they would do things properly, but never got around to it. But they'd been out in the sun for a few days, and they were shrunken and used up, so the flies and the smell weren't as bad.

I had a good look around because recon was my job, and I had more luck. In the shed at the side in the vending machine I found several lemon-lime beverages, generic and sweet, which normally I don't like, and a bag of Doritos. I didn't know why nobody found it before, but I didn't argue with it, because the sun was hot and death was all around.

I thought about everyone who was gone, Raoul who betrayed me, and Bailey who I didn't save, and everyone in the halls and stairs and spread out across the decks who would have liked to live but didn't plan and weren't lucky. I felt bad for them. But I felt respect and something bigger, that I came out on top, with a citrus drink in my hand and a bag of chips. I got further than they did and further really than I had a right to hope, and there was a distance to go and I might make it yet.

From the flight deck I could see water and sky all around and the air was nearly sweet. I wondered if the Company had a plan, or if the big guy made it to land and alerted a squad. I felt that there was room for hope, at least, and I decided I'd make my station up top and watch for signs of life. I thought I'd bring some flares and a mirror and water and food, and I'd scan the horizon for ships and watch the sky for planes. I could be comfortable and wait and hope.

I could hear more sounds from down below, and I wasn't sure what was happening but it sounded unlucky. I realized also the ship was starting to turn or tilt. To sum up: it was no cakewalk and there were no guarantees. But it was a warm day and I had a drink and it was better to be alive than to be dead. So I was satisfied with that.

the station

○ ○ ○

I would like to thank Charmagne, Duncan, Brenda, Todd, Suzanne, and John, who read the drafts and provided much valuable feedback.

I'm also very grateful to Elyse for her long-distance support.

I owe much to Robyn Read, my editor, for her sharp and effective suggestions for revisions.

Finally, I owe thanks and love to my family, Alison and Stephen, my mom and my sweet old dad.

— E.

This book was typeset in Joanna, designed by Eric Gill
and released by Monotype in 1937.